ALEC MACKENZIE'S ART OF SEDUCTION

MACKENZIES, BOOK 9

JENI

D0807229

JA / AG PUBLISHING

BOOKS BY JENNIFER ASHLEY

The Mackenzies Series
(Historical Romance)

The Madness of Lord Ian Mackenzie
Lady Isabella's Scandalous Marriage
The Many Sins of Lord Cameron
The Duke's Perfect Wife
A Mackenzie Family Christmas: The Perfect Gift
The Seduction of Elliot McBride
The Untamed Mackenzie
The Wicked Deeds of Daniel Mackenzie
Scandal and the Duchess
Rules for a Proper Governess
The Stolen Mackenzie Bride
A Mackenzie Clan Gathering
Alec Mackenzie's Art of Seduction
The Devilish Lord Will
(more to come)

Historical Mysteries
Kat Holloway "Below Stairs" Victorian Mysteries
A Soupçon of Poison
Death Below Stairs
Scandal Above Stairs

Leonidas the Gladiator Mysteries
(writing as Ashley Gardner)
Blood Debts
(More to come)

Captain Lacey Regency Mysteries Series
(writing as Ashley Gardner)
The Hanover Square Affair
A Regimental Murder
The Glass House
The Sudbury School Murders
The Necklace Affair
A Body in Berkeley Square
A Covent Garden Mystery
A Death in Norfolk
A Disappearance in Drury Lane
Murder in Grosvenor Square
The Thames River Murders
The Alexandria Affair
A Mystery at Carlton House
Murder in St. Giles

Mystery Anthologies
The Necklace Affair and Other Stories
Murder Most Historical
Past Crimes

Regency Pirate Series
(Historical romance)
The Pirate Next Door
The Pirate Hunter
The Care and Feeding of Pirates

Nvengaria Series
(Paranormal Historical Romance)
Penelope & Prince Charming
The Mad, Bad Duke
Highlander Ever After
The Longest Night

Riding Hard
(Contemporary Romance)
Adam
Grant
Carter
Tyler
Ross
Kyle
Ray

MACKENZIE FAMILY TREE

Ferdinand Daniel Mackenzie (Old Dan) 1330-1395
First Duke of Kilmorgan
= m. Lady Margaret Duncannon

|

Fourteen generations

|

|

Daniel William Mackenzie 1685-1746(?)
(9th Duke of Kilmorgan)
= m. Allison MacNab

|

6 sons
Daniel Duncannon Mackenzie (1710-1746)
William Ferdinand Mackenzie (1714-1746?)
Magnus Ian Mackenzie (1715-1734)
Angus William Mackenzie (1716-1746)
Alec William Mackenzie (1716-1746?)
m.= Lady Celia Fotheringhay

Malcolm Daniel Mackenzie (1720-1802)
(10th Duke of Kilmorgan from 1746)
= m. **Lady Mary Lennox**
|
Angus Roland Mackenzie 1747-1822
(11th Duke of Kilmorgan)
= m. Donnag Fleming
|
William Ian Mackenzie (The Rake) 1780-1850
(12th Duke of Kilmorgan)
= m. Lady Elizabeth Ross
|
Daniel Mackenzie, 13th Duke of Kilmorgan (1824-1874)
(1st Duke of Kilmorgan, English from 1855)
= m. Elspeth Cameron (d. 1864)
|
Hart Mackenzie (b. 1844)
14th Duke of Kilmorgan from 1874
(2nd Duke of Kilmorgan, English)
= m1. Lady Sarah Graham (d. 1876)
|
(Hart Graham Mackenzie, d. 1876)

Hart Mackenzie = **m2. Lady Eleanor Ramsay**
|
Hart Alec Graham Mackenzie (b. 1885)
Malcolm Ian Mackenzie (b. 1887)

Cameron Mackenzie
= m1. Lady Elizabeth Cavendish (d. 1866)
|
Daniel Mackenzie = m. **Violet Devereaux**

Cameron Mackenzie = **m2. Ainsley Douglas**

|

Gavina Mackenzie (b. 1883)
Stuart Mackenzie (b. 1885)

**"Mac" (Roland Ferdinand) Mackenzie
= m. Lady Isabella Scranton**

|

Aimee Mackenzie (b. 1879, adopted 1881)
Eileen Mackenzie (b. 1882)
Robert Mackenzie (b. 1883)

Ian Mackenzie = m. Beth Ackerley

|

Jamie Mackenzie (b. 1882)
Isabella Elizabeth Mackenzie (Belle) (b. 1883)
Megan Mackenzie (b. 1885)

Lloyd Fellows = m. Lady Louisa Scranton

|

Elizabeth Fellows (b. 1886)
William Fellows (b. 1888)
Matthew Fellows (b. 1889)

McBride Family

Patrick McBride = m. Rona McDougal

Sinclair McBride = m.1 Margaret Davies (d. 1878)

|

Caitriona (b. 1875)
Andrew (b. 1877)

Sinclair McBride = **m.2 Roberta "Bertie" Frasier**

Elliot McBride = **m. Juliana St. John**

Ainsley McBride = m.1 John Douglas (d. 1879)
|
Gavina Douglas (d.)

= **m.2 Lord Cameron Mackenzie**
|
Gavina Mackenzie (b. 1883)
Stuart Mackenzie (b. 1885)

Steven McBride (Captain, Army)
= **m. Rose Barclay**
(Dowager Duchess of Southdown)

Note: Names in **bold** indicate main characters in the
Mackenzies / McBrides series

CHAPTER 1

The Attic of Kilmorgan Castle, June 1892

*J*an Mackenzie heard his name like music on the air. He didn't look away from the task he'd set himself, laying each page in its neat stack on the desk, exactly where it needed to go. He knew Beth would come to him the same as he knew when his next breath would be.

She entered the attic with a rustle of skirts, pausing in the open doorway to push a strand of hair from her face. Ian did not have to glance up at her to follow her every move.

"Ian? What on earth are you doing?"

Ian did not reply until he'd laid another page in its stack and squared it to match the notebook next to it. Beth liked him to answer, but Ian wanted to think out the sentences in his head beforehand so he could respond to her satisfaction. What *he* considered the most important part of an explanation was not always what others did.

"Reading," he said after a moment. "About the family."

"Oh?" Beth moved to him, the faint cinnamon scent that clung to her distracting. "You mean your family history?"

Ian had divided the surface of the large kneehole desk, left over from a century ago, into sections, one for every generation of the Mackenzie family. Those sections were divided into immediate members of that family. Papers, letters, ledgers, and notebooks had their own piles in each section, and they were stacked chronologically.

He laid his broad hand on the leftmost pile. "Old Malcolm." Malcolm's wife Mary's journal had provided entertainment for many a winter night with tales of Malcolm's exploits.

"Alec Mackenzie." Ian rested his hand on the next pile then the one after that. "And Will."

"You found their papers?" Beth asked in surprise. "I thought Alec and Will Mackenzie fled into exile after Culloden, when the entire family was listed as dead."

Ian shrugged. "All is here." He didn't speculate on how the letters and journals of Will, Alec, and their families had arrived at Kilmorgan—he only cared that they had.

"Have you read them?" Beth looked over the neat stacks, a little smile on her lips. Ian had come to learn this expression meant she was interested.

Ian didn't answer. He'd of course read each paper, each notebook, before deciding into which stack it should go.

Alec Mackenzie had left sketchbooks full of drawings of his children, his wife, his brothers, his sisters-in-law, his father. Another portfolio held sketches of the skylines of London and of Paris, and of the lands around Kilmorgan, as well as portraits of Alec Mackenzie himself, some of them intimate, Alec only a kilt, a wicked glint in his eye.

Ian opened one of the sketchbooks and pushed it toward Beth. This was of Alec as a young man, dressed in the manner of the early eighteenth century. His pale shirt had cotton lace at the cuffs, his long hair was pulled into a queue, and a strong face laughed out of the picture at them.

"Intriguing." Beth's breath was warm on Ian's cheek. "He was the artistic one, I gather, like Mac." She touched the paper. "But who drew this? Was his wife an artist too?"

"Celia." Ian turned over a page to show a young woman with dark curls under a small lacy cap, a round face, and a rather impish smile. "She drew the cities."

"Oh." Beth clasped her hands as Ian revealed a stretch of London as it had been in 1746. Rooftops marched through the fog—she recognized the view from Grosvenor Square toward Piccadilly and Green Park, but gaps existed where houses were now. "That must be the sketch for the painting that hangs in Mac's wing. How exciting." She looked at Ian with shining eyes. "Tell me about them." Her smile widened. "I know you remember every word of these." She touched the cover of a journal.

For a moment, Ian's interest in his ancestors faded as he lost himself in Beth's brown eyes. Beth was beauty, she was silence, she was the peace in his heart.

She was also stubborn in her own quiet way. She grasped his sleeve and towed him to a dusty settee, one gilded and uphol- stered in petit point, which had come to Kilmorgan straight from Versailles.

Beth nestled into Ian's side and drew her feet up under her, a further distraction from deeds of the remote past. "Go on," she said. "Tell me their story. All the details. I'll let you know which bits to leave out when you tell it again to the children."

Ian pictured the two of them gathering with Jamie, Belle, and Megan in one of their cozy chambers in Ian's wing of the house, plus his son's and daughters' antics and blurted questions as Ian tried to tell them a straightforward tale. Jamie and Belle especially constantly interrupted him, and stories rarely got finished the way Ian planned them. He looked forward to it.

For now, Beth was warm at his side, her hair soft beneath his lips.

"Once upon a time," he began—Beth had explained that all stories should begin with *Once upon a time.*

"A few months after the Battle of Culloden," Ian continued, "Alec Mackenzie left Paris and returned to England, in search of Will, who'd vanished for too long a while. Will's contacts hadn't seen him, rumor had it he might have been arrested, and the family was worried.

"The last place Will had been reported was London, so Alec packed his things, took his daughter, assumed a false name, and went to London ..."

∼

London, 1746

THE SCREAMING WOVE THROUGH ALEC MACKENZIE'S DREAMS AND jerked him from sleep.

For a breath he was back on the battlefield, men keening as they died. Soldiers shoved swords into his clansmen, his friends —never mind they were injured and begging for mercy.

Another breath, and the noise resolved itself into the wail of a child who didn't understand the pain of new teeth.

Alec wrenched himself out of bed, his nightshirt slipping from one large shoulder, his dark red hair tumbling into his eyes. He righted the nightshirt and stumbled into the chilly hall, not worried about trivial things like dressing gown and slippers.

No one stirred in the upper floors of the dark house on

Grosvenor Square. This was one of the square's larger mansions, six stories high, four rooms wide, and several rooms deep. Alec's chamber was one floor down from the attic, his hostess pretending that Alec's position wasn't *quite* that of a servant.

Alec's daughter, Jenny, on the other hand, had to keep to a room in the attics, lest his hostess' guests, the cream of London's intellectual society and patrons of the arts, discover that a *child* actually stayed in the house.

One-year-old Jenny didn't care where she slept, but the positioning of the rooms made it a job to rush to Jenny's side when she needed her da'.

Alec shouldered his way to the back stairs and hurried up a flight. His feet, hardened from running over Highland hills, never felt the roughness of the wooden stairs.

He bolted into Jenny's nursery, cursing when he didn't see the nursemaid Lady Flora had hired. The poor woman needed to sleep, of course, but she was snoring in the next room through Jenny's screams, which were winding up to a pure Highlander howl. Alec's youngest brother, Mal, had screeched like that.

"All right, wee one," Alec whispered in Erse as he lifted his daughter into his arms, her soft warmth against his cheek. "Papa's here."

Jenny continued to cry, but she turned to Alec's shoulder and snuggled down, recognizing her father. Alec held her close, snatching up the bottle of medicine the nursemaid had concocted for Jenny's teething. Swore by it, the woman did.

Alec worked off the cork one-handed and flinched when the acrid stench of pure gin curled into his nose.

"Bloody hell." Alec threw the bottle into the smoldering fire, where it splintered, sending a spurt of blue flame up the chimney. "Well, lass, we'll have to find ye another nursemaid in the morning, won't we? One who won't poison ye with this filth."

In the meantime, there was nothing to soothe Jenny's pain, no other food, drink, or medicine near.

The room was cold as well. The small fire was here at Alec's insistence—Lady Flora's austere housekeeper saw no reason to waste fuel on a babe.

Alec lifted Jenny's blankets from her cot, wrapped her up, and carried her down the stairs to his own bedchamber. He laid her in the bed and then folded his big frame into a chair that he dragged next to it, not wanting to take the chance of rolling on her in his sleep. She was so tiny, and Alec was a bloody great Highlander.

Jenny warmed and calmed, Alec's big hand on her back, and she slept. Alec watched her, knowing that if anyone found Jenny here, he'd be standing before his hostess while she lifted her nose in the air and reminded him exactly how dangerous was his mission and that he should have left his child in France.

His daughter was silent now, sleeping in innocent happiness. Alec pulled a quilt over himself and drifted off, his slumber not quite so innocent and in no way happy.

But Jenny was safe, all that mattered for the moment. Now to make sure the rest of his family was as well.

~

"You're late," Lady Flora, Dowager Marchioness of Ellesmere, said as Lady Celia Fotheringhay hastened into Lady Flora's private salon, Celia's portfolio sliding dangerously from under her arm.

Celia had never been in this room before. Whenever she called upon Lady Flora, she was only allowed into the grand salon, which was two stories high, gilded and painted within an inch of its life, and stuffed with important people.

The *right* important people, Celia amended—the intellectuals and high-minded of the *ton* who supported the Whigs in their power and glory.

Celia had also never been inside this house without her mother, the formidable Duchess of Crenshaw. Lady Flora was said to eat innocent young ladies for breakfast, and so an older, stronger woman was a necessary guard.

For this visit, Celia was on her own and shown into a compact, sunny room on the first floor. This chamber was no less ostentatious than the grand salon, albeit on a smaller scale. The audience took place, alarmingly, at breakfast, and for an entirely different reason than Celia's previous visits.

Lady Flora was forty but her slim body and unlined face compared to a woman of twenty. She wore her golden hair pulled back into a simple knot, and her light blue eyes held as much chill as her voice.

She looked up at Celia from the remains of a repast. Her empty plate was whisked away by a silent footman, while another equally silent footman placed a cup by her elbow. Lady Flora poured thick coffee into it, the trickle of liquid breaking the delicate hush.

Celia's portfolio chose that moment to slip to the floor with a clatter. The clasp broke, and drawings of misty hills, vases of flowers, and Celia's family cat floated across the carpet.

"Drat," Celia said under her breath. The portfolio was awkward—she was always dropping the blasted thing.

To Lady Flora's exasperated sigh, Celia fell to her knees, her striped skirts billowing, to collect the drawings. She heard Lady Flora sigh again, and the two footmen appeared next to Celia, collecting the pages with deft, gloved hands.

The footmen restored the drawings neatly and efficiently to

the portfolio and laid the large thing at the end of the table. A maid appeared out of nowhere for the sole purpose of helping Celia to her feet, then vanished.

"You're late," Lady Flora repeated.

The gilded clock on the mantelpiece gently announced it was quarter past eight. "Mother was in a bit of a state this morning," Celia said quickly as she brushed off her skirts. "There's an important debate today, you see, and Papa was wavering on what he wanted to say …" Her mother's opinion on his vacillation had rung through the house.

Celia trailed off under Lady Flora's glare. Lady Flora obviously had no interest in the Duchess of Crenshaw's machinations regarding Parliamentary debates, at least not at the moment.

"The drawing master I've engaged is celebrated the length and breadth of France," Lady Flora said coolly. "He is instructing you as a favor to me, and to your mama."

Celia knew good and well how obligated she was to her mother and Lady Flora. She'd been told so at least seventy-two times a day for the past several weeks, ever since the Disaster. Drawing lessons with a professional artist was only one idea about what to do with the problem of Celia.

Celia was still astonished that her mother had consented to let her have the lessons at all, but her father had for once squared his shoulders and taken Celia's side against his wife. Then again, when Lady Flora explained that Celia could learn to paint portraits of the great and good of the Whig party, contributing to the cause of making Britain a world power, the duchess had capitulated.

Lady Flora's glare strengthened as Celia stood mutely. The woman was quite beautiful, in a brittle sort of way, which made her more daunting. Celia knew she ought to pity Lady Flora, who'd been devastated when her grown daughter had died a few years ago, but any grief had long since frosted over.

"Well, go on up," Lady Flora said impatiently. "A gaping mouth only lets in flies, so pray, keep it closed."

Celia popped her mouth shut, made a polite curtsy, and said, "Yes, Lady Flora."

As Celia turned to take up her portfolio, Lady Flora said witheringly, "No, no. A *servant* will carry it upstairs."

Celia snatched her hands back from the portfolio and hastened to the door, eager to remove herself from Lady Flora's presence. Before she could leave, however, she had to turn back.

"Um, where *is* the studio?"

Another heavy sigh. "Fourth floor, in the front, near the staircase. The footman will show you."

Lady Flora waved a hand in dismissal—like the empress of a proud Oriental country, Celia reflected as she hurried away. She bit back a laugh picturing Lady Flora in flowing Chinese garments, flicking her fingers while hundreds of lackeys bowed to her on their knees.

Celia lost her smile quickly. The image was far too close to the mark.

She followed the footman in satin breeches and powdered wig out of the room and up three more flights of stairs. Celia was gasping by the time they reached the top, but the footman breathed as calmly as he would after a lazy stroll in a garden.

He opened a door and indicated, with an elegant gloved hand, that she should go inside. Celia scurried past him, and the footman bowed and withdrew, closing the door behind him, the latch catching with a faint *click*.

Celia found herself in a quiet room flooded with sunshine. The chamber held a few chairs and a recamier draped with red cloth, an easel, a table filled with jars and brushes, and another table strewn with square frames of wood, folds of canvas, and a sheaf of drawing paper.

A fire crackled in the hearth, but except for Celia, the room was empty. No artist's assistant bustled about preparing canvases or mixing paints, no artist looked up to comment on her tardiness.

Celia had met portrait painters, including the celebrated Mr. Hogarth, when they'd come to paint her mother, father, brother, and herself, and she knew what artists looked like. Her instructor would either be thin and nervous with a wife and five children to feed, or elderly, fussy, and set in his ways, with a habit of making inelegant noises.

Lady Flora had said the artist was celebrated in France, so Celia pictured a small, dark-haired man with a turned-up nose and a thick accent, who'd click his tongue against his teeth when he regarded Celia's meager efforts.

Celia explored the room and the artist's accoutrements as she waited, hoping to find an example of the drawing master's work, but she saw none.

After a few moments, another footman discreetly glided in and laid Celia's portfolio on a table then glided back out again.

Celia hastened after him to ask if he'd fetch the drawing master, but the footman had gone by the time she reached the hall. Lady Flora's servants were trained to come and go like ghosts.

She hesitated in the stairwell, which was dim after the bright room, the only light coming from a shaded window on the landing.

How long was she to wait? Did the drawing master keep erratic hours, coming and going as he pleased? Was he a famous Frenchman quite annoyed he had to teach the likes of Lady Celia Fotheringhay, an English duke's spoiled daughter? Had he drowned his frustration in wine and now snored away the morning?

Well, he could cease being rude about it. Celia started down the stairs, determined to find another servant to fetch this haughty drawing master. If he lay in bed in a drunken stupor, it would be his own fault when the footman burst in to roust him.

A faint cry made Celia pause. The sound had come from somewhere within the house, behind one of the doors on the very floor she'd left.

Another whimper came to her, muffled but unmistakable. Somewhere down the hall, a baby was crying.

A baby in this refined house was as out of place as a weed that dared show itself in her mother's garden. Celia couldn't imagine Lady Flora letting any of her servants do anything so human as have children, nor allowing a friend's child to visit. Lady Flora's acquaintances kept their children well hidden from the world, in any case, not bringing them to London until they were old enough to be out in society.

Celia rustled back up the stairs and to the nearest door, opened it, found that room empty, and went to the next one. She tried a few more doors, seeing only elegant furnishings in the chambers behind them, all the while the fretful cry continued.

The chamber three down from the studio held the warmth of a bright fire and was filled with sunlight, a beam slanting from the window to touch the deep auburn hair of a man lying on a chair with his head back, fast asleep. A blue and white quilt covered his body, and in the clasp of one big arm was a tiny child with bright red hair. The babe snuggled into him, restless.

The man's face was slack with sleep, but it was strong, square and hard, the nose sharp, once broken. A brush of red whiskers covered his jaw, a brighter color than the hair that straggled across his cheek, and his mouth was a flat, grim line.

He was large-boned, his body taking up the entire delicate-legged chair, the quilt drooping to reveal a wide spread of shoulders in a loose nightshirt. One bare foot protruded from the bottom end of the quilt.

Celia's gaze slid to the foot in fascination. She'd never seen a man unshod before. Even her brother, older by three years, hadn't gone barefoot when they'd played together in the grasslands of Kent.

This foot was broad but well-shaped, the toes curled slightly in his sleep. The strength displayed in that appendage alone suggested that the rest of him would be as powerful. The blunt-fingered hand that cradled the child bore out Celia's observation.

He transfixed her. Celia had never encountered a man as basic, as *natural*, as this sleeping giant. He splayed formidably on the chair, like a lion at rest, not hunting at the moment, saving his strength for later.

Celia's gaze returned to his foot. Her too-vivid imagination pictured him opening his eyes, reaching out his hand to draw her near, sliding his strong foot up under her skirts along her calf. She could feel the warmth of the rough sole through her finely knit stocking, his leg twining hers as he pulled her closer. She'd tumble into his lap, and he'd stroke her hair with the same gentleness as he held the babe, and then he'd smile.

Fire seared Celia's chest. Her breath, which seemed to have left her, came rushing back with sudden sharpness.

She took a quick step back, but something about the man would not let her flee. His presence held her in place as unswervingly as Lady Flora's stares.

If *he* was the drawing master, he didn't look French at all, but Scottish, like those great Highlanders who'd invaded England this past winter. Celia saw no claymore or dirk lying about or any evidence of a tartan to confirm this theory, only a man in a nightshirt under a quilt, holding a tiny child.

Celia could fathom no reason for a Highlander to be here, unless Lady Flora had given him leave. Lady Flora was eccentric enough to do so—she gave sanction to all sorts of scandalous people, like poets and artists, actors and musicians. Lady Flora's lady's companion, Mrs. Reynolds, it was whispered, had once been a courtesan.

Not all Highlanders had tried to rebel, Celia's brother had told her. Half of them had fought for King George and Britain.

Even so, being in the presence of such a man was unnerving. *And,* Celia made herself be honest, *a little bit exciting.* Celia was never allowed to come anywhere near men who might be considered the least bit dangerous.

Celia could, of course, run back downstairs and ask Lady Flora who the man was and why he was here, but she didn't have the nerve to face the reptile in her den again. The lion in this one was less frightening.

She went to the man's side, disconcerted at how warm the air was next to him. The baby opened its eyes, looked up at Celia with complete trust, and said, *"Blurp."*

"Sir." Celia bent down as close as she dared, ready to dart back as she did when she woke her cat too quickly. "Sir."

The Highlander slept on, his lips parting to let out a snore. The snore wasn't loud, but it was deep and low-pitched, a sound only a man could make.

"Sir." Celia poked her finger into his shoulder.

Nothing. He was a lump of quilt-covered rock. His shoulder was hard as granite, her fingers not making a dent.

The baby gurgled at her encouragingly, but if the father would not wake up when his child moved, Celia doubted he'd respond to her soft taps.

Unfortunately for the Highlander, Celia had been raised by a mother who had no patience for anyone in her house, from the scullery maid to the duke himself, being a lie-abed. The Duchess of Crenshaw had all sorts of tricks to drag a person out of sweet slumber.

Celia moved around the bed to the washstand, lifted the delicate porcelain pitcher, brought it back to the chair, upended the pitcher, and poured a cascade of water over the exposed foot.

CHAPTER 2

*T*he foot kicked. The child let out a cry, and the sleeping lion woke, opening eyes of dark gold as he roared.

"Bloody hell, woman!"

He surged from the chair, a giant in nothing but a nightshirt that gaped open at the neck. The thin fabric let sunshine through it, silhouetting a body that was large, taut, and very bare. "What the devil do ye think you're doing?"

The burning in Celia's chest rose to fevered heat. The nightshirt showed her the outline of male legs, hard with muscle, a tight barrel of a waist, and a hard chest. She could see where his legs met his waist, the transition hidden but tantalizingly near.

The man clasped the child securely but glared with eyes that told Celia he was indeed a fierce Highland warrior, come to finish what Bonnie Prince Charlie had begun.

Celia realized her mouth was open. *A gaping mouth only lets in flies.* She shut it with a click of teeth.

"What am I doing?" she asked crisply, hiding the fact that she quavered like the aspic her mother insisted she have for breakfast. "Waking you, sir. We have an appointment."

~

ALEC STARED DOWN AT A WOMAN HE'D NEVER SEEN BEFORE IN HIS life. She gazed back at him, her face flushed, the pitcher of torture in her hand.

Her eyes were hazel, a green-brown mix like sunlight dappling water. Her hair was dark, almost black, the crown of her head covered by a modest cap, the kind unmarried misses wore.

The cap matched the embroidered fichu that lined her bodice and kept male eyes like Alec's from viewing her bosom. It was a fine bosom, the sort a man would like to cup while he drew her close for a taste of her lips. Her gown was a tan and yellow striped cotton without adornment. The dress was drab, very different from the colorful silks dripping with lace and ribbons that Lady Flora draped herself in.

This woman was young, barely into her twenties, with an unworldly air of a person who'd never traveled much beyond her own home. Innocent, yes, but her eyes held the stubbornness of one who would do what she must, damn all censure. Why else would a slip of an English miss dump an ice-cold deluge on him?

"Are you, indeed, the drawing master, sir?" she asked in that clear, clean voice. "You are to give me lessons this morning."

Her words were punctuated by the clock on the tapered-legged writing table striking the half hour past eight. "Damn and blast," he muttered.

Alec realized he faced Lady Celia Fotheringhay, daughter of the Duke of Crenshaw, the man who would be key in finding his brother.

His waking brain kicked him to life. Lady Celia had been brought here by Flora so they could ease into the duke's head and discover all he knew. This charade was for Will's life.

Alec banished his scowl and brought up the Mackenzie charm. Mal, it was agreed, was the most charming of all of them, but Alec came close to his wee brother's skill. He tried a half smile and forced his voice to be light, suppressing his Scottish tones as much as he could.

"My daughter—she was restless all night." Alec lifted Jenny close and kissed the top of her head. Jenny, right on cue, closed her eyes, her small fists clutching his nightshirt in a fetching way.

The young woman simply stared at him, her lips parting. The pitcher was in danger of falling from her hand, so Alec took it from her.

Lady Celia blinked. She jerked once and clamped her mouth closed.

"Go on into the studio, lass," Alec said. "I'll be there after I put her to bed. Promise."

He let his right eye close in the hint of a wink as he set the pitcher on a table and moved past Lady Celia to the chamber door. Lady Celia pivoted as he went by, and her skirts over a modestly round hoop swiveled with her.

She was not what he expected. Alec had pictured a spoiled, pinch-faced harpy, raised to be the privileged daughter of the most prominent duke in Britain. Her father doted on her, *and* he'd likely know whether Alec's brother Will had been captured and where he'd be held if so.

Will's last contact before he'd disappeared had been the Dowager Marchioness of Ellesmere, a grand hostess in London, known to her intimates as Lady Flora.

Lady Flora, as alarmed at Will's disappearance as the Mackenzies, agreed to help. She'd brought Alec to London, given him a new identity and a history, and informed him that the Duke of Crenshaw was the most likely man to have the power over Will's life or death. Lady Flora's plan was to pump Celia for all kinds of information, resorting to blackmail or whatever trickery she could come up with to get it.

If things became desperate, Flora said, Lady Celia could become a bargaining piece. Alec did not want to resort to such measures, but he knew damn well the courts would not spare Will's life when it was discovered exactly who he was and the things he'd done. And Will had done so many things.

Having met Celia now, Alec was certain Lady Flora was too eager to use her. This young woman did not look as though she knew the secrets of the kingdom. She likely had no idea what had gone on during the battles in the far north and the Uprising's horrible culmination at Culloden. She'd probably cheered when it was known that Cumberland had won and sent Charles running. It would have been a cheer of ignorance—the horror of it all would have been kept from her.

Lady Celia studied him, her eyes full of curiosity. No fear at all. This was a woman who'd never faced danger in her life.

Jenny opened her eyes, her whimpers building toward a wail. Alec gathered her close, rocking her in his big arms.

"Hush now, sweet." He turned from Lady Celia and walked with Jenny to the stairs. He began to sing in a soft voice, a song in Erse his mum had whispered to him so very long ago.

Jenny's cries eased into sniffles as Alec climbed higher in the house to return her to her chamber. He was very aware of Lady Celia watching him from the doorway, her gaze fixed on him until he turned the corner of the stairs, and she was lost to sight.

Celia had recovered some but not all of her wits by the time the drawing master reappeared.

He didn't simply walk into the room. He burst into it like a bright comet, stealing the light and forcing all attention to him. At the moment, the attention was Celia's and that of yet another footman who set a pitcher of scented water and glasses on a low table.

The drawing master eyed the pitcher as the footman vanished. He brushed past Celia with a waft of fresh air, lifted the pitcher, and carried it to the other side of the room.

"Don't want to tempt ye," he said. "You have a fondness for throwing water around. Now then, lass."

He looked about the room as though he'd never seen it before, spied her portfolio, and made for it.

He'd changed from nightshirt to knee breeches that looked a bit worn, stockings that had been mended, black shoes he shifted uncomfortably in, a linen shirt, a dark brown frock coat with one patched elbow, and no waistcoat or cravat.

Celia's irritation turned to pity. He was poor, as she'd suspected, a man scraping a living teaching drawing to daughters and sons of aristocrats. Likely he'd left Scotland after the war was lost, looking for work, too proud perhaps, to take a post in the factories and mills. Why he'd left France if he was so famous there, Celia couldn't guess. No doubt he was putting up with Lady Flora now because she could bring him paying clients.

Any idea that Lady Flora was having a scandalous affair with this man Celia did not bother to consider. Everyone knew about Lady Flora. The great surprise was that she'd married at all, but her much-celebrated nuptials—the daughter of a notable earl wedded to a marquess—had made her a powerful woman.

The drawing master reached a broad-fingered hand to Celia's portfolio. Of course he'd be curious about her work, but

Celia pictured him finding her pathetic efforts and laughing out loud. He'd have a booming laugh, and she'd die of mortification. Celia had brought the drawings only because Lady Flora insisted.

She hurried to the table and pressed her hand to the portfolio's cover. "What is your name?" she asked. "Lady Flora did not tell me."

The man's eyes opened and closed a few times, his lashes fair and thick. "Mr. Finn. Ansel Finn."

He spoke the name slowly and carefully as though as uncomfortable with it as with his heavy shoes. It didn't fit him, that name. It was tight and simple, and Celia already believed him much more complicated than that.

Not his fault. He was impoverished, he couldn't help what he was named, and he was under Lady Flora's power. Celia wondered what he'd done to put himself into such a terrible position, but she felt sympathy for him.

He unfastened the portfolio's catch with strong fingers. Celia leaned to press her hand more firmly to the leather top.

"What was that language?" she asked, groping for questions. "That you were singing to your daughter? What was the song?"

Mr. Finn flushed brilliant red, the color blending with the russet hair at his forehead. Then he beamed a wide smile, like sunshine blasting through smoke.

"'Tis very old. Greek, I think."

Celia lifted her hand from the portfolio. "Absolute nonsense. I understand Greek perfectly, and that is nothing like it."

"Ah. Well then." Mr. Finn rubbed his nose. "It's that embarrassed I am, lass. It's Irish. Me mother tongue."

Celia supposed it sounded a bit like what the Irish maids gabbled at each other below stairs. Never in Celia's mother's hearing, of course. In the duchess's opinion, all servants should speak perfect, unaccented English or not speak at all.

"I see," Celia said. "Well, you'd better not speak Irish while you're teaching me, Mr. Finn. Lest my mother, who believes English is the language of God, gets wind of it."

Mr. Finn slanted her a startled look before amusement danced in to cover it. "I will try to remember. What am I supposed to be teaching you?"

"To be an artist, of course." Humiliation bit her. "If I become an eccentric and paint day and night, I will be forgiven all my sins."

Mr. Finn looked her up and down, blatantly so, no politeness. His eyes were the color of gold, or amber, like the whisky her father drank when her mother wasn't home. "What kind of sins can a wee thing like yourself have committed? *I've* done them all, lass."

A lump lodged in Celia's throat, and her breath didn't work quite right. "Apparently, embarrassing my mother is the most grievous sin of all."

Mr. Finn gave her another look of surprise, then he began to laugh. It was a deep, true laugh, crinkling up his face and smoothing its hard lines into something handsome.

"Poor little lass." He shook his head. "You're a charmer, you are. I meant what specifically am I teaching you? Drawing, painting? Landscapes? Portraits? Let's see what ye've done."

He turned swiftly to the portfolio and had it open before Celia could stop him.

"I wish you wouldn't," she said, her face hot. "They're not good. It's only what I've done on my own. I sat in on my brother's drawing lessons, but that was a long time ago ..."

Mr. Finn ignored her as he spread out the drawings—the small sketch of her mother's face that hadn't quite captured her sharpness, the many different pictures of the cat, the buildings of London seen from the garret window, and watercolors of the lands around her family's estate in Kent.

Mr. Finn paused over a careful drawing Celia had done of her father's head and shoulders. She thought she'd caught well his round, affable face, friendly eyes, plump chin, and the wig he liked with two careful curls on either side of his face.

Her father was not a handsome man and preferred the company of his mistress, the boisterous Mrs. Barnett, whom he'd known all his life. All the family was aware of Mrs. Barnett —Celia's mother said it was a relief that Mrs. B. kept her father out from underfoot. The duke was kind to Celia and had taken her side, to her surprise, during the Disaster.

Celia's brother had not. Edward was furious and hadn't spoken to Celia since. That hurt. She and her brother had always been great friends, but she hadn't heard from him since he'd been posted off to France after Culloden to fight in the ongoing war against King Louis.

Mr. Finn studied the drawing of the duke for a long time. His smile had gone and something harsh entered the set of his mouth.

"As I say, I'm not very skilled," Celia said into the silence. "I couldn't get my father to sit for long. He's very busy."

Mr. Finn looked up at her, the flash of bleakness in his eyes like an icy wind on a Highland moor. "Aye, I imagine he's very busy. He's a duke."

"Well, yes. He's on all sorts of committees with ministries and things, when he's not hosting gatherings to support the MPs he champions. He's leader of the party, you know." The last words were spoken with a downturn of voice, Celia finding the situation wearying rather than exciting.

Wearying in the extreme. In her family, every waking moment, every activity, every word uttered, every deed done, had to be for the benefit of the Whigs and the glory of the dukes of Crenshaw. Any indiscretion from Celia, her brother, or her father, any flaw, any wrong turn would discredit the entire edifice.

Hence, Celia's current disgrace. She was a bit amazed they hadn't simply locked her in the cellar and had done.

She felt Mr. Finn's eyes on her. Celia made herself meet his gaze, startled at the deep anger in it. A rage so bitter it made her flinch blazed out, and behind that was fear—stark, cold, bone-shaking fear.

Celia frowned, and in an instant, the look was gone. Mr. Finn's eyes warmed again and he turned to the drawings.

"These are finely done, lass. You have a gift."

Celia shook her head. "You are kind, but ..."

"No, you show talent." Mr. Finn touched the drawings of the cat, each one different. Celia had captured the black and white creature curled up with her tail over her nose, in others stretching, or batting at a fly, or sitting bolt upright like a statue, and finally contorted as she gracefully stretched out a back leg to lick her spread toes.

"Your lines are good," Mr. Finn said. "You can depict an action without overdoing it. Your landscapes show promise— you've got the depth right. This one is particularly good." He tapped the drawing of London rooftops, which her mother said was ridiculous. Who wanted to look at a picture of a city? Especially one seen from a servants' chamber?

"Your portraits, now." Mr. Finn pulled out the pictures of her father and mother and laid them side by side. "You have the outlines of the faces right—you can draw a nose, I will give you that. But I think this is where you can use instruction. How to capture a look, an emotion. I am noticing you have nothing of people save these two faces. No bodies."

"Full length figures are difficult," Celia said in defense. "Especially when no one will sit still long enough for me to draw them." She heard her frustration. Edward, who was a well-muscled specimen, would never give her five minutes for a sketch.

"'Tis why artists hire models," Mr. Finn said. "We pay them to sit still. Mind you, they don't always."

"Do you have trouble with your models, Mr. Finn?" Celia asked in curiosity. "I hear they are ladies of great scandal."

She couldn't keep the wistfulness from her voice. Artists' models led shocking lives, but she admired their ability to do precisely as they pleased. Some of them went on to marry the artists and be celebrated, like Rubens's very young second wife. Those ladies had never worried about their duchess mothers declaring they were no longer of any use to them, or the approbation of society that the Duchess of Crenshaw had such an ungrateful and disobedient daughter.

"No trouble with the lady models," Mr. Finn said without hesitation. "They stay motionless, because the sooner I finish, the sooner they can be paid. I was thinking of my younger brother, who wouldn't stand still if you nailed his foot to the floor. Always moving, is he, even now that he's grown up—" He broke off, bleakness flashing again in his eyes.

Celia wondered what had happened to Mr. Finn to bring him such sadness. Had this younger brother died? Poor man.

To have to scratch a living teaching while mourning his brother and raising a daughter on his own must be very difficult. Mr. Finn had made no mention of a wife—which might mean nothing; some gentlemen never talked about their wives —but a baby would be in the mother's care if the mother were alive, not the father's. Likely he was a widower. Celia's pity escalated.

Mr. Finn clapped his hands together, the sound large, and Celia jumped. "I know where ye need to start, lass. Sit there."

He waved her to a stool before the easel that had been turned to catch the light from the window.

Mr. Finn took up a sheet of thick paper from the bundle on the table and attached it to the easel with swift, sure movements. A large box of drawing pencils, the expensive kind of true English graphite, came out of a drawer in a tall bureau. Mr. Finn extracted two pencils and whittled down the points with the knife for that purpose, lifting the pencils before his golden eyes to study their sharpness.

He handed Celia one pencil and set the other on a table, waiting for her to sit. Celia slid onto the stool uncertainly, jamming her feet on the bottom rung.

"What am I drawing?" she asked.

Mr. Finn slid his coat from his shoulders and dropped himself down on a chair, the gilded thing sliding backward a few inches. His coat landed on the carpet.

"Me."

Celia blinked at him. "To see what I make of your nose?"

Another rumble of laughter. "No, lass. I'm thinking you need a few lessons in anatomy."

He untied his shirt and pulled it off over his head, dropping the shirt on top of his coat, a puddle of pale cloth on black wool.

CHAPTER 3

$\mathcal{C}$elia's mouth went dry as a linen bag.

He sat not five feet from her, a large man with nothing covering his sunbaked torso. He lounged back in the chair, but he was straight and strong, unashamed, elbows on the chair's delicate arms.

The collarbone she'd glimpsed when she'd found him in his nightshirt stretched to his shoulders, one of which bore a small triangular gouge. Red hair curled down his chest to a firm belly, both chest and stomach crossed with scars. The arms that had cradled his daughter held sinewy strength and were brushed with more scars.

He rested his right hand on the chair's arm, palm down, fingers slightly curled. The hand alone was formidable, never mind the rest of him. The wiry hair on his arm was golden red, the hand, at rest, filled with potential power.

His fingertips were blunt, fingers broad. The man claimed to be an artist, but Celia could easily picture this hand around the hilt of a claymore or holding a musket, muscles working as he fought British soldiers to the death.

"Go on then," he said in his rumbling voice. "We've started late, and I have other lessons today."

Celia jumped, realizing her mouth had opened again. She snapped it closed and jerked her gaze from his chest to find him watching her, unsmiling, his golden eyes filled with something she couldn't decipher.

She lifted her pencil and touched it to the paper, but she had no idea how to begin. Drawing had always come easily to her, but at this moment, her fingers would not move.

Perhaps the fact that she was sitting alone in a room with a man who was half naked kept her fingers stiff. The last time Celia had been found in a compromising situation, her mother had tried to force her to marry the gentleman in question. If her mother came upon Celia with *this* man, however, she'd do everything in her power to make certain no one ever knew. Scandal was only acceptable when it was useful.

At this moment, her duchess mother was comfortably far away on the other side of Grosvenor Square, Lady Flora was downstairs, and Celia and the drawing master were quite alone.

She took a deep breath, willed her hand to work, and brushed a dark line across the page.

Her brother's drawing master had taught her to ignore what a thing *was* and to simply draw the form of it. He'd told her to block each part of the object with rough lines before going over them to clarify.

Celia studied Mr. Finn's bare arm, willing herself to see it as a series of shapes instead of the arm she'd imagined pulling her close. The top of his wrist was almost a rectangle and arcs ran from that along his forearm. Muscles curved in long half circles from the underside to gather in a hollow on the inside of his elbow.

Celia slowly sketched the squares and ellipses to represent the hand, arm, and shoulder, but her pencil wobbled and the lines looked wrong. She could not pretend Ansel Finn was so many boxes and circles. She was aware of the blood that flowed under his skin, the heat of him coming to her across the small space, the *aliveness* of him. There was a great difference between drawing this man and sketching a vase of flowers.

"Don't think about it too hard, lass." His silken voice slid into her uncertainty. "Let your mind see, and draw what it tells you."

Celia closed her eyes briefly, then fixed her gaze on his hand again. It lay quietly, the latent strength in his fingers reminding her of the whole man—a lion waiting for his prey.

Her pencil skimmed smoothly across the page, a gray-black line flowing from its point. She formed the curve of his finger, the crease at its middle knuckle, the blunt fingertip.

Celia drew a sharp breath as she looked at what she'd done. Not even a complete finger, but it already held more life than anything she'd drawn before.

She looked up, pleased, and found his gaze firmly on her.

Mr. Finn was sitting completely still, his amusement gone. His eyes were hard, flat, almost angry, and at the same time, full of fire. The fire was banked for now, but what must it be when it blazed?

Celia saw a man holding himself back, hiding himself behind bluster and sudden smiles, neither the bluster nor the smiles the real person. Ansel Finn was not his name. The words were too tame to contain this man.

Not a man. A warrior.

Mr. Finn was no more a poor Irish artist struggling to make a living than Celia was. He'd seen war and death; his eyes had looked upon tragedy.

His bearing, looks, height—all told her he was Scottish, one of the mad Highlanders. The fact that he pretended to be a harmless artist, using a false name and nationality, suggested that he must be one who'd followed Prince Charles Stuart, the Young Pretender, in his march against England.

A traitor to the crown, a crazed fighter—Celia's brother, Edward, had told her about the terrifying Highland soldiers screaming like banshees as they charged the British lines. Their wild cries and fearless attacks had broken the spirits of even the most courageous of Englishmen.

This man had fought and killed, then watched his fellows die and die in the aftermath of Culloden Field. She'd heard all about Culloden from Edward, who'd witnessed the mass slaughter. No quarter given. That had been their orders. No matter that the men surrendered, no matter how much they begged for their lives, the evil Highlanders were cut down even as they raised their hands and pleaded for mercy. The field had been stained red with their blood.

Edward had declared it a great victory. Celia'd had nightmares about it.

She should be frightened to be in the room with a deadly Highlander, and furious with Lady Flora for allowing him near her. There was no doubt that Lady Flora knew exactly who this man was—she was the sort who would find out everything about him.

But then, he *must* be harmless, because Lady Flora would never, ever give comfort to an enemy. She was working hand in glove with Celia's father to make Britain the most powerful empire in the world. She'd been furious about the Jacobite Uprising, happy that the Duke of Cumberland had rushed to Scotland to beat them down.

Ergo, Mr. Finn must not be dangerous.

But the man who looked at her with intense amber eyes, was obviously quite dangerous. It was most puzzling.

Celia cleared her throat. "Shall I continue?"

Mr. Finn lifted his red-gold brows. "Ye came for a drawing

lesson, didn't ye? So we go until it's done. Let me see where you are."

He slid his chair around so that he was next to her. Mr. Finn didn't touch her, but the heat of his skin warmed her through the many layers of her robe à la Française. Celia glanced sideways at the well-muscled shoulder near hers, hard under satin skin. A bead of perspiration gathered at the back of her neck and trickled under her bodice.

Mr. Finn leaned forward to study her drawing, putting his clean-smelling hair in its neat queue nearly under her chin. His hair was dark, but it wasn't brown or black—a definite red hue ran through it like rich mahogany.

"This is well done." He tapped the line she'd made of his finger, which exactly matched the finger that touched it. Then he brushed at the squares and oblongs as though he wanted to erase them, and his fingertips came away black. "*These* are for students who've never drawn before. So that drawing masters can pretend to teach them something. You already know much."

He turned his head to look at her as he spoke, casually, as though sitting next to her half unclothed was nothing unusual. He had no embarrassment about his bare flesh, as if he didn't even notice it.

Celia couldn't cease noticing. The length of his leg rested against her striped skirt, the pressure of it making her heart pound. He was so close she felt his breath on her neck.

She flicked her gaze to his eyes, inches from hers, his stillness returning. The man changed from movement to quietude so fast it was unnerving. Perhaps that unpredictability was what had made the Highlanders so frightening to her brother and his soldiers.

"Edward had a good teacher," she said with difficulty.

Mr. Finn returned to her drawing. The drop in temperature when he no longer focused on her was palpable.

"You've learned much on your own, then," he said. "With more practice, and a better teacher, your talent will shine forth."

"My brother's drawing master was a famous painter," Celia said, suppressing her sudden pleasure at the word *talent*. He must be flattering her so her mother would continue to pay him, but it was nice to hear anyway. "He's done portraits of the king."

"A famous painter doesn't equal a good teacher. They are full of their own genius and have no idea how to convey to others the basics of art. I have no genius, and so I instruct."

Good humor flashed in his eyes, wicked and self-effacing, like a schoolboy who'd made a joke. He'd become warm and friendly again, his distance evaporating. The Highland warrior was gone; the father who soothed his daughter with song had returned.

"What have *you* painted?" Celia asked. "Anything I would have seen?"

Mr. Finn shrugged, muscles moving beneath his shoulders. "Most of my better paintings are in France. But ..."

He snatched the pencil out of her hand before she could squeak in protest. Mr. Finn slid Celia and her chair away from the easel with alarming strength, turned the easel to him, and started scribbling on the drawing paper. He peered at her around it, his arm moving swiftly.

After a few minutes, Mr. Finn clapped the pencil to the table and turned the easel so she could see what he'd done. "Not elegant, but it's the sort of picture I do."

Celia looked into her own face. Not posed and regal, as in the portraits she'd sat for in her father's house, but as she looked at this exact moment. Her lips were parted, her eyes focused, her brows drawn. One curl of her dark hair had escaped the careful knot at the back of her neck and trickled down her shoulder, and the lace cap on top of her head was slightly askew. Celia put a hand to it, and found it out of place in truth.

"That is remarkable," she said in breathless pleasure.

"It's a trick, but one that makes me a living. Now then— you're having the lesson, my lady, not I."

He clipped a new sheet to the easel then picked up the pencil and thrust it back at her. "More than one finger, lass. I want an entire hand."

A grin spread across his face as he spoke, as though he'd said something naughty. Celia's blood warmed, even though she had no idea what other meaning the words could have.

She took the pencil, her suddenly tight stays constricting her breath. Mr. Finn shoved his chair back with strong feet, sliding into the table and slapping his hand to it. Whatever bond held his hair broke, sending a thick red-brown wave to his shoulders.

Celia drew it, then the curve of his jaw, the square of his chin, his eyes full of fire. She was supposed to be sketching his hand, but an abrupt fever streamed through her, moving the pencil before she could stop it.

His face took shape under her fingers, a Scottish soldier, hard and fearsome, yet full of intensity and warmth. The protective look he'd given the child in his arms came through, as well as the teasing gleam he'd reserved for Celia.

Celia's arm ached, her throat was dry, her eyes burning. But she couldn't stop, not until—

"Celia, you are lingering," came a brisk voice. "Your next student has arrived, Mr. Finn."

Celia jerked and dropped the pencil, gasping as her breath poured back into her. The mists cleared to show her Lady Flora poised in the doorway, her wide skirts touching its frame, her eagle gaze fixed on Celia. Every entrance Lady Flora made was a portrait, a beautiful woman pausing in grace before she glided into a room.

Why the devil she'd come to announce Mr. Finn's next appointment herself instead of sending a footman, Celia had no idea. But she was there now, gazing in narrow-eyed disapproval at Celia hunched before the easel and Mr. Finn lolling on her gilded furniture from Paris.

Mr. Finn calmly leaned down and picked up his shirt, bunching it up to pull over his head and settle on his shoulders. Lady Flora watched him then took in Celia's hot face with keen, knowing eyes. She marched over to the easel as Celia slid off the stool, and frowned at what Celia had drawn.

"A good likeness," she pronounced. Her tone betrayed her doubt that Celia could have rendered such a thing. "A *very* good likeness." She glared at Mr. Finn as though annoyed with him.

Mr. Finn returned the look blandly. "Lady Celia has skill."

Celia knew her drawing had caught Mr. Finn well. She'd captured the good humor in his face, his unruly hair, his eyes holding a wicked light as well as an emptiness, as though he had a gap in his soul. Celia had sketched in a quick shadow behind his head to give the picture depth, and now she fancied she saw another in that shadow, a second man as strong as he was, but this one as insubstantial as smoke.

Lady Flora's frown turned to a scowl. She snatched the paper from the easel, the clips that held it down flying. She shoved the picture at Mr. Finn. "*This* much skill?"

Mr. Finn gazed at the picture first in surprise, then with admiration, and finally in dismay. "Mm," he said grimly. "I think we'll abandon anatomy and work on bowls of fruit."

If Celia did have a gift, it was of being able to detach herself from a situation, to see it with the eyes of practical sense instead of emotion. Any of her friends would have burst into tears if Lady Flora and Mr. Finn had looked in such disparagement at her drawing. Celia only watched the two of them, trying to decide what had upset them about it.

It wasn't Celia's talent, or lack of it, she surmised. They weren't condemning the likeness itself, but the fact that she'd caught it.

Why? If Mr. Finn were truly an enemy Highlander in disguise, why on earth would he be here in Lady Flora's grand house on Grosvenor Square, teaching art to ladies of the *ton*? And why would Lady Flora, of all people, invite him to stay?

It was an oddity, and oddities intrigued her.

Lady Flora swiftly rolled the drawing into a scroll. "I will keep this for you, Celia. You must be off now."

As Lady Flora turned away, Mr. Finn caught Celia's gaze. His eyes held understanding and amusement, recognition that both of them were trapped in Lady Flora's snare. Celia flashed a smile at him, acknowledging, and he gave her a swift wink.

Lady Flora turned back, and they both immediately assumed neutral expressions. Out of the corner of her eye, Celia saw Mr. Finn's lips twitch.

Lady Flora waved at Celia with the rolled paper. "Off you go, Celia. Rivers will see you out. Be here tomorrow morning, promptly at eight. *Promptly*, mind."

Celia curtsied and then held out her hand. "Might I take my drawing, so I can study it in the meantime?"

"No," Lady Flora snapped, then she deliberately softened her tone. "No, dear Celia. I will keep it for you, and when you are finished with your instruction, we'll have a little exhibition in my salon. You will like that, won't you?"

Celia was instantly on her guard. When Lady Flora gushed and pretended to be kind, it meant she was up to something.

When Celia didn't answer, Lady Flora became icy once more. "Your mother wishes it," she said. "Go."

There was nothing for it. Celia gave her another curtsy and reached for her portfolio, but Lady Flora closed her eyes in despair and shook her head.

Celia gave up and moved quickly across the room. She turned back at the door and found Lady Flora's glare hard on her. A basilisk had a stare like that.

Mr. Finn had turned away to replace the pencils in their box, his shirt clinging to his back. The sensation of his nearness when he'd sat close to her was still vivid.

He bent to the box, as though making sure each pencil rested precisely in its given slot. He did not look around, did not say goodbye. Mr. Finn was a drawing master and Celia was a duke's daughter, and Lady Flora would hardly approve of any familiarity.

Why then, had Lady Flora said nothing when she'd marched in and found Mr. Finn sitting before Celia without his shirt?

So many puzzles to solve. Celia closed the door and walked to the landing, making certain her heels clicked loudly on the polished floor.

To Celia's relief, Rivers, Lady Flora's stern butler, was nowhere in sight. Celia paused at the top of the stairs, slid off her shoes, and hurried on quick tiptoes back to the studio door.

She pressed her skirts to silence and leaned to put her ear near the keyhole. Eavesdropping wasn't genteel, but Celia had decided long ago that a young lady could learn much if she didn't worry about gentility every single moment of her life.

CHAPTER 4

*W*hat were you thinking?" came Lady Flora's voice, clear and ringing.

"I told her to draw my arm." The Scottish accent Mr. Finn had been holding back flooded out. Celia liked his voice better like this, gruff and growling, holding the rawness of his native land. "I'm thinking she's not an obedient lass." He sounded approving, which made Celia flush, pleased.

"What if she'd showed this to her father?" Lady Flora snapped. "You are reckless—I should have known you would be. So much like your brother."

"Her father has never met me," Mr. Finn answered without heat. "And I dinnae look so much like Will. I only ever looked like—"

The words cut off abruptly, a sound like a cough ending his speech.

"I know." Lady Flora's voice softened, something Celia had never heard in her before. Even when Lady Flora's daughter had died, she had been, if anything, colder and more brittle than ever.

"The lass shouldn't come back here," Mr. Finn said. "We'll find another way."

"Nonsense." Lady Flora's strident tones returned. "If you do everything exactly as I say, all will be well. Now—I should burn this."

Celia couldn't help her tiny gasp. The idea that Flora would stuff the drawing she'd just done into the fire cut off her breath.

When Mr. Finn's eyes had gazed at Celia out of the page, her heart had squeezed into a point of pain. It was the best portrait she'd ever drawn, and she knew it. More than that, she didn't want to lose the image of him, the essence she'd captured. If she was never allowed to see the man again, at least she'd have that.

"No." Mr. Finn's word was a command, quick and sharp. "I'll take it. Best you be about your business, woman."

Celia heard the sound of paper on flesh—presumably Lady Flora had slapped the scroll into his hand.

"Very well. And *don't* call me 'woman.'"

Mr. Finn's laughter rang out. "It's what ye are, underneath all that ice. By the way, I sacked the nursery maid."

"I beg your pardon?" Lady Flora's anger turned to bewilderment. "Why?"

"She was trying to poison my wee one with gin, that's why. I told your under housemaid, Sally, t' take over. She's a bright girl, obviously has looked after children before. Do ye even talk to your servants before you take them on?"

"Of course I do. The nursery maid was a recommendation. Damn and blast."

"Ye take care of the rest of your house. I'll take care of me daughter." Mr. Finn's voice held a growl. "Agreed?"

"Yes, yes. Whatever you like."

Celia blinked. She'd never heard Lady Flora capitulate about anything in her life. The atmosphere in the room had changed— Mr. Finn no longer sounded like a pitiable gentleman grateful for a job, but a man who didn't fear telling Lady Flora exactly what to do. And Lady Flora was letting him, if grudgingly.

How very curious.

Mr. Finn's footfalls approached the door, and Celia realized she'd dallied too long. Gathering her skirts, she scurried for the staircase and snatched up her shoes. She went down the stairs as quickly as she dared, clutching the railing to keep herself from tumbling headlong. Rivers materialized on the first-floor landing, looking up as Celia hurried down, his haughty brows rising.

The main staircase in Lady Flora's mansion gave onto landings that wrapped around each floor. Chairs had been placed along these galleries in case Lady Flora's houseguests grew weary climbing up to their bedchambers and had to pause and rest. The wide sweep of Celia's gown caught on the leg of one of these graceful chairs and sent it tumbling.

Celia tugged at her overskirt the fallen chair had pinned to the floor and heard the India cotton tear—her mother would have a thing or two to say about that. Two footmen materialized beside her, untangled the skirt, and righted the chair.

"Are you well, my lady?" Rivers asked from below.

"Yes, yes." Celia jerked her skirt into place, plunked onto the chair, and thrust her high-heeled slippers onto her feet. She continued her journey down the last flight more sedately, praying her shoes stayed on her feet.

Celia knew Mr. Finn watched from above even before she reached the ground floor and looked back up. He stood four floors above her, his large hand gripping the gallery railing, his dark red hair loose and tumbling about his face.

He remained unmoving, not acknowledging her, but Celia *knew* he knew she'd been listening at the door. Knew she'd heard all he and Lady Flora had discussed.

But he did nothing, said nothing. Celia sent a smile upward

and lifted her hand in a brief farewell. "Good morning, Mr. Finn," she sang out, then she turned for the front door, striving to move with dignity.

Mr. Finn did not answer. Celia felt his eyes on her as a maid helped her into her wraps and she ducked out of the house.

A sedan chair waited on the pavement—because of course a duke's daughter could not be allowed to walk the hundred feet around the square to her father's house. Celia thanked the bearers for waiting, and the footman who helped her in, and the second footman who came out with her portfolio and tucked it into the chair beside her as she settled herself.

Celia glanced up at the house, finding the window that would give onto the fourth floor studio. She couldn't see anything but sun and clouds reflected on glass, but she knew in her heart that Mr. Finn watched her go.

≈

ONCE DARKNESS SETTLED ON THE STREETS, ALEC MACKENZIE departed Lady Flora's house through its back garden and entered a plain black coach at the end of the mews. Not long later, he left Mayfair and then St. James's behind, the coach heading eastward along the river.

At Fleet Street, Alec descended from the coach and melted into the lanes south and east of it.

He'd dressed in dark breeches, plain coat, and sturdy shoes, and pulled his hair into a tight queue, letting the darkness and his hat hide the red of it. Thus garbed, Alec looked like every other working man walking these streets. He was confident that he didn't have much chance of being spotted as a savage High-lander, because most Londoners, especially in this area, had never seen one. They'd met Scots, of course, but those were mostly Glaswegians and other Lowlanders who came looking for work at the docks and in the factories.

Alec was on his way to meet such a Lowlander in a tavern near the river. The man had been another of Will's contacts and might have some idea about what Will had been up to.

The tavern was typical of taverns around dockyards every-where—Paris, London, Edinburgh—didn't matter. A dark interior lit by few lights, a large fireplace with an indifferent fire struggling to burn, plank tables scarred from years of tankards and fists being pounded on them, rushes on the floor that smelled as though they hadn't been swept out and replenished in weeks.

Two harried barmaids sailed among the patrons, swinging away from fondling hands with the ease of long practice. Both caught sight of Alec—one sent him a surly look, and one beamed a smile.

He sent the friendlier woman a nod and seated himself at a relatively empty end of a table. Just his luck, it was the surly barmaid who flowed by and demanded to know if he wanted ale.

"Please," Alec answered. His plan was to speak as little as possible, so his accent wouldn't mark him. Best to sip ale, look unassuming, and wait for his man.

The barmaid gave him an even more sour look and marched away.

Celia Fotheringhay. The name broke into Alec's thoughts, followed by the memory of her hazel eyes, the fearless way she'd assessed him, her interest when he'd begun to instruct her. He'd watched those eyes sparkle with fervor when she'd began drawing in earnest, the passion catching her up before she realized it.

The drawing she'd done of his face had been quite good. It

was as though he'd peered into a mirror or, heartbreakingly, at his twin, Angus, gone forever.

That was the trouble. If the wrong person saw the drawing, Alec Mackenzie was done for.

Lady Celia had caught not only his likeness but showed him for what he was—a Highlander, strong and arrogant, unbroken though Butcher Cumberland had done his best to erase his family from the earth. Celia hadn't sketched in a bonnet and claymore, but she might as well have.

He'd tucked the drawing among his things in his small bedchamber, keeping it safe. Looking at the picture made him remember the truth of himself, and also the pretty young woman who had sketched it.

No dalliance there, though. Celia was the means to an end, the daughter of a man who might know Will's fate. If Alec were cruel, he'd consider using pretty Celia to take his revenge on her ducal father—he admitted the thought had danced in his mind before he'd met her. But the lady was an innocent, ignorant of what had truly happened in the Jacobite Uprising, untouched by it. There was no hatred of all things Scots in her.

An even crueler man would rejoice that she was such an innocent—all the better weapon for tearing down her father.

But Alec was not cruel. In fact, he thought of himself as genial and pleasant, more inclined to flirt with a lovely woman than use her in a dastardly plot of vengeance. Lady Flora was more inclined to the dastardly. He'd have to tell her to keep her scheming fingers off the lovely Celia.

Alec's thoughts were broken when a man sat down next to him and gave him a sullen nod. He was dressed no differently than any in the tavern—linen shirt, homespun breeches, black shoes, worn coat.

But he was Scots, not English. He had the bearing that many Scots in London did, that he was in this country only because he needed the work, that he'd rather be toiling on his farm up north.

The sunny-faced barmaid brought the man a tankard and also carried one for Alec. She gave Alec a warm look and a shimmy of her skirts, but Alec wasn't in the mood for a dalliance. The barmaid departed, looking in no way unhappy that her other services would not be required.

The Scotsman had dark hair scraped into a queue, a rather flat face, and light brown eyes. He took a pull of his ale, grimaced, and nodded at Alec.

"All right?"

"Aye," Alec answered.

They slurped in silence. The ale was watery and tasteless, but that was usual for cheap backstreet taverns. The company wasn't much better—tired men who wanted to drink and then crawl off to their beds.

The man set down his tankard after another long drink and motioned for Alec to follow him. Alec dropped coins for the ale on the table and walked out with him into the night.

They strolled in silence through dark streets lit only by those fortunate enough to have lanterns to guide them. These occasional lamps bobbed along like fireflies in the fog, winking out as their owners reached their destinations and ducked indoors.

Alec's man led him with surety down streets Alec wouldn't have walked alone, and so to the river. Alec had never been through these lanes before but his memory stored up each one, his ability to recall exact details of a place after seeing it only once ensuring he could reach safety in case this man proved to be an enemy. He wouldn't tear around panicked and lost.

The Thames stank, the shingle that lined the shore just as rank. Boats plied the water, their few lights swaying. Alec could just make out the bulk of London Bridge with its pile of houses on top a way down the river, a smudge against the night.

The man halted. Alec kept his hand on his knife, which he could draw in an instant, but his guide did not seem inclined to attack. He spat on the rocks. "Bloody mucky city," he growled in broad Glaswegian. "Stinks like a cesspit."

"This river *is* a cesspit, lad," Alec said. "All the shit gets dumped here. Before you start singing how beautiful and better smelling is our homeland, out with it, man. What do you have to tell me?"

The man spat again. "Heard of men being held," he said. "Not tried, not killed, just held on to. Don't know why."

Alec drew a sharp breath then regretted it as the stench of rotten eggs filled his nostrils. He let it out again, forcing himself to remain calm.

"Held where?" he asked tightly.

The man shrugged. "Might be with a regiment. Might be in a big house of some aristo. Or maybe of a nabob."

Nabobs, those interesting men who traveled to India or the islands of the Caribbean, made piles of money off the backs of slaves, and came home to live like aristocrats but without the title and ancestry. Alec's father had much to say about nabobs, most of it obscene.

A big house—like the estate of a duke? "Whose house?" Alec pressed.

"Dunno."

The man fell silent. Alec waited, but that seemed to be the extent of his knowledge.

Well, it was more than he'd had before. A house, with men held in it. Might be Scotsmen, Frenchmen, or men from the lands of China, for all Alec knew, and these men might simply work there.

But it was something, a tendril to grasp.

The Glaswegian watched Alec, beginning to glower. He'd delivered the goods—now he expected to be paid.

His information was likely worth nothing, but if Alec didn't pay for it, word would get around, and Will's contacts might be less than eager to seek him out.

Alec slid his hand into his coat pocket to find the one coin he'd brought for the purpose. He'd carried money for the ale and for this, not foolish enough to walk about with all his cash in backstreet London.

The moment Alec's hand came out of his pocket, he heard a crunch of boot on gravel, the only thing that saved him.

He ducked out of the way as a cosh came down, the breeze of it brushing his face. Alec dropped the coin and grabbed his dirk, coming around with it up and slashing.

He heard a grunt and a curse, felt his knife bite. The darkness was nearly complete by the river, but the fog glowed faintly with moonlight, letting Alec see the glint of a blade, the swing of another cosh. He counted three men attacking them with deadly intent.

Alec's companion grunted and went down. At the same time, Alec took a punch to his middle, which doubled him over, sending him down on one knee. He dodged as a long knife came at him, and rolled to his feet, striking with his own knife.

More grunts, curses, rancid breath as a man got under Alec's reach, and Alec found knuckles in his face. His head snapped back, but he jabbed at the same time, rewarded with foul words in a broad London accent.

The man Alec had come to meet lay on the shingle and didn't move. Dead? Injured? Unconscious?

The three men were now trying to put Alec into one of these states. He called up all the cunning he'd learned fighting in the streets of Edinburgh and Paris and then again in battle. Strength alone wouldn't help him here, but the wily tricks Will and Mal had taught him would serve.

He elbowed, jabbed, brought his fingers straight at eyes that glittered in the darkness. The men hid their cries of pain in grunts and curses—they must be used to attacking hapless victims in darkness and silence.

Alec ducked away from another blow and came up on his feet, his knife held ready. His back was to the river. The three men advanced with more confidence—Alec had nowhere to go.

To hell with being silent. Alec dragged in a breath and let out a Highland scream, one that had stricken terror into the British at Prestonpans, scattering King George's men like leaves in the wind. He rushed at them, yelling like a demon, his knife raised to deliver killing blows.

The three men hesitated. They were backstreet thugs, going after easy marks—a soldier rushing at them with a murderous battle cry was beyond their ken.

Alec reached the first man and struck. His knife went through the man's coat, cutting to the bone, then he was moving to the second.

Who wasn't there. He and the third man had turned and fled down the shingle to deeper darkness, leaving their unlucky companion to Alec.

Alec took a step back and let his smile spread wide as he lifted his knife. "Shall we dance, laddie?"

The man had his hand on his arm, blood black on dirty fingers. His eyes were so wide, the whites glittered as pale smudges. He turned to flee and gibbered as he slipped on the gravel and went down on his knees.

Alec took two running steps at him. The man managed to gain his feet, and he loped off, limping, holding his arm. Alec stamped on the rocks beneath him, making the sound of giving chase and let himself laugh as the man's struggling gait moved a little faster.

"Bastards," Alec muttered, his laughter dying. "You all right, man?"

He crouched next to his drinking companion, finding him too still. Alarmed, Alec rolled him to his back, his alarm turning to dread when the man's eyes stared motionlessly at the sky. Alec opened the man's coat, pressed his hand over his heart, which wasn't beating.

"Bloody gobshites. Damn it."

Alec balled his fist, sorrow and anger roiling through him. He didn't even know the man's name—the meeting had been set up by a smuggler called Gair, whom the Mackenzie brothers sometimes hired.

If Alec left the poor man here, he'd be stripped of everything by morning, his body left in the river. But if he went for help, he risked exposure. The London watchmen being what they were, they'd more likely arrest Alec for the murder than show any sympathy. And if Alec was arrested ...

Well, he'd be a dead man. No more, no less. And he might bring death on the rest of his family.

But leaving a fellow human being to be picked over by vultures didn't sit well with him. This man might have a wife and children waiting for him at home.

Alec leaned down, slung the man over his shoulder, and trudged with him back to the streets.

He left the unfortunate Glaswegian on the doorstep of a church—they'd know how to care for him and find his family. At least the man could rest the night and release his soul on hallowed ground.

AT EIGHT O'CLOCK THE NEXT MORNING, NOT ONE MINUTE LATER, Celia swept into Lady Flora's house. She'd barely slept the previous night and had risen before her mother this morning, which had never happened in all the years of Celia's life. Her mother had pressed a cool hand to Celia's forehead and asked if she were well.

"Yes, yes," Celia had said impatiently. "Lady Flora scolds if I'm late, is all."

"That she does." The duchess removed her hand, no caresses. "Don't mind her, dear. She's had a bereavement."

Yes, they all tiptoed around Lady Flora, Celia reflected as the door closed behind her in Lady Flora's echoing house. Not only because she was grieving for her daughter, Sophia, who'd been a lovely and charming young woman, but because Flora was what Celia's father called a *femme terrible*—beautiful and frightening.

Celia immediately surrendered her portfolio to the footman and followed Rivers, who appeared at the head of the staircase to lead her up. Celia breathed hard as she reached the last landing, her stiff stomacher squeezing the air out of her.

Rivers, stately and not in the least winded, opened the door to the studio.

"Lady Celia Fotheringhay," he announced as Celia pattered past him into the room. The footman came behind with the portfolio, placed it noiselessly on the table, and withdrew.

Mr. Finn was at the fireplace, his back to her, his hands stuck to the flames. The day was predicted to be warm, summer at last making its way to London, but a fire was always welcome to chase away the damp.

Rivers cleared his throat, but Mr. Finn did not turn, as though he could not absorb enough of the fire's heat.

Celia nodded at Rivers, putting not only thanks and dismissal into the nod but the assurance that she would be well. Rivers made a cool bow before he departed, leaving the door open.

Mr. Finn continued to study the flames. His back in its plain coat conferred strength in its simple lines.

Celia could sketch him from behind, the square of his shoulders, the straight strength of the back that tapered to his waist. His coat, a faded brown wool with the patch Celia had noted yesterday, bore a pleated peplum to make the bottom of the coat fuller, as was fashion. The coat's skirt touched thighs covered with slim broadcloth breeches. The brown of these was a different color from the coat, which meant he'd bought the pieces separately, likely from a secondhand shop, cobbling together a suit.

White stockings hugged muscular calves that immediately marred the portrait of a half-starved man having to work for his keep. Celia had seen the spindleshanks of poor men, whose stockings sagged in deep folds.

In fact, Mr. Finn was robust and in raging good health compared to the gentlemen she and her mother carried charity baskets to at the hospitals and parish poor houses.

He still did not turn, though he knew good and well Celia stood behind him. Celia opened and closed her hands, not sure if she was offended or relieved he didn't acknowledge her. She hadn't made up her mind how to speak to him, what to say. The memory of him sitting so near, baring so much skin, made perspiration bead on her brow, the room suddenly close.

On the other hand, he was being appallingly rude. Celia's father, one of the loftiest men in England, would never stand with his back to a lady. The duke would turn, smile, say something congenial—he did this even for the lowest servant, who was supposed to be beneath his notice.

Celia decided she'd try her father's approach, a kind inquiry. There was a reason her father had so many friends.

She cleared her throat, a much softer version of Rivers's noise. "Mr. Finn?" she walked to him, making her brocade skirts rustle. "Are you well, sir?"

Mr. Finn came to life. He straightened from the fire and swung to her, his smile blazing like the flames on the hearth.

Celia's mouth popped open, damn the flies. Mr. Finn's face was an unholy mess. A large, purpling bruise ran from his temple to his cheekbone, blackening the area under his left eye. Deep cuts sliced his right cheek, the corner of his lip, and his chin.

As Celia stared, Mr. Finn's smile widened.

"Well now, lass, that depends on what you could call *well.*"

CHAPTER 5

*G*ood heavens, Mr. Finn—what on earth happened to you?"

Alec looked into Lady Celia's stunned face and eyes that held deep concern. He'd half hoped she'd grow angry with him when he didn't respond to her presence and stalk away, but he realized that Celia Fotheringhay had more resolve in her than Lady Flora guessed. Studying the fire had given him time to come up with a story.

"Aye, well, an Irishman isn't always welcome in an English tavern, is he?"

Celia's eyes narrowed, and Alec saw with a jolt that Lady Flora had underestimated her perceptiveness as well.

"Hadn't you better give up on the Irishman idea, Mr. Finn?" she said. "We both know you are a Scotsman. It is all right— there are plenty of Scots in London. I know not all fought for the Young Pretender or even condoned his presence. My father has Scotsmen advising him, good and wise men. I will not be frightened in the presence of one."

He made himself look surprised and then grateful. Alec

Mackenzie had indeed fought for Bloody Prince Charlie, if reluctantly, had watched men die for him, including Angus and Duncan, his flesh and blood.

Alec tried to stem his bitterness as he answered, keeping to his persona as Will had taught him. If a man was to live a lie, he had to believe it with all his heart.

"'Tis a relief, I will admit, to have you know the truth," he said. "Please understand, lass, that I'm never sure how an Englishman—or Englishwoman—will respond to me. As happened in the tavern last night."

Celia flushed. "I apologize for my fellow Englishmen. But you must know how very frightened we all were. The army of Highlanders nearly reached London, and we feared we'd be massacred in our beds."

"Ye needn't have worried, lass. It would have taken some doing to massacre *every* person in London. Prince Teàrlach's force wasn't quite that large, so I'm told."

"Perhaps not." Celia gave him a conceding nod. "But men like my father had much to fear. My brother, Edward, fought in many of the battles. His descriptions of Highland soldiers were quite terrifying, and my father ... well, he was afraid he'd be seized and run through, the poor man. He was ready to have us on a ship to the Continent, though my mother pointed out that the French were about to sail against us, and this was no solution. Did you fight on the King's side, Mr. Finn?"

"No," Alec said sharply, then mitigated his tone. "I'm a drawing master, my lady, not a soldier."

"I see." Her eyes held compassion, so much so that Alec burned with it. "Not all Scotsmen fought, I understand, though you feel the consequences of the Uprising. I take it the men you tried to explain this to last night did not listen?"

"They did not." Alec tried a grin, which pulled at the cuts on his face. "And they reasoned they could relieve me of my few pennies at the same time."

"Oh dear." Celia studied him with flattering attention. "Have you put a poultice on those cuts?"

"I'll be well. Now, then, I believe we have a drawing lesson—"

"Wounds can take sick if not properly attended," Celia persisted. "Lady Flora should have prepared calendula for your cuts, and a poultice of hyssop or rosemary for the bruises. Or, rather, she'd have had her cook or housekeeper prepare it. I cannot imagine Lady Flora herself in the stillroom."

Celia's light laughter at her statement trickled into the empty spaces in the man that was Alec Mackenzie and tried to fill them up.

Alec pushed the need for that away with vehemence, at the same time part of him cried out for it.

He'd begun losing what made him whole when Genevieve, Jenny's mum, had died, and then he'd lost Angus, his other self. He and Angus hadn't been the closest of brothers—Alec and Mal had been best mates while Angus had stuck to taking care of their irascible father—but Angus had been Alec's twin.

Alec and Mal had derided Angus for being their father's toady, but the day Angus died, a light had gone out of Alec's life. He hadn't recovered from the blow of his loss and probably never would. Even Duncan's death, as terrible as it had been, hadn't leveled Alec like losing Angus.

He could not allow Celia to take him to a stillroom to nurse him—standing with her in the cool, stone-walled room, dried herbs scenting the air, Celia gently touching his skin would be too bloody enticing.

Alec shoved these thoughts down under the façade he desperately lifted in place. "I'll be well," he repeated firmly. "I heal quickly. Now then, let us draw."

He turned to the easel where he'd already pinned paper. Alec had bullied Lady Flora into lending him a dressing-table mirror from one of her guest rooms—she'd sighed and told Rivers to see to it.

The mirror was about a foot wide by two feet tall perched atop a small walnut drawer, polished and pristine. The drawer pulls were delicate polished brass rings and the drawer had a matching keyhole. The whole thing was meant to be set atop a chest of drawers or dressing table, so a lady could apply her powder or see the effect of her jewelry.

Alec positioned the mirror on the table next to the easel and motioned for Celia to sit on a stool before it.

Celia complied, her green-brown eyes on him. Studying his bruises? Wondering what to tell her father about a Scotsman pretending to be Irish?

Lady Flora was so certain she'd be able to wrap the Duke of Crenshaw around her elegant fingers, certain Celia was malleable and easily led, but Alec was quickly losing his faith in Lady Flora's convictions. No doubt Lady Flora had the *haut ton* of Britain terrified of her, but Celia was proving herself to be far from the mindless young debutante Lady Flora thought her.

Celia perched on the stool and settled her skirts. "Why was Lady Flora so angry at my drawing yesterday?"

Alec hid his start by straightening the mirror. He'd wondered if she'd ask about that. Lady Flora had spoken too openly, underestimating Celia's percipience. "Perhaps she's a wee bit jealous of you, my lady," he extemporized. "Of your talent."

Celia let out another laugh that sounded like music.

Lass, don't soften me. I must be hard as granite.

"Lady Flora, jealous of *me*?" Celia said. "How absurd. It isn't talent—it's a knack. I can catch faces and, as you say, landscapes. The idea that I will draw portraits of famous Whigs was Lady

Flora's, and my mother leapt at the scheme. I must redeem myself somehow, you see."

Alec felt a bite of puzzlement. Celia on her stool was like a flower with her blue and green brocade skirts spread around her like petals. Lace decorated her cuffs and fichu that crossed over her stomacher, but the lace lay quietly instead of standing up in the froths Lady Flora wore. Sixty women in Brussels must slave every day for a month to make enough lace for one of Lady Flora's ensembles.

"Now what can a lass like you have to redeem herself about?" he asked in true curiosity.

"Quite a lot, I assure you," Celia said. "At least, according to my mother. Refusing to run off with a rake is apparently more shocking than remaining chastely at home."

She closed her mouth with a snap, as though she'd said more than she meant to.

There was far more to *that* story, and Alec wanted to know it. "What rake?" The anger that had simmered in him since Angus's senseless death boiled up, the mad Highlander delighted he might have someone to take out his rage on.

Celia snatched up a pencil. "He is not important. Shall I attempt your hand again? As your face is not fit to be seen today. Although ..." Her eyes fixed on him, her focus unnerving, as though she'd decided learning to draw bruises and cuts might be a good thing.

Alec's heart burned at her scrutiny. She was seeing *him* as she had yesterday, below the skin, as her drawing of him had revealed. Celia had caught the true Alec Mackenzie, the man he couldn't contain under drab clothes and pretense, the one he must hide at all costs.

He abruptly turned the mirror until it reflected Celia, her face flushed, her pencil poised. "My face isn't fit to be seen as you say," he said, "so you will draw your own."

Celia stared at her reflection as though she'd never seen it before. "Me?" She blinked, and the reflection blinked back at her. "I doubt my mother sent me to a renowned drawing master to return home with pictures of myself."

Alec minutely adjusted the mirror. "Why? Your mum might quite like a picture of her daughter."

"Her Grace."

"Hmm? What's that, lass?"

"My mother," Celia answered. "She is *Her Grace*. Never Mum. Or Mama. Or even Mother."

Alec stared. "Good Lord, she expects her own daughter to call her *Your Grace?*"

"I avoid the problem by rarely addressing her directly." Celia moved her gaze from herself and rested it on Alec. "What do you call *your* mother?"

"I called her Mum." Alec's mother had been a duchess, as his father was the ninth Duke of Kilmorgan. But it had been a *title* to his mother, not what she *was*. The merry, laughing Allison McNab would never have insisted her sons call her *Your Grace*. Sadness touched him. "She's gone now, poor woman."

"Oh. I'm sorry." Celia did sound sorry—she wasn't mouthing a polite condolence.

"Long ago it was. Me dad, he never truly lived again. He didn't pine away—oh no, that's not his way." Bluster and rage was more the duke's way of grieving. "But he lost himself that day." The one thing saved from the fire at Kilmorgan had been the portrait of Allison, Duchess of Kilmorgan, mother to six unruly sons, only three of which were left. Alec was determined not to make it only two.

"I apologize, Mr. Finn. I did not mean to bring up a painful memory."

Alec blinked, realizing he'd sunk into his real self, leaving

Mr. Finn far behind. Celia had a way of making him forget about everything but the truth.

How did Will do it? Be a different person continuously without slipping back into his own personality?

Alec cleared his throat. "Dinnae worry yourself. She was a happy woman. Now, are we to have this drawing lesson or no?"

"I beg your pardon." Celia flushed and flicked her gaze back to the mirror. "I do not much understand the use in drawing *me*."

"All artists do self-portraits," Alec said. "The great Rembrandt did dozens of them—sketches, studies, paintings of himself in different costumes, making different faces. Daft people say it was vanity, but I think the man was trying to learn to draw many different expressions and was too dirt poor to pay a model."

"I am not the great Rembrandt," Celia pointed out. "I am an Englishman's daughter with rudimentary skill."

"Ye let me be the judge of your skill, lass. *I'm* the master here. Now." He pointed at the blank paper. "Draw."

Celia touched her pencil to the page. Her first stroke was shaky, but Alec watched her grow intrigued as she went along, her determination to get the lines right, the proportions correct. He noticed when she ceased seeing her reflection as *herself* and regarded it as a living being to be rendered on the paper. Her eyes fixed as she concentrated, the tip of her tongue coming out to touch the corner of her lip.

A lovely young woman. Alec was partial to them. He'd have to watch himself.

"Now then. Tell me about this rake ye refused to run away with."

The pencil jerked. Celia hastily lifted it so she wouldn't mar the page, and then she returned to the drawing, becoming absorbed once more in the task.

"The Marquess of Harrenton," she said as she sketched. "He has several immense estates of thousands of acres each, with fine manor houses all over England. He is Whig to the core, a staunch supporter of my father, and an odious man who smells of fish oil. The sordid story, which I am certain you will hear from anyone with a penchant for gossip, is that I was found in a compromising position with him. All would have been well if I had married him, but I refused his gracious offer. Therefore, I am disgraced and ruined, not to mention ungrateful and spoiled." She added a line that defined a curl drooping to her forehead, the stroke swift with indignation.

Alec's anger rose. Compromising position? What did that mean? Had this marquess touched Celia, pinned her against him while he groped her? More still?

Rage climbed as the image came to him, and he overlapped it with one of himself seizing the marquess and slamming his head into the floor. That anyone would dare touch this gentle, pretty young woman made redness dance before his eyes.

He forced himself not to move, but when he answered, his voice was hard. "I'm glad you refused. No lady should be married off against her will to an odious man who smells of fish oil." Who would be dead soon, if Alec had anything to say about it.

Celia glanced at him in surprise. "Well, you are the only one who believes so. Even my brother told me I was ungrateful. I could have been mistress of properties greater than those of my father, a hostess without equal, he said. Though my father's sister left me a small legacy in trust, so I am not penniless, it is nothing to what settlements the marquess could have made. Lord Harrenton is thirty years my senior, my brother reminded me, and so I might not have had to put up with him long. I ought to have gritted my teeth and borne him."

"No' much of a marriage," Alec said his anger remaining

high. Bloody cold English and their bloody cold ideas for matchmaking. "A business arrangement, that is."

"Is it so different in Scotland? Are ladies allowed to choose their own mates?"

Alec had to shake his head. "Not so different. Fathers marry off daughters to strengthen ties to families or to rub rival families' noses in it. My mum defied her family and took up with m' father—she was to have been married into a different clan. In the old days the lasses had no choice. These days ... well, I'm not much in Scotland these days, so I don't know, and I have no sisters. Just as well. I doubt my father would have allowed the poor things to marry anyone."

"Did *you* marry by choice?" Celia asked. "Or was it arranged?"

The image of Genevieve, bright like a shooting star and burning out as quickly, flashed into Alec's head. Her laughter, her white-hot tempers, her vividness—he'd known her so very briefly that some of the memories were slippery, elusive.

"She was a French dancer, and we married on a whim. Ye should have heard my father roar. I left it to my poor younger brother to break the news. The only thing that calmed him was wee Jenny. Now he's a proud grandfather."

Alec forced his tongue to still. His father, as far as Englishmen knew, was dead, on a list of those fallen at Culloden. So were Alec Mackenzie, Will, Malcolm, and Duncan. Dead and gone. Dust.

"She certainly is a lovely child."

Alec snapped out of his thoughts to find Celia's eyes on him again. She smiled, her face softening from her shy wariness.

"Aye, well," Alec tried to sound modest while his heart swelled with pride. Jenny was a bonny lass, there was no denying it. "She's sweet-tempered, that's a fine thing. Though not when the teeth are poking through her gums and making her howl in pain. Strong voice she has." Alec gave up on modesty and ended with a boast.

"You look after her well," Celia said. "For the teething, try chamomile. You steep it in water then mix it with ice—I know Lady Flora has a steady supply of ice, even in the heat of summer. Let Jenny suck on the concoction. It should soothe her."

"You know much of physic?" Alec asked, studying her. "Ye don't look like a midwife. Or the doctors who swan about London in their sedan chairs handing out diagnoses like badges of honor."

Celia shook her head. "Only what my nanny taught me. Every lady has some knowledge of the stillroom, and every estate has one. Who knows how far away the nearest doctor or surgeon might be?"

"Indeed." There had been a stillroom at Kilmorgan Castle, where their cook had prepared vile-tasting remedies to feed the brothers when they'd been sick. Gone now, with the rest of the bloody place.

The stark image of destroyed Kilmorgan recalled Alec to what he was about. He was here to pump this young woman for any information—any inkling of knowledge—of Will. He had no business making a friend of her, no business getting ready to defend her honor against this bloody, vile marquess, whoever he was. Though Alec would not drop the matter. He'd settle it in his own way.

"Now then, young lass, get to drawing," he said briskly. "If we're to make a portrait artist out of ye, it's time to learn." He gestured at the page. "You've caught your likeness well, but there's not enough of *you* in there."

Celia gazed at the paper in perplexity. "What on earth do you mean? I am right there." She tapped the paper with the end of the pencil.

The drawing was good—a young lady frowned in rapt concentration, one curl dangling from under her cap, her lips slightly parted. But whereas yesterday Celia had caught the fire hiding inside Alec Mackenzie, this sketch showed him a woman who could be anyone. The spark that made her Celia Fotheringhay was missing.

"Let me," Alec said.

Before Celia could protest, he dragged her aside, stool and all, scraped another stool to the easel to plant his arse on, and began to add lines to her drawing.

Alec drew in the way light caught on the wayward curl, the slight flush of her cheeks that reddened under his scrutiny, the faint shine of her kissable lips.

The ornate clock on the mantelpiece ticked through moments of silence, the scratch of the pencil the only other sound.

The artistic fire took Alec unawares. He felt it flash through his fingers, pulling the spirit of Celia into them and then out to the paper.

He'd heard that people in some Oriental countries didn't like having their portraits done, fearing the picture would capture and imprison their souls. Alec had thought such a thing interesting but ridiculous at the time, but in this moment, he understood.

He was capturing Celia, as she'd captured him yesterday. She came alive under his pencil strokes—the curve of her neck, the way one corner of her mouth was upturned, giving her an impish look. The shape of her eyes, which weren't identical, the glow in them like a flame shuttered. She had fires inside, one a man might find when he loosened her fichu, eased open the lacings of her stomacher, slid his hand beneath her chemise to seek the heat of bare woman inside.

If seduction were necessary to sway Celia, to be his conduit into her father's mind, Alec wouldn't find it a drudgery. He imagined her in his bed, her body welcoming him, the heat of her lips beneath his, and then the anguished look in her eyes when she realized his duplicity.

Alec made his hand cease moving. She'd already been ruined by one man—could he let it be two?

When he disappeared from her life after that, Celia would go on as she was meant to, painting portraits of her father's dull cronies, withering away in the glittering world of London society. She'd hate the name Alec Mackenzie—or at least Ansel Finn —but Will would be alive and well. Alec could return with Jenny to France and his family.

Celia leaned forward, eager to see what he'd done. Alec studied the drawing with her, watched her reach to touch a line, turn to ask him a question.

Alec didn't want to hurt her. He wanted to befriend Celia, become acquainted with her in all ways, discover what would happen between them.

But she was a duke's daughter, an innocent, and he was a fugitive. That was life as a Scotsman in King Geordie's world. Alec was not welcome in that world, and the sooner he left it, the better.

"TELL ME WHAT HAPPENED TO HER," ALEC DEMANDED OF LADY Flora.

He'd accepted his hostess' invitation to take port while she attended to her toilette later that afternoon. Alec lounged in a silk brocade chair and tried to find comfort against its rigid back.

Lady Flora's dressing chamber was usually filled with friends or the young men she strung on as hopeful lovers—

which always came to nothing, to their disappointment. Her toilettes and salons were famous for discussions of everything from the latest tax on corn to the abolishment of the slave trade to what Chinese ladies wore at their lavish court. Add to this poets, musicians, and artists, and Lady Flora had a mix of company that was shocking, forward thinking, gossip mongering, scandalous, and the envy of all other hostesses.

Lady Flora had already been laced into her stays by her maid, and now she reposed in a robe—a simple name for a vibrant gold and green silk gown that closed in the front and whose voluminous skirts flowed over her legs. At the moment, she had the skirts rucked high as she tied a garter around her right stocking. Her slender leg was encased in light blue cotton, clocked with green embroidery.

"To Celia?" Lady Flora asked as she finished with the garter and tossed her skirt over her legs again. "Why?"

"Because I'd like to know." Alec stretched out in the uncomfortable chair and took a sip of the very fine port, wishing it was Mackenzie malt instead. "Who is this marquess she doesn't want to marry? Was she caught in bed with him? And why was she there, if she finds him odious? Did he rape her? If so, point me in his direction, and I'll hunt up a *sgian dubh* and cut off his balls."

Lady Flora's eyes widened, then she scowled. "Good Lord, you will do nothing of the sort. Celia wasn't found anywhere near his bed. With his hands all over her, yes, but that was a contrivance of her mother's."

CHAPTER 6

*A*lec sat up straight while Lady Flora leaned forward to raise an earring to her earlobe.

"Her own mother set the man on her?" Alec snarled.

Fury gripped him so hard he didn't realize he'd spoken the sentence in Erse, until Lady Flora's cool words cut through his rage.

"I have no idea what you are saying, Alec. And pray, remember that your language is outlawed here. It would hardly do for *me* to be arrested for harboring you."

"Bloody hell, woman," Alec roared in English, coming to his feet. "How can ye sit and tell me something like that without turning a hair? Have ye ice in your veins?"

Lady Flora's look was hard. "I do not, as well you know. I suppose I have become so acquainted with the story it no longer shocks me as it should. Besides, I am not at all amazed Celia's mother concocted the plot. The duchess is a reptile of the coldest nature."

Alec thought of the pencil drawings he'd seen in Celia's portfolio. The unfinished one of her mother had shown a haughty woman, comfortable in her power, while the sketch of the duke made him look like a friendly country squire. Not at all what Alec had expected of either of them. It was no wonder Celia had chosen to draw so many pictures of her cat.

"Tell me the tale," Alec commanded. He made himself sit down again, and he drank deeply of the port.

"It is brief and sordid." Lady Flora leaned to the mirror to slip a second earring into her doubly pierced lobe. "The marquess is wealthy and powerful. A match with Celia would seal an alliance to make the Whigs even more unstoppable than they have become. Nothing in the world is more important to the duchess. Celia, not being a fool, refused to consider the marriage. I do not blame her—Archibald Mortenson, Marquess of Harrenton, has never been prepossessing. He was rather awful in his younger years, never mind now that he's fifty."

"They tried to force the match?" Alec asked, hand tightening on his goblet.

Lady Flora shook her head and slid two earrings, one a diamond stud, the second a dangle of gold, into her other ear. "In England, a young woman can no longer be married off against her will. She can be browbeaten into it, however, and if her parents threaten to toss her out of the house if she doesn't obey, then the choice is a moot point. The duke and duchess presented this match to Celia as though giving her the earth on a platter. When Celia refused, the battle began. Celia can be incredibly stubborn, but so can her mother."

"What about the duke in all this?" Alec asked. "All for trundling his daughter up the aisle in a wheelbarrow if necessary?"

Lady Flora arranged a white-blond lock to droop picturesquely down her neck. "Celia's father, surprisingly, took her side. *We can't force the gel to act against her heart,* were his words. But the duchess was livid. She threatened to lock Celia in her room for weeks, forbade her to go on outings, even with her mother at her side. In short, she tried to keep Celia prisoner until she obeyed. But Celia, in her quiet way, defied her."

She studied her reflection, not with vanity but critically, frowning as she rearranged the lock. "The duchess pretended to relent, but then she and Harrenton hatched a plan. One morning the duchess sent Celia in her dressing gown into a chamber on a pretense that the duchess needed something from within. Of course, the marquess was waiting inside. He seizes Celia and jerks her against him, starting to kiss her. At the appropriate moment, the duchess throws open the doors to let the guests she'd invited witness the tableaux. She'd chosen these guests carefully, from close friends to famous gossips to those known to be opposed to the duke's politics—so she'd have a balance of witnesses. Of course, the duchess expected Celia to break down and beg for a quick wedding to save her reputation. But still Celia refused."

"Good for her," Alec said, pleased he could speak calmly. Harrenton would pay for touching Celia—the man had sealed his own fate.

Lady Flora plucked a hothouse rose, deep pink and overly large, from a vase on the dressing table. She broke the stem at the base of the blossom and pinned it to the top of her bodice.

"The duchess was incandescent with rage. She did lock Celia into her bedroom, but their servants, while terrified of the duchess, dote on Celia. They brought her tidbits from the kitchen, kept her apprised of the goings-on in the house, and smuggled out letters for her. She wrote to an older gentleman, a clergyman friend of her father's who'd been kind to her, told him the entire situation, and asked for advice.

"The clergyman was appalled, visited the duke, and Celia was released. In disgrace, and she is ruined, but the duchess has at last let the marriage matter drop. Celia has a small bit of money her aunt left her, which I am certain bolstered her refusal. But Celia is now to stay indoors and learn to be useful, seeing no one but the immediate family or me. Hence my idea she should paint portraits of her father's cronies, and ..." She waved a languid hand at Alec.

Alec's fury burned in slow fire. "What did the duke say when his friend came calling to ask about the treatment of his daughter?"

"Ah, I forgot the best bit." Lady Flora smiled a cold smile. "The elderly clergyman is a staunch Tory. He and the duke became friends of a sort over their anti-slavery sentiments. In any case, the duke, who hadn't realized the extent of his wife's duplicity—or so he claims—said Celia fought her battle well, and that she'd have made a wily politician."

Alec took another deep draught of port. He thought of the brisk way Celia had said on her first day of lessons, *Apparently, embarrassing my mother is the most grievous sin of all.* She'd spoken quickly, her head up, but Alec had sensed the pain inside her, a humiliation he hadn't understood.

"I'm surprised they didn't send her off to a nunnery," Alec growled. "Pretend they never had a daughter."

Lady Flora's brows rose. "Not the staunchly C of E Duchess of Crenshaw. Popery is a greater taint than debauchery, did you not know? Are you Catholic, Lord Alec?"

Alec shook his head. "My grandfather was Calvinist to his bones. 'Tis why my father is so surly. The rest of us fell out of the habit of churching after our childhood. We attend chapel for Christmas and Easter, and even that is kept quiet. Wouldn't want to catch us actually celebrating anything."

"Odd that you're welcome in France, then. The Huguenots had to flee there not long ago, I believe."

"As I said, we're not much for churching. And we're only visiting."

That was what they told each other, the Mackenzies. That they were in France until outrage at the Uprising faded, until laws became slackly enforced and they could go home again. One day.

"The duchess now prefers to keep Celia at home where she can ensure her good behavior," Lady Flora continued. She slid a diamond bracelet onto her wrist and expertly closed the clasp one-handed. "So she says. Looking for a chance to use her again is most likely."

"As a recluse doing portraits of prominent men," Alec finished. "*You* are using her as well."

Lady Flora turned a serene gaze to him. "As are you. The duke adores her and trusts her. Celia is the best way into her father's knowledge. You must get her to trust *you*. I suppose that was the point of the nonsense of having her draw you without your shirt. How did you convince her? She knows she won't be painting nudes."

"Doesn't matter. She needs to learn anatomy if she's to be any good as an artist. She'll have to understand how the body looks under the clothes, to make the fabric have the right weight and drape."

Lady Flora sent him a severe look. "I know of your reputation with the ladies, Alec. A heart so warm it would melt a breastplate—that is what Will said of you. I believe you once had to be rescued from a man and his five brothers when you decided to dally with his wife."

"And much is made of that tale," Alec said irritably. "His wife had already left him, and she scurried for freedom while I fought him. But I'm not here to make a conquest. I'm here to find my damned brother before it's too late."

"Indeed," Lady Flora said. "If you seduce Celia entirely, please keep it private and make her think it her own idea. I do not need her father bringing a lawsuit against me for not chaperoning her as I should."

"Trust me, any seduction will be very quiet and behind closed doors." Alec would make certain absolutely no one interrupted if he managed to take Celia to his bed. It would be beautiful with her, not sordid. "The woman doesn't need more troubles."

"If she has a child, she will have them," Lady Flora said warningly.

Alec scowled. "I know how to prevent wee ones from coming."

"A mercy you do." Lady Flora returned to her mirror, lifting a strand of diamonds to test against her hair. "Else women would line the roads, hoisting up Mackenzie babes in their arms."

"Exaggeration," Alec muttered.

"Not by much." Lady Flora dropped the diamonds into a tray, rejected. "While you pump Celia for information, I will also be prying it out of my acquaintances. I will host a salon tomorrow evening. You will be there, unobtrusively. You're a gentleman and an artist, eking out a living teaching. No worry any will recognize you—these ladies and gentlemen have never been anywhere near Scotland and couldn't possibly lift a weapon to join a battle. Soldiers and generals never attend my salons."

Alec knew Lady Flora would carefully choose the guests and he would have no reason to worry about arrest, especially if he kept his mouth shut. He'd be Mr. Finn, the talented Irish artist who'd been painting in France and was now down on his luck, helped by the charitable Lady Flora. She was known to give artists and writers she considered had merit a leg up.

Alec lifted his emptied glass. "Here's to it, then."

Lady Flora gave him a nod. Alec wasn't certain he liked the scheming glint he detected in her eyes, but he said not a word.

∼

CELIA PAUSED OUTSIDE THE DOOR TO HER FATHER'S STUDY, VOICES within changing her mind about opening the door. She had always been privileged to simply walk inside as she pleased, but when her father had guests, she politely did not interrupt.

She seated herself in an armless chair in the gallery, her portfolio on the long table next to her. At least here the portfolio did not slip, fall, or spill open—none of the embarrassing tricks it played when inside Lady Flora's pristine house. The landing was darker and colder than usual, and Celia shivered.

The rumbles of male voices came to her through the walnut paneled doors. The flickering light of candles showed under the crack beneath it—Celia's mother thought using too many candles a great waste of money, which was why the hall was quite dark—but the duke had his way on this one point, at least inside his private chambers. Her mother consoled herself that the duke wasn't often home.

"And you are certain they are safe?" the duke was asking.

Celia heard the answer of her father's friend, the Earl of Chesfield. "Of course. We have soldiers there, the best trained. Nothing will be lost."

Celia wondered what precious sort of treasure needed the protection of soldiers. Curious.

Her uncle, her mother's younger brother, the Honorable Perry Waterson, spoke next. "Not to worry, Charles. You leave such trifles to me and go bounce with Mrs. B."

"Really, Perry," the duke said in a shocked voice. "No need to be unseemly."

The Earl of Chesfield chortled. "I'm sure he meant it fondly.

Come along, Waterson, we'll adjourn and let Charles rejoice in the bosom of his family. Or at least *a* bosom."

Uncle Perry sniggered, and Celia went hot with embarrassment. Uncle Perry knew exactly what a mismatched marriage his sister had made, but she wished he wouldn't be quite so blatant that her father sought his comfort elsewhere.

Celia got quietly to her feet when she heard the men make for the study door. She ducked into the next room along, not wanting either of them to see her. She had to leave her portfolio, but the gallery was so dark she doubted they'd notice it in the shadows or have any interest if they did.

The Earl of Chesfield had a booming voice. He was tall, with a large, red face and big-boned body. His wig was always half askew, but for some reason it never looked comical. Perhaps because he was so loud and terrifying—that is, he'd terrified Celia when she'd been a little girl. These days, she found him rude and boorish.

"A very good night to you, sir," the earl thundered to Celia's father. "I suggest you take your brother-in-law's advice. Until tomorrow."

He marched out and made for the stairs. Uncle Perry followed him, but Celia knew he'd stop to visit her mother in her sitting room before departing the house.

When the voices and footsteps had died away, Celia left her hiding place and tapped on the study door.

"It's Celia, Papa."

She heard a sound of delight and then her father's pattering steps before he yanked open the door. "Ah, my dear, how wonderful to see you. Come in, come in. How was the drawing lesson? You must show me what you've done."

"Oh," Celia tried. "It's nothing very ..."

"Nonsense. Is that your portfolio? John—" The duke called to a passing footman. "Be a good chap and carry that in here."

John, in the red silk livery of the Duke of Crenshaw, his wig far more tidy and straight than the Earl of Chesfield's, materialized out of the shadows, snatched up Celia's portfolio, and carried it into the study. John deposited it on the large table in the center, bowed, and glided out.

"Now then." Celia's father, a short man running to fat but not too stout, moved to the portfolio and undid its clasp with quick fingers. He opened the leather case and caught sight of the drawing on top, that of Celia's face. "Oh, my."

Mr. Finn had taken Celia's rudimentary sketch and filled in lines and shadows until the drawing glowed with life. She'd done the same when she'd sketched him, catching the spark inside that made Mr. Finn *himself*. Whatever his true name was didn't matter—the essence of the man had shone in her drawing.

Was this how Mr. Finn saw her? Outwardly quiet but inwardly blazing with restlessness, a need to move, to know, to discover the world?

She did have those desires, Celia realized with a jolt. She'd told herself she'd be content to remain sequestered in her father's house, quietly reading or painting for the rest of her life. But now she realized the confinement of that existence, how she'd have to stifle her own needs all her days. She'd grow more solitary and bitter with each passing year—she'd already begun down that path.

Her thoughts spun until she was dizzy, as the duke gazed, enraptured, at the drawing. "A self-portrait. My dear, how enchanting."

Celia barely heard him. Why the devil had Mr. Finn done this to her—shown her what she could be, what she was losing? This morning, she hadn't mourned her existence, and then in a few swoops of the pencil, Mr. Finn had showed her devastating truth.

"Might I keep this?" Her father lifted the paper, turning it to the light, completely ignoring the stilted sketch of Mr. Finn's arm on the next page. "It is delightful. I shall frame it and hang it where I can look upon it every day."

Celia snapped back to herself. The floor rocked beneath her feet, and she dragged in a breath. Her father was being kind, affectionate as usual. At least Celia had that. Her father bothered with her, a refreshing oddity in a time when so many fathers were sublimely uninterested in their daughters.

"Yes, certainly," Celia said, her voice a croak.

"Thank you. I'll have Matthews take it to be framed. A most lovely gift, my dear."

He patted Celia's shoulder, the closest the duke ever came to making an overture of affection. She'd never seen him so much as touch her mother. Edward always jested that it was a miracle he and Celia had been conceived at all.

Celia patted her father's hand in return and daringly kissed his cheek. The duke jumped and then waved her away goodnaturedly.

"Tell me about your drawing master. This Mr. ... Finn, is it?"

Celia experienced another jolt. She thought of Mr. Finn as she'd left him today, the gleam of golden eyes as he'd swept his gaze over her, the corners of his mouth lifting as though holding back a smile.

He'd made light of his bruises, but she'd known he'd been in a fight for his life.

Did she dare reveal that Mr. Finn was a Highlander, here in London for who knew what purpose, using an assumed name?

She'd tried to ask him about his background today, and he'd answered evasively. But she must be right that he had nothing to do with the Uprising, if only because Lady Flora would never condone a traitor to the crown living under her roof. Not only was she a staunch loyalist, she'd thought the Scottish Prince

Charles a buffoon too young to have an opinion about anything, and the rebelling clansmen foolish and ungrateful knaves. Lady Flora would have found out every scrap of information about Mr. Finn before she let him set foot in the front door.

Mr. Finn had denied fighting for either side of the Uprising and supposedly had been living in France for some years, painting for a living. Then why had he inexplicably decided to travel to London and try his luck here?

None of it added up to anything reasonable.

Celia cleared her throat. "He is Irish, I believe."

"So Lady Flora has said. But I did not mean his nationality. I mean, is he a gentleman? Not a ruffian or a shopkeeper with talent?"

"Oh." Celia hadn't thought about him in those terms. Her father meant—is he one of *us*?

Not necessarily an aristocrat, but at least from an established, landed family who hired people to do anything laborious. Celia thought about how she'd come upon Mr. Finn yesterday morning, sleeping with Jenny in his arms, and the authority in his voice when he'd told Lady Flora that he'd dismissed the nursery maid for giving his daughter gin.

Command had rung in his words, and Lady Flora had responded apologetically, a thing unheard of.

"Yes," Celia managed. "I'd say he was a gentleman."

"I wondered if I might have a word with him—there's an Irish question in debate and I'd enjoy the opinion of a man from there. Straight from the horse's mouth, so to speak." The duke beamed at his own joke.

Celia did not want her father anywhere near Mr. Finn. The duke wasn't a fool—when he engaged Mr. Finn in conversation, he'd soon realize the man knew nothing about Ireland.

"He's spent many years in France," she said quickly. "It's

likely he knows nothing of what is happening in his own country at present."

The duke shrugged. "Possibly. I will have Lady Flora quiz him. She ought to have been an interrogator for the army, that lady. We'd have no more traitors or even any lost buttons if soldiers knew they'd have to face her for it. Eh?"

Celia agreed completely with her father's assessment of Lady Flora. She nodded, and the duke laughed.

"Don't tell your mother I said so. Now be off with you, my daughter. Have a good evening."

"And you, Papa."

Celia gave him another kiss, at which the embarrassed duke shooed her away, and took herself out and closed the door, not bothering with the portfolio. Celia did not trust herself to carry it, and one of the footmen would bring it upstairs later.

The paneled walls of the hall, the large framed painting of their estate in Kent at the end of it, and the high ceiling with its gilded cornice spilling golden vines down the walls, had changed since she'd walked into her father's study. She was trapped inside this cage, Mr. Finn had showed her, a prisoner of her world. Instead of the light and airy feel her mother had forced upon the house when she'd redecorated ten years ago, the atmosphere was heavy, the painting a reminder of the duke's power, and the cornice Celia had always found charming over-wrought.

Like her senses. *There is nothing wrong with me,* Celia chided herself as she made for the staircase to her bedchamber. *Mr. Finn only made the sketch of me better. It has nothing to do with my life.*

But Celia's fingers shook on the stair railing as she ascended, and she knew in her heart that her two drawing lessons with Mr. Finn had already changed everything.

~

CELIA DID NOT HAVE A LESSON THE NEXT MORNING, BECAUSE AT breakfast in the soaring dining room, her mother instructed that she wanted Celia to attend Lady Flora's salon with her that evening.

Celia froze in the act of lifting the pot of chocolate to pour into her cup. "What on earth for?"

The duchess eyed her with displeasure. "Really, Celia, you are in no position to be rude to me. Lady Flora has graciously allowed me to bring you. She has invited the right people for you to be introduced to as a portrait painter."

"But I've only had two lessons." Celia slopped chocolate into her cup and thumped the pot back to the table. She took a sip of the bitter, thick liquid, trying to let it soothe her.

"Do not be obdurate. No one will expect you to whisk out a palette and start in. You will be presented as an artist in training. It is good that you go and ease the stain of your disgrace. These ladies and gentlemen have done far more scandalous things in their lives than be found kissing a man they refused to marry. There will be no debutantes there for you to shock. You will attend."

And that, Celia knew, was that.

When she walked into the salon at nine that evening, wearing the most modest ensemble she owned, her dread fell away and her heart began to pound. In the far corner of the grand drawing room, in the shadows as though keeping to his relatively lowly position, was Mr. Finn.

CHAPTER 7

*A*lec felt the air change when Celia entered the drawing room. A lightness floated through the cloying perfume of the ladies and gentlemen, the scent of powder, the odor of bodies in silk and brocade.

Celia's gown was an olive green open-robe design over underskirts of mustard yellow. Her stomacher was unadorned, unlike Lady Flora's which fluttered with deep pink ribbons marching from abdomen to a very low décolletage. Lady Flora didn't quite let her nipples show at this gathering, but he'd seen her in ensembles that bared her entire bosom.

In contrast to the other ladies here, Celia looked like a nun. Her parents might be too Church of England to send her to a convent, but they treated her as though she were in one.

Celia's dark hair was hidden under a modest cap and she kept her eyes cast down, as befitting one in disgrace. Her mother, who wore a silver and blue gown as dazzling as Celia's was drab, walked next to her daughter like a jailor who couldn't afford to let her prisoner out of her sight.

Celia's head might be bowed, but she was not in any way

submissive. Alec saw the sparks in her eyes as she glanced about, watched them flare when she spied Alec in the corner.

Alec caught her gaze, and in that moment, everything stopped.

In the stretch of time between one heartbeat and the next, Alec saw all the way down inside Celia Fotheringhay—her stubbornness, her determination not to be broken. He saw as well her vulnerability, her awareness that she was trapped, caught in her mother's machinations as well as the hypocrisy of the world in which she existed.

The ladies and gentlemen in this room were not guiltless of sin—in fact, they boasted of their sins, yet at the same time condemned Celia for refusing to be shackled to a man she despised. The difference? They'd capitulated to loveless marriages to please society, while Celia had dared to defy the rules.

Alec's estimation of her rose. The part of him that was Alec the loving man warmed, and he wanted to raise his glass to her. Celia had courage and beauty, and he longed to unleash both.

Another heartbeat and Celia was turning away, shepherded by her mother to a corner. Celia sat on an armless chair, taking the glass of sherry her mother handed her, the duchess not even allowing Celia to be served directly by a footman.

The disgraced wallflower, made to sit amongst those who censured her, to be useful to the people who castigated her, bent her head and sipped her sherry.

Alec saw in her a beautiful woman with fire beneath her skin, the restlessness of a tethered being who yearned to fly. The artist in him wanted to strip away her confining clothes to reveal the beauty beneath, the passionate man in him wanting to touch that beauty, kiss it, taste it.

Little brother Malcolm, the Runt, was right about Alec—when he lost his heart he did it rapidly and completely.

But there was no question of losing his heart, Alec thought reluctantly. Perhaps protectiveness was what he felt about Celia, pity for a vulnerable young woman. Alec would have to find some armor and polish it up if he were going to be a valiant knight to the ladies, like a tarnished Sir Percival.

By the time Celia had been settled, the room had already forgotten her. The salon commenced, ladies and gentlemen discoursing on topics of the moment.

The company was graced today by Mrs. Reynolds, Lady Flora's companion. Mrs. Reynolds was a black-haired, blue-eyed vivacious beauty—some claimed she'd been a courtesan in her younger days. After she'd been widowed and left penniless, Lady Flora, her girlhood friend, had taken her in. Mrs. Reynolds set off her dark looks with a raspberry colored brocade robe à la Française over a shimmering gold silk underskirt, lace adorning her décolletage and three-quarter sleeves.

Mrs. Reynolds had been absent from the house for a few days. Where she'd been and what she'd been about, Alec didn't know, and Lady Flora hadn't told him. Lady Flora had many plots and schemes going at once—helping Alec was only one of them. Alec had learned very quickly not to ask Lady Flora too many questions.

Conversation was seemingly random, though Alec knew Lady Flora directed it with the ease of a master.

At the moment, they were discussing the Venetian painter, Giovanni Canaletto, now a resident of London and painting scenes of London vistas. Lady Flora owned one of his paintings of the Grand Canal in Venice, which hung prominently on the wall opposite her. She'd not seated herself under it, because those who should be looking at *her* might be tempted to admire the painting instead.

"He's come to London because his customers have ceased traveling to Vienna," one gentleman proclaimed. "Too much war on the Continent. Always bad for travel, war, not to mention business."

Alec studied the portly lord who sat steadily consuming food and drink. The man had earlier proclaimed he detested all travel but that between London and his estate in Essex. He'd been invited to the salon because he was a self-proclaimed wit—Alec had yet to hear him say anything witty—and because he sat in on trials of Jacobite prisoners.

"Yes, it's better in jolly old, peaceful England, is it not?" another gentleman said, his voice languid, but he gave the lord-ship a cold stare. "Where all war is in the past, and we never have to worry about our fields being overrun by armies while we sit on our bums eating ices."

"Exactly," the lordship answered.

"No armies overrunning your Essex estate anyway," another gentleman said. "Bloody Scots overran mine in Derbyshire. Picked it clean, stationed troops in my outbuildings. We still haven't cleared up the mess."

A few gentlemen nodded agreement. One of the ladies laughed, a shrill sound that stabbed at Alec's ears. "Gracious, how gloomy you all are. The Scots were easily routed and sent home. Besides, I didn't mind all those handsome men riding down upon us, skirts flying up to show all they had. Such a change from a stuffy Englishman."

"And what stuffy Englishmen are you disparaging, madam?" a younger man asked, turning in his seat to eye her. He wore silk stockings, blue satin breeches, and a long dark blue velvet coat sewn with jewels. His face was whitened with powder, and he wore no wig, his own hair powdered and pulled back into a tail held with a drooping black velvet ribbon. "Not those in this room, I *hope*."

"Oh, yes," the lady said, her eyes sparkling. "I know exactly who I mean."

Mrs. Reynolds broke in. "Forgive us, dear sir. We ladies grow too used to the tame and the civilized. The barbaric excites us. Give us time and we will return to enjoying the civilized."

"Barbaric is correct," the young dandy replied with a sniff. "Those Highlanders ran about in their tartan cloth full of lice, yelling like the devils they are, murdering all in their path. Only the prince was in any way civilized, something of a beauty I understand."

"A *youthful* beauty," Mrs. Reynolds replied. "I prefer a gentleman who has a little more experience of life."

That mollified the gentlemen in the room, most of whom were well thirty.

Alec dared meet Celia's gaze and found her with her fan held to her mouth. The light in her eyes told him she laughed behind it.

He wanted to send her a wide smile, but he kept it a twitch of lips. Her cheekbones flushed brighter.

The talk turned to Prince Charles Stuart—his dress, his manners, his strategies, his charisma. Alec remembered the man too—his pride and arrogance, his inexperience and extreme sense of self-importance that got thousands of good men, including Duncan and Angus, killed.

They discussed Charles's decision to retreat to Scotland. Because these were men and women of some worldliness, they didn't immediately assume the prince had been quaking in his shoes at the idea of stronger fighting if his followers tried to take London. The present company debated the question of why the Scots had turned back, speculating about the prince's own prudence, false reports that French assistance was no longer forthcoming, news that Cumberland's army was on the move.

Alec knew exactly why they'd turned back. Lord George Murray had realized the futility of trying to take the whole of

Britain at once, and had encouraged the retreat to secure Scotland first. If they'd continued, they'd have been cut off from the north and slaughtered to a man. Besides which, the troops, farmers all, had wanted to return to Scotland to secure their homes for the winter. In addition, by that time, enchantment with the young prince had started to wear thin.

Alec hadn't agreed with the adamant MacDonalds and Camerons, or even Mackenzies, who'd backed Charles, but Murray's understanding of Highlanders and what the King's Army could do had saved many a man—at least until Culloden.

None of the gentlemen in this room had ever been soldiers, none had fought either for or against Charles Stuart. None knew of the long marches in the cold, the weariness that seeped into the bones, the energy that had to be dredged up to fight, to live, to defeat those trying their best to kill you.

These men didn't know the brutal reality of looking into the face of a friend, gray and lifeless, or finding pieces of the man you'd drunk whisky with the night before scattered over the grass, the wonder that those pieces weren't you.

They didn't know the anguish of a brother dying in front of them, begging to be killed to spare him the indignity of being gutted by enemy bayonets. Never knew the grief in a father's eyes when he shot his firstborn son, the heir of his body, granting that wish.

Never caught their twin as he slid lifeless from a horse. Never watched a father come apart with loss, heard that father address Alec with his twin brother's name, as though hoping Alec would become him.

Alec found himself clenching his glass of whisky, Scots, which Lady Flora made certain was served to encourage talk of the Uprising. The goblet was heavy crystal, lead bringing out the blue depths of the glass. The facets pressed sharply into Alec's palm and fingers.

"Prestonpans was such a rout of British forces, no wonder there was a run on the Bank of England when he headed south," another man said. "But though they had the keenness, the Scots didn't have staying power when it came to it. Terrified Cope's soldiers though." The man chuckled. "I hear they ran so fast their shadows couldn't keep pace."

Amid the laughter, Alec tightened his hand still more. He'd left Scotland before Prestonpans was fought against General Cope, the man who'd been expected to quickly put down the rebellion. Alec had been heading to France, to find Jenny, Genevieve having died. His heart had been eaten with grief as well as fear for his daughter, and he hadn't given much thought to the Uprising.

Hadn't until he'd returned home in time to watch Angus ride away with Duncan, the last time he'd seen his twin alive.

The situation had been far more complicated than these people knew. The belief that all Highlanders raised claymores to return Charles's Catholic father to the throne to be defeated by English redcoats was too simple. Highlander had fought Highlander, some had closed themselves away from the fighting altogether but had still been punished for it.

Clans had been divided, as had families, including Alec's own.

They'd fought each other and King George's army, had died, and now were being stripped of their language, their plaids, their identity.

"They were brutal fighters," one man said in admiration. "Screaming gleefully as they cut their way through."

"Screamed when they died too," another man said. "So I've been told. Brave fellows, cut down where they stood on the battlefield, never running. Made for some amusing jests—What color tartan do dead Scots wear? Red. What is the sound of a

Highlander begging for mercy? *Do your worst, ye bloody … agh, gurgle, gack."*

And they laughed. Every gentleman and every lady but Celia and her mother laughed, the duchess grimacing as though she found the entire conversation distasteful. Celia's eyes over her fan had turned sad but watchful.

Alec saw Lady Flora dart a glance his way, but she was lost in the red mist that formed before Alec's eyes. Every Mackenzie male had berserker rage inside him, the bloodthirstiness of their ancestor Mackenzie, Old Dan, who had won the family a dukedom.

As laughter surged around him, Alec seemed to float above the room, and the powdered and bewigged ladies and gentlemen reeking of perfume, musty fabric, and unwashed bodies. He wanted to launch himself at them with his Highland war cry just to watch them piss themselves trying to get away from him.

His hand went to his boot without his permission, ready to draw his dirk before he charged.

A cool touch cut through his haze of madness. Alec couldn't turn his head to find the source of the touch—he only knew the mists cleared the slightest bit.

Awareness returned. He was sitting in a hard chair with carved legs, his hand at the top of his boot while he glared at the first man he wanted to gut.

A stomacher of brown and butternut brocade, a skirt flaring from the narrow waist, cut off his view, and breath scented with sherry touched him.

"Mr. Finn," Celia said in a low voice. "Would you be so kind as to show me Lady Flora's gallery?"

CHAPTER 8

*C*elia tensed as Mr. Finn dragged his gaze from Lord Bradford, whom he'd been eyeing like an eagle intent on striking his prey, and fixed on her.

His eyes burned gold, like said eagle's, his breath came fast, and his hand was clenched next to his boot so hard his knuckles were white. One strand of Mr. Finn's dark red hair fell to his cheek, touching his fading bruises, and his lip curled into a silent snarl.

At the moment, he looked like nothing more than one of the brutal Highlanders the gathering mocked.

Celia knew the men made light of the Uprising to hide their fear. Every one of them had scrambled to flee London late last year, when Charles Stuart had been within a hairsbreadth of marching on the city. They'd had ships ready to flee to the Netherlands, Austria, anywhere that would have them. The rumor that King George was preparing to dive into a barge on the Thames and race away had proved to be false, but plenty of the king's supporters had taken their money and made ready to run to the Continent. Now they sat in their comfortable chairs, downing port and sherry and pretending they'd cheerfully faced down the Highlanders by themselves.

Celia kept herself firmly in front of Mr. Finn and his rage. "Please," she whispered.

Mr. Finn rose from his chair, every limb stiff. He didn't so much get to his feet as lift himself, as though pulled by strings. He made no indication he'd heard Celia, did not answer, did not nod.

He turned, his body rigid, and walked to the door behind his chair, a gilded wooden portal that led to the gallery hung with paintings in Lady Flora's collection.

Mrs. Reynolds noticed them go. She shot Celia and Mr. Finn a speculative look. Lady Flora, on the other hand, pointedly ignored them.

Celia shut the door, as Mr. Finn moved down the gallery, his stride swift. Celia rushed to catch up with him, her brocade slippers pattering on the inlaid floor.

Mr. Finn walked past paintings by the artist Rembrandt he so admired, past masterful sculptures by Bernini and Donatello. At the end of the hall another paneled and gilded door led to a tiny withdrawing room, and Mr. Finn made for it.

Celia rustled inside several steps behind him. Mr. Finn stopped abruptly on the far side of the small room, as though suddenly realizing he could go no farther.

He swung around, and Celia froze.

Another lock of Mr. Finn's hair had fallen, this one to his shoulder. Celia seemed to see another man imposed over him, a soldier in kilt and coat, the plaid wrapped around his shoulders, a Scots tam on his head. This vision held a sword in one hand, pistol in the other, the light in his eyes intense and deadly.

Celia took a final stride inside the chamber and closed the door behind her.

"You're one of them, aren't you?" she asked softly. "I know I shouldn't ask you that—you could kill me where I stand. But I have weighed the consequences and decided that, on a whole, such a thing would be preferable to a lifetime in a back chamber at Hungerford Park, my father's estate in Kent. As proud as my father is of his house, every room has rising damp."

Mr. Finn blinked but he remained utterly still. "Ye should not be here, lass." His voice was low, harsh, with a note of fierceness.

"I know. But as I say, I have weighed the consequences ..."

"I mean in this house at all. With me." The last was a snarl.

Celia kept her gaze steady. "I prefer lessons with you, sir, to embroidering with my mother. Here I have at least an hour a day as a respite from the catalog of my shortcomings."

Mr. Finn briefly closed his eyes then turned to the window to stare out at the gloom. Unlike Celia's mother, Lady Flora insisted on lit candles in any room into which her guests might wander. The window panes reflected pinpoints of flame and Ansel Finn's broad-shouldered silhouette.

"This is beyond your ken, lass. Ye should be well out of it."

"Well out of what?" Celia took a courageous step forward. "What of drawing lessons is beyond my comprehension, or a danger? Whoever you are, you are an artist, Mr. Finn. What you did to the clumsy drawing of myself was masterful. You are teaching me, and I wish to learn."

Mr. Finn remained ramrod straight, staring into nothing. Celia moved another step, her heart hammering. "Were you in the battles?" she asked in a near whisper. "Lady Flora should not have let them speak about it, or make cruel jokes. It was unfeeling, horrible."

"Aye, I was in battles." The rumble was quiet, absorbed by the chamber's silk-covered walls. "I killed men. Are ye satisfied now?"

"Of course not. War is a terrible thing." Celia's last step

brought her beside him. Cool air touched her through the window, but Mr. Finn's solid body held warmth. "I saw your expression. You were ready to kill them. Another moment and you might have. You lost family, didn't you? And friends. Those Highlanders they derided were your kin."

Mr. Finn gazed down at her with eyes of flinty gold. "What do ye wish me to say, lass? Aye, I lost m' brothers, and my father is nearly mad with grief. I'm dead meself—the ghost is what ye see. The muster rolls list my name, and every one of my brothers and my dad as killed. If ye tell a soul, they'll hunt me down and make sure my death sticks this time. So run off and blurt out your tale. I'll be gone before those dandies can draw a breath in horror."

Celia's lips parted as she listened, the burning in her chest rising.

"I'd never," she said. "I wouldn't betray you, Mr. Finn. Or whatever your name is."

"Alec."

"Alec." Yes, that fit him. It felt better in her mouth—*Alec*—a name derived from Alexander the Great. Brief but full of meaning.

"Why *wouldn't* ye betray me?" Alec demanded, his eyes hard. "Your father is a powerful aristo who holds the whip over more dogs of the British government than any man alive. King Geordie himself doesn't command such respect. Your father says a word, and my bloody head is falling on the grass. Or my body hanged, drawn, and quartered. It's a traitor I am. Was forced to be. Run from me, lass."

"If you will cease with your terrifying speeches," Celia said, her throat dry, "you will note that I am going nowhere, blurting your tale to no one. You have hidden yourself well, and there is no reason not to remain hidden. But you will have to control your temper around Lady Flora's guests. They are misguided and were much afraid. Bonnie Prince Charlie very nearly did win."

Alec shook his head. "Teàrlach mhic Seamas was a bloody fool who caused the murder of many a fine man. While my neighbors are being executed for it, he wanders the west of Scotland in search of transport. He might be in France by now. If so, I hope my father finds him."

He snapped his mouth closed, his brows drawing down into a fearsome scowl. If Alec's father was half this forbidding, Charles Stuart might do well to fear him.

"If you will be guided by me," Celia said quietly. "Gather yourself. Return to the salon. Smile at them, laugh with them. They are fools, remember. It is the only way." Well Celia knew it. While she'd never been in any danger of being hanged as a traitor, she was permanently in the pillory for her crime of thwarting her mother's schemes.

His scowl deepened. "Why are ye not afraid of me? Now that ye know what I am? Why aren't ye running as fast as those shoes will carry ye?"

Celia could not say why she wasn't worried. She ought to be —he could kill her with his bare hands or the knife he must have in his boot. He'd killed Englishmen before, including men like her brother. Several of her brother's friends had died, in fact, at Falkirk and more at Culloden.

"I am not afraid, because I've observed you." Celia reached up and daringly touched his cheek, his warm hair brushing her hand. "I've seen you with Jenny. And you've been nothing but kind to me. Battle is battle, no matter who you fight for. My brother has killed men, and yet he can be so very gentle."

Fire flared in Alec's eyes. Perhaps the mention of her brother, a soldier in the Duke of Crenshaw's Brigade, had been a mistake.

Alec caught her hand, his fingers strong. She expected him

to shove her away, perhaps even strike her, but he jerked her close.

Celia landed against him, the buttons of his coat pressing through her thin fichu. His eyes held the predatory look of the lion she'd thought of him as on the first day, and they narrowed to slits as he studied her.

Celia was too surprised to try to push herself away. She also had no inclination—Alec's body was strong against hers, and he held the heat of fire. He smelled of wool and man, and the clean linen of his shirt beneath. This close to him, she could see the smattering of freckles across the bridge of his nose and cheekbones, the mark of a man of the north.

She observed all this in a heartbeat before Alec drew her closer still and kissed her.

∾

THE TOUCH OF CELIA'S LIPS SPUN ALEC OUT OF HIS FURY. THE thoughts of the enraged Highlander shattered and vanished.

She was like cool water on a searing day, soothing after a ride through hell. Alec needed her coolness, the peace of her.

Alec Mackenzie would never have peace, but being with Celia could give him a taste of it. Her lips were soft and sweet, fine to lick. Alec nibbled one, liking how she started, how her body moved against his. She tried to catch his kiss and return it, but she was clumsy, having no idea how.

The arrogant duchess might pretend her daughter was a wanton, but Celia was no whore. She was innocent, but interested, and Alec would be her instructor.

His blood went incandescent at the thought. He slid his hand under her hair in its modest knot, sleek, neat. Alec wanted to loosen her hair from its pins, pull it free, let it cascade over him.

He settled for pulling her closer, slanting his mouth over hers, encouraging her to part her lips.

When he dipped his tongue inside her mouth, she jumped again, another fine crash of body against his. Alec touched the corner of her mouth with his thumb, teaching her to open to him.

She caught on, if hesitantly. Alec flicked his tongue over hers, wanting to laugh when she gave the barest flick in return. He swept inside, pulling her up to him, hope rising when she relaxed, her body surrendering even if Celia herself didn't understand why.

Alec had been living like a monk since he'd left France, in spite of Lady Flora offering to send him to discreet ladies for satiation. He'd been too caught up with worry about Will to care about physical needs, and he could not trust himself to remember who he pretended to be in the heat of the moment.

But maybe he should have had a few dalliances, because he wouldn't now have a heavy cockstand while kissing the innocent daughter of an English duke.

Celia rested her hands on his shoulders and then slid them around his neck, holding him. Alec drank her in, tasting sweetness mixed with the sherry she'd sipped. She grew bolder, moving her mouth against his, opening more.

Alec coaxed her into him, showing her how to caress without devouring. Devouring would come later, when he took her to his bedroom, locked the door against all comers, and tumbled down to his bed with her. He'd look upon this beautiful woman and be eased.

Celia drew back and turned her head, her cheeks brilliant red. "Please," she whispered. "I can't breathe."

"Well, you're not to hold your breath, lass." Alec laughed softly as he smoothed the moisture from her mouth. "Kissing would never have caught on if we all dropped dead from it."

"I cannot ... I ..." She pressed her hand to her stomacher, her breasts rising under her fichu.

Alec tucked his arm around her and led her to a ridiculously small settee with a curved back and legs. There was barely enough room for both of them to sink down, Celia's brown and yellow skirts spreading over Alec's thighs. Alec cupped her cheek.

"Better?"

Celia's eyes were wet, candlelight shimmering on the green-brown of them. "I don't know."

"That's the trouble with kissing. Ye sometimes forget where ye are—*who* ye are. Because it no longer matters."

Celia's lips parted as though she contemplated this. "Yes, I see what you mean."

Alec forced down his laughter. She was a joy, and he hadn't found joy in such a long time. "Shall we try it again, love?"

He rested his arm across the back of the settee, leaning into her. In this position, his cock could stay hidden and not frighten her.

"We should not." Celia's lips barely formed the words, as though her heart was not in the protest.

"No, we should not." Alec gave her a gentle kiss. "But *should* doesn't come into it. Only wanting."

Celia nodded, her smile shy. "I think you are correct."

Alec leaned closer, but Celia drew back in sudden apprehension. "My mother did not put you up to this, did she?"

"T' have you caught kissing a defeated, vagabond Highlander? No, lass. This is all my own doing."

"My mother has very odd ideas. I would not be astonished by anything, these days."

"Poor lass. To have your trust taken so young."

"I'm rather old, she would say. Nearly twenty-two and still unmarried."

Alec smoothed her cheek. "Such a terrible thing." He gave her another soft kiss, and then another. "Your husband will be lucky."

Celia copied his brushes of lips, her response rousing Alec's blood. "I shall not have a husband. I've given them up."

He touched his forehead to hers, his heart light. "Good lass. They're nothing but trouble. My brother's wife will tell you so."

Celia smiled into the next kiss. Alec smoothed her hair, dislodging her cap, letting his imagination soar. He pictured her in his bed, her hair spread across his pillow, her face softening as she drew him down to her.

Alec wanted that with a power he hadn't felt in years. What was this young Englishwoman, a hated aristocrat's daughter, his family's enemy, doing to him?

Celia had certainly enchanted him. Alec kissed her again, then moved to lick the shell of her ear. He closed his teeth around her earlobe and suckled.

Celia made a warm sound, and then Alec felt her tongue on his neck.

Into the fire that roared in his ears, he heard the rasp of a latch and the cutting voice of Lady Flora.

"For God's sake." Heels clicked on the polished floor. "Not *now*. Celia, your mother is searching high and low for you. Cease kissing ... Mr. Finn ... before she bursts in here and finds you."

CHAPTER 9

*C*elia jumped, tried to rise, and fell back to the settee in a flutter of skirts. Alec caught her, stifling his laughter as he helped her up and steadied her on her feet.

Bless the lass. Celia had driven away some of the hatred in his soul and returned Alec the painter, Alec the ardent lover. For that he'd be forever grateful.

Lady Flora's icy stare flowed over them. "Mr. Finn, you will make yourself scarce. I suggest the back stairs. Celia, remain here and compose yourself. And straighten your cap. It is awry."

After snapping her commands like a battlefield sergeant, Lady Flora swung away and strode out the door, the slam of it rattling the gilt-framed paintings on the walls.

Celia planted her hands over her face, her cheeks reddening, her eyes wet. But she wasn't crying, Alec realized after a moment. She was laughing.

He caught her around the waist and pulled her down to the settee once more. Celia landed half on his lap, her laughter ringing out.

She had a beautiful laugh. Alec gathered her against him, basking in the vibration of it.

She smelled of sherry and spice, clean silk and linen. Alec kissed her neck, inhaling her beautiful scent. Celia made a soft sound in her throat, her hand on his shoulder relaxing.

Alec nuzzled the line of her jaw, kissed her cheek, and resisted kissing her lips. If he began that, he'd wrap her in his arms and never let her go.

"Lady Flora is right," he said, brushing a kiss to her cheekbone. "Let's have you neat as a pin before your mum finds you."

"Botheration to the lot of them." Celia jumped to her feet, no falling or fluttering this time. "I am a pawn, Mr. Finn, in my mother's games and whatever Lady Flora is currently plotting. Do not look so amazed—Lady Flora is always plotting *something*. Well, I am tired of being a useful but easily discarded piece on their chessboards."

Alec rose with her, her vehemence exhilarating. He'd worried for a moment that she knew about Alec's and Lady Flora's plans but then realized she spoke generally. Lady Flora *was* always scheming—it was how Will had come to know her.

He tugged Celia's cap straight and tucked a stray lock of hair beneath it. "A pawn can bring down a king," he said into her ear. "Remember that."

Celia slanted him a look, her eyes so near. "His royal majesty is in no danger from me. Even Lady Flora can not make me cross the line of treason." She flushed. "Oh, I did not mean—"

"I for one am happy King Geordie remains on the throne. I was only a reluctant Jacobite, to protect my asinine brothers, little good it did me." Alec gave her cap another tug and straightened her fichu on her shoulders.

He lingered as he touched her skin beneath the lace, and he couldn't stop himself leaning down to brush her lips with the briefest kiss.

Celia's mouth was pliant and warm. The kiss threatened to turn deeper, and only the hiss of a guttering candle reminded Alec not to lose himself.

He released her with reluctance. Celia's lips parted, moist and pink, and her eyes held a quietness Alec needed. He longed with all that was within him to draw her into his arms and answer her silent plea for more kisses, but he forced himself to step away.

"I'll leave ye now, lass. I humbly thank ye for your help. Come to lessons tomorrow, and I'll have something special for you."

Celia blinked, popping her mouth closed. "You are still willing to teach me?"

"Of course. I told you—ye have talent. It just wants bringing out."

Celia took a step closer to him and lowered her voice. "Are you truly an artist famous throughout France?"

"Oh, aye. Commissioned by Madame du Pompadour herself to paint a rhinoceros for her."

More blinking. "I beg your ... Did you say a rhinoceros?"

"I did. Haven't ye heard of her? Clara is her name. Brought back from India by a Dutch sea captain, and now she's having a grand tour of Europe. I was commissioned to seek her out and paint her portrait for the royal collection. Louis is trying to bring Clara to Versailles, but I was sent forth in the meantime. Haven't caught up to the beast yet."

"I see."

Her tone told Alec Celia did not quite believe him, but he spoke the truth. Clara was all the rage on the Continent and already had sat—or rather, stood—for several portraits. She'd even been modeled in porcelain at Meissen.

Celia shook out her skirts, sending a wave of brocade over Alec's shoes. "Well, I must decide whether teaching a duke's daughter is one step up or down for you from painting a rhinoceros."

"Ye ponder that all ye like," Alec said. "I already know what I prefer. Come tomorrow at the appointed hour, and see what you will see."

"Not a rhinoceros, I take it?" she asked lightly then her eagerness returned. "Actually I'd quite like to see her. Do you think Clara will come to London?"

"I have no doubt. When she does, we'll visit her, and I'll fulfill my commission for the King of France's mistress. She's been installed less than a year and already wields more power than any queen."

"The famous Madame du Pompadour?" Celia asked. "Or the rhinoceros?"

Alec did not contain his laughter. "Ye are good for me, lass. Ye keep me on this earth. I'll be leaving ye now, before I kiss you again, because I very much want to. I doubt your mother would try to force you to marry *me* if she caught us."

"Of course not. I'm only to fall for rakes if they are highborn and have grand estates."

Alec moved himself to the door but for some reason, he couldn't turn the handle to open it. He *was* highborn and from a grand estate—but he was also Alec the itinerant painter as he now pretended to be.

"God bless you, lass," he said quietly, and finally made himself leave her.

His last glimpse of Celia, watching him with her hazel eyes, her hands in fists, her lips awaiting another kiss, did nothing to calm him. Alec took the vision with him up the back stairs to his chamber, kept it next to him after he kissed his sleepy daughter good night, and let it sustain him in the dark loneliness of his bed.

~

CELIA'S HAMMERING HEART WOULD NOT EASE FOR THE REST OF the salon, so much that she feared she'd need a tonic. Just when she thought she'd calm, she'd feel anew the sensation of Alec's mouth on hers, his tongue sweeping past her parted lips, and the hammering would begin again.

The Marquess of Harrenton's disgusting kisses had been wet and intrusive. Alec's were strong, warm, practiced. A man who knew how to kiss so a woman enjoyed it, how to make her feel beautiful and wanted.

Celia longed to hug herself, laugh, and spin around the room. She restrained herself with difficulty until the interminable salon was over, then again as she rode in the carriage the short way home.

Her mother had been annoyed at Celia for slipping away— apparently no one had noted her leaving, being too caught up in their own conversation. The duchess believed her explanation that she'd been overly warm and also distressed at the topic of discussion. Her mother agreed such subjects were too violent for a young lady, but it was Celia's own fault for throwing away her innocence, and so could no longer expect to be protected from them.

Celia let her mother run on, paying little attention. Her thoughts were all for Alec, her Highlander. He'd worried her with his rage—she'd been certain he would slay every gentleman in Lady Flora's drawing room—but his kisses had been tenderness itself.

Alec was a paradox. Celia had glimpsed the dangerous man inside him, but she wasn't wrong when she concluded him a good father, with kindness in him. But then, his fury at the salon's heartless conversation had revealed an untamed man barely contained.

Celia kept her speculations about what he'd show her at her upcoming lesson at bay during supper but let them run rampant when she lay alone in her bed that night.

For her first lesson, he'd bared his torso and dared her to draw it. Would he do such a thing again? Or perhaps more?

She shivered in warm hope. Alec's body was a fine thing, all tightness and exact proportions. He'd had scars on his arms, deep ones, and now she understood why. He was a fighting man, one who had suppressed that urge to act as a drawing master to earn money for his daughter.

The Highlanders were to be reduced to dire poverty, she knew from listening to her father and Uncle Perry. She'd heard Uncle Perry go on about the Act of Proscription being worked up to take away their language, the plaid cloth that was their national dress, their customs, their land. Uncle Perry had spluttered that some fools in Parliament thought it too harsh. *We need to bring those traitors under our thumb for once and for all,* he'd snarled. As a younger son, Uncle Perry had no seat in the Lords, and when he'd stood for Commons, he'd lost, despite Celia's father's help, and so he was left to helplessly criticize other MPs and badger the duke.

But such measures would never take away the Scots' pride. Alec had an arrogance that couldn't be quelled, a power that would never be quashed. Celia recalled the brusqueness in Alec's voice when he'd chided Lady Flora about his daughter's nurse. Celia had been perplexed at his presumption, but now it was explained—he was used to command.

Regardless, Lady Flora's capitulation was curious. Celia would simply have to watch and listen and find out everything.

❧

CELIA STEPPED OUT OF THE CHAIR AT LADY FLORA'S AT TEN

minutes to eight the next morning. She'd expected to feel embarrassed and worried after kissing Alec so heartily, but her stomach only fluttered in anticipation. Embarrassment was far from her mind.

The flutter increased when she entered the studio high above to find Alec already there.

He straightened from bending over a box about three feet long and one and a half wide on a stand in front of a window, though what was in the box, Celia couldn't see. The large easel with a blank sheet of drawing paper pinned to it obscured whatever he was doing.

Lady Flora's footman silently laid Celia's portfolio on a table and withdrew, closing the door behind him.

Celia rested her hand on her stomacher, a silk concoction of blue with yellow ribbons woven through it. Her maid had tried to dissuade Celia from wearing the bright gown, its deep blue overskirt revealing a gold underskirt embroidered with green vines. Celia's mother expected her to make do with dark and unobtrusive garments now that she was in disgrace, but Celia had wanted to look well for Alec. Another reason for leaving the house early was so her mother would not see what she wore.

Alec barely glanced at her. "There ye are, lass. Come and see."

Celia rustled to him, straightening the lace at her sleeves. What a peacock she was, wishing to strut before him.

Alec stepped aside to reveal the large wooden box on its stand. A flood of sunshine poured in through the tall window, warming the air.

Celia was no more enlightened about the box now that she could see it clearly. And to be honest, Alec was far more enticing to look at. He might dress in plain breeches, linen shirt, and dull brown frock coat, but the man inside the clothes held grace and sinewy strength. He was far more decorative than the dandies at Lady Clara's salon in their bright velvets and gaudy jewels.

"What do you think, love?" Alec asked, watching her with amusement.

Celia started at the word *love* then tried to compose herself. "I think nothing. I mean—what is it?"

"My surprise." Alec opened the box's lid to show the back half of an empty chamber. The front of the box had a hole in it, which Alec had positioned to face the window.

Celia peered inside curiously. "Did it escape? I assume it wasn't a rhinoceros. You'd need a bigger box. And it would need a larger hole."

Alec's rumble of laughter filled the air. "It's a camera obscura. Have ye never seen one?"

"Truly?" Celia peered at the box with more interest. "I've heard of them, but no, I've not seen one."

"Then let me introduce ye."

Alec turned to a low table and opened a smaller box with velvet-lined compartments. He removed what looked like a telescope lens and fitted it into the hole in the box's front. He took a rectangular mirror from the velvet box and positioned it in the back half of the camera obscura, slanting it to catch the light from the hole and throw it to the open top of the box. Then he fitted a frame with glass to the camera obscura's open top.

He gestured to it. "Have a look."

Alec didn't move out of the way, so Celia had to step against him to peer down at the frame of glass. The brush of his coat, the warmth of him inside the linen and wool unnerved her, but then she caught sight of what was on the glass.

"Oh." She drew a happy breath. "How wonderful."

The glass showed her, upside down, the rooftops of Grosvenor Square and the flow of London beyond them. Lady

Flora's huge house was taller than many of its fellows, and the view from her upper floors was vast.

The camera obscura caught the light of the unusually bright day and cast the image inside, the mirror reflecting it to the top of the box.

Though the image wasn't as crisp as the world outside, Celia saw its colors and shapes, as well as the brilliant blue of the sky and stark white clouds.

"Now then." Alec set a piece of very thin paper over the glass. "I saw ye liked painting the city and thought you'd enjoy capturing it precisely. We'll trace the outlines and then make it into a grand painting."

"Like Signor Canaletto's," Celia said excitedly. "I so admire them. My father bought several of his pictures when he was in Venice. And you've seen Lady Flora's."

"Aye, he's fond of the camera obscura. What he does with his tracings is a thing of beauty. I have confidence you could do as well as he."

Celia raised her head. "Me? Paint like Signor Canaletto? Now you are flattering me, Mr. Finn. I suppose you must do so to keep your students paying your fee."

Alec looked hurt. "Do ye not trust me to know talent when I see it? But here's a secret, love—talent isn't all ye need. Ye have to do the work. So draw, lass."

Celia took the pencil he handed her. "You know that I am supposed to be learning portraiture."

"To please your mum, aye. Learn this to please me."

Celia looked up at Alec's face so close to hers, his eyes that interesting golden hue. "What about pleasing *me*?"

"I think this is what ye want too, is it not?"

He saw into the heart of her, how Celia rejoiced at the spread of the world, its many colors and hues, the vastness of it all. How she felt as though she belonged in that vastness, not in the confinement of her father's houses, no matter how magnificent they might be.

Celia wet her lips and resumed her study of the image on the paper. "It's a bit difficult to see clearly."

"For that ..." Alec lifted a thick black drape from a chair. "There's this."

Celia watched, mystified, as Alec shook out the velvet cloth and settled it over her shoulders. The fabric slithered across her silk bodice and cut the chill in this high room.

She was further warmed as Alec pulled the other end of the cloth around himself, the piece so vast it encompassed them both.

"We cut all other light." Alec leaned over the camera obscura, pulling the drape high.

The velvet fell forward over the box, enclosing them in a very small tent. In its darkness, the image projected from the lens was clearer, the colors sharper.

Wordlessly Celia began to trace the outline of the buildings, the horizon beyond, the smoke-filled jumble that was London. Bricks, chimneys, and square or stepped rooflines stretched south toward the Thames, steeples poked up here and there— Grosvenor Chapel, St. Martin-in-the-Fields—the blur of Westminster Abbey.

Celia's pencil outlined them, capturing the strange beauty of London. Her mother could not understand why Celia bothered painting the foggy, dirty city, but Celia found a magic in it, a vibrancy she sensed from high above, one lost when she was on the ground.

Its vibrancy was enhanced by the presence of Alec against her side. Celia longed to know his family name—his clan as they called them, but she did not ask. She had no doubt he would not tell her.

His thigh pressed her skirt, his arm was heavy against hers, and the scent of linen and soap intrigued her—the clean scent of male, unfamiliar to Celia. Her brother, Edward, usually smelled of sweat, hair powder, and the pomander balls he used to keep the odor of London at bay.

Having Alec against her, the light-blocking cloth giving the illusion of privacy, made her heart pound and her blood sear.

"We must look ridiculous from the outside," she said to hide her nervousness. "A drapery with a skirt and a pair of legs."

"And two bums poking at the viewer." Alec's amusement rumbled. "Worthy of a cartoon, is that."

Celia imagined it, exaggerated billows for her back end and his, his well-shaped legs in stockings and large shoes, her skirt ballooning twice its size to add to the comedy. That would be all that the picture showed, and the caption would read—*The Camera Obscura.*

"Shall we draw it?" she asked eagerly.

"And have it printed in newspapers up and down the country?" Alec's grin was visible in the faint light. "Are ye sure ye can stand the notoriety?"

"It wouldn't show our faces, only our back ends. I *will* draw it. You can show it to your daughter when she's old enough to laugh."

"I'll keep it safe 'til then." Alec's voice went soft, the light in his eyes warming. "You've a good heart, lass."

"For an Englishwoman?"

"If you like." He brought his hand up to cup her cheek. Celia jerked, his touch in this confined space startlingly intimate. "Don't move about so," he said. "I only want to kiss you."

Celia swallowed, her chest tightening. "You kissed me yesterday."

"Aye, but that was to calm myself, to keep my anger from killing me. A soothing kiss. This one is just because I want to."

Celia's lips tingled at the remembered sensations of their

encounter in the anteroom. "There are different kinds of kisses?"

"That there are, love." Alec's mouth was an inch from hers. "There are kisses of anger, and of passion. Kisses of friendship, and love, kisses for a daughter, for a sister, for a mother, even a dad if ye can make him hold still. Kisses for thanks, kisses for peace."

Celia's voice slid to a whisper. "Which will this be?"

"I think ... friendship, aye? Maybe a little more."

"Yes," she said, barely able to speak. "I think I'd like that."

Alec closed the last breath of space between them and brushed her lips with a soft kiss, a light touch. The next kiss was as light, but the one after that lasted longer.

Celia's heart pounded as she returned the pressure, or tried to. She lost her balance and fell into him, and the drapery slid down and pooled on the floor at their feet.

CHAPTER 10

*A*lec caught Celia as she fell into him in a soft heap, her skirts tangling the leg of the camera obscura's stand. She began to straighten, to apologize, but Alec pulled her to him, tilted her face to his, and kissed her in the sunshine pouring through the window.

Her lips softened, the protests dying, and she stilled in his arms, her mouth welcoming.

Friendship, he'd said, *maybe a little more.* But this kiss was for enjoyment, to taste a woman, to feel her taste him in return.

He brushed his thumb over her chin. "A kiss for pleasure." He slanted his mouth across hers once more, slowly and deliberately. "A kiss for diversion." Another taste, parting her lips and nibbling the lower one.

"Most diverting, yes," Celia said softly.

Her eyes closed as she sought his mouth again. She bit down on his lower lip, the merest touch, but it sent a hot spike through Alec's every nerve.

She had no idea how seductive she was. Lady Flora had

instructed Alec to flirt with her, flatter her, ensnare her trust, but Alec was the one being ensnared.

Celia continued to nibble, becoming more daring. Alec flicked his tongue across her teeth and caught her upper lip between his. She gasped and began to laugh, then the laughter died when Alec turned to her lower lip, pulling it into his mouth to suckle.

Celia's hands landed on his chest, but not to push him away. Alec felt her breath come faster, her fingers curl on his coat.

He slid his arm around her, drawing her to him, her breasts soft through her fichu. The thin linen, meant to hide her from prying eyes, was a flimsy barrier to his touch. The lace on its edges scratched his fingertips, and her heart hammered behind the fabric.

Alec released her lip then kissed it. Celia's eyes were half closed, her cap falling, her hair mussed. Beautiful.

She didn't hang in his arms like a ravished maiden, she stood upright, clinging to him, strong on her feet. Celia brushed his jaw with her finger, smiling when she found his bristly whiskers.

"I thought all Highlanders wore thick beards, to keep warm."

"Not all," Alec said. "We lads like to be fashionable, and the fashion is to have nothing on the face."

Celia moved her fingers to his hair. "It's also fashionable to shave your head and wear a wig."

"Aye, well, I can't bring myself to let a razor anywhere near m' scalp. Hard enough at m' throat."

"I like your hair." Celia ran fingers through it, gazing at it in wonder, as though she'd never seen a man's hair before, or touched it. And maybe she hadn't. These days, if a gentleman didn't wear a wig, he wore a scull cap over his bald pate.

"My father is bearded," Alec said. "Maybe that's why m' brothers and me shave our faces."

"You said your father is still alive?"

Alec stiffened. He was to pry information from her, not the other way around. He didn't believe now that Celia would race to her father and tell him she'd found a Jacobite in Lady Flora's house—the fact that no one had come to arrest him meant Celia had said nothing thus far. But she might slip in innocent conversation.

"I told you. I lost my family. Culloden killed many a Highlander."

"I'm so sorry, Mr.— I cannot keep calling you Mr. Finn. That's not your name, is it?"

"Then call me Alec. My other names are dangerous for you to know."

Celia shook her head. "I cannot possibly address you by your Christian name. It isn't done. My mother calls my father *Your Grace*, and they have been married thirty years."

Alec's lips twitched. "What does your father call her?"

"Do you know, I don't believe I've ever heard him address my mother directly?"

"Ah, that's sad, that is. But I'm kissing ye, lass. Of course you can use my Christian name when I'm kissing ye—as long as you say it only when we're alone."

Celia touched his chest. "Alec."

Her voice was low, enticing. God help him. "Celia."

The blush that spread over her face told him no man outside her family had ever addressed her thus. The little smile told him she liked it.

"I will keep your secret." She rose on tiptoe and touched a light kiss to his mouth. "This is a kiss of promise."

In more ways than one. Alec needed this woman, and not for having and discarding afterward. Unlike Will, who could move from lady to lady without a qualm or breaking any hearts in the process, Alec couldn't have a woman only once.

If the first time was glorious, the second time would only be better, as he and the lady in question grew to know each other, and what each other liked. He wanted Celia many, many times.

"And this is a kiss of gratitude." Alec followed it with another warm touch of mouths. "And this because you're pretty, and I like it when ye say my name."

"Alec." Her lips curved into a smile.

Alec kissed her again, taking his time, silence reigning in the room. He stroked her cheek, pulling her closer so that her breasts fit against him. He tasted her mouth, coaxed her tongue to tangle with his, felt her breath warm his cheek, her hand grip the lapel of his coat.

When he drew back, Celia's lips were parted, moist, her voice breathless. "What sort of kiss was that?"

"Desire," Alec said in a low voice. "Nothing more."

"I liked that one."

Alec smiled at her eagerness, which made his already hard cock go rigid. He kissed her once again, enjoying the soft response of her lips. "This one is because you've lightened my heart. Have since ye poured that cold water on my foot."

"Gracious." She leaned into him, her fichu crumpling against his coat. "There was no liking in you when you woke that day. But I shall make note that you enjoy such a thing."

"Never said I wanted you to do it again."

Celia laughed softly, a sound that wound through Alec and loosened him. He was a fool—she was his enemy's daughter. But Alec for the first time in nearly a year felt a thread of happiness work its way into his heart.

∽

LADY FLORA APPEARED AFTER THE HOUR WAS OVER TO ANNOUNCE

that Mr. Finn's next pupil had arrived. Alec had no other pupils, of course—Lady Flora fabricated their existence.

She caught Alec and Celia bent over the camera obscura under the drape, laughing like children as Celia very competently outlined the scene. Alec hadn't exaggerated when he'd said Celia had talent, more than her parents or Lady Flora understood.

Lady Flora hemmed loudly, and Celia popped out, her face red, but her eyes starry.

Not until Celia was safely away, Alec watching her sedan chair being carried around the square, did Lady Flora berate him.

"You are taking your time," she said, joining him at the window. "How much have you learned from her?"

Lady Flora's thick perfume was a sharp contrast to Celia's clean scent. "Nothing," Alec had to answer. "Whatever her father knows, he's not let it slip to his daughter."

Lady Flora let out an impatient sigh. "You are to make her pry it from him. At least you have gained her trust."

"Somewhat." Alec closed the camera obscura—he'd removed the drawing and placed it into Celia's portfolio before she went —and folded the drape. "She feels sorry for me, anyway."

"The duke has expressed a wish to meet you, the duchess says." Lady Flora folded her arms as Alec watched Celia descend from the chair on the other side of the square, gathering her blue and yellow skirts as she sped across the few feet of pavement into her father's house. "To quiz you about conditions in Ireland. That would be a disaster."

"Aye." The Duke of Crenshaw would take one look at Alec and know exactly what he was, maybe even *who* he was. "I agree, we must prevent such a thing. I'll have to be ill or exhausted if he decides to call."

"I will keep the duke at bay," Lady Flora said with confidence. No doubt she would. Even the powerful Duke of Cren-shaw quaked in his boots when Lady Flora gave orders. "Mrs. Reynolds has much to tell you. I asked her to wait until Celia's lesson was done."

Alec nodded, curious to learn where Mrs. Reynolds had been and what news she might have. He watched until Celia had gone inside, a footman closing the door, before he turned and followed Lady Flora from the room.

Lady Flora took him to her private sitting room, which held more treasures than a king's strongroom. A painting by Rembrandt van Rijn held pride of place, a portrait of his model, Hendrickje, with her shift hiked high as she waded through a stream. On the opposite wall was a painting of Lady Flora as a younger woman, stiff-backed, haughty, and impossibly beauti-ful. She'd been the most sought-after debutante in London.

The room wasn't crowded but tastefully laid out with a sofa upholstered in silk damask, matching chairs gathered with it so Lady Flora could entertain an intimate group. A clavier stood near the window, positioned so its player could use the light to see the music. A gilded clock stood on the mantel, gently ticking away time.

Mrs. Reynolds was playing the clavier as they entered, the music floating down the hall to embrace them before the footman opened the door—Lady Flora rarely touched a door handle herself.

The piece Mrs. Reynolds played was lively and complicated, executed with such skill that Alec paused to enjoy it. He dimly remembered music at Kilmorgan Castle when their mother had been alive, in the very brief period he'd known her. Imprinted on his mind was a scene in which his mother played a harpsi-chord, serene and lost in the music, while his father watched, lost in her. Alec's father had loved his wife desperately, and had never quite recovered from her death.

The juxtaposition of that memory with Mrs. Reynolds, dark-haired, handsome, her fingers flying on the keyboard, had Alec torn between two worlds.

Lady Flora settled herself on the sofa, stretching one arm across its back as she listened to Mrs. Reynolds. Alec caught his breath as he whirled back to the present—he was in smoky London, hemmed in, relying on a duplicitous Englishwoman for help, carefree boyhood gone.

Lady Flora watched her companion with an expression similar to what Alec's father had worn while watching his wife. Her face was softened, transformed, the woman of ice becoming a human being for that moment.

Mrs. Reynolds continued to play, her eyes on the music. The beauty of the piece caught at Alec's heart, the serenity of it like a smile. He saw not Mrs. Reynolds as he listened, but Celia, her eyes sparkling as she beheld the camera obscura, her laughter as they struggled with the drape, the flare of desire when Alec kissed her, her steadiness when she held him.

His heart gave a painful beat. The piece wound to a close, ending on a firm chord. Mrs. Reynolds gracefully lifted her hands from the keyboard and rose from the stool.

"Lovely, my dear," Lady Flora said. "Your sojourn in Vienna last year was not wasted. Come and sit with us, and tell us all."

Alec went to Mrs. Reynolds and offered his arm to escort her the ten feet from clavier to sofa. Mrs. Reynolds thanked him and sat down, settling her skirts, which came to rest a half inch from Lady Flora's.

Alec folded himself into a chair, resting his hands on his knees, trying to be patient while Mrs. Reynolds thanked Lady Flora for her generosity, and Lady Flora again praised her performance.

When the play of dear friend being kind to dear friend was

at last finished, Mrs. Reynolds gave Alec a knowing look and began.

"I am not sure I discovered anything of use to you, Mr. Finn," she said. Lady Flora had decreed at the outset that they should always use Alec's assumed name, in case a servant might happen to hear and repeat any part of *Lord Alec Mackenzie*, even inadvertently. "I stayed with Lady Westwood, in her husband's house, which lies between Cambridge and Newmarket. A regiment of Foot are billeted there—her husband, Sir Amos, has a large property, and the regiment uses outbuildings on the far edge of the estate. Lady Westwood will certainly not have soldiers in the house."

She and Lady Flora exchanged a look and a smile, old friends discussing people they'd known for years. "Certainly not," Lady Flora agreed.

"But the commander is often invited for supper, being a crony of Sir Amos. He and Sir Amos discuss many a military matter, as Sir Amos served in the same regiment until his retirement. Lady Westwood enters with her opinions instead of sitting in silence, as she has many, and apparently Colonel Graham is used to this, as he speaks openly with her and is not offended. She apologizes to me afterward for making me listen to tedious conversation."

Alec imagined Mrs. Reynolds, with her polite air, pretending to be interested in her roast fowl and sorbet while the colonel and Sir Amos discussed the business of the regiment, all the while listening avidly.

"And what do these military gentlemen have to say?" Alec asked, his fingers tightening on his knees.

"Much about France—they were both at Fontenoy. Colonel Graham returned home with the Duke of Cumberland when he was recalled to put down the Jacobites. The colonel himself did not fight in Scotland, but he helped move prisoners to London for trial."

And execution. The word was not spoken but hung in the air.

Mrs. Reynolds continued. "Colonel Graham was surprised that some of the Scotsmen he escorted were perfect gentlemen, educated and well-read." Her lips twitched into a cool smile. "So many expect all Highlanders to be rough barbarians who can barely speak, and daily crush rocks with their bare hands. Colonel Graham said these men changed his mind."

"Are any of these well-read Highlanders known to us?" Alec kept his tone casual but his heart thumped. Not that he expected Will would let himself be anyone's prisoner for long, and Colonel Graham must be speaking of men who'd surrendered after Culloden or who'd been taken at the forts along Loch Ness. Will had been long gone by then, escorting Mal and Mary to France.

"No." Mrs. Reynolds gave Alec a sad look from her brilliant blue eyes. "I'm sorry, he never mentioned your brother. As I said, I might not have anything to report that can help you. But one evening, Colonel Graham began to speak of a group of prisoners, and Sir Amos cut him off with a significant glance at his wife and me. After that I kept my ears open for any snatch of conversation about it."

She leaned to Alec, pitching her voice so that anyone outside the door would hear only a murmur.

"The colonel mentioned a house, and he spoke of prisoners in the same breath. I don't know what house—whether Sir Amos's or another, I could not discover. But from what I gathered, not all the prisoners were taken to London. There are some that have been neither executed nor tried, nor transported, but are in limbo somewhere. Whether your brother is one of them, I have no idea."

Alec chilled, though his heart beat faster. Was Will among them? Or had he found these prisoners and tried to help them escape—Will would do something like that—and been caught? Captured, or killed in the act?

"A name was also spoken in regard to this house," Mrs. Reynolds went on. "That name was the Duke of Crenshaw."

Celia's father. Alec sat back, waves of rage, worry, and hope crashing over him. A house with Highlanders imprisoned, which might or might not have anything to do with Will.

The Glaswegian he'd met at the tavern had mentioned a house with Scotsmen inside it, and then he'd been killed. Because he possessed information? Or had that fight been a simple robbery? Plenty of footpads roamed London's back streets. Or had Crenshaw sent toughs to make certain any knowledge was crushed out?

The house was worth investigating, Alec told himself, trying to cool his anger. Will had taught him that keeping his head was the wisest thing, no matter how he felt. How Will managed it Alec didn't know. His rage rose, the need to go to that house and tear it open to find out who was inside strong.

He'd have to do more than investigate—if Highlanders were there, Alec could not pluck out Will and leave the others to their fates. Will would be the first to agree. They'd have to all be freed.

Whether or not Will was among these prisoners or had anything to do with them at all, Alec needed to find out more about them. And the knowledge seemed to be lodged in the head of the Duke of Crenshaw, whose daughter had shared with Alec kisses of fiery passion.

~

CELIA SET ASIDE HER NEWSPAPER AND TURNED TO THE DUKE OF

Crenshaw, who serenely buttered toast at the head of the breakfast table.

Her father was not a big man, plump, yes, but small and
round rather than broad. His simple wig was subdued, as were
his dark blue frock coat and waistcoat, his fine cotton shirt and
stock barely visible above the high-buttoned waistcoat. The
Duke of Crenshaw could never be called ostentatious. Yet, his
clothes were made from the most expensive fabric and lace
brought home in the East India Company's ships, so he was by
no means dull or puritanical.

The duke was the perfect statesman—quiet, learned, and
possessing subdued taste but not parsimony. He was devoted to
his mistress, so people whispered, but never let his wife or
family want for anything.

"Papa," Celia said as the duke took a precise bite of his toast.
"Why does this newspaper accuse you of being a Jacobite? That
is hardly accurate when you mustered troops and raised funds
to put down Charles Stuart's uprising."

She waved her hand at the paper, which had printed a fairly
virulent attack on her father, accusing him of wishing to plunge
the country back under Catholic rule, which was ridiculous.
Her father, like her mother, was avidly anti-Papist, and anyway,
he could never accomplish such a thing even if he wanted to.

Instead of looking alarmed or ashamed, the duke chewed his
toast and swallowed. "Take no notice, my dear. I had the
temerity to say that the defeated Scots should not be so harshly
treated. The Young Pretender must be caught and executed, lest
he try again, but those swept into the conflict needn't be unduly
punished. Fined, stripped of whatever title they held, and no
longer given power to command armed troops, of course, but
that should be sufficient."

He took another bite, unworried.

Celia thought of Alec in his shabby clothes, his motherless

daughter with nothing to look forward to but poverty. Alec had not only been angry at the men in the salon, but also at the Scots who'd pulled his family into the conflict and lost them everything.

"This will not hurt you, will it?" Celia touched the newspaper. Though the Whigs held great power at the moment, the duke and the head of government, Pelham, didn't always see eye to eye.

The duke shrugged. "I doubt it. Whenever a man voices an opinion that's contrary to the most popular one, he's called a Jacobite. The word has become meaningless, and the Jacobites' power has been broken for good."

He crunched down another bite of toast.

If the duke knew that a Jacobite, or at least a Highland soldier, was giving his daughter art lessons, what would he do? Arrest Alec? What about Lady Flora, for allowing Alec to live in her house? Celia had no doubt anymore that Lady Flora knew exactly who Alec was. She'd have found out straight away.

Lady Flora was the most puzzling person in this situation. She was staunchly loyal to the Protestant line of kings—King George was in fact quite fond of Lady Flora. She'd held a huge soiree after Culloden, celebrating the British victory and Charles Stuart's flight.

So why had she suddenly invited a Highlander who'd killed King George's soldiers to stay in her house and teach drawing to the daughter of one of the most powerful dukes in England?

The all-powerful duke brushed crumbs from his coat with a buttery hand. "Oh, my dear, I nearly forgot. The most curious thing has happened."

"Yes?" Celia tried to listen, though her thoughts strayed to Alec and his kisses, her anticipation of continuing them today. "What is this curious thing?" It might be Lord Pelham's new wig or her mother actually speaking to a woman beneath her station.

"The Marquess of Harrenton has been laid up."

Celia's chest squeezed, and the eggs she'd eaten seemed to curdle inside her. She did not want to speak of the Marquess of Harrenton. "Is he ill?" she asked politely.

"No, no. It is most astounding. He was waylaid, in Green Park. Set upon by ruffians and beaten quite thoroughly. Nothing stolen, which is the intriguing thing. He was brought down by fists and left on a path for his valet to find. I hear he is abed now, black and blue and recovering." The duke chuckled. "Serves him right."

CHAPTER 11

*C*elia stared at her father in shock. "Set upon?"

She pictured the Marquess of Harrenton, his rotund body spinning every which way as he tried to fend off his attackers. He'd strike out with his long walking stick, his frowsy wig slipping, curses coming from his foul mouth, bathing the miscreants in bad breath.

Why did she imagine one of those attackers as a tall man with dark red hair, large fists flying, his face a snarl of rage?

Had Alec, who'd scowled fiercely when she'd told him about the Disaster, decided to exact vengeance for her? The Highlanders were said to be quite possessive, hold grudges, and enjoy revenge.

No, she was being fanciful. Green Park was notorious for highwaymen, and Lord Harrenton was arrogant enough not to take sufficient care. Alec might have had nothing to do with it.

Celia thought of Alec's scarred arms, his battered and bruised face, his grin shining through his wounds. He was a fighting man—he could cheerfully take down a waddling lordship despite that lordship's walking stick and his footmen.

Celia's fingers shook as she took up her last slice of toast. "You seem gleeful, Papa. Lord Harrenton is your great friend."

"He *was*, indeed. There was much to admire about him. But he dared put his hands on my daughter—I do not care that it was his desperation to break through your stubbornness and force you to change your *no* to a *yes*. As much as I liked the match, he ought to have respected your decision. Had I been a younger man, I would have called him out. As it is, I can only cut him whenever I see him, which is sadly too often."

Celia froze with her toast halfway to her mouth. She'd known her father sympathized with her, but she hadn't realized the extent of his anger. Her father rarely showed that emotion. He and the marquess were still political allies, and she'd thought her father had forgotten the matter.

"I'm sorry, Papa," she said, her throat dry. "I had no idea the incident upset you so much."

The duke's eyes widened. "Well, of course it upset me, child. You're my daughter—the sweetest young lady who ever graced my presence. I want only the best for you. Harrenton is very wealthy and you'd have never wanted for anything, but I'd not have you live in misery with a man you despised. You were quite right to refuse him, your mother wrong to push you at him. I admire your courage in defying them."

Celia's astonishment didn't leave her. The duke spoke with warmth, and that warmth touched her heart. She'd always loved her father, but as he was not an overly sentimental man, she hadn't realized how much the affection was reciprocated.

Her mother was not in love with her father—Celia knew that—nor he with her, but neither the duke or duchess was miserable. The duchess adored being one of the most admired hostesses of the *ton*, while her father found his affection with Mrs. Barnett, a woman Celia had never met.

Celia wasn't quite certain what to say. Her parents didn't

advocate gushings of endearment. Her father might like them, but they embarrassed him.

"Thank you, Papa." Celia smiled fondly, her heart warming. "Unfortunately, my stubbornness has made me ineligible to marry anyone else."

"Oh, I do not believe so," her father said. "One day you will meet a gentleman who will see your fine qualities and wish to marry you regardless—a gentleman you will esteem and like, I mean. When that happens, you will come to me, and I will give you my blessing and make the marriage happen. Never mind your mother."

For all his quietness, Celia's father was a very powerful man. He could shove any marriage he wanted to down society's collective throats, and he'd do it with a smile and a sip of port.

Celia flung down her toast, sprang to her feet, rushed to the head of the table, and squeezed her father in a fervent embrace. He started and blinked, and Celia bent down and kissed his powdered cheek.

"You are the most wonderful father in the world," she declared, hugging him again. "Thank you, Papa."

"Oh. Er." Her father flushed and looked relieved when Celia let him go. "Quite. But—hem—don't mention it to your mother. There's a good gel."

∾

CELIA LEFT THE BREAKFAST ROOM AND RUSHED THROUGH preparations to depart for her lesson. She wanted to demand Alec tell her whether he had anything to do with the attack on the Marquess of Harrenton and also to explain to him what a wonderful gentleman her father was. Alec needed to see that not all Englishmen were cold and heartless.

She bundled herself into the sedan chair and fidgeted as the bearers lumbered around the square with her, arriving at the front door of Lady Flora's house just before eight. The footman admitted her and silently led her, not to the studio but to Lady Flora's breakfast room, where Celia had gone the first morning.

The sun was muted today, dark clouds covering the sky. The gold gilt in the breakfast room, however, shone bright, and tiny mirrors embedded in the moldings reflected the painted blue sky full of cherubs on the ceiling. No need for real sunshine in Lady Flora's house.

Lady Flora was in the act of pouring a dark stream of chocolate into a tiny porcelain cup when Celia entered. "You have no lesson today, Celia." She ceased pouring when the chocolate reached exactly one quarter inch below the cup's rim, and set the pot down. "I had no time to send word before you set off. If you'd like, I can ring for coffee for you and anything you wish to eat."

Celia's breakfast still roiled in her stomach. "No, thank you. Why is there no lesson?" she asked in worry. Had Alec been arrested for beating Lord Harrenton? Or was there another dire reason? "Is Mr. Finn's daughter ill? Is *he*?"

Lady Flora's brows puckered. "No one is ill. Mr. Finn is simply not here."

Celia's fears escalated. "He is not? Where is he?" Had he fled London after attacking Lord Harrenton, was even now pursued by soldiers?

Lady Flora's frown deepened. "I'm certain I have no idea. He did not confide in me, simply told me this morning he had an errand and would return too late for your lesson."

"Oh." Celia drummed her fingers against her skirts. Calmly leaving the house on an errand did not sound like the actions of a man fleeing for his life. Still, something was amiss, she was certain. Why should Alec be running errands before eight in the morning when Lady Flora had a houseful of servants to do it for him? "Where is Mrs. Reynolds this morning?"

Whenever Mrs. Reynolds was in residence, she graced every room Lady Flora did. It was unusual for Lady Flora to breakfast without her.

"My, you are full of questions," Lady Flora said impatiently. "That is unbecoming in a young lady, Celia. Mrs. Reynolds also had an errand, and that errand is none of your business. Now either sit down in a civilized manner and Rivers will bring you coffee, or return home. Your lessons will resume tomorrow."

Celia had no wish to rush back to the cold emptiness of her house and explain why she'd returned. Her father would have departed by now, and Celia would be left alone with the duchess. "May I go up to the studio and draw on my own? Mr. Finn was showing me how to flesh out the tracing from the camera obscura, and I'd like to continue."

Lady Flora waved a languid hand. "If you like, child. But stay there and don't wander the house. It upsets the servants."

"Yes, Lady Flora." Celia babbled the politeness before she turned and hurried out. She heard Flora sigh behind her, no doubt unhappy with Celia's choice, her frenzied pace, and the way her skirts barely missed a delicate table full of porcelain figurines.

Celia hastened up the stairs, aware of the silent footman carrying her portfolio behind her. The footman deposited the leather-bound portfolio on the table in the studio and withdrew, as he did every day. Celia briefly wondered if he'd be happy when the lessons were over.

After the footman departed, she paced the room, trying to suppress her anxiousness and consider things logically.

If Alec had been in fear for his life, surely he'd have run away last night, not retired to his bed and then stepped out on an errand this morning. He might simply be purchasing pigments for mixing paint, or canvases and brushes from merchants who sold that sort of thing. Artists were particular about their accoutrements, and perhaps he didn't trust a servant to buy the correct things.

Besides, Celia had no evidence that Alec had pummeled the Marquess of Harrenton in Green Park. Any footpad might have done so—London was full of thieves and desperate men.

To try to stem her worry, Celia opened her portfolio and spread out the tracings of the London skyline she'd done with Alec the day before. There was not enough light today to use the camera obscura—the fog was lowering, not clearing.

Celia pinned the drawing they'd already begun to the easel and continued to transfer lines from the preliminary sketches as Alec had showed her. The form of Grosvenor Chapel took shape, a newish building with clean lines and a simple steeple tucked among the houses on South Audley Street. The chapel was unembellished inside as well, she knew from her occasional churchgoing with her mother—with clear windows, white-paneled galleries, and a white-painted ceiling. No clutter of popery, her mother would say with satisfaction.

Celia was perfecting the lines of this chapel and trying to decide how to draw the gap between it and the roofline of the houses partly obscuring it, when she heard a commotion in the street below.

Grosvenor Square was full of noises all day long, as vendors sang out their wares, delivery wagons rolled up with the necessities of life, and carriages rumbled through on their way to other parts of the metropolis.

This was different—a clatter of hooves, shouts of men, and what sounded like barked orders. Celia set down her pencil and made her way to the window, resting her hands on the sill as she peered out.

Two horses had halted in front of the house, ridden by men

in uniform, and about a dozen uniformed men surrounded them. They were in a regiment of Foot, from their scarlet coats, but she was unsure which one. Edward was in the Duke of Crenshaw's Brigade, now in France. She was familiar with that insignia but not ones from other regiments.

The man who dismounted was an officer, she knew not only from his sleek wig and the tricorn hat he tucked under his arm, but by his bearing and the deferential way the soldiers stood to attention for him. The second horseman, who dismounted behind the first as Lady Flora's footman came to take the reins of both horses, was also an officer but not as high ranking, apparent from the way he stayed back from the other gentleman.

Nausea bit her stomach. British soldiers preparing to enter a house where a Highlander hid. Had Alec known they'd be coming, and fled?

Celia pressed her hands to her skirts and hurried to the door and out along the hall to the stairs. Keeping to the shadows, Celia peered over the railings as one of Lady Flora's efficient footmen ushered the two officers inside.

Rivers emerged from the back of the house, taking his haughty time. "Good morning. How may I assist you, gentlemen?"

"Captain Jamison of the Twenty-Sixth Foot, at your service, sir." The captain put his hand to his chest and gave Rivers a shallow bow. "I should like to speak to the lady of the house, if it is at all convenient."

"Her ladyship sees no one without an appointment," Rivers said haughtily. "I will convey a message to her if you wish."

Captain Jamison's annoyance floated up to Celia. "My mission is more of a warning to her. Last night, his lordship, the Marquess of Harrenton, was assaulted and robbed. The miscreants were seen fleeing into Mayfair, and more specifically,

Grosvenor Square. We are conducting a search of the area for the culprits. Your ladyship would be wise to remain indoors today."

"Oh dear." Rivers's note of alarm was subdued. Celia had never seen Rivers grow fully agitated about anything. "Very well. I will explain to her ladyship."

"We are also searching the houses, in case the villains have found a corner in which to hide. I will take my men downstairs and root out the fellow if he is here."

An iciness worthy of Lady Flora entered Rivers's voice. "Certainly not. You will need her ladyship's permission, and as I say, she cannot be disturbed. She is still abed."

Both Rivers and Celia knew full well Lady Flora was not in bed, and was likely listening to the conversation from some vantage point.

"We will search below stairs and the public rooms only," the captain said with gruff concession. "The marquess has commanded it. Her ladyship may discuss it with that gentleman if she has a mind to."

Rivers drew a breath for another disdainful reply, but at that moment, Lady Flora herself appeared on the second-floor landing and sent a cold look over the railing to Captain Jamison.

"By all means, conduct your search, sir." She took a few steps down and halted, poised in a chance beam of sunlight through the fog. "I certainly would not like to be murdered in my bed. But please do not upset the servants. Rivers, accompany the men and ensure that they behave themselves."

Her voice was chillier than Celia had ever heard it. When she peered hard at Lady Flora several floors below her, she saw that Lady Flora clenched the railing hard, the fall of lace from her sleeves trembling.

Captain Jamison sent her a look that was not flattering, but he nodded. Celia knew from Edward that soldiers could be unruly, tearing up houses and terrorizing those within on any pretense. The more civilized officers kept such goings-on at bay, but at times the officers could be as unscrupulous as their disorderly men.

Celia had no doubt that Rivers would keep them tame with his cold disapproval, but she wondered what the servants would tell the soldiers. Would they mention Alec? Did they believe him anything other than poor Mr. Finn, Irish drawing tutor? Would he be significant enough for the soldiers to want to question?

She held her breath as the infantrymen moved past the officers and headed for the back stairs. The lieutenant, who'd remained silent the whole time, broke away and strode to the dining room, wresting open its pocket doors to begin his search inside.

Celia's blood went cold. Though Alec might have departed in anticipation of this visit, if he *was* innocently purchasing supplies, he could reappear from his errand and walk right into a houseful of British soldiers. Any of them might recognize a fugitive Highlander when they saw one and arrest him on the spot.

Celia silently fled back to the studio, where she hurried to the window to scan the streets for any sign of Alec. She could signal to him somehow when he appeared, warn him off.

She grasped the window's latch, but it was stiff with disuse. Celia tugged at it impatiently, but it wouldn't move. Why on earth had a window this high off the ground been given a latch? Did Lady Flora fear burglary from a bird?

A cry cut through her nerves as she struggled with the window, a baby's wail, strong and unhappy.

Jenny.

Anxiousness washed through Celia in cold waves. What would the captain do if he heard a baby up here? She couldn't imagine how Lady Flora would explain the child's presence, though she had no doubt Flora would come up with something plausible.

Even so, Celia rushed from the room and up the stairs to the top of the house. A corridor ran under the sloping roof of the garret, which had been partitioned into rooms. Celia traced the crying to a chamber at the end of this corridor.

When she pushed open its door, she found a plump maid— Sally—her cap half fallen from her frizzy brown hair, bouncing baby Jenny in her arms.

Jenny had been swaddled, wrapped tightly from head to foot, a method believed by physicians to help a baby grow strong. Jenny's head, covered with bright red hair, stuck out of the bundle, her mouth wide as she screamed her displeasure.

"I'm sorry, my lady," Sally said over the noise. "She's hurting from the teething, and she wants her dad."

"Here, let me." Celia reached for Jenny, and Sally reluctantly gave her over.

"Lady Flora says I'm to keep her quiet," Sally babbled, wringing her hands. "Mr. Finn gave me the chamomile ice, but she won't take it today."

Poor Jenny must sense something was wrong. Her father absent, soldiers in the house …

Celia began to loosen the tight cloths. She'd not been around babies much, being the youngest child in her household, but she had the feeling Jenny would be much happier if she could move.

"My lady?" Sally cried in alarm. "Should you do that?"

"The poor thing wants a bit of freedom." Celia held the squirming child with difficulty as she tugged off the cloths. "There you are, love." As the last of the swaddling fell away, Celia hoisted Jenny, clad in a thin nightdress, to her shoulder. "Papa will be home soon."

Celia wasn't certain Papa would ever return, and she knew

Jenny couldn't understand her, but she said the words anyway. What would become of this child if Alec was caught and taken prisoner?

Nothing, Celia thought with determination. *I will look after her.*

It was an absurd thought—Celia had no idea how to take care of a child, and her father and mother would hardly let her bring an orphan into their house. But she'd find a way. Alec would never have to worry about his daughter.

Jenny's wails grew fainter as she dug her fists into Celia's soft fichu. A bit of dribble from the child's mouth landed on the embroidered cotton, but Celia only held her closer.

"Give me the chamomile," she said to Sally.

Sally fetched a covered bowl with small balls of ice floating in water, the soothing scent of chamomile wafting from it.

Celia took a chunk of ice between her fingers and offered it to Jenny. "Here, now, love. This will soothe you."

Jenny fretted and cried, but at last she parted her lips, as though curious. She then suckled Celia's finger, and the ice, her sobs quieting.

Sally grinned. "There now. Ye have a way with you, my lady. She likes you."

Celia cuddled Jenny closer. Holding the babe against her heart, Alec's pretty child, sent a warmness through her she'd never experienced. Affection for Jenny grew and swelled.

Yes, she would take care of this child if she had to. It would be a pleasure.

Meanwhile, she glanced out the chamber's tiny window over the gray city and wondered where the devil Jenny's father had got to, and whether he was safe.

CHAPTER 12

*R*ain streaked the carriage windows, the cold making the glass steam with its passengers' breath. Mrs. Reynolds, prim in dark cloak and hood, sat opposite Alec, her gloved hands in quiet repose.

Alec was anything but composed. He craned to look out the window as the carriage bumped over the rutted and rain-soaked road, the outline of a house near the estate of Sir Amos Westwood in the distance.

Mrs. Reynolds and Lady Flora had concluded this house was a possibility for where Scottish soldiers might be held. They knew every estate within a hundred-mile swath outside London, and they'd pared down the possibilities to three. This was one of them. Mrs. Reynolds offered to look it over herself—very few noticed what a widowed lady's companion did—but Alec insisted on accompanying her.

Was Will inside the crumbling brick walls of the Cambridgeshire estate, held in chains? Alec pictured Will's long, lanky body, his red hair coated with dirt and blood, lying on an earthen floor, beaten and starving. *Bloody hell.*

His worry had escalated earlier this morning when Lady Flora had wordlessly handed him a letter from his brother Malcolm.

Mal had written in French, being fluent in the language, and smuggled the letter to Alec via friends of Lady Flora. Very few excise men were willing to search the baggage of an aristocratic English lady landing after a sojourn on the Continent, especially ladies who were close to the daunting Lady Flora.

I don't know whether to give credit to this tale, Mal wrote, *but I heard it from a Borderland lad newly arrived in Paris who was acquainted with Will. He says Will was arrested in the west of Scotland while helping Teàrlach mhic Seamas escape.*

I didn't believe it, but the lad insisted Will jumped in front of a horde of English soldiers, declaring he was Prince Teàrlach himself, and they should bow before the rightful heir to the Scottish throne. The soldiers promptly clapped him in irons. When it was pointed out later by their commander that he wasn't Teàrlach but an unknown Highlander, they took Will off, and the Border lad doesn't know where.

I don't know why Will would do such a daft thing, and the lad might be mistaken, but he swore by all that's holy it was Will.

Dad's out of his mind with worry, and Mary fears he truly is going off his head. Now Dad is convinced King Geordie's men have you as well. Write and tell me it isn't so, so we don't have to lock him in the basement and feed him gruel and weak whisky until your return.

Mary sends her love to you and Jenny.

Your distracted brother,

Malcolm

Alec had committed the letter to memory and burned it.

He could imagine Will popping up in front of British

soldiers to mockingly claim he was Charles Edward Stuart, son of the rightful King of all Britain, because that was the sort of thing Will would do. *Why* was beyond Alec's understanding, but Will did things for his own reasons. If he'd let himself be arrested in the prince's place, it meant he was following some mad plan he'd concocted.

Will would not sacrifice himself out of compassion and loyalty to the prince, Alec knew good and well. Damn and blast him. Will couldn't be bothered to get a message to the rest of them, let them know what he was doing, could he?

"How the bloody hell are we to know if he's here?" he growled at Mrs. Reynolds.

"We don't." She spoke coolly, as calm as Alec was agitated. "We are taking in the lay of the land, reconnoitering, if you will. We should do the same at the other houses and then decide which is best to approach."

"Meanwhile, they drag Will off to a sham trial and hang him," Alec said, scowling at the rainy window. "Or transport him, if they haven't already. Will might not be in any of these places."

"If you rush in and demand to know whether the owner of the house is holding prisoners of war, you'll only be captured yourself," Mrs. Reynolds pointed out. "Wise heads must prevail, my lord."

Alec's father would laugh that a woman was more collected and competent at the spy game than his sons—or maybe he would not. Their mother had been the calm one. It was said that Allison Mackenzie had great intelligence and could debate most men under the table in matters of science, mathematics, astronomy, and studies of the humors. Mal had inherited her logic and intellect, while Alec had been graced with the volatility and restlessness of their father.

No, they all had that restlessness, Alec reflected. Which was what had gotten Duncan and Angus killed, Mal looked upon as a terrifying demon, and now Will taken God knew where.

What would Mal do in this circumstance? Alec missed his favorite brother, but at the same time was glad Mal was in France with Mary, waiting for his first child to be born, all of them well out of danger.

Alec knew exactly what Mal would do, because Will had taught both brothers all his tricks. Mal would sneak through the countryside in the dead of night to lay traps or play pranks to scare the life out of the guards, and slip in to rescue Will.

So Alec would. He'd return, with the help of those he or Lady Flora had already contacted, and reconnoiter, as Mrs. Reynolds termed it. Or Alec would come alone, trusting to his own instincts.

Working with others had already proved perilous. The Glaswegian friend of Will's had been killed, and the two ruffians who'd waylaid the Marquess of Harrenton and beaten him thoroughly last night had nearly been caught. The fools had rushed to Lady Flora's house for sanctuary—and payment—and Alec had sent them off with their money.

Mayhap scouting alone was best.

"I've seen enough," Alec said abruptly. "We should go."

Mrs. Reynolds frowned. "Patience. Let us continue. If there are sentries, that will tell us something here is important enough to be guarded."

Alec meant he'd seen enough to know the lay of the land. He was good at memorizing spaces—he'd noted the position of every window in the house, every tree on the ground, every possible entry into the building, and he would not forget.

The nearby fields, most of which lay fallow, were empty, no farmers tilling them. They'd seen no riders on the road, nobody going into or out of the house. It was strangely quiet here, a good place for highwaymen to lurk.

Highwaymen would get more than they bargained for if they attacked *this* carriage. Alec was on edge enough to become the berserker Highlander, and Mrs. Reynolds carried a pistol tucked somewhere about her person—the woman was reputed to be a dead shot.

They rolled along the tree-lined road, tall grasses bending in the wind and rain. Rain drummed on the carriage roof, and the vehicle bumped hard through ruts, at times nearly dislodging Alec from his seat.

Alec spied a man in a long coat and wide hat leaning against a tree, not doing much of anything. He could barely be seen with his dark garb against the rain-soaked trunk, and Alec might not have noticed him at all if he hadn't been looking.

The man gazed across the rainy fields and didn't turn his head to study the carriage as it went by. It would be less strange if he did stare at them, Alec wanted to tell him. A carriage trundling down a back country road should be of interest to the local men, an event to speculate on. The man's seeming lack of interest betrayed him.

"Well, we know they have a sentry," Mrs. Reynolds said after they'd passed him. "Something to guard. Interesting."

Alec boiled with anger and impatience. "Far more than interesting. The Duke of Crenshaw knows about these places? Were the prisons his idea?"

"I have no notion, my lord." Mrs. Reynolds gave him a steady look. "I can only report what I heard from Sir Amos and his colonel."

"I will shake the duke until he tells me."

"And be arrested alongside your brother or killed where you stand? We must go softly."

"There's no time for that." Alec moved restlessly. "Who knows when the prisoners might be moved or simply executed? And Lord knows what Will Mackenzie will get up to inside a Sassenach gaol. He'll get himself killed before he knows it."

"You must continue as you have. Gain Lady Celia's trust. Her father dotes on her."

"Celia is no fool," Alec said. He already admired her for that.

Thinking about her calmed him slightly. Celia also had a beauty he'd not encountered before in his life, like the sudden gleam of a candle in the darkness.

He'd kissed her in Lady Flora's anteroom in rage and passion, and he'd kissed her in the studio for the fun of it, when he'd showed her the camera obscura. Both times he'd found her kisses soothing, healing.

"No, but she is unworldly and lonely," Mrs. Reynolds said. "Her mother is the foolish one for not recognizing her worth. You are a handsome gentleman, Lord Alec. You could make Lady Celia your servant if you chose—she will be malleable because she's been raised to be. She showed her good sense when she turned down the Marquess of Harrenton, a disgusting man, but that act reveals her romantic notions. She wants a marriage of equals and one of love. She has yet to learn, as I did, that there is no such thing. Her sense of romance is where you will win."

Mrs. Reynolds's words were bleak against the already bleak day. Yes, Celia might have romantic notions, but Mrs. Reynolds's description made Celia sound like a silly ninny, waiting to be swept off her feet, and Alec knew she wasn't. She already had a fairly clear-eyed view of marriage truly in her world.

Mrs. Reynolds continued. "You are not exercising your charm enough on her. You are too angry. Show her the Alec Mackenzie I have heard of, who had the ladies of Edinburgh and Paris happily surrendering."

At one time, before all the sorrow, Alec had been quite the

rogue. Now he was a father, sober and responsible, his roué days behind him.

Except Celia was drawing out the rogue again.

"Seducing information out of Celia will take too long," Alec said. "Lady Flora is a grand plotter, but her plans take time."

"We shall have to think of a way to increase the pace, then." Mrs. Reynolds gave the house receding into the distance one last look. "Celia already watches you with much interest. When she spirited you out of the salon the other night, I wager you rewarded her. She certainly looked flustered when she emerged. One hard push, and you will have her."

"Aye, maybe."

Before he'd met Celia, Alec had planned exactly what Mrs. Reynolds suggested—draw her into his power, no matter what he had to do. But now that he knew her better, his tactics had changed. Celia had been hurt—she was like a wounded bird, afraid to fly again.

Alec no longer had the desire to break her. If he hastened the wooing, as Mrs. Reynolds urged, he would do so in earnest, no pretense. He would make Celia his in all ways, and no matter what happened with Will, he would not give her back.

Regardless of the fact he was supposed to be dead, his family name anathema, his home burned, Alec had money—his mother had settled it on all the brothers long ago. He had plenty squirreled away in many places, including Paris. But he'd have to live out his life there, in exile. Would Celia agree to that?

He'd leave that up to her. Unlike Malcolm, Alec considered himself a simple man. Mal went through machinations and manipulation to get what he wanted. Alec simply took it.

As the carriage rolled through the rain toward London, Alec laid his plans, which he did not share with Mrs. Reynolds. They were none of anyone's business but his own.

WHEN THE SOLDIERS DEPARTED AND JENNY WAS QUIET, CELIA tucked the babe into her cot, kissed her soft hair, and left the nursery.

She descended the stairs, instructing a footman to call a sedan chair for her and have someone fetch her portfolio. Rain had begun in earnest, and Celia had the feeling she'd not see Alec today.

Rivers met her at the bottom of the stairs, his face drawn, his eyes red-rimmed. Celia halted in surprise—she'd never seen Rivers distressed before.

"Is everything all right, Rivers? The soldiers didn't hurt anyone, did they? Or arrest anybody?"

Rivers made a correct bow. "No, my lady. I beg your pardon. Things are a bit at sixes and sevens, but no harm has been done."

Celia frowned at him. "Clearly something is the matter. What has happened?"

Rivers remained stiff, looking down his long nose. "Nothing, my lady." He started to say more, but then his eyes swam with sudden tears. "Truth to tell, my lady, her ladyship has taken to her bed. She is very upset. Mrs. Reynolds can usually soothe her, but she is not here. I'm a bit worried."

The shock of Rivers revealing he had such a human emotion as concern stunned Celia a moment, then she took a breath.

"I can look in on her if you like."

Rivers hesitated, as though wondering what sort of comfort Celia could offer, then he deflated in relief. "If you would be so kind, my lady. It is this way."

He started up the stairs, Celia gathering her skirts to follow.

Rivers led her to a bedroom that was as large and grand as a ballroom. Two floor-to-ceiling windows faced the garden in back of the house, the ceiling painted with the same blue skies and cavorting cherubs as the morning room below it. A circular molding had been placed in the middle of the ceiling, the illusion of a dome with an oculus painted inside it.

Beneath this dome was a bed with gold damask hangings. The bed's canopy was gathered in a ring in the very center, draperies flowing from it over the four bedposts in an elegant cascade.

The rest of the chamber held sofas, chairs, and a writing table. A double door led to an equally sumptuous dressing room where Lady Flora conducted her public toilette, though Celia had never been invited to one.

Lady Flora lay in the bed, her slim form nearly lost among pillows, sheets, and velvet bed coverings. The sound of quiet sobbing reached Celia as soon as she stepped through the door.

The fact of Lady Flora weeping was even more stunning than Rivers's worry. Celia gave a nod to Rivers to leave them alone.

Celia waited until Rivers, with a look of reluctance, quietly pulled the chamber door closed behind him before she approached the bed.

"Lady Flora?" Celia asked softly. "Can I help?"

Lady Flora sat upright with a gasp, her sobs breaking off. Her face was blotchy and swollen, her eyes red and wet, her hair tumbling down her shoulders in tangles. Her poised beauty had vanished, and Celia gazed upon an exhausted, unhappy woman.

"What are you doing in here?" Lady Flora's usual stentorian tones were weak and scratchy. "I will sack Rivers. Get out."

"What is it?" Pity moved Celia to climb the bed step to sit on the mattress and reach for Lady Flora's hand. "Did the soldiers upset you? Did any of them hurt you?"

"No!" Lady Flora sniffled and groped for a handkerchief that was just out of her reach. Celia plucked it up and handed it to her. "It is nothing. I am tired, that is all. I have been staying out too late and not sleeping enough."

Her wretchedness surely had more to it than missing sleep. "Mrs. Reynolds is certain to be back soon. Where did she go?"

Lady Flora snatched her hand from Celia. "Never you mind. Yes, she will return. Rivers will send her to me. She will understand ..."

She broke off, a sob working up through her chest and out her mouth before she could stop it. She squeezed her eyes shut, hiccupping for breath.

"I will stay with you until she comes." Celia rested her hand on Lady Flora's thin back as the woman bowed her head, her body shuddering. "You should not be alone."

Lady Flora tried to shake her off again. "You don't understand. How could you? I miss her. I miss her with every breath. Why did they take her away from me?" The last words rose into a wail.

Celia knew she was not speaking of Mrs. Reynolds, but Sophia, her daughter. Tears of sympathy stung Celia's eyes as she put her arms around Lady Flora and gathered her close. This time, Lady Flora collapsed onto Celia's shoulder and sobbed brokenly.

"I'm so sorry." Celia stroked Lady Flora's hair, no longer timid with her. Lady Flora was a lonely woman, and she grieved. "So sorry."

There was nothing more to say. Sophia had been a beautiful and kind young woman, and she'd died far too young. The cold emptiness of the house was due to her absence.

Celia puzzled over the words *Why did they take her away from me?* Lady Sophia had died of a fever, as had several others in London that year. Celia's father had moved his family to the country to avoid it.

She could mean the men who had taken Sophia's body to be

buried in St. George's burial ground in Mount Street. There had been a tomb prepared at Lady Flora's husband's estate in Hampshire, but the new Marquess of Ellesmere, her deceased husband's great-nephew, and Lady Flora did not get on, as everyone knew. Lady Flora insisted Sophia remain in London, where she would be near, as Flora had use of the Grosvenor Square house for her lifetime. Ellesmere had argued, but Lady Flora had prevailed.

Celia mulled all this over as Lady Flora continued to cry, and Celia rocked her, but she was no more enlightened.

~

BY THE TIME ALEC ARRIVED HOME, IT WAS DARK. HE WENT straight to Jenny, happier once he could hold his daughter close.

She was quiet tonight, and when he remarked on it, Sally told him Lady Celia had come upstairs to calm her earlier.

"Did she, now?" Alec bounced Jenny, making her laugh. "Did ye like her, Jenny? She's a bonny lass, isn't she?"

Sally gave him an aghast look. "She's a duke's daughter, sir."

As far as Sally knew, Alec was Alden Finn, drawing tutor from an impoverished gentleman's family from Ireland. Not good enough for the likes of Lady Celia Fotheringhay.

Alec grinned at her. "Doesn't make her less comely, does it? Don't worry, lass, I'll hold my tongue around my betters."

"She was right good with the babe," Sally admitted. "Jenny took to her, didn't you, Jen?"

Jenny shoved her fingers into her mouth and gurgled around them. She already knew she was endearing and strove to use that fact to her advantage. She was a Mackenzie all right.

It was time for Jenny's supper and bed, so Alec relinquished her to Sally, kissed her good night, and went down to find Mrs. Reynolds to continue their council of war.

Mrs. Reynolds and Lady Flora were at table in Lady Flora's private dining room, the footmen waiting motionlessly near the sideboard heaped with food. Alec was a bit surprised Lady Flora had not left for her nightly round of social gatherings, but no, she sat in her place at the head of the table, nibbling on a feast.

Not eating much, though, Alec saw as he seated himself and accepted a large portion of fish and meat from the footman. Lady Flora appeared pale and unwell, though her eyes sparkled with her usual guile.

Lady Flora dismissed the footmen after they'd served Alec, waiting until they pulled the doors closed behind them before she spoke.

"Mrs. Reynolds told me all," she said as she traced patterns in the butter sauce with her fork. "I agree with her that you must cease dilly-dallying about Celia and bring her under your power."

"I'll not be harming the lass," Alec said quickly, his irritation rising. "She's been through too much for that."

Lady Flora sniffed. Her eyes were strangely pink, her face puffy, which explained why she hadn't gone out. She never left the house unless she was the picture of beauty.

"Celia is resilient," Lady Flora said. "And I did not mean she should be harmed. She has kindness in her—" She broke off and swallowed. "You are quite wealthy, are you not? If you make her your mistress, you could arrange for her to paint leisurely away at a seaside spa for the rest of her life, out of reach of her foul family. How far are you willing to go?"

Alec recalled the ghostly fog surrounding the abandoned house in the country, the rain staining the carriage windows like tears. He thought of Will Mackenzie's sunny smile as he beguiled with one breath and bested you in the next. Was Will in that house, or another like it, waiting to face execution? His smile would be gone, his charm extinguished.

Alec had already resolved that his father would not have to face losing another son. He and Mal would make bloody certain of that.

"As far as I need to," Alec said grimly.

Lady Flora gave him a decided nod. "Good. I have an idea. But you must follow it to the letter. Agreed?"

The shot that had killed Duncan rang in Alec's mind, as did his father's broken voice when he'd looked at Alec moments later and called him by the name of his dead twin.

"Aye," Alec answered, his heart burning. "I'm agreed."

CHAPTER 13

*C*elia returned to Lady Flora's in eager anticipation the next morning.

"Is Lady Flora well?" she asked Rivers as a footman took her cloak and another departed upstairs with the portfolio.

Rivers gave her a nod. His unflappable demeanor had returned, but his eyes held gratitude. "She has recovered. She is breakfasting with Mrs. Reynolds but asked not to be disturbed."

"Ah, it does sound as though she is better. Thank you, Rivers."

Rivers bowed, his evident concern for Lady Flora touching. Lady Flora was a difficult woman, but Celia was glad to see she engendered affection and compassion in Rivers and Mrs. Reynolds at least. It would be horrible to be completely unloved.

Celia's heart beat faster as she made her way to the studio, her anticipation of seeing Alec humming through her. She wanted to make certain he was safe, ask what he'd been doing yesterday, and whether he'd been hiding from the soldiers.

He'd been gone from the house a long time, returning last

evening after dark. Celia knew this because she'd been watching across the square, craning her head to study every carriage that so much as paused near Lady Flora's house. She'd seen Mrs. Reynolds alight a little after eight o'clock, followed by a tall, cloaked and hatted man, difficult to distinguish in the distance, but she'd known it was Alec.

Mostly, Celia simply wanted to see him. To hear him rumble *lass* in his warm accent, to feel the vibration of his laughter, to bathe in his quick smile.

Alec was in the studio when she, breathless from her climb, entered it. Her portfolio was open on the table, and Alec, his back to her, leafed through the pages within.

"I see you carried on with the landscape," he said without turning. "Good. We'll see if we can finish roughing it in today."

Celia went around the table to face him across it. She sent him a shy smile, wondering if he meant to ply her with kisses while they worked.

She hadn't been able to stop thinking about his kisses, his mouth a place of heat, his hands strong on her body. She hadn't understood how fire could rise through her at the touch of a man's mouth, how the places of herself she'd never thought much about could ache for him.

He looked up at her, and Celia froze, chilled as though she stood in a winter breeze.

Alec's eyes were hard, the golden color without warmth. His expression was stiff, closed off, forbidding. His affability had gone, a cold man standing in his place.

"What has happened?" Celia asked in alarm.

Alec shook his head, forcing a quick smile that had no warmth in it. "Nothing, lass." He bent over the drawing, his shoulders rigid as he studied it. "It needs work—but I think when we are finished, you'll have something to be proud of."

Celia curled her fingers against her skirts, her eyes burning.

He was shutting her out. She was familiar enough with the tactic to recognize it—she'd seen her mother subtly and then blatantly cut people when they didn't respond to the subtlety.

Whatever camaraderie she'd begun to form with Alec he'd shut off, like pinching out a candle flame. And it had to do with wherever he'd gone with Mrs. Reynolds yesterday, whatever they'd done.

Her throat tightened. She'd been a fool to think she could form a friendship with this man, but his kisses had awakened something in her she could not dismiss.

She swallowed and tried to breathe. Alec lifted a pencil and handed it to her. His eyes were empty, blank, with a hint of warning that she should accept that he was no longer interested in charming her.

Celia took the pencil with stiff fingers, willing herself not to tremble. If she'd inherited anything from her mother it was pride—she'd never let this man know how close she'd come to making a fool of herself over him. If the kisses meant nothing to him then she would make sure he believed they meant nothing to her.

She forced herself to concentrate on the drawing, to shut out the world and focus on the task, though she couldn't quite with the scent of Alec so close as he advised her on lines and shading.

When the clock struck nine with its muted chimes, Alec straightened. "A little more work with the preliminary drawing, then we'll transfer it to a canvas and learn a bit about color." He cast his glance over her gown, but she knew he saw only the charcoal gray velvet, not Celia within it. "I'll have Rivers find you a smock to protect your clothes while ye learn to mix paint. Your father can provide you assistants for that, but it's best to mix your own at first. Ye get a feel for the colors and the texture of the paint, how it responds under your hands." For a moment, the spark returned to Alec's eyes, his passion for creating art unfeigned. It vanished as quickly. "Off ye go, lass. We're finished for today."

"You missed my lesson yesterday," Celia said, laying the sketches from the camera obscura into her portfolio.

Alec nodded without guilt. "I had a few errands to attend to."

Celia ought to accept this, quietly place her pencil back into its case, and hurry away, saying nothing. Instead she pinched her lips together, drew upon her courage, and looked him in the eye.

"You were gone all day, with Mrs. Reynolds. I saw you return—I can see the house from my chamber window."

Alec's look of wariness reemerged. "Errands, that is all."

"You are lying." Celia lifted her chin. "I will not demand to know what you were about and what has happened to make you angry, but please do me the courtesy of not lying to me. If you wish to cease the lessons, I am certain my mother can find another tutor. Good day, Mr. Finn."

She stalked for the door, ready to exit with her dignity intact, but Alec moved swiftly to stop her.

"We're not ceasing the lessons." Alec's eyes were no less flinty, but the intensity returned, and he spoke rapidly. "I can't tell ye where I was yesterday, and it's my business, but I don't want ye gone. Ye have to come here tomorrow, as usual. Understand?"

Celia didn't, but she caught the adamance in his voice. Something was very wrong.

"I am learning much from you," Celia said with a coolness to match Lady Flora at her most haughty. "Therefore, I would like to continue the lessons. But you really must stay out of pubs and not waylay aristocrats in the park. I will not ask you directly if you beat upon Lord Harrenton, because I do not wish you to have to lie. Soldiers came here to search the house yesterday for the culprits. Quite a mercy you were not here."

Alec flushed. "That it was. And no, lass, I did not put my hands on the marquess."

His words rang of truth, but not the entire truth. Blast the man. He stirred Celia's anger and curiosity in the same measure.

She gave him a nod. "Just so we understand each other. I should depart, Mr. Finn, lest you miss your next appointment."

Alec didn't move. "Ye don't understand me at all." His voice was low, harsh. "But ye can trust me. Believe that." He took a step closer to her. "When those around ye are making your world hell, ye can trust *me*. Promise me you'll remember that."

Celia listened in bewilderment, her lips parting. "Of course," she said with difficulty.

Alec shook his head. "No. I need ye to *promise*. When everything seems at its worst, ye put your trust in me."

He fixed her with a fiery stare, as though her answer was very important. Celia swallowed. "I promise," she said.

"Good."

The one word, spoken in broad Scots, rang through the room. He stood motionless, fingers of one hand resting on his thigh-hugging breeches.

Celia drew a breath, ducked around his unmoving body, and scuttled out. Leaving the warmth of him was difficult, and her breath was ragged as she scrambled down the stairs, snatched her cloak from the waiting footman, and ran out into the rain to climb into the chair.

She had no idea why Alec had made her promise to trust him, but the words, his gaze, the timbre of his voice, had all declared he was a rock she could hold on to. Celia certainly hoped that if it came to it, that rock would not crumble to dust under her touch.

∼

FOR THE NEXT FEW DAYS, CELIA ATTENDED HER DRAWING lessons at eight o'clock on the dot and left again at the stroke of nine. Alec never referred to their discussion about trust and hell, or about his outings, the soldiers, Lord Harrenton, or anything but the picture of London he was helping Celia create.

If not for the undercurrent of tension in Alec, and indeed the entire house, Celia would have enjoyed the instruction. She learned how shadows could be made with only a few lines, altering the entire character of the drawing. How distant objects could be suggested and yet look precise, how to project a grid to the vanishing point yet not make it obvious.

On the third day Alec taught her how to mix paints. It was smelly and messy, the room filled with the sharp odors of linseed oil, beeswax, and the metals in the crushed pigments Alec lay out in mounds on the board.

With a large smock over her gown and her sleeves pushed well out of the way, Celia worked melted wax into the oil and then the pigment, scraping and mixing. After that she'd roll a round glass pestle-like tool Alec called a muller over the paint until it was smooth and glistening. They made burnt umber first, a color Alec said would lay the foundation for the London painting.

He scraped the finished paint into a glass bottle, as the lesson was over, and told her they'd begin transferring her final drawing to the canvas the next day, and begin laying on paint after that.

Celia left, excited, pushing aside her misgivings about Alec and the uneasiness she sensed whenever she walked into Lady Flora's house these days.

Alec had kept himself distant during the lessons, no more flirtation or kissing. The more his bruises and cuts from his fight faded, the more he drew away from Celia. His tension was like a bowstring, one stretched so tight there was an even chance it would snap rather than release its arrow.

There was something about art, however, that cut through Celia's troubled thoughts and became a reality of its own. She could float in the bubble of creation, no matter how difficult it was to make the picture come out to her satisfaction. She even enjoyed the scents and physical sensation of mixing the paint. Alec had been right—she'd *felt* the paint come together, the different textures melding to become a puddle of vibrant color.

Later that afternoon, Celia's anticipation died abruptly when she entered her chamber to find her mother standing over her portfolio, turning the pages within.

"Mama," she said, startled. "I mean, Your Grace."

The duchess did not look at her. "*This* is what you have been doing at Lady Flora's?" She pointed to the master drawing Celia had finished under Alec's tutelage, based on the five sketches she had done using the camera obscura, each from a slightly different position.

"Yes." Celia's enthusiasm bubbled up. "We will start painting very soon. Al— Mr. Finn has obtained quite a large canvas for it, and says it will be like Signor Canaletto's paintings."

"*Mr. Finn* says?" The duchess snorted. "A trumped-up Irishman claiming to know about great painting is like a fish jumping off the plate and explaining how to sauce itself. You are to be learning portrait painting, Celia. Not scribbling pictures of a city anyone can see looking out their windows."

"We *will* do portraits," Celia said, her breath coming fast. "Mr. Finn says I have a talent for landscape that he would hate to see wasted. And I do need to work on faces—though he says I'm good at noses."

The duchess listened to her babbling with a look of exaggerated patience. "That is excellent, I am certain. Let me remind you, daughter, that I allowed this mad idea of Lady Flora's so that you could acquire a useful skill, not to indulge your strange interest in sketching views of London. Your landscapes will never hang alongside Signor Canaletto or Monsieur Lorrain, so let us put a stop to that nonsense at once."

The duchess caught up the pages of the London drawings and began to tear them to shreds.

CHAPTER 14

*C*elia let out a strangled cry as the duchess tore the drawings several more times and hurled the pages to the carpet.

"Mama!" Celia choked out, forgetting she was to address her mother by her title. "How could you?"

Her days of frenzied work, of Alec bringing forth a new world for her, showing her how to translate what she saw onto blank paper, gone in the space of a moment. Alec had opened her eyes to what was possible, and though Celia did not believe she'd achieve the greatness of famous painters, she could at least create something that pleased.

Tears flooded her eyes, and she clutched a chair to stay on her feet. "How *could* you?"

"Do not scold me, Celia. You are an ungrateful and disobedient child, spoilt and indulged by your father. There will be no more drawing lessons. Your uncle Perry and I have discussed what is to be done with you, and we still believe marriage is your best recourse."

"Marriage …" Celia could barely speak the word, could

scarcely breathe. Her heart was breaking, her work torn and trampled by the duchess's high-heeled slippers.

"You took yourself well off the marriage mart by refusing the marquess," the duchess went on. "You are now considered a light skirt, but as the months have gone by, and no child has come of it, other gentlemen not so fastidious will now consider you. Your husband will never trust you, I'm afraid, but if you are obedient and give him an heir, he will perhaps forgive your faults."

Celia's anger flared through her grief. Throughout her childhood, Celia often wondered what she'd done to make her mother dislike her, but in a sudden flash, she realized she'd done nothing at all. Her mother was a single-minded, ambitious woman who did not see Celia as a person, but as a thing to be used to further those ambitions. The duchess had married for the same reason, having no use for the duke once she'd made him her husband and borne two children by him.

"And who is this paragon who will accept me with all my faults?" Celia demanded.

"Keep a civil tongue, daughter. He is not a marquess but the brother of one. A quiet young man who will not amount to much, but at least he has good connections and has said he is willing to marry you. He is James Spencer, younger brother of the Marquess of Ellesmere."

Celia had met this young man once, a few years ago, when the current Lord Ellesmere, great-nephew of Lady Flora's husband, had come up to London to go over some business or other with Lady Flora. Lady Flora had invited the duke and duchess for supper with Ellesmere and his brother, and Celia and Edward had come with them.

Celia remembered a rather vapid young man two years older than herself, with limp clothes, a long, pale face, and teeth already rotting. Rumor had it he was a sodomite, although rumor said that about any gentleman who was not well liked and hadn't yet married.

Younger sons of aristocrats often went into politics or the military, but James Spencer seemed to do not much of anything. He was languid and lazy, and one of the most unprepossessing gentlemen Celia had ever met.

"You cannot mean me to marry *him* ..." Celia's breath went out of her, blackness closing in. Her stays were far too tight, her stomacher cutting into her abdomen.

"Turning up your nose again, are you?" The duchess sniffed. "Haughty creature. Are marquesses and their families beneath your notice? Lady Flora herself proposed the match. Perhaps she is so fond of you that she wishes to call you niece."

"Lady Flora." Celia wheezed the name, fear piling on top of dismay.

"She agrees you are a handful. James lives with Ellesmere on their estate in Hampshire. You will not be a hostess there, of course, as Ellesmere is married, but I'm certain you will be of some use to Lady Ellesmere as her sister-in-law."

Celia could form no more words. Lady Flora intensely disliked the current Lord Ellesmere—which was not surprising, as she had intensely disliked the former one, her own husband. That Lady Flora would believe his brother would make a good match for Celia ... Either James Spencer had much changed since that supper, or Lady Flora had run mad, or else she was setting up this marriage as some machination of her own.

Celia had the sudden urge to discuss the matter with Alec. To pour her troubles out on him, to beg for his advice. To feel his hand on her arm, to hear him rumble, "Ah, poor lass."

But Alec had troubles of his own—he would hardly wish to listen to hers, would he? What would the sorrow of a young gentlewoman coerced into a loveless marriage be to a man far from his home and family, terrified of speaking his own name?

Through the fog in Celia's mind came Alec's quiet but emphatic words from a few days before, when he'd momentarily dropped his cold distance.

When those around ye are making your world hell, ye can trust me. Promise me you'll remember that.

Celia had answered, *I promise.*

Had he known of Lady Flora's and her mother's plans? Had he been warning her?

"Your father has already approached Ellesmere about settlements," the duchess said. "The wedding will be quiet, a special license here at home, and then you will be off to Hampshire. We will take you out into the world a bit to get people used to seeing you again while we make preparations, but you must not expect to be too much in society once you are married."

No, Celia was to rusticate in the country, the family embarrassment shunted aside. "Papa agrees to this match?" she asked in incredulity.

"He sees that it will be best. He indulges you too much, as I say. It will be good for the pair of you to have you out of his influence."

Her mother had bullied her father into it, she meant. The room spun, and Celia had to sit down, though she was never allowed to sit while the duchess stood.

"No, I will not …"

The duchess's lip curled. "Do *not* begin about what you will and will not do. I hope Lord James will cure you of this obstinacy with the back of his hand. If he does not, Ellesmere will. Now, tomorrow night you will accompany me and Lady Flora to the Spring Gardens at Vauxhall. We will go in fancy dress—this will be one of Lady Flora's extravagant outings, and you must be paraded about as Lord James Spencer's betrothed. Have your maid fix you a costume—one of the commedia dell'arte—

Pierette, say, not one so ostentatious as Columbine. Do not speak to me again until then."

So ending her speech, the duchess swung around and strode out of the room. She did not bother to slam the door—a footman closed it decorously behind her.

Celia slid from the chair to the floor. She groped for the torn drawings, the lines and curves she'd painstakingly drawn now forlorn scraps.

No more tears would come. Her eyes burned, her grief twisting inside as she gazed upon the destruction of work she'd labored over for the last week. Celia had poured her heart into the drawing of London, and Alec's hand was in it—it was art they had created together.

As Celia gathered the fragments and held them close another realization poured over her. It wasn't simply the picture she mourned, but what it represented—the hours she'd stood close to Alec, his hand brushing hers as he showed her how to bring the drawing to life, his breath on her skin as he scrutinized her strokes.

He'd been as caught up in the creation as she had been. Time had at once stood still and flown by, magical moments of Alec and Celia working side-by-side, both of them excited about the vista of London unfolding before their eyes.

The duchess had destroyed that beautiful time with each rip of the paper.

Celia could never marry Lord James Spencer. Even if the young man had been a paragon of gentlemanliness, Celia could not pledge her heart, her loyalty, to him. It would be a lie, through and through. She would live in misery, and it would be unfair to James, as unpalatable as he was.

But would she have a choice? Her father must have decided that giving in to the duchess was the quickest way to peace. Celia had watched him give way to her all his life—it was unlikely he'd cease now, no matter how much he sympathized with Celia. And perhaps her father had been convinced that marriage to the brother of a marquess would be better for Celia than no marriage at all.

When those around ye are making your world hell, ye can trust me.

Celia gathered up the pieces of the drawing. She couldn't save it, but perhaps she could save herself. She'd seek out Alec and pour out her tale. Even if he could do nothing to help her, he might have some advice, or at the very least, he'd comfort her in his low, rumbling tones that made her want to stand close to him and simply listen.

She'd dress up and go to Lady Flora's gathering and be sweet as honey, coercing an entry into Lady Flora's house. If the lessons were at an end, she couldn't simply turn up—she'd have to plan a way for Lady Flora to invite her so that she could speak with Alec alone.

Celia restored her portfolio the best she could and lugged it herself out of the room and up the stairs. Her determination was high, but her heart was lead in her chest.

The shaft of light that had kept her life bearable these last days had been suddenly and inexorably extinguished.

ALEC CLIMBED INTO LADY FLORA'S CARRIAGE THE NEXT NIGHT TO find himself facing a lady in a diamond-patterned dress of bright green, red, and black, with a lace ruff at her neck, jewels glittering on the fabric. A tricorn hat rested on Lady Flora's fair hair, and she held a black mask in her gloved hand. Next to her was Mrs. Reynolds in more subdued colors but with the same kind of lace ruff, tricorn hat, and mask.

Lady Flora took in Alec's plain breeches, frock coat, boots, and hatless hair with disapproval. "You are supposed to be in costume."

The coach jerked forward, wheels bumping over cobbles on its way out of the square.

Alec lifted the flap on the pack he'd set next to him, revealing a fold of white velvet trimmed with black. "I'll not ride through London dressed as a clown. Ye have to take me as I am for now."

Lady Flora's eyes tightened in annoyance. She had laid plans, and she didn't like any alteration to said plans. "Make certain you are ready in time. It would never do for Celia to go off with the wrong Pierrot."

Mrs. Reynolds put a soothing hand on her arm. "I will steer her right."

Lady Flora let out a sigh, but sank back into the cushions as the carriage moved down South Audley Street to Piccadilly. From there they wended their way through St. James's to Charing Cross with its pillory in the center, empty tonight. Whitehall took them farther south, past palaces full of British government ministers and the admiralty who would have collective apoplexy if they knew a rebel Highlander rolled in a comfortable carriage through their midst.

Whitehall petered out into meandering streets full of people enjoying drink, cock fights, and general laziness. A few of these denizens ran after the coach to beat on it and demand coin. Lady Flora's coachman snarled at them and flicked his whip menacingly.

The carriage emerged unscathed to Mill Bank where the coachman halted at stairs leading to the river. Footmen who'd clung to the back of the coach jumped down to assist Mrs. Reynolds and Lady Flora, and Alec lent his hand to help them into the hired barge that awaited them at the bottom of the stairs.

The barge was hung with paper lanterns for the occasion, its benches cushioned with velvet. Lady Flora and Mrs. Reynolds settled in, their masses of skirts leaving little room for Alec. He shoved fabric aside with his boot as he sat, chuckling when Lady Flora scolded. The end of this night would work to Alec's satisfaction, and he decided to push aside his anger and enjoy the absurdity.

The river didn't stink quite as much here as it did farther downstream, but even so Alec put his gloved hand to his mouth as the water slapped their barge. Lady Flora and Mrs. Reynolds lifted pomander balls to their noses, the scent of spice and dried oranges drifting through the fetid air. The waterman, used to the stench, rowed on, heading the barge to the opposite bank.

At the stairs on the Lambeth side of the river, Alec helped Mrs. Reynolds and Lady Flora from the barge. At the top of the steps another coach waited, arranged by Lady Flora to take them the short distance to the Spring Gardens.

The gardens at Vauxhall had been popular for some time now—Alec had seen them on a London visit before the Jacobite Uprising had made his life hell. He led the ladies through an open gate in a thick wall, where an acrobat in a backbend scuttled past to encourage them inside.

A long avenue took them to the center of the gardens, where a silken tent in the Turkish style held food, drink, and musicians within its red and black striped walls. More walks led from the central area, some lined with trees, others with elegant colonnades containing marble statues in arched niches, directing visitors down a grand promenade.

The Spring Gardens were free to enter, and the paths were already full. The wine, ale, and food within had to be purchased, but anyone in London could stroll in and enjoy the open garden not far from the stuffy city.

Nature under control. This was the philosophy of English gardeners of the day, especially Lancelot Brown, who busily removed real nature so he could carve landscapes around great houses, and hauled away rocks and woods to put in sweeping parks. Alec had studied his drawings and those of Brown's colleagues to help spark his ideas for the gardens at Kilmorgan Malcolm had asked him to design.

Mal had already laid out the groundwork for a grand house that would take the place of the now-ruined castle. He'd begun having stones quarried when the Jacobite rebellion had disrupted their lives and driven them into exile. Mal, with his characteristic stubbornness, carried on planning the house from afar, urging Alec to continue with his schematics for the garden. The Runt would have his way in the end, Alec was certain. Mal had a knack for it.

Lady Flora's masked guests quickly surrounded her, wishing to show they were intimates of one of the most interesting women in London. Only Mrs. Reynolds saw Alec slip away into the darkness, watching him go without a nod.

CELIA'S PLAN TO SPEAK TO LADY FLORA ABOUT CALLING UPON HER evaporated when she beheld the crush that surrounded her and Mrs. Reynolds. Lady Flora must have invited every single person in her social circle tonight—Celia had never seen so many costumes from the commedia dell'arte in one place in her life.

Lady Flora was Columbine, the lover of Harlequin and as full of schemes and japes as he. There were a quite a number of Harlequins trying to sidle next to her. Many older gentlemen came as Punchinello, each with a different sized hump on their backs. A few ladies were dressed as Pierette, as Celia was, in white velvet gowns trimmed with black braid and pompons. Many of the women wore dominos—a short silk cloak with a hood and a mask that covered the eyes.

Celia's mother staunchly wore no costume but had consented to a domino. Celia wore a black mask and hat, as anonymous as the others.

Celia would have been excited to be at such a gathering earlier this year, at the height of the Season. She'd have fallen in with her friends, whispering and laughing with them about nonsense, thrilling when a handsome gentleman asked to escort or dance with one of them.

Now she watched as an outsider. Most of her friends had already married, or at least were engaged and had returned to their father's estates. Celia hadn't been *entirely* shunned since the Disaster—her parents were far too powerful for society to risk cutting their daughter completely—but she was avoided and talked about.

Celia wasn't as bothered about society's opinion of her tonight, because her thoughts were all for Alec. She found herself looking for him—had he persuaded Lady Flora to bring him along? Was he even now in a Harlequin costume, lingering at the edges of Flora's crowd?

None of the Harlequins seemed right for him—some of the gentlemen had good physiques but not Alec's height. No, dressing up and hovering around Lady Flora wasn't right for Alec. He must be at home with his daughter, or possibly in the studio alone, drawing or painting.

She imagined him in his linen shirt which gaped open at the neck, his eyes focusing as he leaned to the easel to paint something beautiful. He'd absently wipe his cheek, leaving a streak of color on it. Celia's heart gave a painful throb.

"There he is," her mother said into her ear.

Celia jumped, and then sucked in a breath, knowing her

mother could not possibly mean Alec. "Who?" Her voice cracked.

"Your brother, of course. Edward. There."

Celia turned in confusion to where the duchess pointed, the image of Alec dissolving. "How can Edward be here? He's in France with his regiment."

Her mother heaved a sigh worthy of Lady Flora. "Well, now he is *here*. He is granted leave once in a while. He wishes to speak to you, Lord knows why."

Celia hadn't seen Edward since the Disaster, when he'd made it clear he thought her a fool. She'd hoped one day she could make him see her side of things, and they'd be friends again.

She rose on tiptoes to peer eagerly over the heads of the crowd. "Where?"

"Down that walk. He is dressed as Pierrot. Go on—be quick about it."

The duchess pushed Celia in the direction of a tree-lined walk. Not many lanterns hung there, and deep shadows pocketed the way. But if Edward had come, wishing to speak to Celia away from Lady Flora's crush, she'd brave the darkness.

She gathered her velvet skirts and hurried down the path.

When the first shadow closed over her, Celia halted, common sense cutting into her excitement. Why on earth would her mother arrange a meeting between the disgraced Celia and her darling Edward? If Edward wanted to speak to Celia, he'd simply come to the house, or have accompanied them to the gardens. Why don a costume and skulk about in a dark lane? There were easier ways of meeting with her.

Her mother was up to something, wasn't she? The man waiting would not be Edward, but Lord James, and Celia would be caught alone in the dark with him by Lady Flora and all her friends. Once again, Celia would be forced to either agree to marry a gentleman or let herself be shamed.

Being found in yet another man's embrace would clinch the opinion that she was a wanton harlot. Only marriage would save her from being completely ostracized this time.

In rage, Celia swung back. She'd thwart the duchess's scheme and give her a scathing dressing down, never mind her upbringing to honor her parents. Her mother needed to learn a few things about honor.

A gloved hand came out of a black shadow and dragged her from the path. Celia drew a breath to scream, but another hand pressed over her mouth, and a voice sounded in her ear.

"Stop squirming, blasted woman."

CHAPTER 15

*C*elia ceased struggling as Alec half dragged her more deeply under the trees. He wore a kilt belted at his waist, and his coat was red, that of a British soldier—most puzzling. A black tam rested on his head, a dark ribbon fluttering to his neck.

"I thought tartan was banned," was the first thing out of Celia's mouth.

"Not in the regiments," Alec said, words clipped. "I borrowed this from a friend. It's a costume, ye ken?"

Celia kenned nothing at the moment. "My mother is busy trying to disgrace me again. Mr. ... Finn ... will you escort me home? I'd like to speak to you."

"No."

She blinked. "I beg your ..."

Alec tightened his grasp on her arm and guided her to a narrower walk, plunging them into darkness.

"Home won't be safe for ye. I'm pulling ye out of this game. "

Celia inwardly cursed her high-heeled satin slippers, beautiful to look at, horrible to walk in, especially when she had to move swiftly to keep up with the long-legged Alec. "Where else can I go? If you take me to any of my friends, they'll simply send me back to my mother. They'll regard it their duty."

Alec halted and turned her to face him. "I asked you to trust me, aye?"

"And I have decided to. Rather against my common sense, but I feel you *can* be trusted Mr. ... Oh dear, I don't even know your real name."

"Ye flatter me, but it's time for me to decide whether I can trust *you*. You've done me well not rushing home and telling your father a Highlander had swooped down on Mayfair, but will you continue to keep quiet? I want to help ye, but I can't at the expense of my family, or my own life. I have a daughter to look after."

"I would never betray you." Celia looked up at him through her mask, the black silk cool against her cheeks. "I have met cruel men, and you are not one."

"Tell my brothers that." Alec cupped her cheek, his leather glove warm. "If I trust you, and you trust me, we'll go from here and be well out of it. You'll be safe, and do what ye like, and be happy."

Celia leaned into his touch. "Where is this paradise you will lead me to? It sounds impossible."

"I don't know about paradise, but you'll be looked after." Alec brushed a kiss to her lips, stroked his thumb across the mask. "Now let's be off before your mum tries t' get ye married to the Chancellor of the Exchequer and the Archbishop of Canterbury all at the same time."

"You know about her wanting to marry me off to Lord James Spencer?" Celia asked as Alec took her hand and towed her along. "He was waiting for me down that walk in a Pierrot costume, I believe."

"Aye, he was—probably still is. I was to lie in wait down

another lane in the same costume, and Lady Flora was to direct ye to me. Your mum would think the correct man dragged ye off, while it was *me* absconding with ye instead."

"Lady Flora wasn't anywhere near me." Celia quickened her steps, wincing as her shoes slipped and slid. "And you are not dressed as Pierrot."

Alec rumbled a laugh. "Can ye see me tramping about in baggy white breeches with bobbles on m' tunic? I know Flora was laughing about that—in her own way. One of my soldier friends lent me his spare uniform in case I needed it, and I decided to wear it instead. Careful, now."

The path narrowed to nothing, and mud sucked at Celia's shoes. The lane ended in a gate, beyond which was a moonlit field. A carriage waited there, the horses' breaths steaming in the night air. The coach was unmarked, no crest on the door.

Alec opened the gate with ease. Celia was not surprised it would be unlocked—very little about Alec surprised her anymore. A man lounging on the coach's back step hopped down, looming in the moonlit mist like a hunched giant.

Celia took a startled step back, and Alec caught her in his strong grip. The man looked like nothing more than a highwayman, muffled in a greatcoat and hat, his face craggy, one eye covered with a patch. Gray hair straggled from under the hat, and he glared at them both with his single eye.

"All right, then, Padruig?" Alec asked this apparition.

"Aye." The one word was growled and gravelly. Padruig wrenched open the coach door and held out his hand to Celia.

"Don't be afraid." Alec hooked his arm around Celia's waist and half lifted, half boosted her into the coach. "He's the kind one of the pair. Where is your cutthroat partner?"

Padruig didn't look offended that Celia didn't take his hand, only backed out of the way. "Waiting." he grunted. "Won't wait forever."

Celia landed on a soft seat, cushions sliding as she righted herself. Alec heaved himself inside, taking the seat facing her.

"No, he'll run off into the night with my money," Alec said to Padruig as he pulled the door shut. "That's why I pay him only half in advance. A savings if he absconds with it." He knocked on the roof, signaling the coachman.

The coachman clucked to the horses, and the vehicle jerked forward. Padruig waited until the carriage passed him, then it listed as he climbed onto the back.

"Who is he?" Celia asked in amazement.

Alec shrugged. "A useful man. He and Gair stayed well out of the thick of the Uprising and so aren't wanted men. At least not for being Jacobites—they're no doubt wanted for many other crimes. They're friends of my brother Mal's. You'll find that most people the length of England and Scotland are friends of Mal's. He's a frightening lad, is the Runt."

"Runt? Is he so very small?" Nervous laughter threatened to well up inside her. Celia couldn't imagine anyone related to the tall, broad-shouldered Alec to be slight.

"Not these days. We called him that when he was a wee lad and always in mischief. He's still in mischief but not so wee any longer." The warmth that entered Alec's voice when he spoke of his brothers was palpable.

At one time, Celia had been as close to her brother. No wonder her mother had chosen to pretend it was Edward who waited for her—she'd used Celia's affection and need to reconcile with him to manipulate her. When Celia's stunned numbness wore off, she'd be furious.

"Am I allowed to inquire as to where we are going?" she asked Alec. "Is it to meet this Gair?"

"In good time. First I have an errand or two."

"Well, I thank you for retrieving me and preventing a second

Disaster, in any case." Celia peered out the window into the lowering fog, but the only thing she could discern was that they were still south of the river. "Do I understand this mad scheme aright? That Lady Flora's purpose was to have you abduct me? Which you have, only without wearing the Pierrot costume. Why?"

"She is assisting me," Alec said. "But what she thought *her* plans would accomplish, I don't know."

The coach rocked hard over a rut, and Alec used its momentum to leave his seat and drop next to her. He tugged her skirts from under his thigh, and slid his hand behind her head to untie her mask.

Alec caught the silk as it fell away and then brushed her cheek with its end. "She expects me to take you off and have my way with ye."

Celia's heart beat fast and hard, her skin prickling under his touch. "And are you?"

Trust me. The memory of his words drifted to her, as well as the intensity in his eyes when he'd said them.

"I might be." His voice was quiet. "After a time."

Celia swallowed. "And how would you ravishing me benefit Lady Flora?"

Alec's red-brown brows drew down, his eyes dark gold in the gleam of lantern light. "That I don't know. But you and I are out of the game now. The pawn and the ... what piece am I? ... are off the chessboard."

"The knight," Celia said without hesitation. "The warrior who can threaten a queen."

"The queen is the most powerful piece on the board." Alec shrugged. "I don't have the patience to carry on with the metaphor, so I'll just say ye are well out of it."

He fell silent as they wound through dark streets. Near the bulk of Lambeth Palace, the coachman halted, and Alec assisted

Celia out. He flung a long cloak around her, its woolen folds a welcome warmth.

A fishing boat waited for them, one with peeling paint and the permanent smell of fish, a far cry from the decorated barge Lady Flora had sent to ferry Celia and her mother across to the gardens.

The man who waited to hand Celia into the boat was muffled to his ears, only his dark eyes showing between scarf and hat. Alec steadied her as she stepped into the boat, then leapt down after her, landing with easy grace.

Padruig, who'd descended from the coach with them, rested his hand on the hilt of a long knife that hung from his belt. "I'll fend off pursuit, shall I?"

"There won't be any pursuit," Alec said. "Not for a time. Come with us—I'll need a witness."

Padruig shrugged and stepped into the boat with the effort-lessness of a man long used to embarking watercraft. "I'm t' make sure ye get to Gair. He wants the rest of that fare."

"He has no need to worry." Alec guided Celia into the tiny deckhouse, which cut the chill wind on the river. "But don't kill anyone while you're getting us there. I don't need another mess to clear up."

Padruig followed them in and shut the door, leaving the boats' two sailors outside. "Like that Lowlander?"

"Do you know who did for him?" Alec asked, sitting on a bench before the small stove in the middle of the cabin and holding his hands to the fire's warmth. The cabin was filled with junk—nets, fishing poles, crates, bottles, jugs, sacks, wire, and various things Celia couldn't make out in the shadows.

Padruig folded his arms and leaned against the door, blocking the way in—or out. "He had enemies. Could have been any of them."

"But you know which ones," Alec stated.

"Aye, a few men who thought he knew too much. They'll tell no tales." He flicked a glance to Celia, his one eye glittering. Perhaps he thought he needed to make certain *she'd* tell no tales.

Celia shivered as she let Alec tug her down next to him, though she wasn't certain about the cleanliness of the bench. "Never worry, lass," Alec rumbled. "I'll look after ye now."

Padruig snorted, then a draft blew in as he opened the door and faded outside, slamming it behind him.

Celia leaned into the warmth that was Alec, and he wrapped his arm around her. "I am trying to feel alarm that you are abducting me," she said. "I can't bring myself to. But perhaps I am in shock."

Alec sent her a grin. "That's because I'm not much good at abducting. The Runt is the master. The lass *he* abducted never realized it, and now she's in his house in Paris, busily telling the lot of us what to do while she waits for their babe to be born. Mal's the one for intrigue, as is Will." Pain flickered across his face. "Me, I'm a painter, trying to provide for my daughter and keep the rest of my good-for-nothing family out of trouble."

Celia nestled into him. "Does that mean you *are* abducting me or you aren't?"

"Means I'm giving you the choice." Alec raised her silk-gloved hand and kissed it. "I can take you to my friends, trusted ones, who will keep you safe. Ye'd never have to see me again. Or ..."

"Or I can marry you," Celia said.

CHAPTER 16

*A*lec froze with her hand in his, his eyes fixed on her. His chest rose with his breath, the red coat that was the symbol of his enemies moving.

"Or ye can marry me, I was about to say." The words were a growl. "Give a man a chance to speak."

Celia inhaled damp air, warmed by the tiny stove. "I have a small legacy that can help us live—nothing very grand, but it will feed us, and you can continue to give lessons. My money is in a trust, entirely mine, untouchable by my mother or father …"

Alec stilled her babbling with a finger on her lips. "I'm not doing it for your legacy. I want to keep you from your mum's machinations forever. Even if your dad has me killed for it, you'll be my widow and looked after by my da' and brothers."

Celia kissed his finger. "Don't say things like that. All my life I've watched my mother and her friends, including Lady Flora, use marriage as a weapon, or at least a tool to obtain what they want. I say I turn the tables on them, use it as my own weapon."

Anger flared in Alec's eyes. But of course—Celia had just

declared she'd use him and marriage to him to thwart her enemies. What gentleman wanted to hear a woman say that?

The anger vanished with the suddenness of a slap and Alec burst out laughing. His head went back, and his booming laughter filled the room.

"What a woman!" His eyes glowed with golden fire. "I'll show ye off to my family with pride, I will. Yes, I'll marry ye, lass. To hell with the lot of them."

"Good." Celia stuck out her hand. "Seal the bargain?"

Alec pushed the offered hand aside. "I've a better way to seal it than that."

He scooped her up to him and kissed her with a strength that took her breath away. Celia sank into him, sliding her hands under the warmth of his hair. His tam slid off to fall among the detritus, but Alec didn't seem to notice.

He held Celia against him, his arms firm on her back, his body a bulwark in the dark, a solid rock in the swirling maelstrom of her life. Celia kissed him as the boat listed with the current, the strength of the Thames fighting it.

When Alec raised his head, his eyes were dark in the red glow of the stove, the look in them one of triumph, but also one of pain.

Celia wondered at the pain, but there would be time for them to talk, to understand. She touched his cheek, acknowledging what she'd seen, then she kissed him again, seeking the warmth of his lips. They were in this together now, she tried to convey.

Alec's return kiss acknowledged this and made Celia realize that her journey was just beginning.

∼

ANOTHER CARRIAGE WAITED FOR THEM ON THE NORTH SIDE OF

the Thames, at the top of Temple Stairs. Alec tossed the waterman a pouch that clinked as they disembarked, then he took Padruig aside and spoke to him in a low voice.

Padruig looked none too pleased when they finished, but he gave Alec a nod and trotted off into the darkness.

Alec handed Celia into the carriage. She heard him tell the coachman to take them to High Holborn before he climbed in beside her, and they creaked through crowded London streets, neither speaking, Alec gazing out the window.

The house in High Holborn was squashed between its fellows, rising a long and narrow way upward. Alec stepped down from the carriage before it stopped and plied the brass knocker on the front door until a grudging footman opened it a crack.

"We're expected," Alec told the watery eye that peered out at them.

The footman scowled then opened the door all the way, shoving his wig into place as he stepped back to admit them. Alec lifted Celia down, a flash of her clocked stockings and satin shoes showing under her flurry of white skirts.

Alec led her inside, the footman closing out the wind as he shut the door. The interior of the house was quiet, smelling of beeswax and books. Indeed, books were everywhere—in the foyer, in the hall, left in little piles on the bottom step of the staircase.

"Who lives here?" Celia whispered.

"A bishop," Alec said. "Father of a friend, kind to me whenever my mate brought me home with him from Cambridge."

Some bishops sat in the House of Lords, which meant they'd know Celia's father. She wondered if this one supported or opposed the duke, and if he'd simply send the duke word that his errant daughter had turned up, attempting to elope with a Scotsman.

Celia shook out her white velvet skirts. She'd chosen a path —she would take it and make the best of it. Her mother wasn't the only one in the family with steely determination.

The footman returned and told them to follow him up a flight of stairs and into a large sitting room that overlooked the street.

The chamber he ushered them into was sumptuous yet cozy. An arched marble fireplace dominated the room, this one also full of books. The small mirror above the fireplace reflecting Celia, her black-and-white costume peeping from under the dark cloak. It showed Alec beside her, strong and tall in his red coat and plaid. He wore the kilt with ease, looking far more comfortable in it than he had in any of his threadbare suits. The plaid swirled around his strong legs, brushing the tops of his supple boots.

Celia didn't recognize the man who entered. He was small in stature, like her father, and wore a silver embroidered blue frock coat that belled over velvet breeches. His waistcoat, an ecclesiastical purple, strained itself over his ample belly. He wore, as Celia's brother called it, a dog collar, a stiff white band at his throat. A many-curled wig crowned his head above his puffy face, but his dark eyes were gentle as he held out his hand to Alec.

"Well met, my lord. Ah, is this the young lady? How very charming to meet you, my dear."

Celia curtsied politely to his bow, and the bishop looked them over, clasping his hands as though pleased with them both.

Then he patted his pockets. "Ah, yes, I *do* have the license." He pulled out a thick piece of paper, folded into quarters. "And you will have to sign the register, but I think I can manage to lose it for a time. I am the ubiquitous absentminded clergyman, my lady, apt to set things down and not remember where." His eyes twinkled.

He slid the paper back into his pocket and pointed for them to stand on the carpet facing the fireplace. He then wandered the room for a few minutes until he at last took a book from the middle of a stack on a table and returned to them.

"Now then, my lord, you have a ring?"

"I do." Alec removed a thick gold band from his finger and held it out to the bishop.

Celia wondered at the bishop's continuous use of *my lord*. Perhaps he didn't know exactly how to address a Highlander, who must be the son of what was called a laird. A laird wasn't necessarily an aristocrat though, she'd learned, only a land-holder. But perhaps the bishop was merely trying to be polite.

"Excellent," the man went on. "And a witness? I'm afraid I'm the only one in the house at the moment besides my footman. The wife is visiting Thomas—*his* wife is expecting her third child." He beamed, radiating pride.

Alec grinned at him. "Another bairn, eh? Good for old Thomas. Send him my felicitations. I do have a witness—I believe he's just coming up the stairs."

Celia heard the footman berating someone and a growled reply, and then the door was wrenched open to admit Padruig.

"Stay out of there, you!" The footman tried to grab Padruig, but Padruig easily evaded him.

"It's all right, lad," Alec told him. "I told him to come."

The footman, handsome and haughty as good footmen were to be, sent Padruig a disdainful look then Alec one for having such a servant.

Padruig positioned himself behind Alec, his reflected bulk in the mirror incongruous with the luxury of the room. The footman remained, the second witness, Celia surmised, but positioned himself a long way from Padruig.

"I will keep the ceremony short, as no doubt you are in a hurry." The bishop gave Alec a knowing smile. "Now, my lord—

Wilt thou have this woman to be thy wedded wife? ... Wilt thou love her, comfort her, honor and keep her ... forsaking all others ... So long as ye both shall live?" The bishop finished and looked at Alec expectantly.

Alec's gaze was on Celia. "I will." The words filled the room, and Celia flushed with sudden warmth.

"And you, my lady? Wilt thou have this man—"

"I will," Celia broke in quickly. No need for the bishop to say the words again. She'd made her decision.

The bishop lifted his brows but looked pleased. "Very well. We'll move on to the next bit. You must repeat after me, my lord —*after* I have finished, please. *I*—erm—what is your full name, my lord?"

Alec's gaze went to Celia's in the mirror.

"Alec William Mackenzie," he said in a ringing voice.

CHAPTER 17

*M*ackenzie.

Celia gaped at him. She knew that name, and not because half the clan had risen to fight for Bonnie Prince Charlie.

Her mother had her finger on every title and family tree of every peerage in England, Scotland, and Ireland. One never knew when such a person might be useful to her.

There was a Mackenzie that had long ago been awarded the title of Duke of Kilmorgan. The current duke had been one of the handful of Scots selected to attend Parliament in England, after the Act of Union thirty years ago had dissolved the Scots' own parliament.

That duke had been killed, and all his sons with him at Culloden. *Served them right,* her mother had declared with a sniff. *Fools, the whole lot of them.*

The bishop called Alec *my lord.* Not because he was confused about Scottish titles but because Alec, as the son of a duke, would be Lord Alec Mackenzie.

Alec gazed down at her, his tawny eyes glittering. He waited, as though expecting her to shriek, flee the room, or perhaps fall over in a dead swoon.

Celia swallowed hard. The bishop, his eyes on his book, serenely continued, "I, Alec William Mackenzie, take thee ..."

Alec's voice filled the room. " ... Take thee, Celia, to have and to hold from this day forward, for better for worse ... according to God's holy ordinance. And therefore I plight thee my troth."

Troth, the old word for *truth*. It stood for loyalty and honor, binding them with its simple power.

"Now, my lady—erm." The bishop patted his pocket as though ready to consult the license for her name. Would her correct one be there? She'd never told it to Alec.

"Celia Margaret Elizabeth." Her voice was scratched and cracking, nowhere near Alec's firm tones.

"I, Celia Margaret Elizabeth," the bishop went on. "Take thee, Alec, to have and to hold ..."

The bishop carried on, but Celia barely heard him. She was seeing Alec for the first time, every arrogant line of him, the son of a Highland duke, emerging from the shell of the man he'd pretended to be.

But no, he'd never fit as Mr. Finn, poor but talented artist. He was as wrong for that part as he would have been in the costume of Pierrot Lady Flora had expected him to wear tonight. *This* was what Alec was, a Highlander of ancient lineage, the same sort of man as those who'd launched themselves at the British lines at Prestonpans and sent English soldiers fleeing in terror.

Celia realized the bishop had ceased speaking and was looking at her expectantly.

Alec's lips twitched, the hard arrogance softening. He was also the man she'd found protectively holding his child as he slept, his bare and vulnerable foot protruding from his nightshirt.

Celia gulped. "I, Celia Margaret Elizabeth, take thee, Alec ..." Her voice grew stronger as the words tumbled out. "And therefore I plight thee *my* troth."

"And now the ring." The bishop, laid Alec's ring on his book to say the blessing over it, quietly continuing the ceremony he must have read dozens of times in his life.

The band was large and gold, with a square-cut diamond in its center. Celia had never seen Alec wear it before. Her fingers trembled as he lifted it then took her hand, his fingertips brushing the inside of her wrist.

"With this ring, I thee wed." Alec's voice went soft, a bare touch of sound. "With my body, I thee worship, and with all my worldly goods, I thee endow."

He eased the ring onto her middle finger, the only one it would fit. "In the name of the Father, Son, and Holy Ghost," Alec finished. "Amen."

"Amen," Celia murmured, and heard the final word echoed by the footman's whisper and Padruig's growl.

Amen. So be it.

Celia was married.

~

ALEC WONDERED WHAT IT WOULD BE LIKE TO WED IN THE USUAL way, with church and family, a large meal afterward, and then days alone with his bride. He reasoned he would never find out, because this was the last time he intended to be married.

The carriage he'd hired waited outside, the coachman hunkered near the horses for warmth. He drank brandy for even more warmth, which didn't reassure Alec, but they weren't going far.

"All done?" he asked Padruig.

"Aye." Padruig said nothing more, only climbed to the back of the coach.

Alec had given Padruig two sets of instructions, only one to be followed depending on how events unfolded. He knew Padruig would have chosen the correct one once Alec sent him off. The man was no fool, and besides, he liked to be paid.

Alec settled Celia in the coach before he swung in and took the seat opposite hers. Celia held on her lap a parcel the bishop had given her—cakes and bread, which had been left for his supper, but he claimed he had more than he could eat. He'd always been a thoughtful old duffer, not as absentminded as he let on. He'd keep the secret of their marriage, Alec had no doubt.

Celia regarded Alec calmly as the carriage pulled forward, her brown-green eyes assessing. She looked him over as though seeing him for the first time, only now he was her lawful husband, before God and in the eyes of the laws of Great Britain.

"Your father is the Duke of Kilmorgan," she said.

Her voice was steady, but she fidgeted with the ring, her hand resting on the parcel.

"Not my fault." Alec said, trying to sound indifferent. "My dad sired six sons, God rest my poor, dear mum. I happen to be one of them, one above the youngest."

"You told me you were a ghost." Her gaze pinned him. "Now I know what you meant. The Duke of Kilmorgan was killed at Culloden. My father regretted that, as he said we needed good Scots peers, and your father was well respected, even if he turned Jacobite. All his sons were on the roll of the dead as well. The duke and his family are no more."

"Aye, well." Alec rubbed his chin. "It's a bit difficult to tell one dead Scot from the other on a field of battle. One name was true —Duncan, my eldest brother. He died all right. The rest of us

legged it. We have Mal to thank for that, and Padruig, and Will
…"

He trailed off, his heart heavy. Six sons and only three left.
Magnus had died before he'd been twenty, his heart weak.
Angus, shot while helping Duncan chase Lord Loudon across
the northern Highlands. And then Duncan at Culloden.

There was a rustle of velvet, and Celia was next to him,
leaving the parcel behind. "Your family is alive." Her soft voice
brushed him. "You should be rejoicing."

"I am, lass. I am. But …"

If Alec could live his life over again, he'd have persuaded his
father and brothers to travel to France with him and Malcolm
long before Prince Teàrlach set sail for Scotland. There they
could have waited to see what happened with the Jacobite
factions, staying well out of it.

They'd be all together now, Duncan and his father raging at
each other, Angus trying to keep the peace, Alec and Mal
roaming the streets of Paris, and Will …

Aye, well, so Will would have fallen into some sort of trouble, no matter what. The man loved intrigues and kept putting
himself into the thick of them.

Why the devil Will had sprung up and pretended to be
Prince Charles Stuart, Alec still didn't understand. Will must
have been plotting something, or he might have done it to save
others, distracting the soldiers so hidden Scotsmen could get
away. Both, most like.

*Damn ye, Will. If not for you, I could give over all my thoughts to
wooing my bride.*

"My bloody brothers will drive me mad." Alec took Celia's
hands, bringing himself back to the present. He was in London,
the wind was turning cold, and he'd just married a beautiful
young woman. "I can take care of ye, lass. I have plenty of
money salted away, so ye don't have to worry about touching

your legacy. I have a house in Paris, nothing so grand as Lady Flora's or your father's, but it does well enough. Except my whole family lives there at the moment, including my da'. But he'll like you."

Mal's wife, Mary, had softened the old duke in the last year, and the loss of his favorite sons had also taken away some of his bluster. Daniel William Mackenzie, the Duke of Kilmorgan, would never be considered a *gentle* man, but he would be good to Celia—once he got over his apoplexy that Alec had married again, in secret, to the daughter of a man who'd raised an army to fight the Scots.

But one thing at a time.

"Are we off to France now?" Celia asked, eyes shining in the light cast by the punched tin lanterns at their feet. "What about your daughter?"

"I thought Jenny would come with us," Alec said. "Gair might set her to manning the sails. He always needs extra hands."

Celia's laugh was tinged with hysteria. "I meant, will we hurry to Lady Flora's and fetch her?"

"I've already arranged for Sally to bring her to us at the boat. That's where I sent Padruig rushing off to, to tell her the trip to France was going forward."

"I'm glad. Can you trust Sally not to blab to Lady Flora?"

"She's a good lass. She has a brother in France she's been longing to see, so I persuaded her to come with us and look after Jenny." And Sally had no love for Lady Flora. Lady Flora wasn't parsimonious, which was why her servants stayed with her, plus there was a certain cachet that went with working for her. But most of the servants, save for Rivers, stepped delicately around her.

"Good." Celia studied him, her serene face out of keeping with her costume with its old-fashioned ruff and black pompons. "Why don't you look happier, Alec? We've thwarted the scheming queens and will run from the chessboard with Jenny. My father will discover where we've gone soon enough— he has plenty of connections and friends in France, never mind we're technically at war with that country. Wars come and go, but business prevails, is what my brother says. But if I am married, my mother cannot command me any longer. And I don't have to call you Mr. Finn, which pleases me enormously. It was entirely the wrong name for you." Her words ran down as concern entered her eyes. "So why are you not rejoicing?"

Alec lifted her hand that bore his ring and pressed a kiss to her fingers. "Because I'll not be going to France with you. And this makes me sad."

"What?" Celia's eyes widened, but she didn't jerk away. "What are you talking about? Of course we both must go, with Jenny."

Alec shook his head. He hadn't wanted to face a choice like this. On the chilly Paris morning when he'd declared he'd find Will, packed a small bag, and rushed to a boat, he'd somehow thought he'd easily track down his brother, grab him by the ear, and drag him home.

He hadn't expected Will's disappearance to be complicated, that the plans he'd laid with Lady Flora would be even more so. He hadn't expected Celia to be beautiful, intelligent, talented, and a damsel in distress. She was correct when she'd declared Alec was a knight, as in the romances of old, a champion who took on all comers in defense of his lady.

But the world had changed from those faraway days, no matter how many costumes people wore at masked balls, and how much they professed to uphold honor and glory.

Alec had seen, only a few months ago, that all the glory, which was mostly men swanning about proclaiming they were restoring the rightful king, had been brutal and ugly, full of pain, sorrow, rage, and death.

"I can't leave England, lass. Not yet."

"Why not?" Celia pinned him with a gaze that was too discerning. "Please tell me, Alec."

Without lying, she meant. The other day she'd been incensed at his evasion, taking offense that he would be other than open with her.

"I lied to you, because the truth is dangerous," Alec said. "I barely know ye. And you don't know me at all."

"But now we are married." Celia withdrew her hand and touched the ring, the movement equal parts wonder and trepidation. "I admit I have not seen many good examples of marriages, where husband and wife trust each other and confide all to each other. Perhaps such a marriage only exists in stories—I don't know. But I would like to try for such a thing."

"Then you will love Malcolm and Mary," Alec said. "They have complete trust and devotion. Will do anything for each other. It will make ye ill."

"Then we will be like Malcolm and Mary." Celia gave him a small smile. "Alec, please. I can help—I would like to help you. You've already done so much for me, more than you've had to."

"Of course I had to. My fault you're caught in my mess." Alec drew a breath and threw all his planning and caution to the wind. He wasn't one for machinations like Will was—Alec only ever wanted to paint and love beautiful women. *This* beautiful woman. "I leapt at the chance to have the daughter of the bloody Duke of Crenshaw in my power."

"I see." Celia watched him calmly. "I'd say you succeeded. You've married me." She did not appear unduly alarmed by this fact. "And yet, you are nothing like the wicked villains from the plays in Drury Lane. You don't rub your hands and glower nearly enough. Nor are you very happy that you've succeeded in trapping me."

"Because the game changed," Alec growled. "*You* changed it. Which is why I want you out of it."

The carriage listed as they rounded a corner to the Strand, heading for the river. The momentum pushed Celia into Alec, but instead of rising once the coach straightened, she remained against him.

"Tell me why," she said softly. "I shall be a termagant wife, and demand to know all."

To hell with it. Alec sent up a prayer, and cast the dice.

"Because your father knows where my brother is," he said in a hard voice. "He's the most likely person *to* know. Will's been missing for a long time, and I'm not going back to my family without him."

CHAPTER 18

Celia raised her head. The anguish in Alec's eyes pierced her, making her want to reach to him and wipe it away.

But his words were astounding. "*My* father? How on earth would he know where your brother is? Do mean your brother went missing after the battle of Culloden?"

"No—Will escaped—he made it to France. Then for no reason I can understand, he returned to Scotland and—was captured."

The bleakness Celia had seen in the back of Alec's eyes suddenly made sense. He feared his brother was dead, had the terrible emptiness of not knowing what had happened to him. Worried he might never know.

But the notion that Celia's father, her kindhearted, rather browbeaten father, knew the whereabouts of Alec's brother was highly unlikely.

"My father has nothing to do with Jacobite prisoners," she tried to explain. "He did attend some trials, but the glee with which the Scots were being prosecuted upset him, and he ceased going."

Alec shook his head. "Your dad is in charge of a regiment—the Duke of Crenshaw's Brigade. They escorted Scots prisoners back to London before the bulk of the regiment was sent to fight in France."

"My father *pays* for a regiment," Celia corrected him. "He's only nominally in charge. He leaves the running of it to others. At heart my father is a peace-loving man—he doesn't like war."

Alec's eyes glinted. "Nor do I. But war happens. The duke might not give the orders, and he might avoid prisoner trials so he doesn't upset his delicate constitution, but he *knows*. There's a world of knowledge in your da's head."

"I think you're wrong," Celia said. "But there is an easy way to discover if he knows anything about your brother. I can ask him."

"No, lass." Alec's voice was sharp. "What are you going to tell him? *I've married a dead Highlander, Father. Have ye squirreled away his brother somewhere? Oh, the brother's a traitor and supposed to be dead too.*"

"Don't be silly. Now you have to trust *me*. I will think of something ..."

"Ye won't speak to him at all. Ye eloped with me, and now you're going to France with my daughter to live with my family. And there's an end to it."

Celia's temper rose. "I am, am I?" She'd learned to practice meekness with her mother in order to have some peace—the whole family did—but Celia was far from the timid rabbit others believed her. "I might have agreed to obey you in the wedding vows, but not if your orders are unreasonable."

Alec scowled. "I don't remember the bishop reading that part of it."

"Well, such a clause ought to be in there. I believe in a

marriage of partners, not the mismatches so many make to keep power and wealth in the family. I believe a wife should be a helpmeet, not an appendage to put an heir and a spare in the nursery, and then do as she pleases. Lady Flora told me this makes me a romantic, but very well. I am a romantic ..."

She trailed off before Alec's fierce stare.

"God's balls, is that what an English marriage is? A wife to pump out babies and then ignore and be ignored? No wonder so many Englishmen are weedy and pale."

"And all Scottish men are robust?" Celia returned. "Shall I be a Scottish bride and take up my claymore and fight alongside my laird?"

"'Tis not so common anymore." Alec spoke in a forced voice as he tried and failed to lighten the conversation. "Though the wife of the Mackintosh clan chief raised her own Jacobite regiment during the Uprising. When her husband, who fought for King George, was captured at Prestonpans and sent to her as a prisoner, she saluted him and said, *Your servant, Captain.* He bowed back and said, *Your servant, Colonel.*"

Celia had heard that tale, which her father had told her with great amusement. "You see? But do not worry. I'll not lead a regiment against you. I can promise you that."

Alec gave her a dark look. "Don't promise. 'Tis a hard thing, keeping promises."

Celia curled her fingers around the heavy ring. "I already fulfilled one—remember? You asked me to trust you. And here I am. Please, Alec, let me stay and help. I couldn't bear being away from you, not knowing your fate. You're my husband now."

Alec's gaze was piercing. "Aye, and you're my wife. I promised to take care of you, as long as we both shall live."

"And I plighted my troth to *you.* My honor, my loyalty. I will help you, my Alec. Whether you like it or not."

Alec continued to scowl as they wove through the stream of

carriages on the Strand, the traffic heavy in spite of the darkness and fog.

Then a sudden grin broke over his face, like the sun tearing through storm clouds. "Damn it, lass, I'm thinking you'll make me a bonnie wife. And that I made a wise choice."

He rapped on the roof of the coach. A tiny window opened in the top, a patch of the coachman's face appearing. "Guv?"

"Take me to the other address I gave you."

The eye narrowed. "Right you are, guv." The window snapped shut.

Immediately, the coach halted, backed, and turned. Shouts and curses sounded on the street and Celia heard the noise of wheels scraping the cobbles. Sparks flew up, brightening the darkness. Once the carriage righted, they began moving back the way they'd come, heading for Charing Cross.

"Where are we going now?" Celia watched tall houses and black shadows flow past in the night.

"Not to France," Alec said and then fell silent, apparently not about to part with more information.

Celia leaned into him again, uncertainty washing coldness through her. She'd taken an irrevocable step tonight, pledging herself to a stranger from a foreign land, an outlaw in her country.

He was also a warm, firm-bodied man who wrapped his arm around her and held her close, his lips brushing the top of her head. Celia sank into him and let herself, for this moment, feel safe.

~

WILL MACKENZIE KNEW PEOPLE FROM AROUND THE GLOBE—HE had friends from China to the Americas, Africa to the East Indies. He occupied a world Alec didn't understand, but Will made connections with men and women from all strata of life, regardless of whose country was at war with whose, and remained friends with them for years.

Alec knew plenty of people himself, but where Will kept to those who traded information, Alec's circle was in the art world. Not so much the patrons, such as those who graced Lady Flora's salons, but the artists themselves, their models, their assistants —those who grubbed so the patrons could fill their drawing rooms with magnificent paintings.

The woman who owned the house Alec took Celia to had become an acquaintance of both brothers. Will had met Josette Oswald when he was looking for information on the British armies swarming the Continent. Alec had met her a decade ago when she'd been an artist's model in Amsterdam, sitting for painters keen to be the next Rembrandt or Van Dyke. Alec had hired her a time or two, and he and Josette had become friends.

Friends only, never lovers. Whether Josette had been Will's lover, Alec didn't know. Will was loud about visiting brothels or taking mistresses for the fun of it, but any relationship important to him he kept secret.

Alec had no idea of Josette's nationality. Her first name was French, her last English, but she called herself *Mrs.* Oswald, so her maiden name could be of another origin entirely. Or Josette might not have had a husband at all and had simply appended the "Mrs." to her name to give herself respectability, especially after she'd had a child. She spoke French fluently, but her English had a decided London cant. She also spoke Dutch, Russian, and various dialects of German.

When Alec had met Josette, he'd been a lad of eighteen who'd run away to Amsterdam and then France to learn painting. She'd been young herself, a great beauty, but already with a five-year-old child.

Now Josette was near to thirty and running to plumpness,

but she still had the beauty in her round face and glossy black hair that all those artists had tried to capture, on canvas and off. Josette had evaded them all.

She met them in the cramped hall of a house in a lane south of the Strand, the noisome smell of the river seeping to them. Sounds above and in other rooms told Alec her boarding house was full—Josette always pulled in good business.

"I see you decided to risk my hospitality after all," she said as she closed the front door. She looked over Celia in her now-rumpled costume, then Alec in his Highland regimental uniform. "Padruig isn't staying, is he? Only, he frightens my cook—on purpose, the dratted man."

"No, he's off to tell Gair he'll have to wait longer for his payment," Alec said. "We're staying in London a bit."

"I see that. *You* must be the poor thing he married." Josette took in Celia with her shrewd dark eyes. "You'll be wanting a change of clothing, I'll wager. Lord Alec sent for them, and they're upstairs in your bedchamber. You'll want to sort through them—you know how men are. Never pack the right things. My daughter will help you. Glenna!" She called up the stairs. "Come down and assist her ladyship. *Before* the second coming, please."

"Aye, I heard ya."

Down the stairs came a girl with coltish arms and legs, as tall as her mother now. Glenna, the mite who'd been five years old when Alec had painted in the Netherlands, was now a sunny-faced girl of fifteen, already a beauty like her mother.

Glenna curtsied before Celia with respect. "This way, my lady. Mum's fixed a chamber all nice for ya. I'll take your hat—can't have it squashed, can we?"

So chattering, she led Celia up the stairs, slowing her exuberant stride so Celia wouldn't fall behind. Celia glanced once at Alec, who gave her a nod, then she gathered her skirts and skimmed up the stairs after Glenna.

"Mum's been worried all day whether you'd come or not," Glenna said as they went. "Lord Alec couldn't decide whether to stash you here or rush you to Paris. Paris is ever so much nicer, but it's a long journey, with soldiers all over the countryside in France, Mum says."

Her voice faded as she and Celia left the landing, cut off by the closing of a door.

Alec let out his breath. "Thank you, Josette. This is kind of you."

Josette folded her arms over her plain brown bodice, a fichu like the ones Celia wore concealing her bosom. "Kindness has nothing to do with it. I'm worried sick about Willie. You haven't found him yet?"

"No," Alec said glumly. "I have places to look, but no, no sign of him."

He thought of the grim, cold house in the country, and knew he'd be back there, risking his life to find who, if anyone, was in it.

Josette flushed and looked away, her eyes moist, but when she turned back, she'd composed herself. "Did you marry that pretty thing to help in the search? Daughter of the Duke of Crenshaw, eh? Is the marriage even valid?"

Her expression was disapproving. Josette, who'd have done anything to keep her daughter fed, including stealing secrets from a king to hand them to Will, now frowned at Alec, certain he was using Celia and would discard her when finished.

"I married her to take her away from bloody people happy to make use of her," Alec growled. "I tried to send her to m' family, but she wouldn't go."

Josette nodded. "Wise of her. I've met the might of your

family, and it's enough to make even a strong woman flee into the night. Give her time to grow accustomed to you."

"I don't think all the time in the world will do that. The Mackenzies are overbearing bastards. Ye've not heard a word from him?"

"No." Josette lost her smile, fear in her eyes. "Not a dicky bird."

Alec had no idea what Will was to Josette, or she to him. Will left his lovers with ease, and they either remained on good terms or chased him off waving their fists.

But perhaps Josette had been different. She certainly wasn't the same sort of woman Will usually took up with.

Alec gentled his tone. "We'll find him."

The tears that dropped to Josette's cheeks glistened in the light of a single candle on the hall table. "They've probably already killed him. Declaring he was Charles Stuart might have kept him alive until he was taken to a garrison, but once someone in charge knew he wasn't anywhere close to being Prince Charlie, I've no doubt they bayoneted him there and then."

Alec's mind too easily pictured things. He imagined Will, rage in his eyes as his bravado fell away, his glare that changed to agony as the bayonet ran into his heart. Then the life would drain from his face and he'd fall back, bloody and dead, as the soldiers laughed.

Alec clenched his jaw so hard it ached. "We won't let them." He knew he should comfort Josette, but he couldn't move, frozen to the bone. "We'll find him, damn his hide. And then we'll give him hell for worrying us so."

Josette didn't smile. She gave Alec a nod, but it was clear she didn't believe Will was still alive.

He had to be. Alec clung to the hope. If he gave up that hope,

Will would truly be dead and gone, and Alec couldn't face a future that stark.

~

"Even your nightdress is beautiful." Glenna lifted the thin cotton gown from the trunk and laid it upon the bed, smoothing its skirt. "What must it be like to have such clothes?"

Celia had never given her gowns much thought, having been used to sumptuous fabric and the best seamstresses all her life. She had friends who fussed over their clothing and raged if even one stitch wasn't to their liking, but as long as Celia didn't look a mess, she was happy. A quick glance in a mirror or letting a maid straighten a skirt had been enough for her.

But now she looked down at the crumpled, soiled white velvets of her costume and cringed. She'd just been married in the wrinkled garments of a clown.

"I've never been to a masquerade," Glenna said, not noticing Celia's discomfiture. She unhooked the bodice from Celia's skirts, drew off her stomacher and corset cover, and began to unlace her stays. "Mum would never let me. Says men and women who have to pretend to be others for fun are right fools. Says masquerades are excuses to paw at one another's husbands and wives."

Her mother, the beautiful landlady who clearly knew Alec well, wasn't wrong. Celia's mother's masquerades were gatherings of decorum, but Celia had attended others where shepherds chased masked shepherdesses into darkened rooms, and shadows under trees in a garden were filled with people *not* chatting or dancing.

"Your mother is quite lovely," Celia said. Both Glenna and Josette had dark hair and eyes, but the porcelain pale skin of the north. "As are you. You look much like her."

Glenna shrugged. "You're kind, but I know I'm a stick with my hair everywhere." She began to unpin Celia's braids, unwinding them from their tight coil. The loosening of clothes and hair felt good, relaxing on this mad night.

"That is what *you* might see in a mirror," Celia said with conviction. "I see a very pretty young lady."

"Aw, ain't ye sweet. Mum was an artists' model when she were younger. Took off her kit to let men paint her picture. I ask you ..."

An artists' model—this explained how Alec had met her. Which meant Mrs. Oswald must have taken off her kit for *Alec*. Celia tried to decide, through her exhaustion and bemusement, how she felt about that.

She remembered how she'd reflected that artists' models must live exciting lives when Alec had talked about them on her first day of lessons, and how he'd said they sat for him simply because they wanted to be paid. Mrs. Oswald, as beautiful as she was, seemed a sensible woman, at least at first glance, not scandalous at all.

"If you're wondering, my lady, Lord Alec ain't my father," Glenna went on with disarming frankness. "I don't know who is, but it ain't Lord Alec. I was already toddling around before Mum met him." She pulled a brush through Celia's hair. "Just thought I'd set your mind at rest. It's his *brother* Mum fancies. Only never tell her I said that."

"Never." Celia met Glenna's gaze in the mirror and smiled. The girl was easy to like.

Glenna kept up her rapid and cheerful chatter as she helped Celia into her nightdress, but Celia faded back from it, too many things jostling for her attention. Her life had changed tonight, but whether for good or ill remained to be seen.

Yet, she couldn't be terrified. Something had woken in her, defiance and hope, as though chains had fallen away.

She belonged to Alec now, by law, but Celia couldn't believe that a man who'd held his child so tenderly could be cruel to her. Most gentlemen barely acknowledged they had children at all, especially when they were babes. They didn't hold them, bounce them in their arms, and worry about their teething troubles.

At last Celia was ready for bed, her face washed, hair combed and braided. The bedcovers had been folded back, and Glenna competently lifted them so Celia could slide beneath.

The bed had been warmed—Celia's foot touched a cloth-wrapped brick that radiated heat. Glenna lingered for a time, shaking out Celia's white velvet gown and straightening things on the dressing table. At last she departed, sending Celia a grin that was much too knowing for her age.

Celia was married. With all marriage entailed. Her heart hammered, every footfall in the stairwell outside her door magnified.

Would he come? Alec had married her to keep her safe, he'd said, to remove her from the game.

Did that mean in name only? Or would Alec expect his right to her in bed?

Celia shivered. Her mother had explained all about what men wanted from their wives, in explicit detail. The duchess had not wanted Celia to be an ignorant maiden, she said, and told her that the quicker a man was pleased, the more quickly he left her alone.

Lie still and let him do whatever he likes, no matter how repugnant it might be to you, was the duchess's sage advice. *You are there to bear him a son and nothing more.*

Celia didn't want to think about her mother and her disparaging words. She wanted to think about Alec, his breath-stealing kisses, his fine body, his strong hands that could render a beautiful picture in a few deft lines.

Footsteps moved up and down the stairs, some hurried, one tread heavy and slow—a man's. Celia stilled, but whoever it was kept moving, climbing higher into the house.

The candles burned to stubs. Fire warmed the small room, the night dying into silence. Celia determined to stay awake, to wait for Alec, her fingers tingling as she planned every movement she'd make when he came to her.

Those thoughts loosened her body and let lassitude take over. The next thing Celia knew, she was rising from a deep sleep, sunlight pouring through the window.

She became aware of a weight on the mattress next to her. Celia turned her head to see Alec Mackenzie stretched beside her on the bed in kilt and shirt, his arm flung over his face, a soft snore issuing from his mouth.

CHAPTER 19

*A*lec woke to find Celia bending to him, the thick braid of her dark hair falling to his chest like a silken rope.

Her face was shadowed, her eyes alight with green-brown depths. A smile touched her mouth as he focused on her, her face relaxing as though she'd watched him for some time.

"Good morning," she said softly.

Everything wrong in Alec's world dissolved. An angel smiled at him and took the pain away.

"Sorry," was all that came out of his mouth. "There were no other beds in the house. Josette's rooms are full."

A pucker appeared between Celia's brows. "We are married."

The simple statement swept away his apology, as though Celia wondered at his need to make it at all.

"That we are." Alec wrapped her braid around his hand. "But I thought an Englishwoman never shared a chamber with her husband."

Celia studied him, searching for something Alec couldn't put a name to. "My parents certainly do not. Did yours?"

"Aye, they slept in the same bed every night." Alec pillowed his head on his arm. "That's why me poor mum bore six bairns."

"Will you tell me about them?" Celia asked with interest. "Your brothers? I'd like to know. Since I married one of them."

She liked to say the word. *Married.* In her sphere, the state solved many a trouble—though it created plenty more, in Alec's opinion. Marriage in the Mackenzie family had become a source of much shouting by their father. No one was supposed to marry without his permission, yet Alec and Mal kept doing it.

"You want to talk about a bunch of large, noisy, smelly Highlanders? On the morning after your wedding? Before breakfast?"

Another smile. "You can prepare me for when I meet them."

Mal would tease Alec to death but welcome Celia with open arms. His father would like her too, but there would be a long period of bluster and rage before he settled down to get to know her. Will would think Alec a fool for stealing such a highplaced English aristo's daughter, but at the same time would admire Alec's audacity.

Angus ...

"Angus would have liked ye," Alec said quietly. "He was the best of us, the only one who could keep my father calm and happy. We tormented him because he was our dad's pet, but Dad clung to him after Mum died. He was so lost without her, ye see, and only Angus saw that. The rest of us left him to grieve alone."

Celia's eyes softened. "You haven't mentioned Angus before. Which brother is he?"

"My twin." Alec's heart hollowed as he said it, the grief he'd been holding at bay threatening to tear into him. "He's gone— shot by British soldiers north of home in some skirmish no one will remember. It's like there's an empty space right next to me, that will never go away. Angus was always there—we fought, we disagreed—all the time—we were nothing alike. But he was always there ..."

"Your twin. That explains it." Celia's voice was a near whisper.

Alec focused on her with difficulty. "Eh? Explains what?"

"When I drew the picture of you—that first lesson—the one you took away from me. I fancied I saw another man in the shadow behind you, as though there should have been two of you."

Alec's breath caught. "Aye, there was." He trailed off, his eyes wet, but Alec held himself still with effort. The last thing he wanted was his new bride to see him weeping like a wreck.

Celia slid her arm around him and laid her head on his chest.

She said nothing, did nothing, only held him. No inane words that everything would be all right—it would never be—or that she was sorry for him. She was, but what came to Alec was her compassion, her understanding.

This from a woman raised by a cold mother, whose brother had turned his back on her, whose father was responsible for the deaths of Alec's friends and family, even if he'd shunted the duty to others.

That such a family could produce Celia, kind and understanding, proved that God was looking out for Alec Mackenzie.

"You're a wonder, love." Alec brushed her hair back from her face. "Where did it come from? Your gentleness?"

"Hmm?" Celia raised her head. She smelled of warmth and sleep and bare woman. Alec's troubles began to recede as desire pushed through his thoughts. "Am I gentle? I get that from my father, I suppose. Whatever you think of him, he is a kind man, has always been good to me. If you met him, you'd understand." She gave a light laugh. "You will have to meet him, eventually. You stole me away from him."

"That I did." Alec put his hand behind her heavy braid and

pulled her close. "And I'm glad. You might be regretting it, Lady Alec Mackenzie, but I am not."

Celia's eyes widened. "Lady Alec. Yes, I suppose I am now." Her wonder filled the cold spaces in his heart. "A fine name."

Alec hauled her up against him, pushing the covers down until there was nothing but her nightdress between him and the woman inside.

He brushed her face with his thumb, tracing her cheekbone that went pink under his touch. Her lips were parted, red, desirable. Alec gathered her closer and kissed her.

Celia still wasn't skilled at kissing, in spite of Alec's previous instruction. Better, but not practiced. She bumped his mouth, not knowing how to open his lips.

Alec smiled into the kiss, deciding to surrender to her and let her do as she willed.

"What sort of kisses are these?" Celia asked when they eased apart. "Married kisses?"

"Kisses of lovers." Alec skimmed his hand over her hair and drew it down her braid. "Kisses of passion."

"Passion."

Her whisper undid him. Alec was hard for her, need rising fast. Sunshine broke through the rain, slanting through the mist-streaked window to touch her body.

Alec moved his hand down her back, reveling in the suppleness of it, his fingers coming to rest on her hip. "I want you, love. I think I'm dying of wanting you."

Celia touched his face. "Is wanting so very perilous? If so, I am in great danger."

"It's no' funny, lass."

"I know. I am deadly serious."

Then why did Alec want to laugh?

He untied the ribbon that held her nightdress closed, and the loosened gown slid from her as Alec kissed her again, baring her skin. His hands found the smooth flesh of her shoulders, the soft curve of her side, and then the firmer curve of her breast.

Alec cupped it, feeling her nipple drawn to a point, the desire that flowed through him strong in her.

He needed more. Alec bunched the nightdress in his hands, pulling it up Celia's body. He sank into another kiss then lifted her so he could pull the nightdress off over her head.

Celia landed on him again, not a stitch on her now, her face pink with shyness. Alec had divested himself of coat and boots before falling on the bed in his kilt, shirt, and stocking feet. Now Celia worked open the tapes that held his shirt closed, her fingers moving against his chest.

"I was shocked when you stripped off your clothes that first day." She dipped her head to kiss the hollow of his throat. "That was your purpose, wasn't it? To shock me."

"Aye." Alec kissed her hair while she tasted his skin. "The prim duke's daughter. I wanted to frighten you. But you weren't afraid at all. You took up your pencil, and you drew me."

She gave him a self-deprecating look. "Not very well."

"You're wrong about that. That's why we had to take the sketch away from ye. Ye caught me too well."

"I couldn't help it." Celia ran fingertips along the face she'd rendered almost exactly. "You seemed to speak to me, and my hands knew what you were saying. Please tell me Lady Flora didn't burn it."

"I have it safe. 'Tis special to me."

"The man in it is special to *me.*"

Alec's heart pumped hard, his need no longer able to stay quiet. He helped her pull his shirt up and off, Alec tossing it to the floor.

Celia lost herself in exploring his bare chest, touching, kissing, nuzzling. Alec twined his legs around her, positioning himself at her opening. Celia didn't react at first, squirming a bit as she sought to kiss every inch of his neck and chest. Alec let her play, the rub of her against him through the dark plaid firing his need.

She was a beautiful, enchanting woman, a bud ready to flower. No, a better metaphor was one of the fairy folk the villagers of Kilmorgan were always going on about, trapped in a bubble of rain, unable to grow or change until one day, a human touched the bubble, and released the beautiful being within.

Alec would take her to his homeland one day, into the beauty of the wild lands, to listen to the crofters and their tales. But his home was gone, he remembered with a jolt, destroyed.

Celia was his family now. And Jenny, safe in a room above them, looked after by the cheerful Sally.

Family. *My wife.*

Alec ran his hand over Celia's hips, loving her softness, then tangled his legs with hers, rubbing his foot in its cotton stocking up and down her leg.

Celia lifted her head, her eyes sparkling with need but uncertainty. "We will join now?" She wet her lips, a nervous gesture, but it made her mouth moist and delectable. "The man inserts his phallic rod into the woman's receptacle and spills his seed."

Alec stared up at her in amazement. Her expression was serious as she calmly voiced the dispassionate outline of what would happen.

He didn't want to laugh at her—someone had told her that, his Lady Innocence, or she'd read it in a book. But the words, so out of place with the dark heat inside this bed cut through his sphere of anger and heartache. Cut through it like a sword, smashing the shell around him and letting Alec Mackenzie out.

He let out a laugh that built until the bed shook with it and his voice boomed around the room. He laughed for joy and the beauty of Celia, for the warmth of a beautiful woman, for the fact that he could wrap his arms around her and shut out the world.

Celia flushed a dark red. "Is that not what happens? My mother went over it so carefully."

Alec jerked away the pillow beneath his head so he could lie flat and continue laughing. He imagined the cold-faced duchess explaining to Celia her duty to a lust-ridden Englishman eager for his young bride.

His anger at her family returned on top of his mirth, but the morose Alec Mackenzie had fled into the wind.

"Aye, that's what happens, in words." He gently eased her from him and sat up to unfasten the plaid. "But much more than that."

Alec peeled the kilt from his hips and dragged off his stockings. The tartan was the blue and green of the the Black Watch, similar to but not quite the same as the Mackenzies's colors. He imagined Celia rolled up in Mackenzie plaid and his body went rigid.

"On ye come." Alec gathered Celia into his arms and slid her on top of him.

She looked surprised. "I thought I had to be under you?"

More laughter vibrated him. "Oh, lass, teaching you will be splendid. There is so much to learn—it might take us many years. I hope so."

"Well, you were hired to instruct me, weren't you?" she asked, a teasing note in her voice. "I simply didn't anticipate instruction in *this*."

Alec's cock went blood-poundingly stiff.

The fantasy of Celia turning up for drawing lessons, flushed and knowing, shot through his mind. Alec imagined every detail of unlacing her stomacher, unfastening her skirts, peeling her clothes from her, each layer falling to reveal more. He'd take his time with her stockings, sliding the fine silk down her legs, skimming his hand behind her knee to the warmth there.

He'd arrange her on the cushioned sofa he'd prepared while he dropped her silken clothing and stood back, studying her body as an artist, before putting pencil to paper and sketching her. Every line, every curve, every curl of her hair, the arc of her breasts, the proud tilt of her head.

He'd pause from time to time, lay down the pencil, and love her on the sofa until they drowsed in the sunshine.

Then he'd teach her to undress him, and *he'd* be the model. He'd lie back under her scrutiny while she rendered him on her canvas, and then they'd make love again.

Alec's mind, which absorbed and remembered every facet of a situation, played the scene to him in vivid precision. His entire being willed him to make the fantasy truth.

He pulled Celia down to him, loving the warm weight of her body. Her breasts pressed his chest, her nipples points against his skin, as he moved one hand to the soft round of her buttocks.

"I won't hurt you, love."

Celia gave him a tight nod. "I can bear it."

Alec caressed her cheek. "I don't want ye to *bear* it, my lass. I want ye to love every second of it."

She nodded again. "I'll try."

Laughter threatened to overwhelm Alec, but he held it back. This was too important.

He parted her legs with his hand and eased her very carefully over the tip of his cock. Alec bit back a groan as he felt her liquid heat, but he resisted simply thrusting into her. He had to go carefully, letting her understand, and trust.

"Oh," Celia said. Her eyes widened as Alec slid in the barest inch. "*Oh.*"

"There now," he said softly. "I'll let you grow used to it."

He held himself rigid as Celia stiffened, then her face softened. She was tight, squeezing his tip, fanning his hot desire.

The same desire flushed her as she bent her head to kiss him. When her teeth latched onto Alec's lip, he lost his tight control and slipped another inch inside her.

Celia gasped, and Alec froze. His body was on fire, the need to bury himself inside her strong.

"All right?" he asked. "Am I hurting ye?" It would kill him to pull out, but he'd do it if she felt any pain. He had no intention of Celia looking at him in fear every time she remembered this day.

"No." She drew a breath. "Not really. It feels odd."

"Odd? Put a man in his place, why don't ye, lass?"

Celia gave him a sudden grin. "I rather like the place you are in, my husband."

"Ah, damn." Alec shuddered, flashing hot at the same time. "Why do ye say things like that?"

He balled his fists as he slid ever so slowly in the rest of the way, watching Celia's eyes soften, her thoughts scatter. Alec held her there, letting her feel full, waiting for her to understand what it meant for him to be inside her.

Celia braced herself over him, shaking her head as though trying to comprehend what was happening to her.

She made a soft moan that nearly undid him. Still, Alec held himself in check, determined not to make this beautiful moment a horror for her.

Outside, the city continued to wake, the rising voices of the vendors who strolled the streets coming to them. Their chants rang out, offering strawberries or coffee, or to take rags or grind knives, blending with the rumble of carts, the shouts of drovers, the clank of chains as a boat was unleashed from the strand and pushed into the river. London was always alive.

Inside the room with Celia was quiet. The fire snapped on

the hearth, and the ropes that held the mattress in place creaked. Celia let out a sigh that blended with a groan, and Alec stroked her hair again.

"What do I do?" she whispered. "I feel strange ... and wonderful."

"Ye don't have to do anything, love." Alec's hand drifted down her back. "Ye can do all, or nothing. That's the beauty of loving."

"It's not what I thought it would be."

Alec grinned. "It never is."

He gradually raised her until she was straddling him, on her knees. Celia's eyes widened again, another new sensation flooding her.

Alec lifted his hips, sliding deeper into her. Making love in this position was always a challenge but his reward was Celia swaying on him, a cry issuing from her throat as she relaxed onto him.

Her long braid snaked down to him, smooth against his side. Celia rocked on him, letting out another cry, her fingers biting his chest. Her breasts moved, her nipples dark and tight, the beauty of her no longer hidden.

"Alec," she whispered. "I love—"

She closed her mouth over the word, as though she hadn't meant to let it slip out, and Alec's self-control splintered. He drove into her, his hips coming off the bed, his own shouts blending with hers.

Celia arched back, and Alec caught her hands to steady her. He twined his fingers through hers, holding tight as she rode him, the two locked together—hands, legs, bodies.

Alec let out a growl. He clasped her around the waist and rolled them so he was on top of her. Celia looked at him in bewilderment, then her smile returned as he thrust into her.

A few quick moments, and it was done. Alec's seed left him,

but his hips continued to move, Alec wanting to stay with her, in her, she around him, forever.

Celia's smile dissolved into soft cries of delight, which melded with his groans until their voices at last wound into silence.

Alec crashed next to Celia and pulled her close, surrendering himself to peace.

∼

CELIA LAY AWAKE FOR A LONG TIME, WATCHING ALEC SLEEP. HIS face was quiet, his dark red-brown hair falling into his eyes, his lips slack. Unshaved whiskers darkened his jaw but burnished red in the firelight.

Her Highlander. Celia brushed his shoulder, feeling strength beneath smooth skin. Alec was one of the barbarians who'd charged at her brother's regiment, screaming insanely, and cut down all in their path. They'd followed Charles Stuart far into England, threatening all she knew.

And she couldn't be afraid of him.

Alec's eyes flickered. In the next moment, she looked into the golden depths of them, his slow smile lifting the corners of his mouth.

"All right, love?"

CHAPTER 20

Celia grew hot with embarrassment, remembering her unrestrained cries, but her chagrin dispersed under his gaze. She was warm and comfortable, happy in spite of it all.

She smoothed a tumbledown lock of his dark red hair. "I don't wonder that men and women seek to take lovers. To have that ..." She gave a warm shiver, remembering the sensation of him inside her, the explosive joy of her surrender.

"That's only the beginning, love." Alec kissed her fingers. "I have much more to teach you."

"You do?" she asked shyly. He'd already showed her so much —first that being with a husband was nothing to fear, and second, that far from being a chore or a duty, lying with Alec had been beautiful. The pain she'd expected had slid away on a wild elation, her body taking over and doing things she'd never known it could do.

"Oh, yes." His voice was dark. "I'll give you all kinds of instruction, my love."

For answer, Celia leaned and kissed him. His lips caressed hers, the kiss leisurely, his mouth hot.

"What sort of kiss is this?" she asked softly when they finished.

"The after-loving kind." Alec smoothed her hair. "When you're warm and open, and the world doesn't exist beyond this bed."

That was it exactly—nothing mattered but this, and being with him.

Before Celia could form thoughts into words, Alec kissed her again, then came down with her into the mattress, his strong body covering hers.

When he slid inside her this time, it was different—slow, enjoyable, not like the crazed wildness of an hour ago. Alec stretched out on her, his weight comforting, shielding.

Celia moved with him, groaning with him as excitement built and then surged. Alec thrust into her faster and faster, their voices joining, until they collapsed together, laughing and kissing.

Celia fell into deep slumber after that, and when she awoke, the sun was nearing its zenith, and Alec was gone.

CELIA FOUND ALEC WITH JOSETTE IN A SMALL DINING ROOM ON the ground floor, directed there by Glenna, who helped her dress. Glenna's smirks and innuendo kept Celia blushing furiously, as the girl brushed out her hair and wound it into a competent knot. Really, a fifteen-year-old maiden should *not* know so much about the marriage bed.

Alec was making his way through a plate piled high with eggs, sausages, and toast, with a slab of meat pie awaiting his attention at his elbow. As Celia entered, he looked up and smiled at her, his eyes full of wickedness.

Another blush, this one scalding her. How was she to ever be in the same house with him when every look reminded her of her wantonness? She ought to be ashamed of her behavior with him, but shame couldn't last in the face of the deep contentment in her heart.

Josette's breezy voice cut through her thoughts. "There you are, love. Plenty of victuals on the sideboard for you. Eat up. You'll need your strength if you're to be married to Alec."

Celia didn't think her face could become any redder, but a glance at the mirror above the sideboard proved her wrong. She filled her plate with a shaking hand, while Alec chuckled.

Pretending nonchalance, Celia sat across from Alec. The room was small, the table taking most of the space, with the sideboard squeezed into the corner. The table was of fine mahogany with serpentine legs ending in dainty feet, but the chairs were mismatched—some had thick spindles, some had elegant carving, and two were plain chairs that looked like they came from a farmer's kitchen.

The crockery was mismatched too, with one or two fine pieces of porcelain interspersed with heavier stoneware.

"How is Jenny this morning?" Celia asked Alec as she took a dainty bite of eggs mixed with cheese, finding it quite good.

Another man might grunt something in indifference, but Alec beamed a proud smile. "Cooing and happy. Ate a large breakfast with the appetite of a Highlander. I think she likes being out of the cold mortuary of Lady Flora's grand mansion."

Indeed, Lady Flora's house, while containing the most expensive and tasteful objects of the day, was chill and empty. Josette's boarding house, in contrast, was cozy, with its worn furniture and small rugs overlapping each other, the smell of cinnamon and coffee overcoming the stench of London outside.

"Would you mind if I looked in on her?" Celia asked as she scooped up another forkful of eggs.

"Why should I mind, love? She's your stepdaughter now."

Celia blushed again. "Oh, yes. I suppose she is."

Josette's eyes twinkled. "You've found yourself an enchanting bride, Lord Alec. From the sound of things coming from upstairs, you're enchanted with her too. I had several complaints from my regular boarders."

Alec gave Celia a wink as she heated until she thought her blood would boil. "I don't think she's used to unseemly talk at the breakfast table," he observed. "Or any other table."

"Nonsense." Josette lifted a porcelain cup decorated with a spray of roses. "Rapport in the bedroom can lead to rapport in the rest of life. Not that I had that in my first marriage, God rot that man's poxy soul. I married a scoundrel, my lady. One day he set off for parts unknown and managed to get himself killed. Good riddance, I say."

She spoke airily, but Celia saw the flash of anger, old pain buried deep.

Celia was curious about Josette's history, but this was not the time or place to pry. She cleared her throat.

"After I visit with Jenny, we must turn to finding and freeing your brother," she said to Alec. When Alec and Josette exchanged a swift glance, Celia sent them an exasperated look. "Did you suppose I'd sit in my room by the fire while your brother might be in danger? I told you I could help find him, and I will."

Alec scowled. "And I remember saying you should stay well out of it."

"Because my father might be connected to all this? I believe that is why I *should* involve myself. I don't believe for a moment Papa is hiding any prisoners, which is why I will ask him straight out."

Alec held up a hand, which was filled with his coffee cup. "Prudence, love. Let's not rush to make me dead in truth. The sooner you and Jenny are off to my family in France, the better."

Celia eyed Alec calmly, though her agitation rose. "We had this argument last night, I believe. I am your wife now. I stay with you. I have no intention of betraying you or your family—I can discover things without ever mentioning your name. As far as my father is concerned, you are Mr. Finn, the drawing master, and now I am Mrs. Finn. For the time being."

Alec pushed aside his empty plate. "Josette, lass, talk sense into her."

Josette looked wise. "It is not for me to insert myself into an argument between husband and wife. But consider, Alec. She is well placed to gain information. That is why you decided to give her the drawing lessons in the first place."

So Alec had implied. *I leapt at the chance to have the daughter of the bloody Duke of Crenshaw in my power.* Celia sipped her coffee, determined not to feel hurt that she'd been looked upon by Alec and Lady Flora as a means to an end.

"That is before I knew her." Alec slanted Celia a glance full of heat. "Before she stole my heart away. Now I want no one to touch her, not her mum, not Lady Flora, not her dad. My father is a difficult man, but he'll honor you as my wife, lass. And Mal and Mary will look after ye well."

Celia clicked her cup into its saucer. "I am not leaving, Alec, and that is final."

Alec let out a sigh, but he didn't appear very surprised. "Aye, well, I suppose this house is safe enough for now. Josette is a good sort, and not fool enough to let slip that a man such as me stays here."

"Thank you very much," Josette murmured.

"What ye need to do now, my wife, is write your old dad a letter," Alec went on. "One that tells him you're safe and well, so he doesn't send the army out to tear up London to find ye."

Celia nodded. "Yes, I want to. I'd not like to concern him unduly." She spoke as though indifferent, but her heart constricted. She loved her father and knew he would worry. He'd fear that Celia had been abducted—it happened, and vagabonds and thieves could turn violent. Tales of murders and other terrible crimes frequently blared from the pages of the newspapers.

Alec watched her, his eyes quiet. She wished she could make him believe in her father's kindness, but she conceded her father *might* know who was keeping his brother prisoner—if Will Mackenzie was still alive—even if the duke wasn't aware of the significance of the information.

When Celia finished her breakfast she asked Josette for pen, ink, paper, and jar of sand, and after Glenna brought the things, Celia composed the missive right there at the table. She wrote swiftly, sprinkled the sand onto the ink, shook it off, and handed the letter to Alec.

He didn't reach for it. "I don't need to read your post, love. I trust you not to tell him ye married a traitor."

"Please." Celia laid the paper before him. "I want no secrets between us."

Alec's eyes narrowed, but he pulled the letter to him and read. Celia had kept her message simple:

Dearest Papa,

I am safe, dare I say happy? I am married. Mr. Finn, Lady Flora's guest, saved me from a dire situation and protected my reputation by making me his wife last night. We were married by the Bishop of Arden, by special license.

Mr. Finn is a gentleman, and you need have no worry for me. You once promised me you'd give me your blessing if I found a man I esteemed and liked. I ask this blessing now, and your forgiveness.

We will withdraw for a while, until society calms from this interesting on dit, *if they even notice what the eccentric Lady Celia has done now. I will miss you, dear Papa, but one day we will reunite, and I can express my fondness for you that these words are inadequate to convey.*

God keep you.

Your loving daughter,

Celia

Alec's eyes were soft as he handed the letter back to her. "I hope someday I will be worthy of what you write."

"You already are, else I would not have written it." Celia folded the paper lengthwise, then in thirds and wrote her father's direction on the outside. Josette brought her wax, which Celia melted with a candle's flame. The signet with which she usually sealed her letters was at home in her writing table, so she simply dribbled wax over the crease to hold it closed.

"Can someone deliver this?" she asked Josette. "I have to confess I've never sent anything through the post myself. My father francs all my letters and puts them on a tray for the butler. There they mysteriously disappear and find their way to their recipients."

"Of course," Josette said, amused. "I'll have a lad run it there for you." She glanced at the direction. "Grosvenor Square. My, my." She turned to Alec. "Trust a Mackenzie to fly so high."

"The flying isn't the difficulty, lass. It's the falling and crashing. We do that often enough."

"Aye, I hope Willie hasn't done so." Josette's teasing fled, and she sat down heavily. "His friends have had no word?"

Alec shook his head. "I met with a Glaswegian who'd heard of men being held in a house, and then Mrs. Reynolds, Lady Flora's companion, told me the same story."

"What Glaswegian?" Josette asked quickly. "He might know more."

"Not this lad. We were attacked, the pair of us—by thieves, his enemies, who knows? And he got himself killed."

Celia's gasp made both Alec and Josette jerk to look at her, as though they'd forgotten her presence. "So that is what you and Padruig were talking about," she said to Alec. "And why you were all battered that morning. I knew it was more than a disagreement in a tavern."

Alec nodded, looking unhappy. "I carried the Glaswegian to a church, left him on their doorstep, and rang the bell at the vicarage. I hope they did right by him. Couldn't have left the poor man on the bank of the Thames to be picked over by thieves."

Alec's sadness caught at Celia's heart. Here was a man who'd had to make hard decisions, and was still making them.

"I'm certain they took care of him," Celia said. Dead beggars were put into pauper's graves, she knew from her charity work, but at least prayers were said for their souls. The vicar would likely assume this was another such poor vagrant. "I am sorry."

"Not your fault, lass. London's full of villains. The entire world is, truth to tell. Now to wrest my brother away from them."

"How?" Josette asked.

Celia noted the despair in her eyes. She was extremely worried about Will, and Celia remembered what Glenna had said the night before—*It's his brother Mum fancies.* Celia regarded her with sympathy. It was also clear that Josette did not want to admit what she felt.

Alec drew a blank sheet of paper toward him and picked up her pen. "I saw a house, east of Cambridge, with a long outbuilding, abandoned." He sketched a rough map with London and Cambridge, and an X where the house must be. He made X's in two other places, one in Kent, heart-stoppingly close to where Celia's father's estate would be, and one north and east of that, in Essex.

Alec then drew the outline of a house, filling in windows,

trees, sky, grounds, scrub, all in easy, competent lines. Celia watched the scene come alive as though she peered at it through a window.

"This is the house Mrs. Reynolds and I drove by," Alec said when he finished. "We didn't see much of anyone, but there was a sentry, and that road was a lonely one. I haven't seen the other two houses yet, but I intend to."

The house Alec had drawn looked familiar, but then England was dotted with large homes in similar styles as men who made fortunes around the world built mansions for themselves and their families. Celia's mother sneered at these upstarts, men of no title or background, basing their dynasties on nothing but money. Celia's father, more pragmatic, said it was the times they lived in, and if these fellows were lucky enough to make a packet, they ought to enjoy it. Celia's mother only sniffed and condemned him with a glance.

"Who lives in the houses?" she asked.

"This one is rented out by Sir Amos Westwood, but I don't know about the others," Alec said. "I am not acquainted with all the aristos in England."

"But I am," Celia said eagerly. "If you show me these houses, I can tell you who lives there or nearby and whether they are likely to have Scottish soldiers kept prisoner in their outbuildings."

"Lady Flora also knows them," Alec pointed out. "I'd rather risk *her* jaunting about the countryside, not you. Or Mrs. Reynolds, whom Lady Flora will likely send in her place."

"Bugger that," Celia said decidedly.

Alec's eyes widened, then a sparkle lit their depths.

Josette burst out laughing. "You've shocked him, my dear. I never thought it possible to shock a Mackenzie."

Celia shrugged, but she felt amused triumph. "My brother is a soldier. He taught me all sorts of bad words. I'll not sit here and embroider, Alec Mackenzie, while you risk your neck poking around places guarded by British soldiers. In fact, *I* ought to go scouting with Mrs. Reynolds while you stay well out of sight. If *we* are caught, the guards will roll their eyes and send us two lost gentle-born ladies on their way. *You* would be clapped in chains the moment you opened your mouth."

Josette continued to chuckle. "She has a point, my friend."

Alec's brows came down. "Like hell I'm letting ye rush about the countryside on your own. Mrs. Reynolds is a competent woman, but every highwayman from here to the coast will sniff out a fine carriage with only two ladies inside."

"You could send your man, Padruig, to protect us. I don't believe highwaymen would bother *him*."

"*If* I can find him, *if* Gair will spare him, and *if* I didn't think Gair would gouge me for every shilling I had. No, if you're determined then I and my pistol are accompanying you, wife."

Celia lifted her coffee cup, pleased. "That is settled then."

Alec studied the ceiling. "May God grant me patience. You are right, lass, that ye'll know the countryside and the people living in it better than I. But ye stay *in* the coach, no matter what we find, no matter what I decide to do. Agreed?"

"I doubt rushing about through wet fields would be good for my constitution," Celia said. "And Mrs. Reynolds is always good company. Do you know, she's been to China? How exciting."

Josette began to laugh again as Alec looked pained. Josette beamed at Celia, which made her lovely face even more beautiful. "I do believe you will be very good for him, my dear."

≈

ALEC TOOK CELIA UPSTAIRS TO SPEND THE NEXT HOUR WITH Jenny. Josette had sent off a lad to deliver the letter to Celia's father, and Alec sent a verbal message by a man he knew and trusted to Lady Flora, telling her he wanted to further explore country houses. She'd know what he meant. Now to wait for her response.

Jenny sang out when she saw Alec, squirmed down from her chair, and took two toddling steps toward him. Alec caught her in his arms and lifted her high.

Jenny clung to him and pressed a very wet kiss to his cheek, then she pushed from him and launched herself at Celia.

Where did tiny children come by such strength? Jenny was out of his arms before he could stop her, and Celia staggered as she caught the babe.

Celia laughed, her face lighting. She didn't seem to mind the drool coming out of Jenny's happy mouth to stain her fichu, or the way Jenny burrowed into Celia's shoulder, her tiny hands clenching the finely woven wool of Celia's gown.

Sally hovered nearby with a distressed expression, but Celia only held Jenny more securely and looked down at her with wonder. "Good afternoon, little one," she said, her voice holding a tenderness Alec hadn't heard in it before. "I'm your new Mama."

Jenny cooed, pleased. When Celia looked at Alec, her eyes were shining with tears.

Alec drew both Celia and his daughter into the circle of his arms, a pain that had been lodged in his heart for a long while easing.

∼

THE COACHMAN WHO'D MET THEM OUTSIDE THE GARDENS AT Vauxhall halted at Josette's door an hour later. Celia, wrapped in a dun-colored cloak, her hair covered by a broad-brimmed hat, took Alec's hand to let him help her in. He sprang up behind her, wearing Mr. Finn's brown, rather worn frock coat and breeches she'd first seen him in, and boots rather than stockings and shoes.

With his hair tied back in a simple tail and a tricorn pulled low over his forehead, Alec looked like any other man hurrying about London on a weekday morning. Alec and Celia might be a plain middle-class husband and wife running errands, deciding what sort of furniture they'd like for their house, and what food to buy for the baby.

It was a strange sensation, being like everyone else. Celia had been shut away in a cushioned world of privilege her entire life, servants at her beck and call to bring her anything she wished. This could have turned her into a horrible, spoiled shrew, but the example of her haughty mother had made her shrink from it. Celia had aimed to be more like her father, conscious of his own position but also conscious of his duty to use that position to benefit others.

Alec took the seat next to her, his warmth and strength bolstering. Celia flushed, remembering the cries she hadn't been able to suppress when he'd loved her, but she leaned against him, liking that she could.

Alec threaded his fingers through hers and held her hand on his lap, an intimate gesture of a lover. Fire spread through her.

"I know why Josette is anxious for you to find your brother," Celia said to keep from making a fool of herself and reaching for him. "She seems quite fond of Will. More puzzling is why Lady Flora decided to help you. It is a most curious thing for her to do."

Alec shook his head even as he stroked the backs of her gloved fingers. "I don't know, love. Lady Flora was one of Will's contacts in London. I'd say she was his lover, except …"

"Except that she and Mrs. Reynolds are lovers." Celia stated this in a matter-of-fact tone, then laughed when Alec stared at her. "Oh dear, I do believe I've shocked you again, Mr. Finn."

CHAPTER 21

$\mathcal{A}$lec continued to stare as Celia collapsed into laughter. "You must be very prim and proper in Scotland," she said, wiping her eyes. "Everyone knows about Lady Flora. We say nothing, of course, but everyone *knows*."

Something sparked in his eyes. "Lass, if ye think Highlanders are prim and proper, prepare yourself for a shock. Even the most Calvinist of them set aside their prudery when there's bairns to be made. But I thought you Englishwomen had cold blood and no notion of what went on outside a drawing room."

"Then you have not been to the same drawing rooms I have." Celia tilted her head back to study him from under her hat. "I wasn't meant to see, but even my mother's salons have turned bawdy when ladies and gentlemen sneak away to play. Unbeknownst to my mother, of course. She'd have exposed them and thrown them out."

"I'm sorry your mum wasn't warmer to ye," Alec said in a soft voice. "She has such a fine daughter—I don't know how she could treat you so."

"I wish I could say I was well rid of her." Celia twined her gloved fingers more tightly through his. "And I know, with my head, that I am. But she's my mother. I only ever wanted to please her."

"As is natural. But she abused that trust. You might forgive her, but I won't."

Celia made a faint shrug. "I am a duke's daughter. I was to marry not for my own happiness but to strengthen the family, and the dynasty. My aunt—my father's sister—understood this, because of course she was a duke's daughter as well. That's why she left me the legacy."

"Which I won't touch," Alec said, the words firm. "It's yours, and I'll have my man of business make sure it remains yours. Then you'll have something if I'm arrested and dragged away."

Celia shivered, clasping his hand as though she'd be strong enough to prevent a soldier taking him. "Please don't talk like that."

"'Tis only practical. I promised to endow you with all my worldly goods, remember? And I have plenty of them, so you keep your legacy and do with it what you please."

Celia snuggled into his side. "Well, if Scotsmen don't have prudery, I know one thing you do have."

"What's that?" Alec asked in sudden suspicion.

"Pride."

Alec huffed a laugh. "You're right about that, lass. And I'm the least proud of the family. No one can match me da', unless it's Malcolm—the Runt is full of himself. Or Will ..." He trailed off.

"We'll find him," Celia said.

She wished she could promise that. But life was never certain, war was savage, and the aftermath could be worse.

"You ought to have told me about him right away," she continued in a gentler tone. "I could have made discreet inquiries from the first day."

Alec's growl returned. "And I know I'll be arguing about this with ye the rest of my days. I didn't know if I could trust ye, it's dangerous, and even now, I don't want you in it."

"You've made that very clear." Celia rubbed his shoulder then rested her cheek on it. "But I believe that whatever you are *in* from now on, Alec, I'll be there too."

"Even in shite?" Alec asked, his voice vibrating her.

"I'll wear stout boots."

His laugh sounded through the carriage. Alec turned her face up to him and pushed away the distancing hat. "I am right that you've stolen my heart."

He kissed her, thumbs at the corners of her mouth opening her to him. Celia tasted his desire, thought of the dark passion of that morning, and her body dissolved into heat.

Alec continued the kissing, with hands skimming her bodice, unpinning her fichu to nip his way across her breasts, as the carriage moved east through the Temple Bar to Fleet Street and then up around the glory of St. Paul's to Cheapside, and an inn there where Mrs. Reynolds was to meet them.

Alec helped Celia re-pin her fichu and restore her hat over her now-mussed hair by the time they stopped, and Alec stepped down to find Mrs. Reynolds. He'd proved that gloved hands on her skin could be a powerful sensation.

Celia knew she was still flushed and unkempt when Mrs. Reynolds ascended and sat next to her on the forward facing seat—where ladies sat—because Mrs. Reynolds assumed a slightly disapproving expression as she looked Celia over. She said nothing, however, only waited for Alec to climb in and take the rear-facing seat.

Alec's eyes glimmered with mirth, he not the least ashamed that Mrs. Reynolds guessed he'd been fondling his bride.

Mrs. Reynolds said nothing until they'd wound their way

through Cornhill and Leadenhall Street to Whitechapel, through that district to Mile End Road. At the turnpike gate, the coachman paid the toll, and they were through into open country.

Staying north of the river, the road took them through Middlesex toward Essex and the sea.

"Lady Flora was most astonished to receive your message," Mrs. Reynolds said, fixing Alec with a sharp gaze once they were surrounded by farmland. "And a bit put out."

"Livid, ye mean," Alec said, unabashed. "She knew when she met me that I'd follow my own path."

Mrs. Reynolds turned her sharp gaze to Celia. "You are well, my lady?"

"Of course," Celia said. "Lord Alec has explained everything to me, including Lady Flora's plan for him to put me into his power utterly."

"Which he has done," Mrs. Reynolds snapped. "Quite thoroughly, it seems."

Alec said nothing, only gazed out the window, as though he saw no reason to justify himself.

"In a kinder way than Lady Flora had in mind," Celia answered. "Why should Lady Flora want to see me ruined? Does she hate me so? I can't imagine what I've done to earn her wrath."

Mrs. Reynolds let out a sigh. "It's nothing to do with you, Lady Celia. Flora—her ladyship—is distraught. I am afraid she saw you as a means to an end, that is all, and she thought that if Lord Alec made you afraid and dependent on his good will, you would be more biddable. I am sorry—truly. I tried to make her see reason, but ..." She swallowed, the cool, poised woman shaken. "I am pleased Lord Alec has proved himself a gentleman."

"I usually do," Alec said, leaning back and closing his eyes.

"I'm not the rogue Will is. To be fair, his ladies go to him most willingly—he's a charmer, not a rake."

Mrs. Reynolds continued to look distressed, and Celia patted her hand. She wasn't certain what to say—how did she respond to an apology about a plan to have her seduced and abandoned? The fact that Lady Flora had nothing against Celia herself did nothing to mitigate Celia's anger and bewilderment.

She thought of how Lady Flora had wept after the soldiers had searched her house, how pathetically she'd clung to Celia. Lady Flora had always been arrogant and haughty, and Sophia's death and her grief had turned her ruthless and harder still. The sparkle that had drawn all society to her had become deadly lightning.

Celia wished she could explain to all of them that she wasn't the giddy halfwit they imagined her. She'd known quite well her risk when she'd asked for Alec's help, but she'd known her trust in him hadn't been misplaced.

She'd grown up watching calculating men and women thrust and parry in order to rise in power or help their sons, daughters, and friends do so. There were people in her mother's circle who—like Lady Flora—would stop at nothing to further their ambitions, no matter who they hurt in the process. Others were equally as determined but held themselves to principles that they would not compromise. Those men and women had honor, and were recognized as such.

Alec was in the second category. Celia had seen this from his affection for his daughter, his true interest in Celia's art skills, his rage at the guests at the salon, his impatience with Lady Flora's high-handedness, his gentleness with Celia, and his protectiveness toward her against Lady Flora and her mother.

Celia had not refused Lord Harrenton solely from a maiden's disappointment that she'd marry an aging man. She'd seen his shallowness, his lechery, his greed—he'd even asked her father, in Celia's hearing, whether her legacy would be turned over to him. If Lord Harrenton had been a kind and caring man, Celia might have accepted. Lord James, her mother's next choice, had the same shallowness and lack of integrity.

Celia wanted the duchess and Lady Flora to understand that she made choices for reasons and not whims, but she supposed they never would. To them, Celia had been vulnerable and pliable, but that was over now. She was wife to a man she'd pledged her loyalty to, a man who'd earned her respect.

The road led off into farmland, and after that, marshes that ran along the river. The stink of the city fell behind, though the marshes weren't much better—foulness from the dockyards flowed downstream to the sea.

When it grew dark, the coachman clattered into the yard of an inn, one of the coaching houses along the turnpike. Traveling at night brought many dangers, and Alec, it turned out, had already arranged accommodation along their route.

Celia shared a tiny bedchamber with him, most of it taken up by a large bed.

"A gentleman, ye ladies decided I was?" Alec asked as he skimmed out of his clothes and slid bare under the covers with her. "Ye flatter me."

"You are." Celia's heart beat faster, her body moving against his of its own accord. "Whether you like it or not."

"What I like is *you*, my wife," Alec whispered, and then he loved her as the candles burned and sputtered out with the acrid odor of tallow.

In the morning, they went on, after a hearty breakfast brought up by the innkeeper's wife. The food was plain but good, and the innkeeper's wife flushed when Celia praised it.

Alec had styled them as a squire and his wife, with Mrs. Reynolds a widowed friend and companion to Celia. He seemed to revel in the deception, speaking little, looking confused when asked too many questions. The innkeeper and wife were indulgent to him, probably thinking him a bit slow in the head. Alec laughed as they rolled away, Mrs. Reynolds frowning at him.

"I understand why Willie likes the games he plays," Alec said, then his laughter died. "Though his games can be deadly, the bloody fool."

If the errand weren't so dire, Celia would be rejoicing in the country drive. June was marching on, the time when her father would be finishing up his business in London and moving them to the country for the rest of the year. Soft warmth touched the land around them, the fields blushing green, the trees beyond the marshes growing thick with foliage.

The Crenshaw estate in Kent, Hungerford Park, was beautiful, with a grand garden and grassy lawn, rambling hills excellent for long walks or rides on the duke's horses. The house was the largest in the area, a stone villa with rows of glittering windows, galleries of paintings, and books—so many books. On rainy days, Celia and her father shut themselves in the library and read all day long.

She would miss that. A qualm touched her, but she refused to give up all joy in her life because her mother had shoved her down a path—quite literally. She would prove that Alec Mackenzie was no traitor, his family would be restored, and he and her father would come to know and like each other. Harmony would return to life, she was certain of it. The alternative was too painful to face.

They followed the river and its waving marsh grasses to Tilbury, but they moved on through that town, not stopping until they reached a tiny village called Stanford le Hope. Here they found a small inn happy to take their custom.

It was such a different thing to travel as a married woman, Celia realized. She'd always been rather an appendage when she journeyed in her father's coach, her father and brother being the most important members of the family.

At the turnpike inn and now the inn at Stanford, the landlady assumed Celia would make all the important decisions—what was to be done with the baggage, what food would she like brought, and what sort of chambers did she wish to take?

Mrs. Reynolds slid into her relegated position as lesser person without fuss, and remained silent as Celia answered the landlady's questions. Alec again became the hearty if dim country squire, deferring all decisions to Celia. He was masterful at puckering up his face as though thinking hard and then shrugging and saying, "You must ask my wife. Yes, she will know what to do."

"You're horrible," Celia said when they lay in bed under the eaves. She poked him playfully in the chest. "I've never had to give such commands before. I'm terrified I'll choose wrong."

"I'm not." Alec gave her a smile that fired her blood. "You've a wise head on your shoulders. You can look after your doltish husband with no trouble."

"They pity me, I think. I see the landlady's sympathy when you clutch your head and walk away. You're enjoying it."

"Aye, a bit of playacting is a welcome diversion. And it keeps them from asking questions."

He had a point. "But you refused to dress up as Pierrot in the gardens," she reminded him.

Alec gave her a long-suffering look. "There are limits, my wife. It was hard enough putting on the uniform of a Scot whose job it is to put down other Scots."

Celia regarded him in puzzlement. "I thought you said the man was a friend of yours."

"He is. But he's fighting Frenchies and their allies on the Continent, not striding about the Highlands. Hence, we became friends. He lent me the uniform in case I needed to be a Scot while in England, but not a feared one."

"You are a complex man, my Lord Alec." Celia traced designs on his bare chest, enjoying the planes and curves of him.

"Not really. But I'll present whatever face I have to." He nuzzled her. "With you, I can be the real Alec. Thank you for giving me that, lass."

Celia kissed him. "I like the real Alec. Do you like the real Celia, I wonder?"

"I have all this time." Alec ended the conversation by rolling her onto her back and sliding inside her, loving her in swift silence.

~

IN THE MORNING, ALEC WOKE WITH CELIA'S WARM HAIR SPREAD across his shoulder, and his protectiveness surged. The thought of taking her close to the house they'd explore today, possibly putting her near soldiers, a pack of restless young men away from home, made every misgiving rise. If they were guarding prisoners and spotted and arrested Alec, what would they do to Celia?

"Stay behind today," he said as Celia blinked open her eyes. "Hide away here, and let the landlady look after you. Mrs. Reynolds and I will explore and return."

"Absolute nonsense," she said at once.

The heat of her defiance didn't really surprise him. "It will be dangerous, love." And if he lost her, no words would describe the incredible emptiness and grief that would be Alec Mackenzie. He'd already lost enough.

Celia sat up, the covers falling enticingly from her body. "I have already told you. I am here to help you. I will, no matter how small my assistance might be. I want you to find your brother. Besides, leaving me here is no guarantee of my safety. Plenty of dangerous people come to inns and taprooms. Who knows if the landlord can be trusted to guard me?"

Alec's rumble of anger shook the bed, but he realized their argument would quickly escalate to a shouting match, for which he didn't have time, and conceded.

He took in her flushed face, flashing eyes, and clenched fists and decided that later he might enjoy continuing the row. Even her triumph as Alec growled that she might as well accompany them made him want to kiss her. A full-blown argument would probably have an even better ending.

Celia scrambled into the coach when they went down after breakfast, as though worried he'd tell the coachman to rush off and leave her behind. Alec said nothing, only helped Mrs. Reynolds in and took his seat, and they were off.

The house the coach bumped toward was south of Stanhope near the village of Mucking, which ran along a creek emptying into the Thames. Farms spread from one side of the village, lush and green, and marshes, gray tinged with green, lay on the other.

Closer to the river, on the road to Tilbury, the coach creaked onto a tiny lane scarcely wide enough for the vehicle. Lined with brush that slapped against the wheels, it ran alongside the creek. The roof of a large house appeared over the brush, but this road skirted rather than approached it.

"Is this the house?" Celia asked as Alec tensed. "I know this place. It is Lord Spalding's estate."

Alec nodded. "Aye. The second possible prison is just beyond this."

CHAPTER 22

*C*elia leaned forward to take in the stone chimneys rising above the close-growing trees. "Lord Spalding and my father don't get on. Lord Spalding is obdurate in the question of banning slavery completely, even in the colonies. They quarrel about it endlessly."

Alec said nothing as he studied the house, committing every stone of it to memory.

The road curved past the house and headed toward fields, which were sprouting whatever Englishmen planted in this part of the country. A wall separated the grounds from the lane, and beyond the wall was a smaller building, long and low, one story high, that stretched across the bottom of the garden. Alec knocked on the roof of the carriage and asked the coachman to stop.

"The orangery," Celia said, looking out with him. "Very lovely inside, with lavish rooms where Lord Spalding holds banquets when the fit takes him. He keeps his orange trees in there too, but they are incidental."

Alec huffed a laugh as he ran his gaze over the arched, many-paned windows on the orangery's ground floor. The foundation bore small windows, which presumably opened to a kitchen and other storage rooms.

"As deathly quiet as the house in Cambridge," Alec observed. The building was meant to be festive, but under the leaden skies it was drab and forbidding.

"Most families are in London still." The scent of rosewater Celia had bathed her face in that morning touched Alec as she leaned to him. "There will be a few more grand balls in the city, then we'll start heading to estates for summer fetes and house parties, and when it gets colder, hunting and shooting."

"Not much different from what we do in Scotland," Alec said. "Summer and fall is for growing and harvesting, January for swanning to Edinburgh, putting on silk stockings, and pretending to be dandies."

"I look forward to that," Celia said in a light voice.

Alec liked that she assumed all would be well sooner or later, that normal life could resume for him. Alec was skeptical, but having her optimism about him was refreshing.

"Shall we drive on?" Mrs. Reynolds asked in impatience from where she sat on the cushioned seat. "In case they have guards?"

Alec knocked on the roof, and their journey resumed. They continued the drive, pretending to be nothing more than an idle family traipsing about the country, reveling in its natural beauty —a popular pastime—before they returned to Stanhope to sleep.

The next morning they headed south. A ferry at Tilbury took them with the carriage across the river to Gravesend, and in a village not far south of that, they crossed an ancient road that had lain here for seventeen centuries.

"This is the road that took pilgrims to Canterbury in the days of Mr. Chaucer, my brother told me," Celia said, indicating the large, flat stones with grass growing up between them. "And the Roman legions marched over it from the sea to London—Londinium—and back again."

Alec gazed down the faint line of stones, placed there by men of the Roman army nearly two millennia ago. His brother, Malcolm, had a fascination for history and antiquities—the discovery of the ancient city of Herculaneum near Naples excited Mal to no end. Only business at the distillery and then the Jacobite Uprising had kept him from rushing there and burrowing into the earth himself. He'd do it one day soon, no doubt.

Alec took his notebook from his pocket, opened to a blank page, and quickly sketched the road. He'd fill in more later from memory—the vast gray sky, the contrast of the very English farm village around it, the ghostly auras of the legionnaires as they tramped after their commanders.

Their coach left the road behind and turned south and west, moving slowly through farmlands interspersed with wild country. Alec hadn't been in this part of England before and wondered at the odd, squat houses with brick roofs topped with large, conical chimneys that rose from the grasses from time to time.

"Oast houses," Celia said, noting his puzzlement. "For drying hops, which many farmers grow in Kent. They spread the hops on a drying floor, and heat comes up through cracks beneath and disperses through the chimneys."

"Hops, eh?" Alec asked. "Are you a brewer?"

Celia dimpled in amusement. "Of course not. But farmers on my father's land grow hops, and I am curious by nature. My brother and I made nuisances of ourselves when we were younger, and the oast house workers showed us everything, likely to keep an eye on us."

And a good landlord knew exactly what his tenants grew and how it was processed and when crops were good or bad. The same way a good laird helped when times were hard and shared the rewards with his men when times were easy.

Alec sharply missed the life at Kilmorgan, when he and his brothers worked alongside their tenants and celebrated when the work was done. They would have that back, Alec vowed. One day.

They traveled a dozen miles in total, spending the night at Wrotham, which was near Celia's father's estate and not far from Sevenoaks. Celia went to their private chamber quickly, Alec noted, now worried she'd be recognized.

They kept to their chambers for meals and sleep, and left again in the morning, heading for the last house on Mrs. Reynolds's list. This was a castle, or an imitation one, near Shoreham.

They entered another turnpike road, and the coachman handed over the shilling and sixpence for their coach and four horses. Wits in London liked to say that while highwaymen robbed you only once, turnpikes kept on robbing you, sanctioned by Acts of Parliament.

Plans were in motion to extend turnpikes and wider roads up into Scotland, another attempt to tame the Highlanders. They'd tried this with the Wade roads after the 1715 uprising, but this time, Alec reflected, they wouldn't stop until the Highlands were paved and its inhabitants beggared or driven out.

They came upon the ruin of a real castle, now a lump of stone with one tower still standing. Alec was surprised to see even that, as local men would have absconded with the stones—why leave perfectly good building material to disintegrate in the rain?

The man who'd built the manor house just south of this must have tried to emulate the castle—the house was red brick and rambling, with false turrets here and there poking up over the wall around it.

"Home of the Tate family," Celia said. "The Earl of Chesfield, one of my father's friends. The earl has strong anti-Jacobite feelings and helped my father fund his regiment."

"A good candidate for holding Scotsmen prisoner, then," Alec said, tasting sourness.

Mrs. Reynolds calmly watched the brick crenellations of the walls flow by. "Let's not jump to conclusions. Careful observation will help us at present."

"I won't go bursting in waving my claymore, if that's your worry," Alec said. "But if I find out they're holding Will, I'll get him out of there, whatever it takes."

"I am certain you will," Mrs. Reynolds said in cool tones.

He noted Celia's look, which held understanding. In that moment, Alec realized he was no longer alone. The emptiness of his existence since Angus and Duncan had died began to fill again.

The road went past the house to the lands behind it. The Earl of Chesfield's estate didn't have a grand orangery or ornate gardens, but it did have an extensive park and woods that ran to the end of the property. At the edge of these woods was an older house, possibly the original manor before the current earl had built his monstrosity.

The old house had two floors, the ground floor with small windows closed by heavy shutters, a relic of the times when a home was a fortress against one's neighbors. The upper floor contained a row of dormer windows, also shuttered.

The mists that wound through the trees, blurring the light brick and black roof, was picturesque to an artist, disquieting to a passerby. To Alec, the house was merely a pile of stones that might hide his brother.

Alec opened his sketchbook to a blank page and drew the scene in quick, bold lines, adding in the trees that grew up to its walls. The house must have once lain in a clearing, but time and neglect had let the woods return and overrun it. All the better for secrecy?

He did not like the feeling he got from the place, a miasma of isolation and uneasiness. Difficult to believe they were a mere twenty-five miles or so from London, and very few miles from the thriving spa at Tunbridge Wells. This place was eerie, lonely.

When they emerged from the woods, the narrow road ran down a short hill to a chapel that lay in ruins, its roof gaping to the sky. Most likely it was a remnant of a monastery or nunnery that had been closed and gutted by Henry the Eighth when he'd had his tiff with the Catholic Church. Again, most of the stones had been carried away by locals, but enough remained of the abandoned chapel to add to the forlorn note of this part of the journey.

They circled back south to Shorham, where they put up at yet another inn.

Celia and Mrs. Reynolds descended and Alec moved to speak to the coachman, at the same time a man in a scarlet coat, a soldier of some regiment, came out of the taproom and into the yard, settling his hat as he made swiftly for the gate.

Celia's eyes widened and she swung around, quickly bowing her head and staring fixedly at the coach's wheels. The man gave them an uninterested glance as he went past, finding no significance in the travelers.

Alec had begun to relax when the soldier halted. The man remained in place, his back to them, as though thinking something over, and then he swung around. He was young, with hair the same color as Celia's, a frown creasing his face as he looked her over.

"Celia?" he said with incredulity. He strode to her before Alec could get between him and her, and swung her around. "What the devil are you doing here?"

CHAPTER 23

*C*elia stared in dismay at her brother, Edward Fotheringhay, Captain in the Duke of Crenshaw's Brigade, who gazed down at her in bafflement.

His expression held no outrage, she realized in the next heartbeat. He must not have heard of her elopement.

"What are *you* doing here?" she countered. "I thought your regiment was in France."

"On leave," Edward said quickly, but his eyes flickered.

Edward had always been bad at lying. Something was not right. "Then why not stay at the house?" Celia asked. "Or is the ale tastier among villagers?"

She put a teasing note in her voice, and Edward looked relieved. Celia perceived that Edward was more disconcerted that she'd seen *him* than that he'd seen her.

"As you say," Edward answered, but distractedly. He caught sight of Mrs. Reynolds and frowned anew. "Why is Mrs. Reynolds chaperoning you? Is Lady Flora here?" He looked about more swiftly, nervously, as though ready to flee on a moment's notice.

"London was growing too hot and close," Celia said, waving her hand. "I wanted to come home for some air."

Again, Edward looked relieved, and nodded. "Mother is very angry with you." He spoke offhand, as though searching for something to say.

"So are you—I thought."

"I was. I mean, I am." Edward dragged forth a scowl, but he seemed preoccupied. "You were too hasty and obstinate. I have forgiven you, because I'm so fond of you, Ceil, but you know you ruined your chances. All you can do now is wait upon Father and Mother, or hope that a steady gentleman someday will overlook the incident and take you on."

Celia was sharply aware of Alec, who'd kept himself near the coachman, his back turned. But he listened, his stance tense, boots planted firmly on the yard's dusty stones.

Mrs. Reynolds said nothing at all, fading politely back a few steps, as would be expected of a mere companion. No help would be forthcoming from her.

Celia could put Edward off and hope he went about his business, whatever it was, but if he was on his way to Hungerford Park, he'd be puzzled if she didn't accompany him. He would also discover, sooner or later, that Celia had run off with Mr. Finn—a letter might be heading to him even now.

Might as well get it over with. "Edward, I'm married," Celia blurted.

Edward blinked, as though this were the last thing he'd expected her to tell him. "I beg your pardon?"

"I married. A few nights ago. To a drawing master." Celia gestured to Alec who was now patting the horses, every line of his back rigid.

"A drawing master?" Edward's eyes widened, and his distracted air fled. "Have you run completely mad? Really, Celia, you have gone too far. Papa will annul this marriage right away —if he refuses, I will insist."

Edward's hazel eyes, so like Celia's, blazed, his chest puffing out with indignation.

"You will do no such thing," Celia said hotly. "It is a legal marriage. Mr. Finn is a gentleman, and none of the conditions of annulment can be met." She flushed as she spoke the last.

A marriage could be annulled upon one of three conditions —if a man were already married, or if the couple were too closely related, or if the man were impotent. Alec had proved fairly often the last few nights that he was not the latter.

Edward couldn't meet her eyes. "Celia, you are unseemly."

"I am practical," Celia said. "The marriage is true and will remain so. Not the brilliant match everyone expected, I know. I'm certain Mama will write reams to you about it, once she ceases raging. But I am happy. I hope that is enough to assuage your anger. "

Mrs. Reynolds broke in gently. "Perhaps an inn yard is not the place to quarrel about it. Lady Flora speaks highly of the man. Would you be willing to shake his hand?"

Celia did not want her brother, a soldier who'd fought under Cumberland to come face to face with Alec Mackenzie, but on the other hand, the sooner, the better. No one knew Alec as Alec —as far as most of the population of Britain was concerned, Lord Alec Mackenzie was no more.

Alec turned from the horses and came forward, hand outstretched. He'd pressed his hat firmly down to his ears, and took on the befuddled expression he'd been using with the innkeepers.

"Good afternoon, sir," he said to Edward. "How do you do?"

Edward peered under the shadow of Alec's hat as he accepted his outstretched hand, as though trying to decide what to make of him. "So you have married my sister, have you?" he asked in a stern voice. "Is she correct that you make her happy, or will I have to call you out?"

Alec flinched, the very picture of alarm and confusion. "Good heavens, no. Of course not. I am very much in love, sir. Very much in love. I wouldn't know one end of a sword from the other." He chortled nervously. "I believe *Mrs.* Finn is pleased with me. At least, she has said so."

Celia, her tongue stuck to the roof of her mouth, could say nothing at the moment.

Edward withdrew his hand, disapproval in his eyes. "A drawing master, eh? That sounds as though you don't have many coins to rub together. How will you support her?"

Alec produced a convincing blush. "Oh, ah. Her ladyship, Lady Flora, has found me well-paying pupils, and I do have a small inheritance from my father. Enough to keep Mrs. Finn in fresh linen and decent wine, don't you know."

"Finn. Sounds Irish."

"My father has a small landholding in that country. Very small. Nothing to what your father has. No, no." Alec gave a breathy laugh, his expression holding just the right amount of humility.

Edward peered again beneath Alec's hat brim, and this time, his eyes widened. "But you—"

He stood staring at Alec, mouth open, while Celia held her breath. Mrs. Reynolds had her hand in her muff, where Celia knew she kept a pistol. Alec had tensed, his hand edging to the top of his boot.

Then Edward shook himself. "No, no. Forgive my bad manners, Mr. Finn. I understand now why you didn't continue to the house, Celia. Best to stay apart, let Mother and Father grow used to the idea—am I guessing correctly that they did not condone this marriage? That you eloped?"

Celia dropped her gaze, pretending shame, which was what

Edward would expect. "We did. Mama was going to push me into yet another unfortunate match, and I'm afraid I ran away. I had already developed an attachment to Mr. Finn, and he had the kindness to help me."

Every word true, except Alec's name.

Edward kept his reproving expression but at last gave Celia a nod. "I understand. But *you*, sir, if you cause my sister any unhappiness, you will have to discover which end of the sword to hold and answer to me."

"Yes, yes, indeed." Alec bowed nervously. "Of course, your lordship. I am quite aware of the honor, Lady Celia has bestowed upon me, quite aware—"

"Enough." Edward took on his bluff, superior tones. "Good day, Celia. Mr. Finn. Mrs. Reynolds. I hope we all may meet again in happier times."

Edward tipped his hat then swung around and strode again for the gate, the tails of his red coat stirring.

Celia let out a long breath. Mrs. Reynolds moved swiftly into the inn, requesting rooms for them, and Celia followed. Alec hung back to confer with the coachman, who'd also watched the conversation with great uneasiness. Celia realized that all three of them—Mrs. Reynolds, Alec, and the coachman—had been prepared to kill or at least incapacitate Edward if he'd guessed who Alec was.

The knowledge shook her. She had married Alec, and she was falling in love with him, but Edward was her brother. Would it come to making a choice between them?

She prayed not. She also sent up a brief thanks to the Deity that no other soldiers were in the halls of the inn, or the taproom—she glanced inside as she passed. Edward had been alone.

And then that fact bothered her—Edward was always accompanied by his batman or some servant, and usually a friend or two. So what was he truly doing here, alone in this inn, instead of riding straight for Hungerford Park? She mulled this over as she followed the landlady to her rooms above to wait for Alec.

Celia was washing her hands and face in the basin when Alec came in. Celia turned to him, her face dripping, and reached for the linen towel that hung at the washstand.

Alec closed the door quietly and tossed his hat to a hook, but his face held grim tightness, and his eyes sparkled with fury.

"It's here," Alec said as Celia dried her face and came to him. "Will is in that house, Celia. I feel it in my bones. And your brother knows all about it."

$\sim$

CELIA'S DISTRESS REACHED ALEC AS THEY ATE THE MEAL HE barely tasted and on into the darkening night, but Alec couldn't concentrate enough to reassure her. He knew in his heart Will was in that old manor house, and it was all he could do not to ride off immediately and rescue him.

At a certain time in his life, Alec would have torn off at once, damn the consequences. Only experience and what he'd learned from Will himself stayed his hand.

If he charged through the woods, no matter how stealthily, the guards who were certain to be posted would stumble upon him, and if he wasn't shot outright, he'd end up inside the prison, keeping Will company.

He needed a cool head, and a plan.

Alec stared out the window, though he couldn't see much but the corner of the yard. He half expected Edward to return, bringing a contingent of soldiers with him. He was certain Edward had realized Alec was a Highlander, and had thought one of the prisoners had escaped.

Celia remained on the stool at the fire, staring into the flames, an untouched cup of coffee on the table.

Alec pried himself from the window and went to sit with her. "I'm sorry, love."

Celia looked up at him, and Alec was startled to find her eyes full of anger. "Not your fault if Edward has a part in locking men into secret prisons. Oh, Alec, if he has done this, what am I to do?"

"I wish I could tell you." Alec rested his hand on her cold one. "My only worry at the moment is to decide how I rush in and take my brother out. I won't have the wherewithal to ponder the grand implications of it all until later. That's why I'm sorry."

Celia let out a breath. "I've always admired my brother. So proud when he decided to become an officer instead of idle away his time like so many first sons do, waiting to inherit. We were so fond of each other as children. He was angry at me, yes, when I wouldn't marry Lord Harrenton, but I held out hope that we'd reconcile." She shivered. "But I couldn't forgive this."

"We don't know for certain your brother is involved," Alec said. "I know I said that, but I could be wrong." Alec didn't think he was, but Celia's anguish cut at him.

"He was very nervous," Celia said. "Far more worried about me catching him here than I was of him. It took him a few minutes to realize he ought to wonder why I'd come. Then when he looked at you ..."

"I know," Alec answered. "It was a bad moment."

"So, what do we do?"

Alec lifted Celia's hand and kissed it. "For that, I have a few ideas. We need a council of war—I'd like Mrs. Reynolds in on it, if ye don't mind. She and Lady Flora are a devious pair."

Celia agreed. Not long later, Mrs. Reynolds entered the

room and they gathered around the small table, speaking in low voices.

Mrs. Reynolds, now that they were in private, lost the quiet deference she assumed even in Lady Flora's house. She gave Alec a blunt stare and declared they should all return to London at once.

"Aye, I was thinking so," Alec said.

Celia flashed him a look of surprise. "I thought you wanted to investigate the house. You said you felt it in your bones—are you thinking that perhaps your bones are unreliable?"

Alec gave her the ghost of a smile. "No, I still believe Will's here. I can feel it. Mal's theory is that because I'm quick to learn the layout of a place and remember it that I catch clues that most people miss—even I miss them until I reason out what I've seen. However, you are right. I can't say for certain he's there. But it's only a matter of getting close enough to find out."

Celia shuddered. "Please go no closer than this, at least not tonight."

"Not with your brother roaming about. He might have alerted the soldiers." Alec leaned across the table to her. "I have an idea how we might search. You won't like it, love, but I can think of no other way."

"What?" Celia asked, torn between curiosity and anxiety. "Disguise ourselves as farmers and pretend we're looking for lost cows?"

Alec's eyes crinkled. "I like that, but I don't believe I could be convincing. No, lass, I was thinking we'd return to London, as Mrs. Reynolds suggests, and you face your mum and dad, and ask for their blessing."

CHAPTER 24

*C*elia sat in cold shock while Alec outlined his plan, which was both calculating and terrifying.

She knew he was right—she would have to face her parents sooner or later. What she'd hoped was that they'd find Alec's brother, fetch Jenny, hop into a boat for the Continent, and from there she could write a long letter to her father, a lengthier version of the note she'd sent him from Josette's boarding house.

She and the duke would correspond for a time, years perhaps, before she returned to London. By that time, the scandal of her elopement would have worn off, and she and her father could laugh about it.

"What if they refuse to see reason?" she asked in near panic. "Have you arrested for abducting me?"

Mrs. Reynolds broke in. "Do not fear, my lady. We will have Lady Flora on our side. She will make your mother understand that accepting Mr. Finn and blessing the marriage will be the least embarrassing course for her all around. Who knows? If your father declares he will make something of Mr. Finn, groom him as an MP or some such, then your marriage will be seen as a boon rather than a misalliance."

It was not a misalliance. Celia's father and Alec's were of equal rank—whatever the English might think of a Scottish title —but that was hardly the point.

"Until my father's men of business discover there is no Mr. Finn, small landholder in Ireland," Celia pointed out.

"But there is such a man," Alec said calmly. "I've a friend called Alden Finn, whose father recently passed and left him a bit of land in County Cork. There's even a ruined castle on it to give it éclat."

Celia let out her breath in irritation. "I ought to have guessed. You have friends who lend you uniforms, boats in which to escape, and now a name and family history."

Alec nodded, far from contrite. "I knew there'd be a risk that some clever-wit would look into the background of Mr. Finn. So I made certain he had one."

"Bloody cheek," Celia growled.

Alec grinned at her exasperation. "You're very beautiful when ye glare at me like that, lass."

"If we may resume," Mrs. Reynolds interjected, while Celia's face heated. "Lord Alec is correct. We must return to London, make your parents swallow your marriage without fuss, and carry on with the plan. Lady Flora, as I say, will be a great help. She can be very persuasive."

All three of them nodded thoughtfully.

"Well then," Alec said. "We leave at first light. If we change horses often enough, we'll reach London by midnight. My daughter is waiting there, impatient for her da'."

And Alec keenly felt the separation, Celia could see.

Mrs. Reynolds departed then, and Alec ate heartily of the supper the landlady had provided. Celia's interest in food revived as well—deciding to act was certainly preferable to brooding.

She and Alec made love well into the night, and both were red-eyed and exhausted by the time they piled into the coach, driving out of the inn's yard as dawn broke.

~

THE JOURNEY TO LONDON WAS SILENT, NO ONE WANTING MUCH to speak now that plans were laid. Celia went over and over the speech she'd give her father when they arrived, telling him how she'd allowed her heart to decide her happiness, how her natural prudence had first made certain Mr. Finn would make a good husband.

With Alec, Lady Flora, and Mrs. Reynolds playing their parts, Celia believed they'd get away with the deception for now. But how long would that last? One day, Alec would be known as a Mackenzie—they could not live a lie forever.

One thing at a time, Celia told herself. First, they must see that Alec's brother was safe, then they would decide how they would live. Exile was the most likely choice. Celia's heart sank at the thought, but she steeled herself. She was no wilting weed— her family was old and powerful, and she possessed their strength and steadfastness that had let them survive for centuries.

The first stop when they reached London was Josette's house. Alec declared he and Celia would not be going back to stay with Lady Flora, and he wanted to make sure Jenny was well. Celia had a wash before she climbed to the nursery to find Alec holding his sleepy daughter, speaking in a low voice to her.

"What is that language?" Celia asked as Alec's musical words washed over her. "You told me Irish when I first met you—after you tried to make me believe it was Greek."

"Erse," Alec answered. "Which is similar to the Irish language —I did not mislead you much. Both tongues have a common origin. Erse is the language of my fathers, and I want Jenny to know it."

"It will be banned, won't it?" Celia said. "Everything about being Scots will."

"Yes." Alec's tone was grim, yet he showed nothing but tenderness as he looked down at Jenny. "But this little one won't grow up in fear, denying who and what she is."

"We'll have to live on the Continent a long time then," Celia observed.

Alec sent her a startled look, followed by a grin. "My ever practical Celia. One thing I love about you."

Love. Celia suppressed the jolt that ran through her. He'd said the word when he'd spoken to Edward—*I am very much in love, sir. Very much in love.*

But he'd been playacting, hadn't he? Saying what would keep Edward calm, and fooled. Alec tossed the syllable out as though it was nothing.

It was everything to Celia.

And yet, Alec was a loving man. He demonstrated it all the time with Jenny, showed it in his terrible fear about his brother, and in the fact that he had raced across the Channel to find Will, leaving his younger brother safely behind. He'd also been married before, and grieved his wife's passing.

"Tell me about Jenny's mother," Celia said softly. "What was she like?"

"Genevieve?" Alec opened his mouth, paused, closed it, and frowned. Jenny burrowed into his shoulder, making contented noises.

"The truth is, I barely knew the lass," Alec said, candlelight playing shadows across his face. "She was a dancer in the opera. A wild thing, flittering and fluttering, her feet never touching the ground. I chased her—she chased me. We had an exciting affair, and I talked her into marrying me—I suspected she was carrying my child." He splayed his hand across Jenny's back. "We married but we never settled down. I thought there'd be plenty of time for that later. I went back and forth from France to Scotland, and when Prince Teàrlach crossed to Scotland and stirred up trouble, I told Genevieve to remain in Paris. We'd reunite after the Uprising was settled one way or the other."

He let out a breath, his gaze going remote. "And then she was gone. A man brought a letter to me while Mal and I stood in the street outside our house in Edinburgh. The letter said Genevieve died bringing in our babe but that Jenny was alive and well. Malcolm put me on a ship, and I went to find Jenny.

"Genevieve's family had already buried her by the time I reached Paris, and I realized how little I knew about her. I didn't even know her sisters and brothers or her friends, and most of those friends weren't aware she'd married me." Alec shook his head. "It was like a dream, or a play. Just when you begin to know the actors, the curtain closes, and the fantasy dissolves."

He trailed off, his voice glum, his words blending into the shadows closing on them.

"Jenny didn't," Celia said quietly.

Alec's eyes softened. "Except Jenny. Aye, she's real enough. The first night I knew her, I changed her nappy three times, and her screams went right through my head. She's a Mackenzie all right, making sure she's center of everyone's world." Alec kissed her hair, and Jenny gurgled.

"You are good to her."

Alec's brows went up. "Of course I'm good to her. I'm her dad, aren't I?"

Celia knew full well that many a gentleman wouldn't bother with an unexpected child, especially a girl. Alec could have denied Jenny was his and thrust her upon Genevieve's family, or left her with a parish as a foundling.

Or he could not have gone to Paris for her at all, leaving Jenny's fate in others' hands. Instead, he'd rushed across the water to find his daughter, to make sure she was taken care of. Alec was a rare man, and Celia's heart warmed.

He held Jenny close and spoke to Celia over her head. "You should go down to bed, love. It was a long journey."

"I know, but I wanted to say good-night to Jenny."

Alec's eyes flickered. "You're the one who's good to her, lass."

Celia mimicked his earlier words. "Of course I'm good to her. I'm her mama now."

Alec's expression held gratitude as he handed Jenny over for a quick hug, but his tone remained brisk. "Say your good-night then, and off to bed with ye."

Celia kissed Jenny's softly scented cheek, then she kissed Alec's as she returned Jenny to him. He turned his head and caught her lips.

The kiss was brief but held passion. The kiss ended when Jenny squealed with impatience, and they broke apart, Alec's laughter rumbling.

Celia's lips tingled as she turned away to descend to their bedchamber, as did her body from the heat in Alec's eyes. Not long later, he joined her, and the promising look he'd given her in Jenny's attic room became truth.

～

THE ENCOUNTER WITH CELIA'S FAMILY TOOK PLACE AT LADY Flora's. Alec arranged them in a tableaux in Lady Flora's private sitting room, the one that held a portrait of Lady Flora as a young woman, a regal beauty.

Alec seated Celia on a gold damask settee near the window

and stood behind her, his hand on her shoulder. He'd dressed in dark brown, his coat without frills, embroidery, lace, or trim. He'd found a white wig that settled over his dark red hair, two rolls of small, tight curls on either side of it.

Alec fixed his expression into that of a muddled country squire who was wondering what his steward might be up to while he was away. Celia wore one of the gowns Alec had asked Sally to bring to Josette's along with her portfolio, a light summer cotton with gold and green flowers—becoming, simple, modest.

The duchess led the way into the room at high speed, and under Alec's hand, Celia tensed. She lifted her chin, however— no crumpling under the duchess's enraged stare.

"Explain yourself, Celia," the duchess commanded in window-rattling tones.

The duke entered behind his wife, briefly taking in Alec before his eyes settled on his daughter.

The look of relief and love that came over the duke startled Alec. For such a long time, Alec had been picturing the man as a dire villain, one who hid away captured Jacobites for whatever nefarious purpose he had in mind.

What Alec saw was a short, plump man with a round face that held no malevolence. He had lines about his eyes, etched by a life of responsibility, not to mention marriage to a high-handed wife. At the moment, the duke's attention was all for Celia, his expression one of thankfulness that she was well and unharmed.

The duchess moved her glare from Celia to Alec. Her face was narrow, her nose long, the eyes above that nose holding a coldness Alec had seen over a musket aimed at him on Culloden field.

It was a saying in the Highlands that a man should take a good look at his sweetheart's mother before he stole her away, to get a glimpse into his life to come. Alec decided the saying wasn't quite accurate—he saw nothing of Celia in this woman and nothing of her in Celia. Celia must take her kindness from the genial-looking duke and probably her interest in art and curiosities from him as well. The duchess held only coldness and ruthless ambition.

"Who *are* you?" the duchess demanded of Alec.

Lady Flora and Mrs. Reynolds had come in behind the duke, the mitigators in this tricky situation.

"You know who he is, Your Grace," Lady Flora said. "Mr. Finn, the drawing master from Ireland, lately from Paris. He is a gentleman with a bit of land."

"Barely a gentleman." The duchess sniffed. "But I mean, *who* are you? What sort of land do you have? How many acres? How many in the arable? What sort of income will you be giving my daughter? Or will you be rushing to us in a few years from your Irish retreat with your hand out?"

"Now, Freya, let us not be hasty," the duke said.

The duchess's eyes went frosty, and Alec remembered Celia telling him her father and mother rarely used their given names with each other. A special occasion indeed.

"Hasty?" the duchess snapped. "She has defied me at every turn, and now she disgraces herself completely by marrying a ... a *nobody*. But not for long. Your father will have the marriage annulled."

Celia went pink, no doubt recalling the conversation with her brother about how they had no grounds for annulment. Alec drew a breath to begin the embarrassed and blundering speech that he'd prepared to argue against annulment, but Lady Flora cut in.

"Perhaps not the best recourse, Your Grace," she said. "This step need not be a humiliation, you know. Mr. Finn *is* gentleman born, and could be a good resource to you. Your

Grace will suffer less indignity if you put it about that the match is part of your plans. Mr. Finn can be given a courtesy title if you have approval—there is precedent for such things. And think of what you might make of the grandchildren."

The duchess did not look mollified by Lady Flora's words, but Alec watched the wheels begin to turn behind her eyes. If Celia had sons, she must be thinking, though they wouldn't be in the direct line for the dukedom, they would be more people for her to manipulate.

"Hmph," the duchess said.

Throughout this exchange, Celia looked not at her mother, but at her father. "Papa?"

"Are you happy with this man, daughter?" The duke spoke with resignation.

Celia reached up and took Alec's hand. "I am, Papa."

The duke gazed hard at her and then at Alec. Finally he sighed and nodded. "I did promise, didn't I? Very well, Celia. You have my blessing."

Celia's mother scowled at her husband. "I see nothing blessed about it. This young man already has a babe. Celia will be a drudge to it."

"No, indeed. Jenny is lovely," Celia put in quickly.

"There is nothing lovely about babies." The duchess sniffed. "I ought to know—I bore two of them. Good Lord." She pressed her hand to her face, her eyes widening. "How will I break this news to Edward? He will have apoplexy."

"He already knows." Celia squeezed Alec's hand and he squeezed back in reassurance. "We saw him—in the country, near our house. Al—Mr. Finn and I were looking for possible places to live while in England."

"Nonsense," the duke broke in briskly "Your home will be with us, of course, at Hungerford Park."

The duchess ignored him. "What on earth is Edward doing

home? I thought he was campaigning in France and the Nether-lands." She spoke ingenuously, apparently entirely forgetting she'd told Celia Edward waited to speak to her in the Spring Gardens at Vauxhall.

"He said he was on leave," Celia said.

Both duke and duchess looked perplexed, and disquiet touched Alec. He'd suspected Edward of being complicit in capturing Will, but then why wouldn't the duke know about it? His wife, a plotter if Alec ever saw one, was equally nonplussed.

"All the better that he is in England," Lady Flora broke in. "You must have a grand celebration, a wedding reception, at Hungerford Park—your first ball of the summer—to show how pleased you are at this marriage."

"That my daughter disobeyed me at every turn and ran away with a parvenu?" the duchess asked in incredulity.

Celia drew herself up to speak, but Alec stilled her.

"It's all right, my dear." He spoke in the breathy, self-depre-cating voice that he'd assumed as the dithering Mr. Finn. "I am a man of no consequence and we know it. It was a love match, Your Grace ... And Your Grace." He nodded to Celia's mother, then her father. "I am a fortunate man indeed."

The duchess gave him a chilly look. "More than fortunate. You have your hands on a duke's daughter and her legacy."

"No, no," Alec said quickly. "My man of business will see to it that her money in trust is beyond my reach."

"Then what on earth will you live on?" the duchess asked. "Yes, Charles, you will have to fashion some sort of position for him so they will not starve altogether." She swung to Lady Flora, eyes blazing. "I agree, Flora, that we must show the world we are not completely disgusted with this turn of events. Husband, put it about that you've had your eye on this man Finn for a time, and that we arranged the marriage. I will throw myself into planning a grand soiree, and perhaps the labor involved will help me forget my anguish that my daughter has destroyed all my hopes."

With a swish of skirts, she sped past Lady Flora and out of the room, shrilling for her footman to attend her.

Mrs. Reynolds watched her go, a look of satisfaction on her face. Lady Flora, serenely cool, betrayed no such triumph.

Celia rose, breaking the tableaux. "Papa."

The duke went to her, and Celia took his hands. They were of a height, the duke's brown-green eyes so like Celia's own. He had an ingenuous face, a man not gifted with extreme intellect, but Alec noted that he'd looked at each person in the room as a unique being without instantly categorizing them as the duchess did.

The duke touched his cheek to Celia's. "Daughter. I am pleased to see you so happy."

He gave her a warm smile and then held out his hand to Alec over the sofa. "I greet you, sir. *Son.* I hope that we may have a long and satisfying acquaintance."

Alec clasped the duke's hand, and the duke pressed his other hand over it, squeezing in friendship.

"As I do," Alec answered politely.

The duke looked straight into Alec's eyes, but Alec saw no recognition dawn, no sudden awareness that Alec was a Scotsman from the rebellious Highlands. There was no duplicity in the duke's gaze, only tentative camaraderie and optimism.

Either the duke was a superb actor, or Alec had misjudged him entirely. Alec saw no cruelty or callousness in this man, and he realized in that moment that he'd been completely wrong— the Duke of Crenshaw had nothing to do with capturing and imprisoning his brother.

CHAPTER 25

*T*he Duchess of Crenshaw's summer ball was remarked upon for years to come, but not for the reasons, Celia knew, that the duchess could have foreseen.

In less than a week's time, Celia and Alec were installed at Hungerford Park, a house that dated to the fourteenth century but had been built over and around so many times that the original stones could only be found in one of the cellars. Ten years ago, the facade had been redone so that rows of tall, narrow windows flooded the house with light. Celia's father complained about the window tax, but Celia's mother had overridden his objections.

The ballroom, on the end of the first floor and lined by three walls of these windows, had been dusted and polished, new candles set in its five chandeliers that dripped with crystals. An orchestra tuned in a gallery above, and the double doors were thrown open to a terrace that overlooked the formal gardens. Chinese paper lanterns hanging from branches of trees down the garden's center lit the fountains and the walks.

The furnishings of the public rooms had been released from

their drop cloths, the rugs beaten and relaid, the gilded frames holding precious paintings rubbed until they glowed.

The duchess had accomplished all this by bullying her staff unmercifully, and bullying her friends into accepting her invitation on short notice. It would not be forgotten, the duchess had implied, if the recipient of this invitation made their excuses or simply didn't turn up. More than half of London society was dependent on the duke's support, and so they duly arrived.

The Earl of Chesfield, of the red face and booming voice, arrived with his wife and sister in tow. With him came officers —a colonel, a captain, and a young lieutenant—from the regiment that boarded in his house. Uncle Perry, more refined than the earl in a neat wig and tasteful blue frock coat, greeted Chesfield and his officers and fell into conversation with them.

Celia's father, who disliked large gatherings but suffered them for the sake of the Whig party, stood uncomfortably next to his wife, his face pink, and welcomed his flock.

Alec had managed to beg off standing in the receiving line with the duke and duchess, giving his opinion that the duke's friends might be offended if forced to greet a nobody. A gradual introduction might be better, he suggested in his breathy, deferential voice.

The duchess agreed with Alec, looking a bit surprised he understood his lowly position. She did tell him, however, that he needed to attend in suitable attire. This she delivered with a pointed glare at Alec's well-worn suit.

The duke offered his tailor in London. Alec hadn't told Celia what the tailor had come up with, but when he emerged from his bedchamber to escort her downstairs, Celia saw that Alec had decided to err on the side of ostentation.

His frock coat was black velvet, but that fact could scarcely be discerned behind the silver embroidery and gold-threaded lace that covered every inch of it. Lace flowed over Alec's blunt-fingered hands and spilled out from the top of his waistcoat. The coat's peplum had been starched to bell out around his breeches, which were silver and gold brocade. White stockings clocked from knee to ankle covered his strong legs, and his brocade shoes were topped with buckles four inches square that glittered with diamonds.

Celia, who'd instructed her maid to dress her in modest attire—dark green velvet overskirt over a blue silk underskirt, and a fichu to cover her shoulders and bosom, stared at Alec, open-mouthed.

"Good heavens, Mr. Finn," she exclaimed. "If you stand under a chandelier, the company will have to shield their eyes."

"Exactly, lass." Alec was flushed with anticipation, his eyes glittering as much as his shoe buckles. "They'll see the hideous costume, not the man inside it. It's what a gentleman of little means would purchase when he was told there was no limit to what he could spend. He'd go mad for a time. The tailor was a happy man."

Celia looked him over, wanting to laugh. "I wish I could say you will be the most overdressed gentleman at the gathering, but I fear that will not be so." She tucked her hand through the crook in his arm, thrilling, as she always did, at the strength under the soft velvet. "Every dandy and fop in London will be here, wanting a look at the man who stole away the Duke of Crenshaw's daughter." She leaned close. "I doubt any of those will recognize you, but what about the Earl of Chesfield and his officers from the regiment?"

"This is where you will help me, my wife. You will cut them off whenever they try to get near me, or tell them I just stepped out of the room when they ask to meet me. And when it's time for me to vanish for good, you will claim I am with those who scuttled off to view paintings or exotic plants or whatever entertainments are to be had in this vast house."

Celia tightened her hold. "Do you truly have to go alone? This is too dangerous."

"We've been through the plan." Alec pressed his hand over hers. "Padruig will help, and if Will *is* in that house, we'll save time if he doesn't have to be convinced by strangers that I'm waiting for him. He'll flay me alive for coming after him, but at least he'll be free to do it."

Determination burned through him. Celia wasn't so foolish to insist on accompanying him—she'd hardly be helpful in her skirts and wide panniers, blundering through a dark woodland full of soldiers. Her part was to distract her mother's guests from cornering Alec or noticing when he'd gone. When the house was thronged, the dancing fully commenced, Celia would slip away and meet him in the appointed place.

The entire ball, in fact, was a diversion. Alec, Lady Flora, and Mrs. Reynolds had planned down to the minute what each of them would do. Celia had watched Alec grow grim as they plotted, the warrior in him erasing the smiling charmer Alec could become. He was a dangerous man, as Celia had sensed the first day she'd met him.

However, even with the officers attending the ball, and the soldiers likely slacking while their superiors went off to an entertainment, Alec would have to move like a ghost as he scouted the old house for a sign of his brother.

"You'll gleam in the moonlight." Celia said. "You won't even need a lantern."

Alec chuckled. "I have hidden plainer clothes in the woods. Don't worry about me, wife. I have done this before."

"That is hardly reassuring."

Alec slid his arm around her and scooped her to him for a long kiss. The silver threads of his coat and the gold in the lace scratched her skin, and the entire garment reeked of perfume.

But Alec's kiss was his, hot, commanding and giving at the same time.

Celia curled her fingers into the lapels of his coat, drinking in the kiss, memorizing the feel of him against her. If he was caught—

It didn't bear thinking about. Celia's heart beat faster as she released him. "Godspeed," she whispered.

Alec kissed her one more time and then, hand in hand, they descended the stairs.

≈

"OH, I QUITE AGREE," ALEC SAID TO EDWARD AND A LONDON FOP who'd been at Lady Flora's salon. "Suppression is the only thing to do. In Ireland as well. The natives there can be quite unruly at very just laws passed to keep the peace. They need to understand those laws are for their own good."

He sniffed, drew a large handkerchief from his sleeve, and touched it to his nose.

Edward frowned at him in disapproval, but whether at his words or the fluttering handkerchief, Alec had no idea.

"Indeed," the fop said. He spoke with a nasally lisp. "If the Irish or Scots stir up trouble, they will be crushed underfoot. They must be. If God had not intended us to be their masters, we would not be."

Ah, yes. The "what *is* must be right" sentiment. Alec had the feeling that if this young man woke up every morning in a black stone house with a leaky roof and nothing to eat all day but nettles, he might begin to question the rightness of the world.

Alec suppressed his derision and laughed inanely. Edward frowned more, as though having second thoughts about the suitability of Mr. Finn as a husband for his sister.

Alec finished the conversation by drifting away, saying

something about finding his dear wife. He scanned the room for her as though out of his depth without her.

Not difficult to feign—he didn't like Celia being too far from him. Alec strolled through the crowds, nodding and smiling, his wig askew, his handkerchief pressed often to his face. The duke's cronies eyed him sharply, but he watched the impression that Mr. Finn was an affable fool take hold. Alec knew that an impression, once embedded, was hard to shake off, which suited his purpose. The London *ton* would look upon him with arrogance, feel superior, and dismiss him.

Lady Flora arrived—late—surrounded by Mrs. Reynolds and an entourage of ladies who styled themselves, along with Flora and the duchess, as the leaders of society. The attention they drew allowed Alec to slip from the ballroom to a side corridor, where all was in shadow.

Celia watched him go. Alec caught her glance across the room, but she, bless her, made no obvious sign she'd seen him. They shared a brief look.

Alec knew, in that moment, with perfect certainty, that he loved her. Had for some time, since she'd caught the fire in his eyes in her drawing, when he'd seen the fire in *her*. Her clear thinking, her straight-faced jokes, her shrewd observation, and her gentle caring had wrapped around his whole being, had become part of him.

He'd finish this mission without being caught, because he would do whatever he must to return to her, his beautiful wife, the joy he'd found when he'd expected only sorrow.

I love you, my Celia, he whispered in his heart, then he made himself turn and go.

He'd explored the entire house in the days before the ball. This hall led past the room where pastries and drink were kept ready to replenish the tables in the supper room and thence to a staircase leading all the way to the cellars.

Alec headed down the stairs, which ended in a stone-clad passage connecting the servants' hall with the kitchen. A door halfway down this passage opened outside to stone steps going upward to a gate in a high hedge that led to the garden. Thus, guests at a garden party could have food and drink brought to them seemingly out of nowhere.

The main part of the garden lay beyond this hedge, screened from the working side of the house. Tonight, the ball's guests ambled along paths around pattering fountains, their way lit by colorful paper lanterns. Already ladies and gentlemen were seeking the darker reaches of the lanes for a stolen kiss, a tryst, or other secret meetings that might involve coupling or politics —the Duchess of Crenshaw's gatherings engendered both, according to Celia.

He skirted the edge of the garden, keeping to the shadow of the hedge. At the garden's far side was a wood, one that reached Lord Chesfield's lands, beyond which was the old house they'd passed the week before.

Alec had left a bundle at the end of the garden when he'd rambled over the estate like an excited pleb. Here he stripped out of his garish jacket and waistcoat and donned a dark, close-fitting coat, sliding his ostentatious breeches off to reveal a skintight pair of dark leather ones beneath them. He tugged off the wig, which would be a white smudge in the darkness, and made sure his hair was bound tightly out of his way. His shoes he replaced with a stout pair of boots.

Alec straightened up when he finished dressing and hiding his ballroom garb, turned around—

—and came face to face with an Englishman who recognized him at once, no question.

He was the Earl of Wilfort, Malcolm's father-in-law, who'd lived with the Mackenzies for months before his rescue by the British soldiers who'd burned Kilmorgan Castle.

Wilfort knew Alec, no disguise would aid him, and it was too late to hide.

"Alec Mackenzie?" Wilfort asked in a ringing voice. "What the devil?"

~

CELIA TURNED HER BACK ON ALEC SLIPPING OUT THE DOOR AND continued speaking brightly to her girlhood friends. The pain in her heart on seeing him go was greater than she'd expected. She'd thought herself sanguine with the plan, but now her mouth was dry, her throat tight, and she found it difficult to draw a natural breath.

It was all she could do to suppress the vision of the peril he headed to and focus on her friends' conversation. She forced her lips to smile, her voice to be light, as she chatted with them, wondering that she'd ever looked forward to their inane conversation.

Now that Celia was respectably married—though the ladies made certain she understood she'd made a grave mistake marrying so far beneath her—her friends no longer shunned her company. Of course, each young lady in the circle made it a point to mention *her* husband's or affianced's house, lands, investments, and gifts, and to flash her jewels as often as possible.

Celia countered this by remaining modest, quiet, and admiring, and exuding—when she could get a word in edgewise—that she'd married for love.

"Mr. Finn and I have discovered an enjoyment in strolling along together, speaking of anything and everything," she would say. Or, "Mr. Finn is teaching me the most marvelous techniques of drawing—he is quite talented, and is helping me with my small skill." Or, "Mr. Finn and I discovered we both very much enjoy reading. I know I am a bit of a bluestocking about books, but it is fine to have someone with whom to discuss them on a quiet night."

By the end of the conversation, several of the ladies looked wistful.

Celia tried not to glance at the tall, ornate clock in the corner of the ballroom, or even look at the door through which Alec had departed. She continued to chatter with her friends, but her lips were stiff, and her heart jumped and banged. She wasn't certain whether she hoped Alec found his brother or that the house would prove to be empty.

Celia noticed after a time that Lady Flora too had disappeared. Her friends remained, commanding plenty of attention, but Celia saw that Mrs. Reynolds, drifting from group to group, gazed about in some concern.

The dancing would not begin until after supper. Celia and Lady Flora had convinced the duchess to not have a sit-down meal, but for guests to eat as they wandered about, as though this were an indoor garden party. That way, there would be no pairing off to go into the dining room, when Alec's absence might be noted.

Celia wondered now whether Lady Flora had yet another plan up her sleeve—had she come up with the idea of no sit-down supper so her *own* absence wouldn't be noticed? And where the devil had Edward got to?

Mrs. Reynolds worked her way through the crush to Celia, putting a hand on her arm and giving her a look that said she needed a quiet word.

Celia walked away after her, pausing to speak to friends as she passed them, so it would not appear as though she was hurrying out with Mrs. Reynolds. At one point, Uncle Perry's sons—Celia's vapid cousins—stalled her to tell her at length their opinions on her misalliance, but at last she broke away and left the ballroom.

Mrs. Reynolds waited for her at the stairs, and they ascended to the relative privacy of the gallery.

"I can't find her." Mrs. Reynolds said in a whisper, and Celia realized the woman trembled. "I know why Lord Alec wanted Lord Chesfield to bring the regimental officers with him tonight—but I fear ... Flora has been behaving so very odd lately."

They were alone in the gallery, away from the stairs and the noise from the ballroom below.

"She has indeed," Celia answered. Lady Flora's entire part in this affair had been odd—from her allowing Alec to stay in her house at all, to her broken sobbing after the soldiers had searched her home, to her idea for Alec to abduct Celia and put her into his power. "Tell me what you fear."

Mrs. Reynolds shook her head. "She is fixated on the regiment at Lord Chesfield's. I don't know everything, but this week she's been very excited, and she ceased talking to me. I very much worry that ... We must find her. Please help me, Lady Celia."

Her eyes glittered with tears, alarming in a woman usually so unruffled.

"Where did you see her last?" Celia asked.

"I thought she came up the main stairs. I do wish your mother would have set lights up here."

"And waste the candles?" Celia lifted her skirts, panniers creaking as she started down the gallery. "One can peer at my father's paintings just fine in the dark."

Mrs. Reynolds's heels clicked as she hurried after Celia. "Yes—Flora must have suggested they view the collection."

"Suggested to whom?" Celia asked in bewilderment.

A male voice roared down the corridor, as though in answer

to her question. "What the bloody hell are you doing, woman? Put that down before you hurt yourself."

Mrs. Reynolds increased her pace, passing Celia in a graceful flash. Celia kicked off her useless shoes and ran after her, stocking-footed, her skirts swaying like a galleon in high wind.

At the end of the hall, double doors led to an anteroom where, in the days of Charles II, courtiers would remain while the king viewed the duke's extensive collection of paintings in relative privacy.

Three people stood in the high-ceilinged little room tonight, which was lit by candles they must have ignited. One was the colonel billeted with Chesfield—Kell, Celia believed his name was. The other man in the room, also in a scarlet regimental coat, was her brother, Edward.

Lady Flora faced them both, a polished flintlock pistol in each hand, their mother-of-pearl handles things of beauty in the candles' flickering light.

CHAPTER 26

*T*he Earl of Wilfort continued to stare at Alec through the gloom of the woods, his eyes gleaming in the moonlight.

"What has happened?" Wilfort demanded swiftly, more concerned than outraged. "Why are you in England? Is Mary—"

Alec pushed Wilfort into the shadows, cutting off his panicked question. "Not a word. Not a sound."

Wilfort's words died away, the man astute enough to realize when silence was necessary. Mal's father-in-law was a slim man with wiry strength, much of that strength from his character. He was dressed in fine clothes, obviously one of the guests at the duchess's ball, his neat wig tied with a black ribbon.

Alec gripped his arm and guided him into the woods until they were well away from the garden. He stopped at the tree beneath which he'd hidden a dark lantern, but he didn't release Wilfort to look for it.

"Your daughter is perfectly safe," he said in a low voice. "She's in Paris, growing thick with Mal's babe. What are *you* doing skulking at the end of the Duke of Crenshaw's garden?"

"The duke's crushes weary me." Wilfort adopted the same soft tones. "I attended tonight only because I need to show my interest in his offspring's tiresome new husband, an Irishman of no note. One glimpse of the colorful popinjay was enough."

Alec couldn't suppress his grin. He let go of Wilfort's arm to sketch a fussy bow, à la Mr. Finn.

Wilfort's eyes widened. "Good God. I thought there was something familiar about the man, but I never got close enough to observe you clearly. Do you mean to say you tricked Crenshaw's insipid daughter into believing she is your wife? What on earth for?"

Alec lost his smile. "Celia is not insipid. She's worth a thousand of the duke and duchess and her rather dim brother. It was no trick. I married her in truth."

Wilfort's bafflement deepened. "Then why are you still in England? I understand about the disguise—your life is forfeit if you're caught. But why did you not abscond with her out of the country the instant you married her?"

"What do you know about Crenshaw's regiment?" Alec countered.

"Little. The duke raised it to fight in France, but after Fontenoy, it was diverted to Scotland with Cumberland. A contingent is billeted nearby, I believe."

"On the Earl of Chesfield's land. I suspect they're holding my brother."

"Malcolm?" Wilfort's question rang with horror.

"Not Mal. Will. I made the Runt stay with his wife."

Emotions flickered through the earl's eyes, he not one for demonstrating either great fear or relief. He settled on amazement and disapproval. "You are creeping over to try to free him? Are you mad?"

"I need to discover if Will is there at all, and if so, how to get him away. If you have any fondness for our family, you'll help me—namely return to the house and escort Celia safely to our rendezvous."

Wilfort's mouth firmed. "I'll accompany you, if you don't mind."

He stated it politely, but Alec knew he meant he'd follow whether Alec liked it or not.

"I can move quicker on my own," Alec protested.

"And if sentries spy you, they'll respond to an order from me more readily than an explanation from you. I can walk right in without challenge if I declare that the duke or Chesfield sent me to look over the prisoner."

"We believe there's more than one prisoner. I heard that several Scotsmen were being held. Why, I've not learned."

"All the better. I will say I was sent to observe what is being done with the prisoners."

"Too bloody risky."

Wilfort gave him a deprecating look. "I suppose you intend to pick a lock or break open a window? I'd believe it of Malcolm or William, but you have always seemed more civilized."

"If by *civilized* ye mean weak, you're wrong."

Wilfort shook his head. "I did not mean that at all. I mean that picking locks and breaking windows is not in your character. If you charge in there by yourself, you'll end up fighting for your life."

Alec ground his teeth, but he knew in his heart that Wilfort was right. Will and Mal had inherited the cunning and crafty nature of their ancestor, Old Dan Mackenzie, the first duke, who'd come by the title in ways best not looked into. Alec had always been more straightforward. He encountered a problem, he beat on it until it solved itself or went away.

"How can I know you won't simply turn me over to them?" Alec asked. "We get inside the prison, and they lock me in as well?"

"Because of my love for my daughter and my unborn grand-child," Wilfort said sternly. "And my respect for your brothers and father. Besides, I know that if I betray you, you'll slice me open on the spot. I want to live to see Mary again."

"Aye, well. You have a point."

Alec crouched down and reached beneath the leaves. Wilfort took a step back, as though worried he'd come up with a sword, and relaxed when he saw the lantern.

Alec took flint and steel from his pocket, struck a spark, and lit the candle inside. The dark lantern had three sides solid iron, and the fourth side could be quickly shuttered.

"Stay quiet," Alec ordered, and then led the way through the wood in the direction of the old house.

~

"FLORA!" MRS. REYNOLDS'S ANGUISHED CRY BROKE THE SILENCE.

Lady Flora did not flinch. Her pistols remained trained on Edward and the colonel. Colonel Kell had a hatchet-like face and at this moment he glared at Lady Flora in rage.

"Lady Flora," Celia said in dismay. "For heaven's sake—please, don't hurt my brother." The simple plea was uttered without rancor. Edward's eyes were wide with fear, but also shame.

"He was *there*." Lady Flora's voice shook. "He knew what happened. When *this* monster ..." She broke off and advanced until the pistol was leveled at Colonel Kell's chest, though she remained just out of his reach.

"What on earth did he do?" Celia asked.

But in a flash, she understood. Lady Flora had collapsed in despair when the soldiers had gone through her house, though she'd been cool and tart while she'd spoken to them. She'd wept unrestrainedly afterward, sobbing that she missed her daughter. *I miss her with every breath. Why did they take her away from me?*

"Flora, no." Mrs. Reynolds started forward, but Lady Flora stilled her with a quelling glare.

"Please," Mrs. Reynolds went on, her eyes shining with tears. "If you kill him, you'll hang. Please don't do this. I can't bear to be without you."

"He touched her." Lady Flora's voice rang clear. "My Sophia. The breath of my life. *He* put his filthy hands on her." She waved the pistol at Colonel Kell's head. "She sobbed it out to me, how he'd found her alone in Lord Chesfield's bloody house, how she resisted his flirtation, until he dragged her off and had his way with her. Drunk and disgusting, and when she screamed, he laughed."

The colonel's face drained of color. Celia didn't know Colonel Kell well, but she'd seen him with Lord Chesfield. Celia had overheard her father say that Kell had acquired his rank more through money and position than the ability to lead.

"Oh, God," Kell said with realization. "Is that who she was?"

"Yes, *that was who she was.*" Lady Flora's eyes were dark with pure fury. "She had a name. Sophia. Say it."

Colonel Kell gulped. Edward, Celia was troubled to note, continued to look ashamed. Had he known?

Lady Flora pointed her second pistol at Kell's groin. *"Say it."*

"Sophia," the colonel babbled. "Her name was Sophia. I had no idea she was your daughter, my lady. I'd never have touched her."

"Bastard." Lady Flora spat at him. "She was light and life, and you took that away from her. She showed signs of your disgusting pox, which even now rots your blood. The child she carried died inside her. In despair, my dear, beautiful, sweet Sophia, took a pistol and ended her life."

Colonel Kell swallowed. "I didn't know. I swear to you."

Lady Flora had put it about that Sophia had died of an illness, nursed to the end by Flora herself. No one had been allowed to see her, to go near her. The illness, Celia now realized, had been Sophia's pregnancy and miscarriage as well as her knowledge that she carried a disease that would slowly kill her.

"I'm so sorry," Celia whispered, aghast.

Edward now looked shocked. He must not have known the whole truth.

"Flora, please don't do this." Mrs. Reynolds moved to her. "There is another way. We'll accuse him, humiliate him, ruin him—"

"And have my daughter's name dragged through the dirt?" Lady Flora asked in imperious tones. "No. He is scum, and scum must be cleansed."

Lady Flora leveled the pistol, her finger squeezing the trigger. Mrs. Reynolds flung herself at her. At the same time Edward barreled into Kell, shoving him to the floor.

Behind Celia, a puzzled voice said, "Good heavens, what is happening?" and Celia's father hurried into the room.

The pistol Lady Flora began to fire ended up pointing straight at the Duke of Crenshaw. Celia screamed and ran at her father, just as the gun went off.

Blood spattered Celia's white fichu and her father's pristine silk cravat as the two of them toppled to the floor. Celia gasped but felt no pain, only lightness.

"Celia!" The duke caught her in his arms, cupped her face. "My darling girl, are you all right?"

"I seem to be ..." Celia trailed off as she saw the gouge in her father's face, the blood. *"Papa."* She quickly stripped off her fichu, wadded it, and pressed it to his cheekbone.

The duke blinked, his eyes flooding with pain. "Oh. Bloody hell."

"Arrest her!" Colonel Kell spluttered as he climbed to his feet, pointing a shaking finger at Lady Flora. "She is a madwoman. She has shot the duke."

"I'll arrest *you*, sir," Edward growled, springing up beside him. "For rapine and dissolution."

"All that will do is shame Sophia," Lady Flora wailed. "My way is better. I don't care if I do hang!"

She brought up the second pistol and fired it at Kell.

Celia and Mrs. Reynolds had caught both Lady Flora's arms at the same time. The bang of the gun burst in Celia's ears, but the bullet went wild, striking a thick molding that framed the windows.

Celia twisted the spent pistol from her grasp. "Lady Flora, for heaven's *sake*. Edward, see to Papa."

"I am all right." Her father sat down suddenly on a chair, the linen pressed hard to his face. "I think. 'Twas only a graze. I had worse as a young man in the army."

"*You*, sir, are going nowhere." Celia stepped in front of the colonel, who was trying to flee out the door.

Mrs. Reynolds stood beside her, the two of them making a formidable wall. Behind the colonel, Lady Flora sank to the floor, head in her hands, weeping.

"Don't worry, Flora, dear gel," the duke said weakly. "We will not have to put him on trial. He can be ruined all the same, when it's put about that he's a rakehell and a wastrel, not to be trusted around decent women."

"I keep explaining, I did not know who she was," Colonel Kell said in desperation.

"That is hardly the point." The chill in Edward's voice was worthy of their mother. "A man of honor would not touch a woman, no matter what her status. We take our orders to protect the weak, not be as horrible to them as any enemy."

Lady Flora raised her head. Her face was blotchy with tears, her eyes red and streaming. "It's worse. He and Lord Chesfield are keeping prisoners—not ransoming them or trying and executing them. Keeping them penned up day after day, probably torturing them, terrifying them. Monsters."

"Lady Flora," Celia said, her eyes widening. Even now Alec must have reached the house where the prisoners were—did Flora mean to send Colonel Kell and all his men rushing there at this moment?

Lady Flora pointed a long finger at the duke. "And *you* condone it! You are as guilty of horrors as he is."

The duke blinked over the now-bloody linen. "What are you talking about, my dear? What prisoners? We housed some temporarily, yes, but they're gone now. Transported, or pressed into the army. We need such bloodthirsty fighters on our side."

Edward shook his head. "No, Papa. They are still there. I saw them—I heard of some odd goings-on, so I came home to investigate. Lord Chesfield and his friends have three prisons, and they move their prisoners from place to place whenever they fear they'll be discovered. These men—Scots all—have been thrown into foul cells, each put to the question several times a day. Lord Chesfield explained that they are trying out new interrogation techniques on the prisoners, to see what is the most effective. Monsters, indeed."

Colonel Kell sneered. "*They* are the monsters. You fought them, Captain," he said to Edward. "You saw their brutality."

Edward looked down his nose at him. "Fighting on the battlefield is a damn sight different thing from banging up a man and torturing him, instead of giving him the clean dignity of an execution."

"You're soft, like your father," Kell snarled. "I am not afraid of you, whelp."

"You ought to be," Edward said, his aristocratic hauteur rising. "*I* will be Duke of Crenshaw one day, while you will be the trumped-up country squire you always have been. You and Lord Chesfield will have those men transported or tried and executed, immediately. We will start in the morning."

Celia's heart thumped. If Alec could not find Will and get him free tonight …

"Papa." She swallowed. "Can you not do something? *You* have nothing to do with torturing prisoners, do you?"

"Of course not." The duke looked indignant. "I'd never condone such a thing."

Celia believed him. Her relief that her father was as guiltless as she'd always thought him made her knees weak.

"But who did?" she asked, her curious mind surging ahead. "Lord Chesfield does not have that power, not without Papa's permission—"

Edward was shaking his head again. "Not Father," he said, his voice quiet. "Uncle Perry, pretending he had Father's authority."

"Oh." Celia felt sick, the pistol heavy in her hand. She recalled the bluff conversation she'd overheard between her father, Chesfield, and Uncle Perry, where they'd advised her father to go play with his mistress and leave the difficult decisions to them. "Oh." Her anger rose. "Damn him."

"*Celia.*" Edward looked shocked.

He opened his mouth to say more, but was interrupted by the arrival of Uncle Perry himself, Lord Chesfield at his side. Celia heard others coming, the gunshots having attracted attention.

"Sir." Colonel Kell snapped off a salute to Lord Chesfield. "They know, sir. About the prisoners."

The duke levered himself to his feet and lowered the cloth, unmindful of the amount of blood that had poured out of his cheek.

"Explain yourself, Perry," he said in a severe voice he rarely used. "And you, Chesfield. You both told me the Highlanders would be taken to trial right away. And now I hear you've been using them to practice interrogation and torture? Taking orders from Perry in my name? I'll not stand for this. Where is the honor in it?"

"They're *traitors*," Uncle Perry said in the condescending tone he habitually used to explain things to Celia's father. "They deserve to die vicious deaths, but only after they suffer a while first."

"These are not barbaric times," the duke snapped. "I fought under Marlborough, against the mighty Louis of France—the current Louis, his great-grandson, is a pale imitation. And even then we were not so merciless to our prisoners. War has rules for a reason."

"Highland soldiers are not *men*," Uncle Perry said with exaggerated patience. "They are animals. They don't feel things and understand them the way we do. Leave the thinking to me, Charles. It's always best."

"Not this time." The duke drew himself up. "*I* am the head of this regiment. None can countermand my orders but the king. If you'd like to draw *him* into this, I am happy to send a messenger and invite him to the discussion."

Lord Chesfield and Uncle Perry exchanged glances. "Now, don't be so hasty, Charles," Lord Chesfield began.

Uncle Perry set his jaw. "If you are that much of a stickler for the rules against filthy brutes that nearly overran us, brother-in-law, then yes, we will have them executed. We will do it right now." He picked up the pistol Lady Flora had dropped to the floor. "Give me that gun, Celia. Come along, Charles. You can be witness to our mercy as we shoot the bloody lot of them."

CHAPTER 27

*T*he sentries, as Alec had suspected, had taken advantage of their officers being away to gather for a celebration of their own. Their sergeant joined them as they passed around a fat jug of something, laughing together in a circle of firelight, well away from the house.

One of the men was about to go on leave, to return home where his wife had borne their first child. He took a lot of teasing, growling at their remarks, but he remained good-natured.

They were, in short, bored soldiers who'd taken the King's shilling for the pay, and didn't much care whether they guarded a house in the English woods or camped in mud in the middle of France. They obviously were not worried about their captives escaping or of anyone walking in to rescue them.

Malcolm might have set off an incendiary device deep in the woods to attract their attention, but Alec did not want these lounging soldiers to come alert. He'd had a better idea when he'd seen the penned-up sheep on the farm at the other end of Hungerford Park, which were released during the day to keep the lawn trimmed.

Padruig had not been happy with his part to play, but he took Alec's coin and melted away to obey.

Timed to the second, the sound of bleating filled the woods, and the soldiers groaned. "Bloody hell," the sergeant snarled. "That's the second time this week. Can't the man fix his fences? He's a bleeding duke after all. Go on, corporal—take your men and herd them back. Next time, we'll dine on fresh mutton and to hell with it."

Most of the guards trudged into the woods, making plenty of noise. The sheep, happy with their midnight freedom, dashed hither and yon, leading them on a merry chase.

The door sentry left to help.

Alec darted out of the shadows, sank down, and inserted a stiff wire into the back door's lock. Wilfort stepped in front of him, hiding him from anyone who might happen to glance from the woods. After a moment or two, the lock clicked open.

Wilfort stayed behind as a lookout as Alec slipped inside. The story Wilfort would tell if caught was that he'd grown bored with the duke's ball and had taken a walk—more or less the truth.

Alec moved swiftly through an empty hall that ran the length of the house, doors on either side of it. None were locked, he discovered, but the rooms held no Scottish prisoners. He found cots, a makeshift kitchen, an office—the barracks of the soldiers.

Two doors very close to each other opened to stairs, one flight going up, the other going down. Alec had reasoned they'd keep the prisoners in the cellar, but a muffled groan from above changed his mind. He started up silently.

At the top was another hall, also lined with doors, but each of these had been fixed with a solid wooden bar that rested in slots in the doorframe, bolting them firmly shut. A man inside might pick or break open a lock, but escaping through the thick bar would be a different matter.

The doors were paneled and painted, once elegant, but the bolts fixed on them were roughhewn, the effect like a lady covering a lovely gown with a course, homespun cloak.

The hall held a dozen doors. Will might be behind one of them, or not here at all.

Alec grunted as he heaved the first bar out of its slots and then picked the lock. He swung the door open but took a quick step back as a thick miasma of unwashed bodies and un-emptied slop pails wafted out at him.

No light flickered here, and the shaft from Alec's dark lantern barely illuminated two unmoving lumps of men, chained, on the floor of a room devoid of furniture, the window shuttered and covered with iron bars. The men wore linen shirts and breeches and were barefoot, with no blankets against the cool of the night. Their hair was thickly matted, beards hid their faces, and each had one hand manacled to an iron bar in the wall.

They didn't stir as Alec looked in on them. Neither of the men was Will—they didn't possess the length of limbs or flame-red hair of his brother. Alec moved inside, removed another tool from his pocket, and unscrewed the manacles.

The men never woke. Alec left them and went to the next room to find a similar scene. This time, when he went to loosen the manacles, a hand came out to seize Alec's throat in a surprisingly strong grip.

Alec looked into blue eyes, which widened. "Alec Macken-zie?" came a hoarse whisper. "Bloody hell."

"Stuart Cameron?"

A Highlander, friend to Will, a man Alec had seen often enough in his lifetime. Stuart's face was covered with a filthy beard, his face creased with blood and dirt, but his eyes held fire.

"Aye, that's me, as much as they try to make me forget me name. Ye best go from here, lad, lest they chain you up with us."

"Rot that." Alec unscrewed his manacles. "Can ye stand?"

"I'll do."

Alec pressed the screwdriver into his hand. "Free the others. I'm looking for Will. Is he here?"

Stuart shook his head. "I only ever see *him*, and the bloody Sassenach soldiers." He gestured with his foot at the unconscious man next to him. "They put me in here with a McTavish. Can ye credit it?"

"There are horses at the edge of the woods. A boat waiting in the Thames. Sentries are distracted. Get yourself and as many as you can out of here. *Now.*"

Stuart had enough raiding and fighting days behind him to know how to move rapidly. He nodded and had the second man unscrewed and shaken awake before Alec made it to the hall.

He tried three more doors, finding the same behind each—a pair of men, chained and asleep, barefoot, beaten, starved, and exhausted. Alec hurriedly loosened their manacles with a second screwdriver in his pocket—Mal had taught him to always bring more than one tool, just in case.

Alec moved to the next room on the corridor, making himself go methodically through each one. He didn't want to miss Will or make too much noise because he got in a hurry.

When he opened one door and went through, a man rose up behind him, wrapped chains around Alec's neck, and pulled them tight.

Alec fought hard, but the hands on the chains were relentless. The man on the floor rose, also inexplicably free of his manacles, and plunged a dirk at Alec's heart.

At the last moment, the blade halted. "Will!" the man with the dirk cried in a hoarse whisper. "Leave off! It's Alec!"

For a second, the chains didn't waver, then they rattled and fell away. A pair of raw, red hands spun him around, and Alec looked into the face of Will Mackenzie.

Alec barely recognized him. While his beard had not grown as thick and tangled as the others', his face was covered with scraggly whiskers that could not hide the bruises and raw wounds on his face. His fingers trembled as he held Alec, and his breathing was shallow.

His eyes, though, Mackenzie gold, burned like living fire.

Without a word, Will dragged Alec to him, closing his arms around him in a rib-crushing hug. Alec held him in an embrace for a long moment, rejoicing that his brother was alive, solid, real.

They pushed from each other at the same instant, their relieved looks turning to glares.

"Come on, man, we're going," Alec said.

"What the devil are ye doing here?" Will growled at the same time. "Get out before ye ruin everything."

"What do ye mean, ruin everything? I'm rescuing ye, ye ungrateful bastard."

"Who asked ye to? I'm trying to figure out what these poxy Sassenach soldiers are up to. A few more days, I'll know."

"They're up to executing you, that's what," Alec snapped. "We're going."

"Ye don't understand—"

The man with the dirk cut him off. "We have enough, Willie. It's too risky to stay."

Will scrubbed his hand through his hair in a familiar gesture that made Alec's heart squeeze, and let out a snarling groan.

"Aye, you're right. I'll free the others. Alec, go on before you're caught. I'll be along."

"Stuart Cameron is letting out the others. I have horses waiting and vehicles for those too weak to ride. Gair's on the Thames, ready to float us off."

Will shook his head. "Wagons will be too slow."

"Not wagons. Chaises and coaches, pulled by fast horses." Alec took Will's arm and swung him around. "Now, go!"

Will's cellmate pushed past them both with a fierce look and headed into the corridor. Will and Alec followed, and they found the other men freed, Stuart Cameron herding them to the stairs, the more injured slung over the shoulders of the less injured.

The house remained quiet as they trundled out, but Stuart halted after a peek out the door. "There's an Englishman out there."

"Aye. It's Wilfort—Mal's wife's dad," Alec said. "He's with me."

"Wilfort?" Stuart asked, startled. "I remember him from when Murray banged him up at Holyrood. Are you sure?"

Will waved him on. "He's a decent man, for an English aristo. Besides, when couldn't ye outfight and outrun one lone silver-haired gent?"

"When soldiers started poking me with bayonets to see how long it took me to scream," Stuart said, but he made the decision to dart through the door, the others following.

The Earl of Wilfort turned to them and pointed through the trees. "That way. Hurry! I hear others coming."

The sheep were still bounding through the woods, the shouts of the soldiers faint as they pursued them. What Wilfort had heard, and what Alec did now, was the jingle of harness and the rumble of wheels as a carriage came their way, moving rapidly on the rough road.

The Highlanders dispersed, fading into the mists as silent as smoke. Will looked around, listening. "Sheep?"

"Aye." Alec took the time to grin. "A good distraction, I thought."

Will gave him an admiring look. "Did Mal do all this? Where is he?"

Alec scowled. "No, *I* did, ye ungrateful sod. I have a mind to put you back in there and chain you up myself."

For a moment, Will looked thoughtful, as though seriously considering the idea. Then he sighed. "No, they'd just kill me now. Wilfort," he greeted the man as he jogged past. "Pleasant to see you again. Mary was well, last I saw her."

"So I hear," Lord Wilfort said. "Both of you, go. I'll stave off whoever is coming…"

Alec paused to press the man's hand. "Thank you. I thought Mal was mad to steal away your daughter, but you've proved a good friend to us."

"I thought the same," Wilfort said with his dry humor. "Now I have a pack of crazed Highlanders for in-laws. I look forward to renewing our acquaintance when I am next in Paris."

He sketched Alec a bow. Alec shot him a salute and turned to run after Will.

He saw his brother flitting from shadow to shadow, as agile as ever, thank God. Alec's brain hadn't quite caught up to the fact that he'd accomplished his mission, but his blood was pounding, his exhilaration high. Celia would be waiting at the boat, as would Jenny, all prearranged and planned to the last detail.

Alec heard a shout. He turned as the carriage, its lamps flaring, surged along the narrow drive to the old house. Alec saw the large frame of the regimental colonel drop from the box, along with what looked like Celia's brother. He then saw Lord Chesfield emerge from the carriage, followed by the Duke of Crenshaw.

The colonel and Chesfield yelled for the sentries, bellowing orders and curses. The duke slammed the carriage door but remained behind, arguing with someone inside the coach, not noticing Wilfort approach him.

The carriage door opened again, and Alec went cold as he saw his wife emerge and climb to the ground in a flurry of skirts.

~

"PAPA, YOU HAVE TO STOP THEM," CELIA CRIED AS SHE SPRANG from the carriage's lower step, clutching at her father to keep from slipping. She'd found and restored her shoes, but they were useless in the churned-up mud.

The duke steadied her with concern. "I see no sentries or soldiers—something is wrong. But do not worry, my dear, I won't let them execute the men tonight. I will see that they're conveyed to London, where they'll have a proper trial."

Her father did not understand it had gone far beyond that. Uncle Perry and his pet colonel were crazed with hatred.

Celia clutched his sleeve. "Alec is in there—I mean Mr. Finn. He's gone to find his brother. You can't let them kill him, Papa —please!"

The duke's eyes widened. "Child, what are you saying? Why would Mr. Finn's brother ...?" He trailed off as realization grew. "Mr. Finn is a *Highlander*? But—I thought he was Irish."

Celia was too anguished to worry about explaining. "You have the power to stop them. Please do not let Uncle Perry kill my husband!"

The duke gaped at her for a moment longer before he squared his shoulders, turned, and cupped his hands around his mouth. "Perry! Chesfield! Come back at once!"

Colonel Kell and Edward returned to the carriage before the others, the colonel with his pistol out. "They've gone—escaped,"

Kell snapped. He took in the duke's expression and abruptly trained the pistol on him. "You did this."

"Oh, for heaven's sake," Celia said heatedly. "My father didn't even know the prisoners were here."

Uncle Perry rushed into the light thrown by the coach lamps. "What are you doing, Kell? Get out there and hunt them down."

"No," the duke said in a hard voice. "Let them go."

Uncle Perry spun to face his brother-in-law. His dark eyes held the same chill as Celia's mother's. "And let them burn and pillage their way through the countryside, raping and killing as they go?"

"They are broken wretches who will flee the country," the duke said. "If they even live to reach the coast."

"Have you lost your mind, old man?" Uncle Perry roared. "I'll tell Freya to declare you insane, and *I'll* take over your command. You are a bloody, weak fool, and the sooner you step aside, the better."

"I believe *I* am my father's heir," Edward said with quiet fury. "When he is gone, you will answer to *me*."

"I made you, Edward," Uncle Perry's eyes glittered with triumph. "You are mine."

"No one made me." Edward's voice was quiet but strong. "I have listened to you disparage my father and sister for long enough. You are nothing, and now you are finished."

Uncle Perry's eyes burned first with fury then calculation. "No matter. The Highlanders have escaped, and they are murdering as they go. What a pity the duke and his son were caught in the melee."

He aimed his pistol at Edward, and gave the colonel, who still had his gun aimed at the duke, the nod to fire. Celia shouted and lunged for Perry.

Two horses charged out of the darkness. One bowled right

into Colonel Kell, sending him into Edward, who grappled with him as they went down. The second horse skimmed past Uncle Perry, a fist coming down to slam into the side of Uncle Perry's head.

Uncle Perry dropped, the pistol falling uselessly from his grasp. The duke cried out and threw up his hands in defense, but Alec galloped past him and then wheeled his horse and returned, reaching down for Celia.

"Are you mad?" she shouted at him. "I can't possibly—"

Edward and Colonel Kell continued to wrestle. The colonel rolled on top of Edward, and now the pistol pointed at Edward's head.

The man on the first horse leapt from it, tackling the colonel. Edward grabbed at the pistol, but Colonel Kell held on to it as he clawed and kicked and fought both Edward and the very dirty and battered man who'd landed on him. The three men tumbled and tangled, the battered man gaining his feet again, just as the pistol went off.

"Edward!" Celia screamed.

Alec slid off his horse. He caught Celia as she rushed to her brother, moved her gently aside, and ran to Edward himself.

Alec and Will rolled Colonel Kell from Edward. Edward grunted and pushed the colonel away, coming to his feet, his wig hanging from the epaulette on his shoulder. His white cravat was now scarlet, but Edward stood upright, breathing hard.

"Bloody hell," Edward said. "Bloody, bloody hell."

Colonel Kell, the man who'd violated Lady Flora's daughter, who'd caused Sophia's death and Lady Flora so much grief, was dead, a bullet from his own pistol in his chest. Lady Flora now had her revenge.

The Highlander who seized Uncle Perry by the collar and hauled him up was tall and grim, and had eyes so like Alec's

Celia knew at once who he was. Those eyes held impossible fury as he shook Uncle Perry until Perry woke with a gasp.

Uncle Perry gazed at Will for a stunned second, and then a look of terrible fear came over him. "No," he croaked, before Will Mackenzie's fist caught him on the side of the face once, twice, thrice.

Again and again, Will hit him, until Uncle Perry's face was covered with blood, and he collapsed once more into a senseless heap.

Will let him drop, kicked the man's ribs, spat on him, and turned to Alec, fierce satisfaction in his eyes.

"There. Now, I'm ready."

Will flowed up onto the horse and turned it, nudging it forward. Alec once more held out his hand to Celia.

The duke gave Celia a look of such distress that her breath caught. She went to her father and took his hands.

"I'll come back, Papa. One day, I promise. But Alec is my husband. I pledged myself to him with all my heart—and I love him." There, she'd said it.

The duke's eyes moistened. "But how will you live? He's an outlaw ..."

"I will provide well for her," Alec said. "My real name is Alec Mackenzie, and my father's a duke. I have a fair bit put by, all safe in France and the Low Countries. She'll live like a princess. My da' and brothers would let me do nothing less."

The duke swallowed, blinking back his tears. "Go then, my dear. I'll deal with your Uncle Perry. And your mother."

He lifted his chin as he said this last. The worm had turned, Celia decided. She knew her father was stronger than he let on —a learned man, preferring his books to people, he nonetheless had power, and he knew it. To keep the peace he let others do as they wished, but Celia had a feeling that peace had come to an end. She almost wished she could see her mother's face when the duke confronted her.

Almost. Alec was her husband, and she was leaving with him.

"I'll look after him," Edward told her. He caught Celia in an embrace. "Be well, sweet sister."

"Thank you." Celia kissed his cheek. She turned from him and seized her father's hands again, pressing a kiss to each one. "I love you, Papa. Come and visit me in Paris."

As usual, her father looked embarrassed at her open display, but his smile was warm. "I will be there, daughter."

And she knew he would be.

"Come along, my love." Alec guided her with his arm around her waist to the horse. "Before my impatient brother drags me off by the hair. Ah, here he is."

Will had galloped back, a pistol gripped in his hand. "Time and tide, brother."

Alec swung onto the horse. He reached down for Celia, who had to kick off her brocaded slippers to put her foot on his boot and let him haul her upward. Her skirts billowed, making the horse dance. She wished she'd been able to change to the more sensible clothes she'd planned to wear to the boat, but it couldn't be helped.

"What are you doing?" Will demanded as the horses sprang forward. "Carrying her off, are ye? Isn't that going a bit too far?"

"She's my wife, ye ass. I'm not leaving her behind."

Will whirled around, barely missing a low-hanging limb. "Your wife?" His eyes widened as he took in Celia, Alec holding her close. "Good Lord, you're quick off the mark. It's only been a month since I last saw you. When did you find time to get yourself married?"

"'Tis a fine tale," Alec said. "One to tell to while away a sea voyage. *If* we ever get there."

Will gave Celia one last amazed look, then he turned and urged his horse onward.

Alec laughed as he followed, holding Celia rock steady on the saddle. She relaxed back into him, curling her stockinged feet in the cool air, knowing he'd never let her fall.

CHAPTER 28

*G*air's ship, waiting in the Thames, was small and ramshackle, but Celia, who'd voyaged to and from the Continent several times in her life, recognized it as a seaworthy craft. The ropes were firm, the sails whole, and the boards of the ship, while not polished like a naval craft's or a grand merchantman's, held no holes or rot.

Celia found herself surrounded by Scotsmen, all of them injured in some way, many of them too ill to lift their heads. Gair, a slightly built, evil-looking man with a thin queue of hair hanging from a mostly bald head, complained incessantly that his hold was taken up with filthy, stinking Highlanders, but Celia noted that he found a hammock or pallet for every man and made sure they were tended.

During the trip, Celia assisted in nursing them, bathing wounds, helping men shave themselves, or covering them with warm blankets at night. Her heart went out to these Scotsmen, hurt, starved, a long way from home and journeying even farther from home to save themselves. They didn't complain, they made jokes—usually bawdy ones—and settled in to heal.

Will Mackenzie recovered quickly, as did his friend Stuart Cameron. The big men were rough speaking and joined Padruig in toasting their freedom with Scots whisky—the ship seemed to carry many casks of it.

Gair gave over his captain's cabin to Alec, Celia, and Jenny, but not, he warned, from the goodness of his heart. The cabin would cost them extra. Alec only nodded and promised the money when they reached shore.

"Never pay Gair up front," he explained as he and Celia sat in the bow, Alec wrapped in a dark green plaid he'd brought out as soon as they sailed. "If he finds a cargo that will make him wealthier halfway to your destination, he might send you off in a skiff and take on the more lucrative cargo."

"Would he truly do that?" Celia asked, glancing at the man chivvying one of his sailors up a mast. "I'd think no one would trust him after a time."

"No one does. I exaggerate to make the story better, but not by much. Gair prides himself on being underhanded."

They'd slid down the Thames under cover of darkness, Gair competently avoiding naval ships at Gravesend and Southend, slipping through marshland and mist, heading to open water as the sun rose. The Channel tossed the boat wildly, and the freed men groaned, seasickness not helping their weakened state.

Alec slid his arms around Celia, holding her close, as the wind of their passage chilled them. They could have hunkered below, but Alec had said he wanted clean air, and Celia agreed.

Will found them, dropping onto the board seat opposite them, wineskin in hand. "Now is time for that story, Alec." His eyes were alight, his jaw clean and shaved, showing a sharp Mackenzie face, albeit one bruised and cut. "Rescuing a pack of Highlanders *and* finding yourself a bride in the space of a few weeks? Tell me everything."

Alec shrugged. "Why don't we wait until we reach home? I'll only have to explain all over again to Dad and Mal and Mary."

He teased—Celia had sensed the lightness in him since they'd made it on board. Will scowled. "I can always beat it out of you, little brother."

"Ye can try, ye mean. Why don't you tell *me* why the devil you were so angry at me for turning up to free ye? Did ye enjoy being prisoner of British soldiers ready to flay ye alive? And why the devil did ye spring up in front of a troop and tell them ye were Prince Teàrlach?"

"So they'd capture me, of course." Will took a pull from the wineskin, which Celia knew held whisky—Mackenzie malt, Alec had told her.

"Of course," Alec repeated with a scowl. "Who were ye protecting? Teàrlach himself?"

Will shook his head. "I never saw the man. He's gone to ground well and good in the western Highlands somewhere. Good luck to anyone trying to find him. Of course, the soldiers were certain I knew where he was, so they took me to their special interrogation prison, which was all to my plan."

Alec spoke into Celia's ear, his breath warm against the sea wind. "He's a madman. Only explanation."

"Only a little mad," Will said. "I'd heard rumor of men high-placed in Prince Teàrlach's army who were being kept in a secret prison. They'd vanished—no one knew what had happened to them, not even their own families. Stuart Cameron was one of them, and he's an old friend, for his sins. Also Mackenzies who didn't get themselves murdered on the expedition looking for French gold."

Will paused, his expression bleak. Celia had heard the story of a ship carrying gold from France and other weapons and supplies that had landed in the north of Scotland, the gold and goods immediately seized by Highlanders loyal to King George.

Jacobites who'd gone to find the gold had been cut down nearly to a man. The gold had been the last hope of the Jacobite army, according to Edward, and that hope had died, making their defeat at Culloden inevitable.

"I heard that rumor too," Alec said. "Which is why I was looking for you. But I stayed in a comfortable house and questioned people instead of jumping in front of a troop to get myself captured."

Will shrugged. "I like to be more direct. Anyway I found the prison. They moved it about, from house to house, so if anyone got wind of it, they'd be gone before the area could be searched. The men running it were very aware that they risked their careers, because it wasn't sanctioned by King Geordie or even Cumberland, as much of a bastard as he is. The plan was to ferret out everything these men knew and present it to the king, in hopes he would lavish them with rewards, money, whatever a greedy man wishes for. Your uncle is ambitious, lass. He also very much enjoyed thinking of ways to torture us." He rubbed the side of his head, which was crossed with contusions under his scraggly hair. No wonder Will had punched Uncle Perry so thoroughly.

Celia nodded glumly. "He has always been envious of my father, always pushing in on everything he did. My father let him, because he is generous. I suppose Uncle Perry wanted power of his own—perhaps he thought the king might give him a title. Being brother-in-law to a duke isn't the same as being a duke himself."

"And ye couldn't find this out skulking around and listening at keyholes?" Alec demanded of Will.

Will opened his eyes wide. "Is that what ye think I do?" His face was different from Alec's, narrower, his nose longer, but they both had the dark red hair, smattering of freckles, and the Mackenzie golden eyes.

"All right, there's some of that," Will conceded. "But I wanted to know exactly what Lord Chesfield and the Honorable Perry Waterson were up to. What better way than to make them think me in their power? You can find out much about interrogators from the questions they ask."

"Ye can also get your head bashed in," Alec growled. "Here I am, running up and down England looking for ye, while you're sitting all cozy in a cell gathering information."

Will's expression cleared. "And I am grateful, Alec. I wasn't quite sure how we'd all get away—I knew *I* could, but I did not want to leave the rest of those men to their fate. I planned to use the grand ball at the duke's to my advantage, but I had no idea you'd decided to use it for *yours*."

"Alec planned the ball in the first place," Celia said, rising to his defense. "He had Lady Flora convince my mother to hold it, and then he arranged for the horses and carriages, and for Gair to be waiting with his boat. Mrs. Oswald—Josette—assisted us." Celia watched Will as she spoke this last, gauging his reaction to the name.

To her satisfaction, Will's eyes softened. "Ah, Josette. How is she?"

"She appears to be well," Celia answered when Alec remained silent. "She was quite worried about you, and a great help." Celia wasn't quite sure all Josette had done, but the woman had been genuinely concerned about Will. She'd have to write her and tell her Will was well and free. "Alec and all his acquaintances spent a long time planning your rescue," Celia went on. "He even married me as a part of it all."

Alec laughed, the sound rich. "No, lass, marrying you was a selfish ruse." He kissed her neck, his mouth hot. "To get ye all to myself."

Celia flushed as her skin tingled. Will watched them, then

his face softened and he lifted the wineskin in a toast. "Ah, Alec, 'tis good to see you happy again."

"'Tis good to be so, brother mine."

"What *did* my Uncle Perry want to find out?" Celia asked Will, curious even as she warmed to Alec's touch. "Did he think you had Bonnie Prince Charlie hidden away somewhere?"

Will shook his head. "Funny, they didn't seem interested in the prince at all. The sooner he fell into a bog or headed back to France the better, as far as they were concerned. No, what they asked most about was the gold."

"The French gold?" Celia asked. "Good heavens."

"Aye," Will said. "It was never found, you know. Mal and I suspected it was stolen by the Highlanders who intercepted it, and they've now spent it on ostentatious things like food and clothing to keep them warm through the winter. But Lord Chesfield and your uncle are convinced the gold is still floating about the northern Highlands. They were so adamant, they've nearly convinced me as well."

The end of Will's nose twitched, as though he were anxious to dive overboard, swim ashore, race to Scotland, and start hunting for lost gold.

"And then I came along," Alec broke in, "to put an end to your information gathering. And to save your life and that of twenty Scotsmen at the same time. I can see why you're cursing me."

Will's grin flashed. "Truth to tell, I was bloody glad to see ye. Ye did a fine thing, Alec. *And* ye got yourself a wife in the bargain." He looked Celia over, his pleased expression warring with one of curiosity. "We'll be having a grand celebration when we're back in the bosom of the family, I'm thinking."

"Aye, that we will," Alec said. He gathered Celia close, the fold of his plaid coming around her shoulders. "As I introduce to them the woman I love."

"Love?" Celia asked, her heartbeat speeding.

She hadn't meant to blurt the question, especially not in front of Will. She flushed, but she studied Alec—he could use the word so casually.

"Yes." Alec's golden eyes held fire, passion, truth, and a hint of challenge. "I love you, my Celia."

"Oh." Celia burned all over, any hesitancy, fear, and trepidation dissolving at the heat in his voice. "I love *you*, my Highlander. My Alec."

A huff of laughter accompanied a swirl of plaid as Will took himself away and down the deck, leaving them alone.

The wind from the sea to the north was brisk, sending rain through the Channel and rough water. The boat tossed, the cold bit at them, but as Alec leaned to kiss her, Celia had never felt warmer in her life.

~

THEY LINGERED ON THE COAST OF FRANCE, GAIR AGAIN AVOIDING British ships prowling the waters in their ongoing war with King Louis. Will had a hideaway near Le Havre, and there the men rested and recovered. Most had a broken bone or two, and some were simply too ill to move.

Alec watched Celia come into her own as she bathed wounds, wrapped limbs, and bullied the landlord who ran the house into scrounging up clothes, medicines, clean bedding, decent food, and hearty ale. She did it all in perfect French, ordering large, strong men about with the intensity of a battlefield general. Perhaps having something of her mother in her wasn't a bad thing.

After two weeks, the Highlanders improved and grew stronger, and talked about what they would do. Some wanted to brave going home, to make sure their families were well. Others planned to settle in France or find their friends who'd gone to the Low Countries for life in exile. Stuart Cameron was one who planned to return to Scotland, though he promised he'd keep his head down and not require Will and Alec to rescue him again.

Letters had gone back and forth between Le Havre and Paris, Mal telling Alec he had everything ready for Alec's return with his bride and daughter. Celia insisted on writing to her father to ensure him she was well, and Will got the letter smuggled across the Channel.

They set out on a fine summer morning in a chaise Will had procured, one with good springs and soft cushions. Sally rode inside with them, she and Celia cooing over Jenny, who loved every moment of attention. Alec and Will rode facing the two ladies, the brothers traveling in companionable silence. Will looked his old self again, his beard long gone, his red hair trimmed, his eyes as animated as ever.

The journey went in easy stages, Alec not wanting to tire Celia, Sally, and Jenny. He liked the slowness, which gave him time to talk at length with Will and discover everything he'd learned since they'd last seen each other.

The Mackenzies would have to lie low in Paris for a time, Will said, though Lord Wilfort was subtly pulling strings to have the family cleared of treason and slowly brought back to life. Will, for his part, preferred to stay dead—he could travel about and poke into things easier if everyone thought Will Mackenzie had perished on the battlefield.

Alec didn't mind one way or another—he had Celia and Jenny, a place to live, time to pursue his painting and raise his daughter. One day, he would return to the lands of his ancestors, but for now, he'd while away his time in Paris, not a bad city to spend an exile in.

He also liked the time to lie abed with Celia, learning her

body, teaching her to explore his. Sunlight lingered into the night at this time of year, which let him enjoy her in the long dusk, her body a place of light and shadow.

Paris unfolded like a smoky smudge on the horizon after a few days. The outskirts were thickly clustered with houses, the buildings rising higher and becoming more lush as they neared the Tuileries, Palais-Royal, the Louvre, and the squat towers of Notre Dame. Tall houses crowded onto the Pont-au-Change and other bridges, the Seine beneath as smelly as the Thames.

Alec took them to a house in the Saint-Germain district, a confection of stone and painted shutters that rose to a mansard roof. The main door led to a courtyard, beyond which was a large garden shared by houses in the square.

A door in the courtyard sprang open as soon as the carriage pulled into it, and out came Malcolm Mackenzie, the Runt towering over Alec as he pulled him out of the coach and smothered him in a hug.

He shoved Alec aside and yanked Will out next, giving him the same crushing embrace.

"I was sure you were both dead," Mal declared at the top of his voice. "Without me there to look after ye."

A young woman with very blond hair and a quiet manner stepped out of the house after Mal, beaming her wide smile on Alec.

"I knew you'd prevail," she said, rising on tiptoe to kiss Alec's cheek, then Will's. "Mal worried every day, but between you and Will, I was sure you'd be right as rain."

Mary stepped back and took them in, and Alec saw the smudges of worry that had stained her face, despite her glib words. Alec also noted that her gown was cut to hide her thickening belly, and Mary touched her hand to her stomacher. "He kicks something lively," she said. "A Mackenzie without question. Now, where is she?"

Mary reached Celia before Alec could, the two greeting each other with enthusiasm, as Alec helped his wife from the coach.

"You could have knocked me over with a feather when Mal told me Alec had married Lady Celia Fotheringhay," Mary exclaimed. "I thought you betrothed to that horrid Lord Harrenton. We *must* talk."

"Watch yourself," Mal warned Alec, standing shoulder to shoulder with him. "That's a bad sign."

"You love listening to Mary chatter, Runt," Alec returned. "Don't pretend you don't. I imagine the house will be filled with chatter now, and babies crying. We won't be able to think."

"There's always whisky." Mal clapped both brothers on their shoulders. "I am bloody glad to see you both, I won't deny it."

Sally emerged from the coach with Jenny, and Alec took his daughter gladly into his arms. At the same time, a rumble filled the courtyard as Daniel William Mackenzie, Ninth Duke of Kilmorgan, barreled out the door.

"Did anyone bother to tell me they were here?" he bellowed. "It's more gray hair you've given me, Willie, you and Alec both. I can't spare any more sons, damn the lot of ye. Is this the wife?"

Alec held Jenny securely, she observing the duke without fear as she chewed on one fist with new teeth. Alec put his arm around Celia, and Mary remained steadfastly on her other side.

"This is Celia," Alec said. "Your daughter."

The duke, who'd glared so hard at Mary when she'd first appeared in his house, sent the same glare to Celia, but his eyes quickly softened.

"Well now." The duke cleared his throat. "Ye appear as though ye can look after my good-for-nothing son. Got a bit of steel in you, I warrant. You'd have to, t' run off with him."

"I hope so," Celia said. She made a very proper curtsy. "I am happy to meet you, Your Grace."

She held out her hand. The duke took it, but instead of

bowing over it, he tugged Celia close and enclosed her in an embrace. He said nothing, but his eyes were moist when he released her.

"She's too damned fine for the likes of you, Alec," he said as he straightened. The duke surreptitiously wiped his face, muttering something about dust.

"Don't I know it." Alec grinned at Celia. "That means he likes you."

"Humph." The duke set his face in its habitual scowl and stormed back into the house. "There's a feast waiting for ye. Make Mary happy and come and eat it."

"Ah." Alec said as he followed the grumble into the house, Celia at his side, Jenny on his arm. "'Tis good to be home."

EPILOGUE

*B*eing part of the Mackenzie family was a considerable change for Celia. Alec's persona of artist who struggled to find work to feed his child fell away, revealing a man of sought-after talent who lived in one of the most sumptuous houses in Paris.

They quickly settled into a routine, though Celia realized Alec was simply picking up where he'd left off. He spent the morning at the top of the house in his studio, taking advantage of sunshine pouring in through the skylight. Celia made the habit of leaving him alone to paint for an hour or so, and then joining him.

Watching him work in bare feet, breeches, and smock that slid from his wide shoulders was a joy in itself. Once Alec was satisfied with his morning's work, he'd turn to teaching Celia.

Her portfolio had been among the things Alec had ordered taken to the boat, and they did their best to restore or copy the sketches Celia's mother had destroyed. Celia now used a camera obscura to draw the Paris skyline, and Alec showed her how to translate what she traced onto canvas.

He resumed his instruction on mixing paint, the latter ending up very messy, their bodies paint-streaked, the two of them breathless with laughter and bright-eyed when they emerged for dinner. It took Celia a while to find all the places the paint had smeared her skin from their wild lovemaking on the chaise.

Alec, Mal, and Mary showed her Paris, its decadence, its beauty, its gardens. Alec continued to work on plans for an extensive garden for Mal's glorious house, which they'd build on Kilmorgan lands one day.

Celia watched, her heart full, as the brothers put their heads together over their designs, making and scratching out notes, arguing or agreeing. Mal and Alec belonged together, and she and Mary had made a pact that they'd not be separated again, not for long stretches anyway.

On occasion the duke invited in the Scottish families who also now made their homes in Paris, and they'd have a dance. Plaids filled the main salon, emptied of furniture, and the music of bagpipes, drums, and fiddles invaded the house. Men and women caught hands and danced in circles, then twirled each other, kilts flying, laughter gilding the air. Alec taught Celia how to dance in the Scottish fashion, which was robust and heady, pure enjoyment.

She also had the pleasure of watching Alec perform a sword dance one night, his tall body steady as his feet moved in complicated patterns between a pair of crossed swords. He kept his gaze on Celia, his smile widening as the dance wound to a frenzy.

When he finished, he caught her around the waist and spun her away, his kisses as hot as the dance. He loved her that night with equal passion.

Will was a frequent visitor to the palace at Versailles, and on occasion he took Alec and Celia with him. Alec was welcomed by Louis himself—Alec tutored the king's offspring from time to time. The king's beautiful mistress, Madame du Pompadour, was charming to Celia, and asked Alec for suggestions on what paintings to purchase for his majesty.

On one visit, Celia at last was introduced to Clara, the rhinoceros.

The king had set up a menagerie at the end of the gardens, and Clara had her own pavilion. The Dutchman who was her caretaker kept a protective eye on her.

Clara of the delicate name was enormous. Her horn had been trimmed down, but she had a great wide head, a huge body and thick hide, and large flat feet. No claws, Celia saw, though she'd seen rhinos depicted with such things before.

Her dark eyes sparkled as she looked over the many gentlemen who'd come to draw her, resting on Celia in her blue and green skirts as though puzzling about them.

The odor in the pavilion was strong, but Celia seated herself to sketch the beast, Alec on a stool beside her making his own drawing. Clara watched them, placid and hardly vicious, closing her eyes in pleasure when her keeper scratched the side of her face.

Their subsequent paintings of Clara hung in the stairwell of the Mackenzies's home, and became Jenny's favorites.

Another benefit of living with Mackenzies was the letters. They flew thick and fast between London and Paris, never seeing a post office, as messengers smuggled them past guards and censors.

Celia received letters from her father, who told her he was well, missed her, and that her mother had buried herself in charity work and didn't say much these days about Celia, marriages, or Uncle Perry and his ruthless machinations to rise in power.

Uncle Perry had recovered from his adventure and gone on

travels—he was currently on his way to the American colonies, so said the duke. The king and prime minister had heard about the imprisoned and tortured Scotsmen, and Lord Chesfield was having to explain himself.

The scandal wasn't made much of, Celia's father went on, as most Englishmen were not sympathetic to Jacobite Highlanders these days, but the decisions about the regiment were returned firmly to the duke's hands, the soldiers redeployed to the Continent. Edward had been promoted to Major, and he would soon command a troop in the Netherlands, continuing to fight for Maria Theresa of Austria's right to keep her throne.

Edward wrote of his mother and Uncle Perry, but in less couched terms than their father.

> Uncle Perry scuttled away to the colonies with his tail between his legs. The king and prime minister are not so much concerned with the horrible things he'd done to the men imprisoned, but that he assumed any power at all. He is a nobody and should behave so, was their final word.
>
> Mother too, has been quite subdued. Father put his foot down, it seems, and she has ceased to cross him. She now asks what he thinks anytime she has a scheme, but mostly she keeps to herself. The house has never been more comfortable.
>
> I hope to see you, dear sister, sometime on my travels.
>
> I remain, ever your
>
> Edward

Mrs. Reynolds wrote only one letter, a brief one. In it she said that she and Lady Flora were on a rambling holiday to the west coast of England, and that they would remain away from London until Lady Flora's nerves were better. Mrs. Reynolds ended the letter by wishing Celia and Alec much happiness.

∽

As summer drew to a close, Celia lay with Alec in their room near the top of the house, late evening sunshine drifting in to touch them.

They'd worked all morning on a portrait of baby Jenny—Celia had made a series of sketches that Alec was now helping her render into a painting. All the sketches were hurried, as the girl could not sit still for more than a minute or so.

Most of the sketch sessions became a game of Jenny running mightily from her father, who would swoop down upon her and lift her to the ceiling. Jenny would laugh and squeal and then wait for her opportunity to run again.

Alone in their chamber now, Alec lazily kissed Celia's breast, his warm weight at her side. He trailed fingers down Celia's abdomen to touch the dark curls damp with their loving.

"Jenny's picture will be beautiful," Celia said, sighing happily. "We'll have to hang it in a sunny room in the new house at Kilmorgan."

"If it's ever built," Alec said, letting out an exasperated growl. "Mal's changed his mind on the plans *again*."

"There's time." Celia touched his face, loving the friction of whiskers beneath her fingertips. "I don't mind staying in Paris for a while."

"Aye, I suppose we have more choice of what we eat here. But too much of a good thing wears on a man. I haven't had porridge and sheep's entrails in an age."

Celia grinned. "Mal says you never touch such things. You certainly shoveled in the roast pork with endives in butter at supper tonight."

"Ah, I must make the best of what I have."

Celia nipped his shoulder. "You are the worst liar I have ever met."

"No, I'm not." Alec rolled onto his stomach, propping himself on his elbows. "I played the befuddled Mr. Finn well enough."

"True. But not for me. I saw through you the first day I met you."

"Ha. That's because ye poured ice-cold water on my foot, woman. A man can't keep up his disguise when he's cursing and sopping wet."

"I'm glad you didn't." Celia smoothed his hair, which had come loose from its tail. "I'm glad I came to know the real man, Alec Mackenzie, my wild Highlander."

Alec turned his head and kissed her fingers. "My prim, stuffy duke's daughter turned out not to be so prim."

"Or stuffy," Celia said, pretending offense. "I am quite open-minded."

"Aye, about drawing a man with his clothes off. I was pleased ye didn't faint dead away."

"No indeed. I was quite interested. I'd never seen a man without his shirt before." Celia let her gaze run across his shoulders to his back and down to his smooth buttocks. "It was most intriguing."

Alec's gaze went dark. "And look where it's led you."

"To Paris. Where I believe this conversation began." Celia studied the round of his hips, the strength of his thighs. "I would not mind taking up my pencil and drawing you again. More of you, this time, I mean."

Alec gave her a slow smile. "Prim and proper you are not, my wife. I suppose I could be your subject. Shall I fetch you paper now?"

"I believe I'd prefer to do it in the studio in the morning, with all the sunshine."

Alec flushed, and Celia's heartbeat quickened. She imagined Alec lounging on the chaise, his body bare, one leg dangling over the chaise's edge as he bathed her in a sinful smile. It was enough to make her wish the night would speed through and the sun rise swiftly.

"Have I embarrassed you, husband?" she asked.

"Not I. I'm looking forward to it. You'll draw me in the morning, and we'll work on Jenny's portrait in the afternoon. That is, if we have any strength left."

Celia gave him a mock astonished look. "Are you proposing we do something unseemly in the studio?"

"We'll see about that, won't we?"

He moved to kiss Celia, but she put a hand out to stop him. "Alec," she said. "I'd also like to do a portrait of both you and Jenny, for the family."

Alec nodded. "We'll do one with all three of us. We'll take it in turns."

He said it offhand as he rolled Celia down into the bed.

"All four of us," Celia said. "Sometime soon."

Alec kissed her lips as she spoke, then he froze, his mouth fused to hers. After a moment, he carefully raised his head. "Four?"

"Yes, indeed. I talked it over with Mary, and we have decided that I am increasing. The child will probably arrive in early spring."

Alec's lips parted as he stared down at her, his freckles standing out on his paling cheeks.

"Bloody hell," he whispered.

"It is the sort of thing that happens when a husband and wife enjoy each other as much as we do."

"Bloody hell," Alec repeated. His voice grew louder and more hoarse. "Celia."

"Yes?"

His arms came around her, and he lifted her to him, pressing his face to the curve of her neck. "Celia, if I lose ye …"

Jenny's mother had passed bringing her in. She sensed that worry in Alec take shape.

"I am quite robust," Celia assured him. "And I have the determination of my mother. I will be fine, I have decided."

Alec lifted his head. Tears stood in his eyes, which shone with hope and fear. "I'll look after ye. Every day and every hour. You'll have your portrait of the four of us, I swear it."

"Excellent." Celia drew him to her. "Until then …?"

Alec growled. He came down on her, kissing her hard, but he was gentleness itself as he slid inside her.

"I love you, my Celia," he groaned.

Celia's heart sang as she let him fill her, reveling in the beauty of her husband. "I love you too, my Highlander."

Alec kissed her lips, her face. "My beautiful lady, my light. Thank ye for saving my life."

"I always will, my love." The words were meant to be tender, but as Alec's thrusts began, Celia's desires rose in a sweeping wave, and they came out a cry.

She gave up on words, and wrapped herself around her husband, the two of them entwined in heat and love as the twilight slid away and moonlight bathed them.

~

Kilmorgan Castle, 1892

BETH MACKENZIE GAVE A CONTENTED SIGH AS HER HUSBAND FELL silent, the story finished.

"I love a happy ending," Beth said. She and Ian were on the floor now, on a pile of worn rugs that had adorned Kilmorgan in one decade or another. Ian leaned against the desk, Beth lounging with her head on his shoulder, her plaid skirts billowing around them.

"Aye," Ian said, his voice quiet.

"But don't stop there," Beth said. "What happened to Will? Did he marry? Was it Josette? Alec and Celia wouldn't have mentioned her if she weren't important, would he?"

Ian waited patiently until Beth's questions faded. "None of that was in Alec's or Celia's journals that I found." He caressed her arm with his thumb. "Though it might be in their papers I still haven't decoded."

"Decoded?" Beth sat up, her interest caught. "Some of them were in code? What sort of code?"

"A simple number and letter substitution. Many of the letters Will wrote after they settled in Paris are in this code. He couldn't risk the letters the family sent to England or Scotland being intercepted."

Beth's fascination increased. "How intriguing. And you broke it?" She laughed and sank back to Ian and the comfort of his arm around her. "A foolish question to ask a man who uses Fibonacci sequences to send me notes."

A hint of amusement glinted in Ian's eyes. He enjoyed writing out the messages as much as Beth enjoyed receiving and untangling them.

"Will Mackenzie came up with the codes," Ian said. "His personal ones are complex, but he also invented one his brothers, sisters-in-law, and father could use for their correspondence. I broke them using much hard work and patience." Something like a twinkle entered Ian's eyes. "And the key Will left for them."

"Rogue." Beth studied him. "If I didn't know better, I'd say you were teasing me."

Ian gazed down at her, his golden eyes intense. Beth loved it when he looked directly at her, which grew easier for him each year. She knew he saw only *her*, not anything else around him or what called to him inside his head.

"Aye," Ian said. "Have I done it right?"

Beth snuggled into him. "You've done it marvelously. You know jolly well what happened to Will, and Alec and Celia's children, and everything else I want to know, don't you?"

Ian nodded. "But it isn't in Alec's story. It's in Will's."

"Well then …"

Ian glanced at the skylight, which had darkened. Beth had lit lamps as Ian had told his tale into the dusk of the summer night.

"It's late," Ian said. "Another time. We'll tell it all to our children—both stories."

Beth nodded against him, his strength beneath his coat intoxicating. "Yes, you are right. That will be better." She made no move to rise though. Leaning against Ian was not only comfortable but desirable.

Then she heaved a sigh. "I suppose we'd better go downstairs before your brothers begin searching for us."

"Hart knows where we are." Ian's voice rumbled beneath her. "He knows to leave us be."

"Of course." Ian would have told his oldest brother not to let anyone up to the attic if Beth came to find him—and Ian had known she would come.

"You planned this in advance," she said with sudden clarity. "Luring me into the attic, keeping me here with your fascinating tales of your family."

Ian's slow smile spread across his face. "Maybe."

"You're incorrigible, Ian Mackenzie."

"Incorrigible." Ian's brows drew together. "You think I'm unreformable? Irredeemable? That's what *incorrigible* means."

"Exactly." Beth slid her arms around him. "I wouldn't have you any other way."

Puzzlement flickered on Ian's face, then it cleared as all interest in the past fled. He focused on Beth alone, his golden eyes darkening, the passion in him as strong as when they'd first met.

Beth found herself on the rugs, Ian's warmth coming down on her, his hands loosening buttons, hooks, and laces, his kilt spreading to cover them both.

Beth welcomed Ian into her, holding the husband who was her life and breath, as they joined together under candle flames that flickered as golden as his eyes.

AUTHOR'S NOTE

*T*hank you for reading! I am thrilled to be able to return to the Mackenzie family and tell more stories about Ian Mackenzie's ancestors. I had planned to write only Malcolm's story (*The Stolen Mackenzie Bride*), but as I learned more about Alec and Will, I knew I needed to tell their tales as well. Will's book (*The Devilish Lord Will*) is next—follow and see what trouble Will Mackenzie can get himself into.

As you might guess, the Mackenzie family is very special to me. They walked into my head a long time ago, Ian demanding my attention, his brothers there to protect him. I knew everything about Ian, Mac, Cameron, and Hart before I ever put pen to paper.

From there, the series grew as I included the story of Daniel (Cameron's son, *The Wicked Deeds of Daniel Mackenzie*), and the McBrides, who intrigued me when Cameron's heroine, Ainsley, talked with such fondness about her brothers.

I hope to do more Mackenzies as time permits. There are Mackenzies of other eras, including Old Dan, the original Duke of Kilmorgan, back in the 1300s. The Mackenzie children will be adults in the Edwardian age, and then there are other characters who pop up (David Fleming and Cameron's Romany groom) who might want tales as well. (Please see the **Mackenzie Family Tree** at the beginning of this book to keep everyone straight!)

Historical notes: I love writing about the eighteenth century, which was a period of great change, from the growth of travel and tourism, to wars that reshaped countries and empires all over the globe, to new discoveries in science that forever changed our understanding of the physical world. Art, music, and architecture became the light and airy style called rococo, and discoveries of Herculaneum and Pompeii revived interest in history and classical design. It was an exuberant, vibrant, dangerous, volatile age I have long had interest in, and very much enjoy exploring this amazing century.

Clara, the rhinoceros, is a true historical figure. She was orphaned in India as a baby, and rescued by the director of the Dutch East India Company, who raised her. He gave her in turn to a Dutch captain (Douwe van der Meer), who took her back with him to Europe and showed her off to fascinated artists and monarchs. Very tame, Clara traveled with van der Meer all over Europe, did visit France and Louis XV, and ended her days in England, looked after by her Dutch sea captain until her death. I found the beguiling Clara so fascinating I *had* to include her in the book!

I hope you enjoyed Alec and Celia's tale, and I hope to be writing Mackenzies for a long time to come.

ALL MY BEST,
Jennifer Ashley

ABOUT THE AUTHOR

New York Times bestselling and award-winning author Jennifer Ashley has written more than 85 published novels and novellas in romance, urban fantasy, and mystery under the names Jennifer Ashley, Allyson James, and Ashley Gardner. Her books have been nominated for and won Romance Writers of America's RITA (given for the best romance novels and novellas of the year), several *RT BookReviews* Reviewers Choice awards (including Best Urban Fantasy, Best Historical Mystery, and Career Achievement in Historical Romance), and Prism awards for her paranormal romances. Jennifer's books have been translated into more than a dozen languages and have earned starred reviews in *Booklist* and *Publisher's Weekly.*

More about Jennifer's series can be found on her website:
www.jenniferashley.com
Join her newsletter
http://eepurl.com/47kLL
And follow her on
Bookbub:
www.bookbub.com/authors/jennifer-ashley
Facebook:
www.facebook.com/JenniferAshleyAllysonJamesAshleyGardner
Twitter:
www.twitter.com/JennAllyson

Made in the USA
Middletown, DE
14 November 2017